GW01454908

A VERY VEXING MURDER

A VERY VEXING MURDER

By Lucy Andrew

First published in paperback in Great Britain in 2026 by Corvus, an imprint of Atlantic Books Ltd

10 9 8 7 6 5 4 3 2 1

A CIP catalogue record for this book is available from the British Library.

Paperback ISBN: 978 1 80546 418 1
E-book ISBN: 978 1 80546 419 8

Printed in Great Britain.

Corvus
An imprint of Atlantic Books Ltd
Ormond House
26–27 Boswell Street
London
WC1N 3JZ
www.atlantic-books.co.uk

Product safety EU representative: Authorised Rep Compliance Ltd., Ground Floor, 71 Lower Baggot Street, Dublin, D02 P593, Ireland. www.arccompliance.com

[*Dedication – to follow*]

CHAPTER I

Rule number one: Don't commit yourself to disposing of your client's rivals unless you're sure they deserve it (or you've been paid an obscene sum to do so).

'Miss Harriet Smith?'

Her booming voice reverberates around the room and it takes all my years of training not to flinch as she addresses me. She's a dragon of a lady, with enough money to earn epithets like 'distinguished' and 'refined', and she has ice-cold eyes that look through you, as if you aren't worth the bother of looking at. Which is a bit rich, given that *she's* the one who summoned *me*. There's a huge portrait of Mrs Churchill on the wall behind her – a younger, thinner incarnation in her wedding clothes, thirty-five years earlier – with that same glazed expression as the woman herself. It's not quite as imposing as its flesh-and-blood counterpart. She's dressed in a charcoal-grey gown of half-mourning which adds to her gravitas. I wish there was something more between us than the narrow mahogany desk that wobbles dangerously as she leans across it, her fingernails tapping out an erratic rhythm. The teacup beside her rattles with every beat, setting my teeth on edge.

I don't let her see any of this, of course. Instead, I smile sweetly, inhaling the cloying scent of lavender that wafts through the room, and answer her question as cryptically as possible. 'For now.'

'Not your real name, I presume.'

'That's very astute of you, ma'am.'

If she perceives my sarcasm, she doesn't acknowledge it. She leans back in her plush, velvet chair, squinting against the sunlight that streams through the window. I think about offering to draw the curtains but, on second thoughts, I'd rather she didn't look at me too closely.

'Names are important among my set, you understand. A name can tell you a lot about a person, don't you think?' She pauses for a moment, as if she's expecting a response, and so, of course, I say nothing.

She continues, apparently unperturbed by my silence. 'I knew a Smith once. Gardener,' she booms, and this time, I nearly do flinch. 'An odd fellow, but *I* never had any trouble with him. There was a regrettable incident involving his daughter and a member of the local regiment. Dreadful business. Naturally, I had to let him go. A shame, really. He was an artist with the pruning shears.' She stares wistfully out of the window, presumably thinking of better days and neater rosebushes.

'You may be wondering, Miss Smith,' she says, her distaste for my pseudonym only too palpable in those two sharp syllables, 'for what purpose you have been summoned.'

I am curious, I'll admit. (But not to her.)

'You come to me by personal recommendation from a most distinguished individual.'

She waits for this to impress me. It doesn't. I've dealt with many *distinguished individuals* in my time and they're all the same. Abrupt. Demanding. Looking as if they'd sat on a cactus but were far too well bred to do anything about it. And, considering that I've spent half my short life conning them out of their undeserved fortunes, I can't imagine that many of them would be willing to give me a glowing reference for anything other than lying, thieving and, in recent years, seducing their husbands. Of course, since the Derbyshire disaster, I have stooped to taking on a few jobs on behalf of ladies and gentlemen who have a problem to solve and don't want to get their hands dirty, but I doubt any of them would be likely to share their secret shame with Mrs Churchill.

'I never do anything without personal recommendation, you understand,' my would-be client continues.

Rich people never do. I can think of a few recommendations I'd like to put to the lot of them, although none of these are polite enough to record here. Besides, it wouldn't be professional.

I offer her a deferential nod. 'I'm honoured, ma'am, I'm sure.'

Her eyes sweep over my face, taking in every detail. 'I must say, I was expecting someone more experienced.'

'I'm quite experienced enough, Mrs Churchill. I've been working in this business these past nine years.'

I don't mention the fact that I was eight years old when I started. My youth has given me many advantages in my line of work, but since I stopped working with my father and started seeking out my own clients to make my living, I've found it's better to keep my seventeen years to myself.

There's a paper knife on the desk in front of her, its hilt bedecked with wonderful jewels – emeralds and rubies and pearls. Beautiful. Exotic. Completely over the top. I covet it. She sees me looking, perhaps, because her fingers are upon it as she continues. 'My friend. The one who recommended you. She tells me … She tells me that you observe people. Find. Things. Out.'

That's one way of putting it. And I'll give them this, if there's one thing the rich excel at (besides taking and making recommendations) it's a good euphemism. Observe people. Find. Things. Out.

'That's part of it, ma'am.'

She squints at me over her pince-nez, bosom heaving as she leans across the desk again. 'Of course, I know all about her little . . . problem.'

I doubt that very much, whoever this mystery friend is.

'I am her confidante in all things.'

I doubt that too, but I don't let on. 'I'm relieved to hear it, ma'am.'

'Relieved? Why should you be relieved?' She brandishes the paper knife like a dagger and, with the pointy end a few inches from my face, I decide I don't want it so much after all.

I stay calm. Stand my ground. (Well, I'm sitting down, but you get the picture.)

'Because, ma'am,' I say, ignoring the paper knife, 'it saves me from having to deny your request for the particulars of her little problem. Client confidentiality, you understand.'

'Indeed.' The paper knife retreats an inch or two. 'She spoke highly of your . . .' she searches for yet another of her charming little euphemisms, 'discretion. What I am about to tell you goes no further.'

'May I assume you're ready to agree terms?'

'You may be assured I will make it worth your while. We can settle the details later,' she says with a wave of her hand. The paper knife comes perilously close to the end of my nose. I still don't flinch.

'I would prefer to settle them now, if you please.' I take out my pocketbook and slide it across the table. 'Here is a list of my rates.'

'Rates?' The letter opener makes a satisfying clank as it lands next to my pocketbook.

'You will find them very reasonable, I'm sure.' I give her my best Harriet Smith wide-eyed innocent look and flutter my eyelashes for good measure.

'I shall review your rates at my leisure. In the meantime—'

'I have taken the liberty of drawing up a contract for your convenience.'

'Contract?'

I push it towards her. 'It only awaits your signature, ma'am.'

'Don't you want to hear the details first?'

'We can settle the details later, can we not? Besides, I never commit details to paper. It's imprudent in my line of work.'

Except for details of payment. That's very important.

She looks as if she's about to raise an objection but, whatever it is, she must have thought better of it, because she's reaching for her pen now. 'Very well.' She dips the nib into the inkwell with such violence it makes me glad she's not still holding the paper knife.

'Emily!' she barks.

The maid is beside her mistress so quickly I can only assume she's in the habit of listening at keyholes.

'Mend my pen,' Mrs Churchill demands. 'Or, better still, fetch me a new one.'

'Emily hasn't been your maid for sixteen years, ma'am. *I* am not Emily,' the maid remarks as she bends over to examine the pen, wrinkling her button nose. Her face would be pretty if it wasn't for the permanent frown etched across it.

'No, well, you couldn't be, could you? Emily was far too well bred to answer back. If only she hadn't run off with that dreadful coachman.' Mrs Churchill stares off into the middle distance, her expression grave.

'A lucky escape, I assure you,' not-Emily says under her breath as she hands the pen back to her mistress.

Mrs Churchill is roused by the tinkle of broken glass in the hallway. Not-Emily sighs. 'That will be Matilda. Again. She's not cut out to be a housemaid. I can't imagine what tempted you to hire her in the first place.'

'That is all,' Mrs Churchill snaps, gesturing towards the door. The maid departs, taking her dark mutterings with her.

Mrs Churchill sniffs loudly. The pen hovers as she squints at the contract. 'An advance on expenses?' she says with a frown.

'Naturally, there will be expenses,' I reply, keeping my expression neutral.

And I have no money of my own to pay them.

'I shall dictate the amount,' she says, and I can't exactly object, so I don't.

I love that sound. The scratching of pen against paper. It's the sound of adventure. Possibility. The glorious satin reticule I absolutely can do without but, then, why should I when I have rich society ladies throwing money at me? Well, one, at least.

She pushes the contract back towards me, determined not to look at it, as if any kind of financial transaction is beneath her notice. I sign my own name on the paper, blot it, fold it neatly and slip it into my pocketbook, leaving a second copy on the table for Mrs Churchill's own records. To business, then.

'Now, what is it I can do for you, Mrs Churchill?'

She's fiddling with the catch of a silver snuffbox that

looks as if it cost more than my entire wardrobe. Finally, it's open and she takes from it a portrait miniature and flings it in my direction. The young woman in the picture has an elegant kind of beauty. Her face is pale and aristocratic, but there's a softness to it which tells me she hasn't lived among the Churchills of this world. The playful glint in her eyes and the curve of her lips suggests she's privy to some tantalising secret – the kind of secret that, should she care to reveal it, would bond us together, for ever. I picture us walking through the Bath Assembly Rooms, arm in arm, fending off an army of eager suitors. The best of friends.

'Her.' Mrs Churchill leans forward and taps a gaunt finger against my would-be best friend's forehead. 'Miss Jane Fairfax.' She pronounces every syllable as if it's poison on her tongue. 'I want her gone.'

'I think you misunderstand the nature of my business, Mrs Churchill.'

'Jane Fairfax will soon be visiting her aunt in the village of Highbury. You have a contact in Highbury, I understand – a way in. It's one of the reasons I chose you for the job. My friend said you can make problems go away. Well. Jane Fairfax is my problem. And I would like you to make her go away. I don't care how you do it. Publicly humiliate her. Pay her off. Send some scoundrel in to seduce her, for all I care.'

'Goodness. What has the poor girl done?'

Mrs Churchill snorts. 'Do not be fooled by her delicate

looks, Miss Smith. She is not the sweet girl she would have everyone believe. She is like you.'

Charming.

'A swindler,' Mrs Churchill clarifies when I don't respond. 'The other reason why I hired you.'

'I prefer the term con artist.'

'You can call it whatever you please. But the truth is, she's managed to get her claws into my nephew—'

'Frank Churchill?'

'You know him?' Mrs Churchill demands. She looks mildly alarmed at the prospect that I might move in the same social circles as her dear nephew.

'I know of him, of course.'

I know he's an absolute scoundrel with a wandering eye and a gambling habit.

She relaxes a little at this. It's perfectly acceptable for me to gaze admiringly at Frank Churchill from a distance, it seems.

'Well, this Fairfax girl has Frank in her power. They met in Weymouth last autumn and have corresponded ever since. In short, he means to marry the wretch.'

Now we're getting somewhere.

'I see. Has he announced his intentions?'

'He has not,' Mrs Churchill barks. 'But I know what he is planning. He has been out at all hours. Smiling too much. Yesterday, I even caught him *whistling*,' she adds, as if this is incontrovertible proof of his marital plans.

'And what makes you think Jane Fairfax is a swindler? Could she not just be a girl in love?'

'In love? She's as poor as a church mouse.'

'And poor women, of course, have no feelings.'

Mrs Churchill's eyelid twitches. 'I think you understand me, Miss Smith. It would be a very good match for her. You are perhaps not aware that Frank is much more than my nephew. He is my ward. My husband's sister was something of a free spirit. A rebellious girl who thought more of her own immediate pleasure than familial duty. She married a most unsuitable man – a Captain Weston – who could not keep her in the manner to which she had been accustomed. They lived beyond their means, were dreadfully unhappy and she died before her poor son Frank had left infancy. We offered to take him in, of course, and to make him heir to the Churchill fortune on the understanding that he took on the Churchill name. Well, his father was glad to be rid of him. So you see, it is vitally important that he marries the right sort. Frank will come into his inheritance at five-and-twenty. In less than two years, he will be master of this estate.'

'I understand you perfectly, Mrs Churchill. But if marrying for money were a criminal offence, half the young women of England would be under lock and key.'

'It is not about money, Miss Smith. It is about legacy. Frank must take a suitable wife for the preservation of the Churchill line. Of course, there is a stipulation that Frank will not inherit unless I approve of his choice—'

'Then, pardon my ignorance, Mrs Churchill, but why do you need *me*? Why do you not just simply withhold your approval?'

Mrs Churchill raises an eyebrow. 'If I thought it were that easy . . . My nephew has inherited something of his mother's stubbornness. I fear that if I oppose the match, he will surrender his claim to the Churchill estate and run away with the girl. And this house and everything that comes with it would pass to the Eddowes, a vulgar family, barely related to my husband, who are in trade and hail from *Birmingham.*' There's a tremor of rage in the final word. Birmingham is apparently a step too far for Mrs Churchill.

'And so the Churchill line would come to an end,' I muse. I see that this would be a fate worse than Jane Fairfax for Mrs Churchill. I know her type. She had married into the great Churchill family and out-Churchill'd them all. For there's no one more zealous than a convert.

'There is also the matter of the missing jewellery,' Mrs Churchill says, eyes narrowed. 'Two pearl necklaces, a gold locket, a pair of diamond earrings.' She counts them off on her fingers. 'Family heirlooms, passed down from my late husband's great-grandmother. They would have gone to Frank's bride eventually, but not to the likes of her.'

'You think your nephew has given them to Jane?'

'Where else would they have gone? She has bewitched him. He has lost all sense of reason and duty. You will retrieve the jewels. I will not have them round the neck of a mere lieutenant's daughter,' she says, conveniently forgetting that *she* is the daughter of a mere apothecary. (I do my research.) 'I will not let her take Frank away from me. I will not—' She breaks off in frustration, clearly sensing my lack of investment in her plight. 'She is poisoning him against me.'

The venom in her assertion does nothing to help her case. I've heard it so many times before. From overprotective mothers. Jilted lovers. Jealous wives.

'I see from your expression that you think this an exaggeration.' She removes her pince-nez and looks at me – really looks – for a good few seconds, as if weighing up whether to let me in on some terrible secret.

I do my best to look sympathetic and trustworthy in equal measure.

She returns the pince-nez to the tip of her nose and reaches her hand towards a cup of tea that must have long since gone cold.

'Speaking of poison.' Gently, triumphantly almost, she places the cup in my outstretched hands.

I smell it as soon as I lift the cup. The unmistakable almond odour.

'Cyanide.'

It's not a question, but she answers it anyway.

'She means to secure Frank's fortune and *I* am the only obstacle left in her way. Marrying for money may not be a crime, but murder certainly is.'

'You're suggesting that Jane poisoned your tea?'

'I am not suggesting it, Miss Smith. I know it to be true. Jane Fairfax is trying to kill me. And *you* are going to stop her.'

CHAPTER 2

Rule number two: When seeking help from unwilling sources, ambush them in the middle of the night. It's harder to say no when you're half asleep.

'For the love of all things holy—'
    There's a tell-tale squelch as I jump down from the stile. I withdraw my nankeen boot from the pungent, slimy substance and drag my heel across the grass.

Please don't be ruined. I can't afford another pair right now.

I squint against the darkness, arms out in front of me to ward off insomniac cows. I don't trust cows. Their eyes are too big and their moos are too loud and—

I squeal as something huge, rough and wet swipes at my hand. The licking. *That's* the worst part. The cow lets out a low bellow as I push my palm against her muzzle. 'Get away!'

And now I'm covered in mucus as well as saliva.

She licks me again.

'No wonder we eat your kind,' I mutter as I inch away from her, attempting to keep eye contact, which is difficult considering that I can't actually see her eyes in the near-blackness. I can feel them on me, though, as I take another backward step. When I'm certain the cow-beast isn't following, I turn around and run like hell for the gate. I clamber over it, boots crunching on the gravel as I tiptoe towards the farmhouse.

Mrs Churchill was right. Not about her nephew's fiancée trying to kill her. (Well, she might be right about that – only time will tell.) But about the other thing. I do have a way into Highbury. Unfortunately, that way involves scrambling over a rusty stile, traipsing through cowpats and nearly being licked to death by an overexcited Welsh cow.

That's the easy part. The real challenge is waiting for me behind this door. The lights are out, but I know he's there. Alone. I checked. His mother and sisters are visiting a cousin in Bath who is ready to give birth any day now.

My hand hovers over the doorknocker.

Here goes.

The door swings open before I even knock.

'No. No. No.' He rakes his fingers through his chaotic curls and scrunches his eyes shut, as if he hopes that I'm just a dreadful hallucination.

Afraid not.

Robert Martin: tenant farmer, frustrated writer and now (much to his dismay) general lackey, sole confidant and best friend of Harriet Smith. (Although I'm not sure he'd agree with the best friend part. Not after what happened aboard the *Harlequin*.) Unlike me, Robert is making the dishevelled look work for him. He isn't every woman's dream, but he has a certain rustic charm. Short, tanned, well built, a scattering of freckles across his nose and a mess of chestnut curls that are begging you to run your fingers through them. (Not that I've ever tried.) And, at four-and-twenty, he thinks himself infinitely more mature and sensible than I am and doesn't let me forget it.

I fold my arms. 'I haven't asked you anything yet.'

He opens his eyes and lets them rove over my body, taking in my flushed cheeks and haphazard attire. It's not exactly the vision of loveliness I wanted to present to him but, then, I hadn't factored in the field full of monsters. Thank goodness it's dark, at least.

'The first no was an objection to your presence. The second was a pre-emptive no for whatever insane favour you're about to ask me.'

'And the third no?'

He shrugs and offers me his trademark lopsided smirk. 'That one was just for emphasis.'

'Well, will you at least let me in? I need to clean my boots and wash the cow saliva off my hand.'

'There's a pail of water in the cowshed. Goodnight.' He attempts to close the door, but I anticipate the move, pushing my full weight against it until my leg is wedged in the gap.

'Look, I appreciate we didn't leave things on the best of terms ...' I slide my body all the way across the threshold and into the farmhouse kitchen while Robert is distracted by his own indignation.

'The best of terms? Harriet, you left me aboard a ship full of drunk, angry sailors in the middle of the Irish Sea—' The glow of the lantern on the kitchen table illuminates his features well enough for me to see that I have some work to do to placate him.

'Yes, well, there was a very good reason for that.'

'Let me guess. You thought you saw your father?'

There are two crucial things to know about my father. Firstly, he's a brilliant con man who taught me the tricks of the trade while I still had my milk teeth. He's as cunning as they come: a consummate liar; an expert thief; a master of disguise. Secondly, he's excellent at holding a grudge and he has a very big one against me right now. If he ever catches up with me, he'll make me pay for what happened on our last job. Our final job.

I betrayed him, I suppose. But he betrayed *me*, too. He was conning some great lady in Derbyshire and I was left to seduce her supercilious nephew. But then I fell in love, confessed all, and the gentleman still wanted me. We were going to run away together. Leave behind the world of exploitative fathers and overbearing aunts. But Father wasn't willing to lose me and my talents to a rich toff, so he did what any devoted father would do: drugged me, paid a cad to seduce me and ensured that my lover walked in on the scene. It didn't turn out so well for my father in the end. No longer bound to me, my lover immediately revealed my father's intentions to his aunt. But I should have known my father wouldn't make it to a jail cell, let alone the gallows. He conned his way out of it, went on the run and now he's out there, somewhere, hunting for me. And knowing Father Dearest as I do, he won't rest until he has destroyed my life as thoroughly as I have destroyed his.

Luckily for me, the man my father paid to ruin my one chance at happiness – an opportunistic leech called George Wickham – was exactly the kind of man to brag to his friends about his planned exploits. And while Wickham's best friend, Reuben Denny, thought that a drugged seventeen-year-old girl was fair game, Denny's lover, Robert Martin, did not. Robert may have been infatuated enough to desert his farm and pursue Denny one-hundred-and-fifty miles across the country, but he wasn't so far gone that he would fail to act when he discovered Wickham's intentions. And so, if it hadn't been for Robert's poor relationship choices, but essentially good character, things would have been a lot worse for me that night at the Featherstones' ball. He stepped up when every gentleman of my acquaintance had abandoned me. Despite my intoxication, I'll never forget the hard set of his mouth and his eyes full of righteous indignation as he pulled Wickham to his feet and punched him in the face. Afterwards, when I was alone, penniless and desperate, Robert helped me get back on my feet, which, much to his dismay, meant back on the con. But conning people isn't so easy without my father by my side and so I've fallen into the habit of turning to Robert every time I get myself into a scrape. Robert has become my saviour. My ever-reluctant safety net. Unfortunately for me, this means that I have to put up with his smug I-told-you-sos and the constant crick in my neck from gazing up at him on his moral high ground.

'I swear, I really thought it was him this time—'

Robert shakes his head. 'Like the time you saw him at the Derbyshire militia camp—'

'Ah, well—'

'—and at the Bath Assembly Rooms—'

'You see—'

'—and in that gambling den in Westminster Abbey.'

'I'll admit that one was a bit of a stretch.'

Robert throws up his hands. 'Harriet, this obsession with your father – it's not healthy.'

Robert's right. Ever since I fled from Derbyshire, I've seen my father everywhere thanks to my overactive imagination and guilty conscience. But my father is going to track me down eventually.

'Look, I'm sorry for abandoning you but, in my defence, it did look an awful lot like him and please don't pretend you didn't enjoy being stranded on a ship full of burly sailors at least a little bit.'

Robert smirks. 'It wasn't all bad. But the answer's still no.'

'Please, Robert. It's just one tiny favour. I have a job in Highbury and I don't even need you to find me somewhere to stay.'

'What kind of job?'

'Nothing big,' I assure him. 'Just breaking off an engagement. Retrieving some jewels. The usual kind of thing.' I don't mention the attempted murder, or the promise I've made to catch Mrs Churchill's would-be killer before they strike again. The truth is, seduction and thievery *are* my areas of expertise. Murder, not so much. And while poisoned tea and wicked women is exactly the kind of fare Robert would put in his strange, experimental novel (which I'm not convinced the English public are ready for), in real life, he's a bit more squeamish. He thinks my work is dangerous enough as it is. If I confess that I've been hired to catch a killer, he'll refuse to help me at all.

'Where are you staying?' Robert asks reluctantly.

'Mrs Goddard's school. She's taken me on as a parlour boarder and my expenses from my employer barely cover it, so I really do need this new job to work out. There's good money in it if I'm successful. I just want to get the lay of the land.'

Robert leans against the wall, fingers drumming on his thigh. 'You want gossip on my neighbours.'

'Not even that, really. Just *one* of your neighbours.'

He hits me with his holier-than-thou stare. 'Who?'

'Jane Fairfax.'

'Jane Fairfax? For a start, she's not my neighbour. She doesn't even live in Highbury.'

'I know that.'

'Then why are *you* in Highbury?'

'She'll be here soon. Trust me.'

'Well, it seems you're better informed about Jane Fairfax than I am,' he says, grasping my elbow and steering me towards the door. 'Goodnight.'

I press my back up against the door as Robert reaches for the doorknob.

'Please, Robert,' I say, placing my hand against his chest and pushing him further into the kitchen. 'I just need to get a feel for her. Who are her friends? Enemies? Who will know her deepest, darkest secrets? That sort of thing.'

Whether or not she's capable of murder, Mrs Churchill is convinced that Jane is responsible for the attempt on her life, so much so that her instruction was not to catch the poisoner, but to stop Jane Fairfax. She can give me no proof that Jane was anywhere near Enscombe on the day of the poisoning, but that doesn't seem to bother Mrs Churchill. Jane is guilty and that is that. I suppose it's as good a place to start as any. And, while I can't yet prove Jane had the opportunity to do the deed herself, she certainly has a good motive.

Robert sighs. 'From what I know of her, Jane Fairfax isn't the kind of girl to have any deep, dark secrets. Or enemies. Mr Knightley speaks very highly of her,' he adds, a blush rising to his cheeks.

'Ah, the famous George Knightley.'

It turns out that Robert is madly in love with his landlord and I, for one, cannot blame him. Judging from his portrait miniature and his great estate, Mr Knightley has two of the best qualities a man can possess: high cheekbones and an even higher income. Even though he's twenty years my senior, I think I might be half in love with him myself, if I were in the market. I'm not, of course. Love and con artistry make strange bedfellows.

'Jane's an orphan,' Robert says. 'She was taken in by her father's friend. A colonel, I think.'

'Colonel Campbell.'

Robert frowns. 'I thought you needed information on her?'

'I do,' I insist. 'But I didn't come in completely blind. I'm not an amateur.'

If I'm honest, there's not much Robert could tell me about Jane Fairfax that I don't already know. But I'll need him soon enough, so I may as well get him used to the idea of helping me.

'Well, you probably know she has an aunt and grandmother in Highbury, otherwise you wouldn't be here.'

'Yes. The Bateses,' I say.

'I warn you, Miss Bates is a bit of a talker.'

'All the better for me. And then there's Emma Woodhouse: the young heiress of Hartfield. She's the same age as Jane. They are friends, I imagine?'

Robert snorts. 'I'm not sure Emma Woodhouse *has* any friends. Apart from her old governess, Mrs Weston, but I don't think that counts.' There's an uncharacteristic sneer in Robert's voice. He's a hard man to make an enemy of (I'm living proof of that) so whatever Emma

Woodhouse has done to offend him, it must be particularly egregious.

'Ah, yes. Mrs Weston. Recently married to Mr Weston of Randalls. He has a son, doesn't he?'

Robert huffs. 'Apparently. Not that Frank Churchill has ever graced us with his presence in Highbury. Mind you, he gave up his father's name easily enough, so I suppose he's not in a great hurry to visit him, either. Mr Knightley thinks it's most undutiful of Frank to neglect his father's new wife. He didn't even turn up for the wedding.'

'Well, you can hardly blame him for that. His father gave *him* up easily enough to his wife's rich relations. The Churchills have been better parents to Frank than Mr Weston ever was. It wasn't that he couldn't afford to keep Frank at home. He just found it more convenient to pack him off to the Churchills.'

Robert narrows his eyes. 'As much as I would like to debate with you the respective familial duty of Mr Weston and Frank Churchill, I have to be up at four o'clock to milk the cows.'

I bite my lip against the twitch of a smile. 'I think that's enough to be going on with. Frank Churchill: undutiful son; Jane Fairfax: poor orphan girl; Emma Woodhouse: friendless heiress; Miss Bates: garrulous spinster; Mr Knightley: absolute heaven. Does that sum it up?'

Robert blushes again. 'Perfectly,' he says as he hooks his arm around my waist and reaches for the doorknob.

'Oh, one more thing,' I say, inhaling the scent of sweat, cow dung and vegetable soap that emanates from Robert. It's strangely intoxicating. 'The Bateses – where do they live?' I ask as he pushes me through the door.

'On the high street, above the milliner's,' Robert says, slamming the door in my face.

'Lovely. I'll start with them,' I announce to the door-knocker.

✳

'Miss Smith – I do hope you are settling into Highbury – so kind of you to visit – and when you have only been here two days – I'm sure you must have more exciting things to do than call on us.' Miss Bates gestures towards her mother, a birdlike old woman who is snoring into her morning tea. 'MOTHER!' Miss Bates shouts.

Mrs Bates snorts and upsets her teacup, splashing milky brown liquid over her shawl. She raises her head, staring blankly at her daughter.

'KIND,' Miss Bates shouts, 'OF MISS SMITH,' she nods towards me, 'TO CALL UPON US.'

'Very kind,' Mrs Bates agrees, glancing at me and then settling back in her chair, eyes closed.

The apartment is spotlessly clean, but depressingly cluttered, and there's a musty scent hanging in the air which no amount of polish could dispel. Miss Bates must be in her forties, but has the deportment of a much older woman. She possesses the plain face and drab clothes of a seasoned spinster, and tries to make up for her dullness by speaking a mile a minute about whatever topic happens to be in her head at any given moment.

'You mustn't mind Mother,' Miss Bates says, steering me towards the threadbare chintz sofa. I ignore her offer and instead seat myself in a hard-backed chair by the window which gives me a good view of the high street. People-watching is a hobby of mine and, if Miss Bates is the chatterbox she's reputed to be, I might be grateful for the distraction. 'Mother's not been sleeping well. Not since I let slip about Jane's cold,' she adds, lowering her voice as she perches on the edge of the sofa.

'Jane is your niece, is she not?' I thought I would need to work up to this, but I've clearly underestimated the magnitude of Miss Bates's familial pride.

'Yes. How clever of you to know! Such a kind girl – and so talented – particularly at the pianoforte. But you must not tell her I said so – she is the picture of modesty.'

Hardly the portrait of a scheming murderess, but I suppose Miss Bates is somewhat biased. Her face takes on a youthful glow as she talks about her niece. 'Jane is – *was* – my sister's child – that is to say, my sister is no longer with us – such a sad story—' She glances at her mother.

'Yes, I heard that Jane was an orphan,' I say, determined to head off whatever longwinded tale Miss Bates is about to embark upon, 'but I'm sorry to hear she is unwell. I hope it's not serious?'

'Oh – so kind of you – not serious at all – just a trifling cold – but she has not been quite well since her visit to Weymouth—'

My fingers twitch at the mention of Weymouth – the place where Jane fell for Frank Churchill. Or his money, at least.

'I said to her – well, I wrote to her, rather – Jane, I said, I shouldn't wonder about you catching a cold after what happened on that dreadful boat trip.'

'Boat trip?' She has me at a disadvantage here. It's not a place I care to be.

'Really quite shocking – frightened me half to death when I found out – Jane would have plunged into the water if it hadn't been for Mr Dixon – such a jolt and she was thrown about – thank goodness Mr Dixon was there to catch her.'

I glance over at Mrs Bates. Her eyes are still closed, but her snores are a little too loud to be natural. I suspect she's not as deaf as she makes out. Not that I can blame her. I suppose that *I* might develop a convenient hearing defect if I lived with Miss Bates.

'Mr Dixon?' I ask, as I peer through the window at a lithe young woman in a scarlet pelisse.

'Yes, he is Miss Campbell's husband – well, I should say Mrs Dixon now, shouldn't I? Mrs Dixon is Jane's particular friend – the daughter of Colonel Campbell, Jane's guardian. They're more like sisters, really. And Mr Dixon – a wonderful young man. Irish. Jane was invited to Ireland by the Dixons but, well, you see here,' she says, moving aside a lace doily as she sifts through papers on the side-table. 'Not this one – not that – ah!' She waves the letter around triumphantly before pushing it into my hands. 'We've just had word that Jane has declined the Dixons' invitation and is coming to stay here instead. And she'll arrive as soon as Friday or Saturday!'

Mr Dixon saving Jane Fairfax's life? I might be able to use that.

The woman in the scarlet pelisse has stopped to examine the window display at Ford's, the haberdasher's shop. In profile, she looks magnificent with her aquiline nose, strong jawline and a single blonde curl trailing down her neck. She has the appearance of a woman who knows her own worth and is quick to remind others of it too.

Miss Bates hovers beside me, pointing out pretty turns of phrase in Jane's letter. 'Oh!' she exclaims, gripping my arm as she follows my gaze out onto the street. 'There's Miss Woodhouse – she'll be delighted to hear about Jane.' Miss Bates leans over my chair and throws open the sash window. 'Miss Woodhouse! Miss Woodhouse! Do come up!'

Emma Woodhouse catches my eye as she waves at Miss Bates, a flicker of curiosity in her expression as she sweeps past the window.

'Oh. Well – I expect she didn't hear that last bit,' Miss Bates says.

Some more selective deafness.

As Emma ducks out of view, I have the sudden urge to pursue her. I've already secured an invitation to Hartfield to meet her, thanks to my landlady, Mrs Goddard, but patience isn't one of my virtues.

'It's been so nice to make your acquaintance, Miss Bates,' I say, rising from my chair and slipping Jane's letter into my pocket in one smooth movement, 'but I really must be going. I need to run some errands for Mrs Goddard—' I'm at the door before she's had chance to draw breath. 'Good day to you,' I say as I retreat to the stairs.

'Oh, Miss Smith, must you really be going? Such a shame – but you must call again when Jane arrives.'

You can be assured that I will, Miss Bates.

I slam the door with more force than I'd intended as I step out into the street.

'Goodness, was it really that bad?' Emma Woodhouse is leaning against the window of the milliner's, smirking.

'Oh, Miss Woodhouse! I did not see you there!'

'You are Miss Smith,' Emma states. 'Mrs Goddard was to introduce us at Hartfield.'

'Oh, yes. Mrs Goddard is very kind,' I say, sounding just like Miss Bates.

'Well, it seems we do not need her.' Emma leans forward and lowers her voice. 'Tell me, what do you think of Miss Bates?'

I sense that the extent of our friendship rests on how I answer this question. 'Oh, well, she is perfectly nice, although she does talk rather a lot.'

Emma grins as she links arms with me and steers me away from the Bateses' apartment. 'Lord, she didn't read you any letters, did she?'

I laugh. 'She did, actually. From her niece, Miss Fairfax.'

Emma rolls her eyes. 'Of course. The great Jane Fairfax.'

'You are not friends?' I hazard.

'Friends? No. Miss Fairfax has never much liked me and she knows how to hold a grudge. And sometimes grudges can go too far.' Her smile fades. 'Still,' she says, rousing herself with a shake of her head, 'she's hardly ever in Highbury so we're not much thrown together.'

'Oh, well, you'll be thrown together soon,' I say, watching Emma carefully. 'Miss Bates tells me she's just had word from Jane that she will be arriving imminently.'

Emma's grip on my elbow tightens. 'Jane Fairfax? Here? I think you must be mistaken.'

'I do not think so. I saw the letter myself.'

Emma stops, drops my arm and turns towards me. 'You are sure?'

'Quite sure.'

'Well,' Emma says, with forced cheerfulness, 'in that case, I don't suppose you need to hear *my* opinion of Miss Fairfax. You will see for yourself soon enough. It was nice meeting you, Miss Smith. I'm sure we'll be the best of friends.' She turns away, chin raised, and strides off down the street.

If I'm looking for someone who might agree with Mrs Churchill's assessment of Jane Fairfax, Emma Woodhouse is that person. There's a history there. Something for me to dig into. But to do that, I require one vital ingredient: Miss Fairfax herself.

CHAPTER 3

Rule number three: *If you want to know a lady's deepest, darkest secrets, steal her letters.*

The post office is a wonderful establishment. Letters travelling from one end of the country to the other with such regularity, and hardly a single one going astray. The post keeps us connected. It is the agent of business deals, the purveyor of family gossip, the abettor of love affairs. In a letter, we can confess our true feelings away from pricked ears and prying eyes. In a letter, we can be ourselves. We trust the post office to place our letters into the hands of our intended recipients. Most of the time that's exactly what happens. But, if your name is Frank Churchill or Jane Fairfax, today is not one of those times.

'You're early this morning, Miss Smith,' says Mrs Leech, the buck-teethed postmistress, as she squints over the counter at me. Mrs Leech is a widow who lives for her Irish Setter and news from her married daughter in London. 'I haven't even finished sorting through these yet,' she adds, gesturing to the haphazard mountain of mail in front of her.

This was exactly my intention. In my experience, it's much easier to steal someone's correspondence when the post office is in its early-morning disarray. My eyes sweep over the counter, deciphering the names scrawled across the letters until I find the one I'm looking for: Miss Fairfax.

Finally.

I've been anticipating a letter for Jane Fairfax since Miss Bates announced her imminent arrival when I met her on Monday. Today is Thursday. Jane is due on Friday or Saturday. And if Frank Churchill is as love-struck as his aunt insists he is, he'll ensure there's a letter waiting for Jane, discretion be damned.

'Just the one for Mrs Goddard today,' Mrs Leech says. I slide the coins across the counter as she hands me the letter.

I don't turn around as the bell rings. I don't need to. I know exactly who has entered the post office, because I bullied him into it.

'Good morning, Mrs Leech. Miss Smith.' Robert gives an awkward bow and then trips over his own feet on his way to the counter.

Smooth.

'Mr Martin. Another early customer.'

'Yes,' Robert says, a little too loudly. 'I was just walking past and I thought, I wonder if there's any post from my mother and sisters in Bath.'

I slide my hand across the counter towards Miss Fairfax's letter.

'You must be missing them, Mr Martin?' Mrs Leech replies.

'Yes,' Robert says, his voice rising half an octave as he sees my fingers on Jane's letter. 'I hardly know what to do with myself.'

You can stop acting like a maniac, for one thing.

'It must be busy for you on the farm on your own. Elizabeth does so much. But I expect Mr Ingleby is helping you out, isn't he?'

'Mr Ingleby. Yes, very helpful,' Robert agrees, eyes darting from the counter to Mrs Leech and back again.

Mr Ingleby is Elizabeth Martin's fiancé – Robert's soon-to-be-brother-in-law. His father rents the neighbouring farm from Mr Knightley, but Mr Ingleby Senior is in no rush to hand over the reins and so his son has set his sights on the Martins' farm as his best chance of advancement. This works out nicely for Robert because he's far more interested in his literary aspirations than tilling the land. It's even better for me because it means I can drag Robert away from the farm at a moment's notice, safe in the knowledge that he can't fob me off with the tired old excuse that there's no one to feed the pigs.

Mrs Leech plucks a letter from the pile and squints down at it. 'There is one for you, Mr Martin, although it looks a bit careless for your mother's hand.'

Robert snatches it up with a deep blush and muttered

thanks, managing to knock an entire pile of mail onto the floor in the process, Jane's letter included.

The bell rings again as I stoop to retrieve Jane's correspondence. I have just enough time to slide it into the copy of *The Monk* I'm carrying for such emergencies when a pair of dainty hands in the softest kid leather gloves I've ever encountered brush against mine. The dainty hands are attached to a pair of slender arms, square shoulders and an exquisite neck, which is crowned by one of the most beautiful faces I have ever seen. Alabaster skin, vermillion lips and smoky-grey eyes with all the appeal of an autumnal night by the fireside, curled up with an Ann Radcliffe book.

I admit, I may be getting a little carried away.

'Let me help,' says the goddess, scooping up an armful of letters and placing them on the counter with a grace that perfectly matches her appearance. I'll give her this, she doesn't *look* like a con woman but, I suppose, neither do I.

Robert's face is ashen as he stutters his response. 'J-Jane Fairfax.'

'Mr Martin,' she says, with an elegant curtsey, as Robert clambers to his feet and all but throws a pile of letters at poor Mrs Leech.

'You're not supposed to be here yet.'

'Yes, I am a day early. The Colonel's carriage became available and I did so want to surprise my aunt and Grandmama,' Jane says, doing an impressive job of ignoring the fact that Robert is gawping at her as if she's some sort of bizarre circus exhibit.

33

I clear my throat loudly and, when that doesn't work, I drop a large parcel on Robert's foot.

'I'm so sorry, Mr Martin,' I say, catching his eye as I bend down to recover the parcel. 'How very clumsy of me. I do hope it didn't hurt.'

'Not at all, Miss Smith,' he counters with a stiff smile.

Jane tilts her head at Robert. 'How did you know I was early?'

Robert opens and closes his mouth like a beached salmon.

Honestly, do I have to do all the heavy lifting?

'I should think the whole of Highbury knows when you are due to arrive, Miss Fairfax. Your aunt has spoken of little else since your last letter.'

Jane turns towards me, searching my expression for signs of spite. When she finds none, she hits me with a smile so dazzling that I begin to understand why Frank is ready to defy his aunt and relinquish his fortune for her. 'That does sound like Aunt Hetty,' she agrees. 'Jane Fairfax,' she adds, 'though you obviously already know that.'

'Harriet Smith. I'm a parlour boarder at Mrs Goddard's school.'

'Pleased to meet you, Miss Smith,' she says, sounding like she actually means it.

'You too, Miss Fairfax.'

There's something about Jane, beyond her pretty face, that draws me in. Some kind of connection between us. She's an orphan. Her parents died when she was three years old – her father as a soldier in service, her mother from grief. I have few remaining happy memories of my own mother and, given what's happened with Father, I suppose I'm now an orphan too, of sorts. But it's more what we don't share – the different paths we trod. Jane was rescued by Colonel Campbell to repay a life debt he owed to her father. My father's debts were my damnation. I had no handsome soldier to save me. Jane Fairfax is my other self – the me I could never be. A sweet girl with people who love her. The hope of a happy ending. Or, she is a fellow con woman with a heart harder than mine and a murderous streak to boot.

'It seems we are all early this morning, Miss Fairfax,' says Robert, waving his arms around as if he's fending off a swarm of aggressive bees. 'You're early to Highbury. I'm early to the post office. Miss Smith is too. It's a complete coincidence that we find ourselves here, together, at the same time.'

One thing I didn't consider when I coerced Robert into helping me with my postal theft was that he's an atrocious liar. You would think an aspiring novelist could come up with a convincing enough reason for an early-morning trip to the post office or, at least, not draw unnecessary attention to it. But if there's an easy route to success, Robert Martin will be sure to blunder off in the opposite direction.

Jane stares at Robert in puzzlement and, as he opens his mouth to say something else that will no doubt add to the impression that he's an utter lunatic, I step in to rescue him.

'You're expecting a letter so soon, Miss Fairfax?' I ask with a meaningful glare at Robert.

'Not as such,' Jane says, still watching Robert, 'but my friends in Ireland may have sent something ahead of my arrival.'

'Miss Fairfax. Miss Smith. I must leave you,' Robert announces gravely. 'Good day to you, Mrs Leech,' he adds, hitting his head on the bell as he shuffles backwards through the door.

'I do worry about him, with his mother and sisters being away,' Mrs Leech says as we watch Robert stumble off down the street. 'I'm sure there's a letter here for you somewhere, Miss Fairfax,' she adds. 'I'll check in the back.'

'He did seem a little out of sorts,' Jane muses, turning towards me.

'Hmmm,' I say, wondering how best to explain Robert's lunacy. 'Well, I did think perhaps— But no, I'm quite sure it's just my imagination.'

'What?' Jane says, a glint in her eyes that makes her whole face come alive. For some reason, I really want to keep it there.

'I thought perhaps— Oh but, Miss Fairfax, you will think me so vain.'

Jane smiles. 'You think he likes you?'

'Perhaps a little,' I own, holding my breath until my cheeks are as pink as a summer rose.

'I think you might be right. It certainly wasn't for my benefit that he was so flustered.'

'Oh, Miss Fairfax, it is kind of you to say so, but I don't think—'

'Do you like him?' she asks, ignoring my protestations.

'Perhaps. But, please,' I add, finally meeting her gaze, 'you must not tell Miss Woodhouse. She does not approve of Mr Martin. I think she might have someone loftier in mind for me.'

This is not entirely untrue. I've known Emma Woodhouse for less than a week and she's already marrying me off to the local clergyman, Mr Elton, in her head. There's more chance of me marrying *Robert* than Mr Elton, but there's no sense in telling Emma that. She's a woman who is accustomed to getting her own way. And by playing meek little Harriet Smith – always in agreement and forever in the thrall of Highbury's undisputed queen – I have access to everyone and draw the attention of no one. So I'm quite happy to defer to Emma's apparent wisdom – until it gets in in the way of my own plans, that is.

The smile drops from Jane's lips and her eyes flash with anger at the mention of Miss Woodhouse. Apparently, she's about as fond as Emma as Emma is of her. She looks rather sinister for a moment, like the kind of girl who might slip a dose of cyanide into her enemy's tea.

'I'm sure Miss Woodhouse means well,' says Jane, in a tone that suggests the exact opposite, 'but you must learn to know your own heart and make your own decisions in matters of love. Do not let friends or family make them for you. That will not lead to happiness.'

Happiness. There was a time when I believed I could have it. But it's better this way. It makes life less complicated. There's nothing for anyone to hold over me now. No distractions. I am my own mistress. I am in control. I have given up on happiness. I left it back in Derbyshire and there's no retrieving it now.

Mrs Leech bustles back to the counter, empty-handed. 'I could have sworn there were some letters for you, Miss Fairfax, but my eyes must have been playing tricks on me for there's nothing here.'

Jane's shoulders sag. 'Oh well. Maybe tomorrow.' She looks so disappointed that I'm almost tempted to open my book and slip her correspondence onto the counter while she's looking down at her gloved hands.

Jane's eyes dart to my book as if she's read my mind. 'Oh,' she exclaims, '*The Monk*. Have you finished it?'

I'm so relieved at this unexpected line of questioning that I nearly hand her the book there and then.

'I have read it three times over,' I say in the hushed voice that one uses to discuss books as licentious as *The Monk*. 'It's not so good as Mrs Radcliffe's tales, but it's plenty shocking.'

'Ah yes. Mrs Radcliffe,' Jane replies, eyes gleaming. 'I am very fond of *Udolpho*, but *The Italian* is my favourite, although I lent out my copy several years ago and it was never returned. My friend Mr Dixon has read *The Monk*, but he would not share it with me, or his wife. He said it was not becoming of a young lady to read such stuff.'

Mr Dixon again.

'A young lady has as much right to read it as a young man,' I say, forgetting myself for a moment. I'm not sure Harriet Smith would hold such views.

'That's just what I think,' Jane says. 'I should very much like to read it.' She stares wistfully at the book. 'If only to shock Mr Dixon.'

I jerk the book away. 'I will happily lend it to you when I've finished it. We can't let Mr Dixon have all the fun, can we?'

Jane pulls back her hand, eyes narrowed. 'I thought you said you had read it three times over?' The warmth in her tone has evaporated.

Damnation.

Trust Jane Fairfax to be an attentive listener.

'I have. But, well, it's silly, really. It's just that this book belonged to my mother and she did not leave a lot behind to remember her by.'

In truth, my mother was never much of a reader. She was wholly consumed by her music. It was her passion. Her purpose. I'm not proud of my lie to Jane but it was the only thing I could think of that would be sure to work on her. Dead mothers have a way of tugging at the heartstrings. Particularly when you have one yourself.

Her expression softens as she reaches for my hand and squeezes it gently. 'I quite understand, Miss Smith. You must keep your book. Good day to you, Mrs Leech.' She nods in the postmistress's direction. 'Miss Smith,' she adds, squeezing my hand again.

I had hoped to be better prepared for my first encounter with Miss Fairfax, but perhaps a chance meeting in the post office wasn't such a bad start to proceedings. It gave me the opportunity to observe her at close quarters, without half of Highbury between us. And, I have to say, I'm struggling to detect any signs of the conniving con woman Mrs Churchill painted her as – and *I* am far better placed to make this judgement than Mrs Churchill. It takes one to know one, after all. Mrs Churchill's words ring in my head.

I want her gone.

The problem is, *I* don't. Not now I've seen Jane in the flesh. I wait until she has disappeared down the street before making a move. 'Good day, Mrs Leech.'

Mrs Leech is so busy sifting through piles of letters, muttering to herself about Jane's missing correspondence, that she doesn't acknowledge me as I reach the door.

Once outside, I hurry into Mr Cole's stable yard, heading towards a row of empty stalls and breathing in the sweet scent of horse manure. I open up *The Monk* and withdraw Jane's letter.

'You got it, then?'

I whirl round to face the disembodied voice, nearly dropping the book in my haste. 'Jesus Christ, Robert! What are you doing lurking back there?'

'Waiting for you,' he says with an infuriating smirk.

'Well, as you've been so kind as to seek me out, perhaps you would care to explain what the hell all that was in the post office?'

'All what?' Robert asks, the picture of wide-eyed innocence.

'You practically told Jane we were there to steal her love letters.'

'Well, pardon me for having a guilty conscience.'

'It's all right,' I say, patting his shoulder. 'I covered for you by explaining you're madly in love with me.'

'And she believed that?'

'Why wouldn't she?' I ask, arms folded. 'Are you saying I'm not lovable?'

'You're a delight, darling.' Robert snatches the letter from me, still smirking. I try to snatch it back, but fear I might tear it so, in the end, I settle for standing on tiptoes and reading it over Robert's shoulder.

My dearest Jane,

It seems an age since I held you in my arms. I have missed you every day since my return to Yorkshire. You will be in Highbury when you read this and, where you lead, I will follow. I would follow you anywhere, my darling. I would have followed you into the very depths of the ocean that day in Weymouth, had Mr Dixon not stepped in to save the day. I knew when I saw you in his arms that I could not lose you now. I could not allow you to reject my suit yet again with all your talk of duty and propriety. And you did not. You could not resist me then any more than I could resist you. I will see you soon, my love. And soon you will be mine.

Yours always,

F.

'He's laying it on a bit thick, isn't he?' Robert says, handing me the letter. 'The lover doth protest too much, methinks.'

Hmmm. It *is* rather florid for my taste. And a little bit desperate. Possessive, even. There's something not quite right about this boating accident. Of course, if Jane *is* a con artist, then she could have orchestrated the whole thing to ensnare Frank. I'm sure that's what Mrs Churchill would suggest. But, if Frank's letter is anything to go by, I wouldn't put it past *him* to have arranged this little 'accident' to encourage Jane to accept him. Life is short, *carpe diem*, and all that nonsense. It's what I would have done. But I wouldn't have let Mr Dixon play the hero. I would have been there to rescue Jane myself.

Nevertheless, the outcome was the same. Jane accepted Frank's proposal. And Frank Churchill strikes me as the kind of man who gets exactly what he wants.

'It's not the letter I would have written,' I say, when I realise that Robert is still waiting for a response.

Robert rubs his thumb across the base of his neck. 'Would you like me to return to the post office with you and throw some letters around to distract Mrs Leech again?'

'I think you've done enough damage for one day, thank you,' I say, slipping the letter into my book.

Robert reaches for my hand. 'You will return it, won't you, Harriet?'

I squeeze his fingers. 'Of course. Now, get back to your dull agricultural reports, or cow-wrangling or whatever you do on that farm of yours. You can't leave Mr Ingleby to do all the work or else you might not have a farm to return to.'

'Don't tempt me,' Robert replies, giving me a jaunty salute as he heads off towards Abbey-Mill Farm.

I *was* going to take the letter back. Honestly. But now Robert has planted the idea in my head, I wonder if it might be better if Jane didn't receive Frank's latest declaration of love – and the warning of his arrival. I want her on the back foot and, besides, his repeated avowals will only break her heart harder when I have to wrench them apart.

I reach for the letter concealed beneath Frank's love note. A different hand, written in haste and with a sense of urgency.

Jane,
Colonel Campbell informs me that you are planning to stay
with your aunt in Highbury. I know why you have gone there
and I beg you to reconsider. It is too dangerous after what
happened in Weymouth. You must come to Ireland. You will be
safe here. You must leave Highbury, before it is too late.
Your friend always,
William Dixon

Hmmm. Mr Dixon clearly knows something I don't. Danger? In the sleepy little village of Highbury? I don't see it. Unless you count the possibility of being trampled by Robert's overzealous cows or being talked to death by

Miss Bates. I thought *I* posed the biggest threat to Jane Fairfax and her earthly happiness. But, if Mr Dixon is to be believed, there's something wicked waiting for Jane in Highbury. Something worse than me.

CHAPTER 4

Rule number four: *Know thine enemy.*
Intimately.

Miss Smith,

I had hoped for an update on your progress by now. I am sure that there is plenty to keep you occupied in Highbury but, while you are in my employ, I must insist that you focus on the task for which I am paying you. I will not sleep soundly until I am assured that the threat has been removed. As you have evidently not yet recovered my jewellery, I have enclosed some sketches and more detailed descriptions of the pieces to help speed up the process. They will not be hard to find among Miss Fairfax's paste jewellery. You have had ample opportunity to amuse yourself. The time has come to get results.

Mrs Churchill

'The time has come to get results!' I shout in my best Mrs Churchill boom. 'Get results? What does she think I've been trying to do? And, besides, it's been all of one week since Jane Fairfax arrived.' I pace up and down the yard and narrowly avoid mowing down a harassed-looking chicken. The chicken squawks at me as I leap aside.

'Mmmm,' Robert says. He's sitting cross-legged on the ground, bent over a notebook and chewing on the end of his pencil. Two fields away, Mr Ingleby is doing something far more industrious (although I'm not sure exactly what) with the cows.

I've been on high alert since Mr Dixon's warning to Jane that something is rotten in the village of Highbury. But nothing whatsoever has happened. Jane has settled into a routine of tea with her aunt, visits to her neighbours and daily walks to the post office. She has done nothing out of the ordinary – no plotting or poisoning or anything more nefarious than ducking behind a tree to avoid Miss Woodhouse. And no one has done anything remotely threatening to Jane. There's nothing to report to Mrs Churchill. Which is hardly my fault, is it?

'The cheek of the woman. To suggest I'm lounging around, frittering away my expenses.'

'Mmmm.' Robert is scribbling away in his notebook now, lips pressed together in determination.

'Robert, are you even listening to me?' I wave the letter in his direction.

'Frittering away expenses,' he mumbles, still scribbling.

'Robert!' I stamp my foot with such force that he flinches as he's finally forced to acknowledge me.

'Hold it right there.' He stares up at me as if I'm some fascinating sculpture and then he's scribbling furiously in his notebook once more.

'What on earth are you doing?' I fix him with my best I-don't-have-time-for-this-nonsense glare.

'That look, right there. I'm trying to capture you, my darling.' His eyes glisten with mad enthusiasm. 'It's the exact look Henrietta will give George when he suggests that Lord Reginald's body isn't actually under the floorboards at Waverley Manor, as she suspects, but concealed in a tea chest in the local magistrate's stables.'

'And George is?'

'The hero of my masterpiece.'

'Right.'

It would have to be George, wouldn't it? Apparently, Mr Knightley is starring in more than just Robert's fantasies. Sometimes I wonder what world Robert Martin actually comes from. Or lives in, for that matter.

'I hesitate to ask you this, but all this business with people running round poking dead bodies and digging up evidence – is it really the thing? What's wrong with a nice haunting or a ruined castle?'

Robert snorts at me. 'That's a little last century, don't you think? Times are changing, Harriet. People are fed up of revolution, war and the Prince Regent's never-ending string of mistresses. They want order, rationality, somebody to set things right. They need a hero like George Squire.'

George Squire? Lord, give me strength . . .

'Robert, I don't have time for your silly stories right now. This is real life.'

Robert sighs and puts down his notebook, reaching for a stray chicken that's pecking at his boots.

'What have I done? I'll tell you what I've done, Mrs Churchill,' I say, resuming my frantic pacing. 'I've followed Jane back and forth to the post office, watching her sad little face as she comes away empty handed; I've stolen her letters; I've listened to Miss Bates sing her praises, Emma list her faults—'

'I thought you returned her letters?' Robert says, scooping up the pecking chicken and carrying it over to the henhouse.

'I know everything there is to know about Jane Fairfax,' I say, waving away Robert's accusation. 'I know she is proficient at the pianoforte and can sing Thomas Moore's *Irish Melodies* from memory. I know that her handwriting slants to the left and she crosses her t's very low on the stem. I know that her favourite poet is Mary Robinson, her favourite author Henry Fielding, although she is also partial to Ann Radcliffe. I know she has an intense dislike for Emma Woodhouse and there is a childhood grievance between them – some nonsense about a music master, or so I've heard, although I'm sure there's more to it than that. So you see, Mrs Churchill, I've done rather a lot, and none of it has been remotely entertaining.' I stop pacing and put my hands on my hips in a gesture of defiance, dropping Mrs Churchill's letter in the process.

Robert stoops to retrieve it. 'What's this?' he asks as a loose sheet of paper flutters to the ground.

'Oh, her dreadful sketches and descriptions of some jewellery that Frank has supposedly stolen and given to Jane. She wants me to recover it in addition to breaking off the engagement.'

She wants me to prove that Jane is a thief as well as a poisoner.

'And?'

'And what?'

'Have you recovered it?'

'Well, how could I? When I haven't been trailing Jane, or digging into her past, I've had Emma parading me around like a show pony and the two of them are particularly skilled at avoiding each other, so I haven't had much opportunity to root around in Jane's jewellery box.' In actual fact, I've been putting most of my efforts into trying to find Mrs Churchill's poisoner – which you'd think she'd be more bothered about than a few jewels – but I can't tell Robert that, can I? One thing's for certain, if Jane tried to kill Mrs Churchill, she had an accomplice. For, courtesy of my vast network of informants, I have it on good authority that Jane was busy helping the Campbells pack up their house in London when someone slipped a dose of cyanide into Mrs Churchill's tea.

'Anyway, it's not as if Mrs Churchill needs the jewels,' I add. 'Honestly, if my father could see me now. He trained me to relieve disgustingly rich women of their unnecessary jewellery, not steal it back for them.'

Robert sighs. 'Wouldn't you rather be doing something more noble?'

'Noble?'

'These Gothic novelists you so enjoy. Your Radcliffes and Lewises. The women they create are either virtuous, empty-headed maidens who stumble across a mystery only to faint from the exertion of it all, or manipulative, worldly women who prey upon the innocent and use every situation to their advantage.'

'And I'm the second of the two, I suppose?'

Robert ignores the charge. 'I see a third way. A girl who is neither the terrorised nor the terroriser. A clever girl who uses her gifts to seek truth and justice and protect the innocent. That's how I would write my heroine.'

'Seeker of truth and justice? Protector of the innocent? It would never catch on.'

'No. Not while there's no real-life figure to model her on.'

Well, this is really too much. I was not put on this earth for the sole purpose of inspiring the experimental scribblings of a tenant farmer.

'I am not one of your heroines, Robert Martin. You have no right to be disappointed in *me*.'

And yet it rankles, all the same.

Besides, I *am* seeking the truth. And I may not have found it yet, but I'm sure I'll be much closer to it once Frank arrives. Because, if Jane has an accomplice, Frank is the most likely candidate. He has as much to gain as she does from Mrs Churchill's death. And he has much more ready access to his aunt's tea. I managed to ascertain that he was at Enscombe on the day of the poisoning, but once Mrs Churchill realised why I was asking, she swiftly shut down that line of enquiry.

Although there is one small issue with the Frank-as-poisoner theory. As quiet as she no doubt tries to keep it, Frank must know that his aunt's father was an apothecary. And the daughter of an apothecary could sniff out cyanide a mile off. Which leaves me with three possibilities:

1) Frank poisoned the tea as a threat to his aunt, rather than an attempt to kill her.
2) The poison *was* meant to kill Mrs Churchill, but it wasn't Frank who put it there.
3) Mrs Churchill never intended to drink the tea and put the poison in it herself for dramatic effect.

'You're sulking,' Robert observes as he scoops up another rogue chicken.

'I'm not sulking. I'm thinking.'

'About what?'

'Mr Dixon's letter to Jane—'

'The letter you stole—'

'I returned that one. Anyway,' I say, moving on before Robert notices my latent confession, 'if Frank arranged the boating "accident" in Weymouth to encourage Jane into accepting his proposal—'

'That's a big if, Harriet—'

'Well, *if* he did, it's likely the danger to which Mr Dixon was alerting Jane was from Frank. That makes the most sense. I've been following her around like a lost puppy all week and nothing has endangered her at all, unless you count the possibility of her being bored to death by that dreadful sermon from Mr Elton's stand-in on Sunday.'

Mr Elton has disappeared to Bath in something of a hurry. Emma keeps giving me doleful looks, as if I should be affected by his absence. I suppose, in her fevered imagination, I'm madly in love with him. It's obvious to me what has happened. Mr Elton has finally made his move on Emma and she has rejected him. And now he's flounced off to the Bath marriage market in search of a substitute. I don't fancy his chances of finding a bride of Emma's pedigree. A mere clergyman is no more likely to ensnare a rich heiress in Bath than in Highbury. But he'll find *someone* who'll take him.

'I don't know where they stumbled across this rector, but if he gives another sermon like that one, I'm going to have to write to Mr Elton and beg him to return. I'm almost certain I heard Mrs Goddard snoring.'

'Oh, speaking of letters,' Robert says, rummaging around in his pocket and drawing out half a carrot and a crumpled piece of paper, 'a messenger delivered this for you last night.'

'And you're just giving it to me now?' I hit Robert with my copy of *The Monk*. (I'd been planning to drop in on Jane today and the book would offer me good cover if she caught me snooping around in her bedroom. *Oh, Miss Fairfax, I felt so bad about not lending it to you in the post office. You are so kind and I knew you wouldn't accept my mother's book if I offered it to you. So I thought I'd just leave it here.*)

Robert shrugs as I snatch the note from him. 'It was late. I forgot all about it. If it's so urgent, I don't know why you're getting your messages delivered here. A huge boy – frightened me half to death. And he expected payment.'

'Well, I can't have messages arriving at Mrs Goddard's in the middle of the night, can I? People would talk,' I say, ripping open the letter and decoding the spidery handwriting.

Frank Churchill at Randalls.

My informant may be huge, but he's not big on words.

'Brilliant.' I scowl at Robert. This is all I need.

'What?'

'Frank Churchill is at his father's house. You really should have passed this on sooner, you know.'

'Well, you have it now.'

'Yes, but if I'd known Frank had arrived, do you really think I'd be standing here talking to you?'

'I'm sensing from your tone that the answer is no.'

'But, of course, Mrs Churchill didn't bother to inform me herself, did she?'

'Perhaps she doesn't know.'

'Oh, she knows. Frank wouldn't step foot in Highbury without her express permission. No, she's probably sent him on purpose to see exactly what her money is buying for her.'

Not that I've been paid yet, beyond my advance on expenses.

I snatch up Mrs Churchill's letter and slip it into my pelisse. 'If you'll excuse me, I have an engagement to break off.'

And a poisoner to catch.

✳

I squint against the sunlight as I stride into Highbury. My breath mists in the icy spring air. I ignore the sharp pain in my chest as I quicken my pace. I really should have known that Frank was here. If only Robert had been more efficient. I aimed to be one step ahead of Frank, but now I feel like I've been ambushed.

I enter the high street just as Frank is leaving the Bateses' apartment. Because, of course, Jane would be the first person he called upon in Highbury. I duck behind a grey slate wishing well, taking in Frank's tight breeches and perfectly coiffed hair as Jane rushes out after him, cheeks flushed, mouth set in a hard line. She looks both ways before grasping his arm and dragging him into Mr Cole's stable yard. I wait until they've disappeared inside and creep after them.

The Coles' stable yard is a good place for a lovers' tryst. The Coles made their money in trade and, in true nouveau-riche style, they try to make everyone forget it by parading their wealth around in the most tasteless manner possible. The horses are more for display than actual use and they only have one groom, a lazy lad with a squint who spends more time in the local tavern than the stables. That's probably where he is now, because the yard is deserted, except for two bay geldings who poke their heads over their stall doors at the sound of footsteps. Jane drags Frank to the end stall before turning to face him with an expression that would have terrified many men into submission. But apparently, Frank Churchill is made of sterner stuff, because he simply grins at Jane before pushing her back against the wall.

I inhale the sweet scent of hay and horse manure and slide into an empty stall, shutting the door behind me. I feel a huff of warm breath on my neck as I take a backward step. The stall isn't empty after all. I turn towards the dark muzzle of a grey Lipizzaner stallion that wouldn't be out of place in Mr Knightley's stables.

The Coles are clearly going up in the world.

The stallion tosses his head and whinnies softly as I trail my fingers through his mane. I retreat from my new friend and peer out of the stable to see Jane still pinned against the wall, making no attempt to free herself as Frank's hand cups her chin. I close my eyes, pushing away the image of a different hand, a different face – a love that was similarly doomed.

'Come away with me,' Frank murmurs as his fingers grasp the back of Jane's neck. I hear in his tone the possessiveness that I detected in his letter to Jane.

Finally, Jane pushes him away. 'I can't.'

'You can,' Frank insists, clutching her hands in his. 'We can. I can get the money.'

Jane shakes her head and pulls her hands free. 'Money doesn't solve everything, you know. There are other considerations. The scandal. The harm to my reputation. I will not do that to Aunt Hetty or my grandmama. I will not go against your family, either.'

'My aunt will never give her blessing.'

'I know. But I won't do it. Not like this. *I* have nothing to be ashamed of,' she says, raising her chin.

Frank grabs her arm. 'You suppose I'm ashamed? Of this? Of you?'

'Your behaviour suggests it. You have not told your aunt we are engaged.'

'I didn't expect such judgement from you.'

'Frank, you're hurting me.'

My fingers curl into a fist. I can't stand by and watch Frank treat Jane like this. He's a bully. A spoilt rich boy used to getting his own way.

Not this time.

I unlatch the stall door, ready to leap to Jane's defence.

'Fine. Have it your way,' Frank says, dropping Jane's arm. I withdraw to the shadows just in time as Frank turns on his heel and storms out of the stables.

Jane's hands are shaking as she lets out a strangled sob. She closes her eyes and takes a deep, calming breath. I find myself breathing in time with her. One of the bay geldings whickers and nuzzles at Jane's palm as she absently strokes his muzzle. The Lipizzaner snorts and paws the ground beside me. I duck down behind the stall door as Jane raises her head and turns in my direction. I hold my breath at the soft tread of her approaching boots. She stops outside my stall, clicking her tongue at the Lipizzaner.

I exhale gratefully as Jane slips out of the stable yard and back onto the high street. This exchange has been very informative. I see exactly how it stands between Frank and Jane. She is all goodness and restraint. *He* is the embodiment of recklessness. Jane Fairfax poisoning Mrs Churchill to ensure that she can marry Frank? I can't see it. But Frank Churchill poisoning his aunt to ensure that he can marry Jane? Much more likely. Of course, the thought must have crossed Mrs Churchill's mind, but she'll never admit that to me. Mrs Churchill wants a scapegoat and Jane is a convenient target. Pointing the finger at Jane kills two birds with one stone: it absolves Frank of the blame, while also getting rid of his unsuitable fiancée. It's the perfect solution for Mrs Churchill.

But not for me.

I scramble to my feet, catching up with Jane as she reaches her aunt's apartment.

'Miss Fairfax.'

She pretends not to hear me as she fumbles with her key.

'Miss Fairfax.' I step up beside her and take the key from her still-shaking hands, inserting it in the lock.

She nods her thanks, clearly not trusting herself to speak.

'I'm so glad I caught you,' I say as the door swings open. 'I have been meaning to call by all week, but Miss Woodhouse has kept me rather busy.' Mainly, I've been listening to Emma's endless speculations about whether Frank Churchill would finally grace us with his presence. As I've spent most of my waking hours wondering the same thing – but for very different reasons to Emma – the never-ending cycle of Churchill chatter has not done much to settle my nerves. 'I have scones,' I announce, fishing around in my reticule, 'although I'm afraid they might be a bit squashed.'

Jane looks down at the crumbling scones and back up at me. 'Would you like to come in, Miss Smith?'

I nod and follow Jane upstairs. The Bateses' apartment feels brighter now Jane has arrived. The parlour smells of freesias and apples, spring air wafts in through the open window, and the fading chintz sofa is covered in intricately embroidered cushions which are obviously Jane's handiwork.

'Do sit down, Miss Smith,' Jane says, gesturing towards the sofa. 'I'm afraid my aunt is over at Mrs Goddard's and Grandmama has gone for her nap.'

I try not to look too relieved at this announcement, but the twitch of Jane's lip suggests I haven't quite managed it.

'Thank you for the scones,' she says, taking them from me. 'I'll just put them in the kitchen.' She makes no attempt to move.

'Miss Fairfax, are you all right?'

'Am I all right?' Jane's eyes narrow.

'You look a little out of sorts. As if something has upset you.'

Jane's lip wobbles. She places the scones on the tea table and perches on the arm of the sofa. She takes a deep breath and leans towards me. 'Can I ask you something?' she says in a near-whisper.

'Of course.' I'm careful to hold her gaze.

'Would you—' She clears her throat and tries again. 'Would you like a cup of tea, Miss Smith?'

I would rather you confessed your secrets, Miss Fairfax, but if tea is all that's on offer, I will take it. It might at least give me the chance to look for Mrs Churchill's precious heirlooms.

'Tea would be lovely.'

As Jane retreats into the kitchen, I slip into the room I suppose to be her bedroom, taking my copy of *The Monk* with me as my cover. I should just about have time to make a cursory search for the jewellery. Jane's bedroom is depressingly plain. Only her dressing table offers an indication that somebody lives here. A tallow candle, a hairbrush, a silk reticule and two neat piles of books: Homer's *Odyssey*, Shakespeare's *Complete Works*, Fielding's *Tom Jones*, Robinson's *Sappho and Phaon* and Wollstonecraft's *A Vindication of the Rights of Women* are in one pile; the other consists entirely of Ann Radcliffe's novels, minus the lent-out copy of *The Italian*. I lay down *The Monk* on Jane's dressing table and trace my fingers across the cover of the first volume of *The Romance of the Forest* – my favourite. There's an inscription on the title page.

To my darling Jane,
All my love,
Henry

My first thought is that Jane is having a sordid affair with a man who has very good taste in literature. My second thought is that this is exactly the kind of conclusion to which Emma Woodhouse would leap, which means it's almost certainly erroneous. Besides, the ink of the inscription is fading, the pages musty and yellowing. This isn't Jane's book. It's her mother's – a gift from Jane's father, Lieutenant Henry Fairfax. I close the book with a new-found reverence and a sense of guilt. No wonder she bought my story about *The Monk* so readily. It didn't belong to my mother, of course. She despaired of rogues and romance and rollicking adventures. The real world, she insisted, was much more mundane and disappointing. No, I stole this book from the library of some ancient duke who I'd just conned out of half his fortune. But I've added an inscription to it now – just to make it convincing.

I return *The Romance of the Forest* to the pile and open Jane's dressing table. I find her small jewellery box – plain mahogany, lined with fading red velvet. Mrs Churchill is right – it's mainly paste jewels, but there are a couple of finer pieces. An emerald brooch. A ruby cross on a gold chain which has been well cared for, but the clasp is stiff, as if it hasn't been worn for a very long time. There *is* a string of pearls, but they are yellow and peeling – definitely not the Churchill jewels. I check the other drawers in Jane's dressing table. I even look under the bed.

Nothing.

If Mrs Churchill's jewellery is here, it's well hidden. The rattle of china from the kitchen tells me my time is almost up. I take one last look around the room, searching for inspiration. I find it on Jane's dressing table in the form of a rosewood writing box, inlaid with a mother-of-pearl fleur-de-lys design that looks vaguely familiar. I open the box and remove the two empty inkwells. There's nothing else inside. I try the drawer at the bottom, but it only opens an inch or two. There's a piece of paper wedged inside. I bend over to inspect it. There's something else there too. Something shiny and black. I prise my fingers into the drawer and pull out the mystery object.

Attached to its ridged, black body are eight beeswax-yellow legs, two huge pincers and a thin, black tail, tipped with a toffee-coloured stinger. It takes me a moment to realise that the tail is twitching. I let out a yelp loud enough to alert Jane in the kitchen as I drop the scorpion onto the floor and leap backwards. I have just enough time to retrieve my copy of *The Monk* from Jane's dressing table and hold it to my chest as I tiptoe around the scorpion.

Jane stands frozen in the doorway, pale-faced and trembling. Eyes hard, lips pursed, she watches the scorpion scuttle across the floor. She balls her hands into fists, as if readying herself for a fight. My yelp must have woken up Mrs Bates, because she's in the doorway now, beside her granddaughter. She glances at Jane and then at the scorpion. Jaw clenched, she takes a step forward, raises the heel of her slipper and, with a surprising show of strength, stamps down on the scorpion, over and over, until all that remains is an ink-black stain, oozing across the floor. She nods grimly on that final blow, a gleam of satisfaction in her eyes as she bends to remove her slipper, squeezing Jane's arm as she hobbles from the room.

CHAPTER 5

Rule number five: A little stalking goes a long way.
But only if you're persistent about it.

'Splat!' I slam my palm against the table with such
force that the tea slops over the side of my cup
and forms a muddy moat in my saucer. 'All over
the floor. Innards everywhere. You don't want to get on
the wrong side of Mrs Bates. You should have seen Jane's
face. It was whiter than a spring snowdrop. And she was
trembling so violently you would have thought *she* had
been the one to pick up the scorpion.'

It's strange – her reaction was so extreme I wonder
if there was some special significance to the scorpion. It
seemed personal to Jane. As if someone was sending her a
very specific message.

'I, on the other hand, behaved with admirable calm,' I
add, as I attempt to mop up my tea with the edge of the
tablecloth.

'I think it's perfectly acceptable to blanch at the sight

of a scorpion. Horrible creatures with their great pincers and all those legs.' Robert waggles his arms around in what he evidently thinks is a scorpion-like manner.

'Well, yes, they're hardly fluffy kittens, but it wasn't that bad.'

'What *I* want to know is how on earth the scorpion got there,' Robert says, pouring cream into his tea with wild abandon.

I shrug. 'I asked Jane about the writing box – told her I'd opened it because I heard something scrabbling around inside when I went in to leave my copy of *The Monk* on her dressing table. She claimed she had never seen the box before, but she looked as if she knew who had put it there. And Mrs Bates confirmed that there were no callers that morning, other than Frank. Although I suppose someone could have crept in while she was asleep.'

Robert raises an eyebrow as he pours yet another helping of cream into his cup.

'Yes, I know,' I say. 'Frank does seem the obvious candidate. He was awfully keen to get Jane to elope with him. He could have slipped the scorpion into her room as a scare tactic to make Jane think someone was out to get her. The sooner they get married and she's under his protection, the better – that sort of thing. Besides, it's probably not the first time he's pulled that tactic.'

'The boating accident in Weymouth.'

'Exactly.'

Robert frowns. 'I think it's fairly likely Frank planted

the scorpion. What I meant was how did the scorpion get here? To merry old England. I've never encountered one in real life.'

'Oh, there's a whole colony of yellow-tailed scorpions in Kent and East London,' I say, with a wave of my hand. 'Apparently they stowed away on some Italian masonry a few years back and moved into the shipyards.'

Robert's grip on his teaspoon tightens. 'How do you know all this?'

I shrug. 'My father once posed as a naturalist in an attempt to seduce a particularly eccentric duchess. And, of course, he left *me* to do all the research. Actually, it was rather fascinating.'

'I'm sure,' Robert mumbles, studying me as if *I'm* some kind of venomous creature.

'Don't worry. Yellow-tailed scorpions are not one of the deadly species. Their sting is no more painful than a bee's. And it won't kill you – unless, perhaps, you're very young, or very old. So you'd most likely be fine.'

'That's a relief.'

'Unless you have a particularly weak constitution. Then it could kill you, I suppose.'

'You're such a comfort, Harriet,' Robert says. He takes a long gulp of tea and sets down his cup. 'Well, Miss Bates keeps droning on about the horrible cold her niece caught in Weymouth. It's clear that Jane isn't the healthiest of specimens. If she's as fragile as her aunt insists, perhaps that's why she was so bothered by the scorpion.'

'I hope not. Because that would mean someone isn't trying to scare her. They're trying to kill her.'

I wonder if Mrs Churchill would still pay me if Jane suddenly dropped dead.

I fear Robert might be able to read the thought from my expression, but he's too busy staring over my shoulder at our quarry.

'What's he doing now?' I ask.

Robert scowls at me over his monocle. Yes, monocle. He's wearing a false moustache, too, and I'm determined not to allude to it. I'm sure he hasn't quite recovered from our recent quarrel about Gothic heroines and morally acceptable occupations for a young woman and he only agreed to this assignation so that he could thoroughly show me up. It's all right for Robert. All he had to do was borrow a horse from his beloved Mr Knightley for an imaginary trip to the cattle market. *I*, on the other hand, had to beg the use of Emma's carriage to convey one of my fellow parlour boarders, Miss Bickerton – a notorious gossip and tremendous bore – to visit her sick aunt in London. Of course, there's nothing wrong with her aunt or, at least, there wasn't when I left Miss Bickerton on her doorstep. I can't guarantee that this will still be the case after a few hours in Miss Bickerton's company . . .

My disguise is much more subtle than Robert's. My best auburn wig and some carefully applied cosmetics. A scattering of freckles across my nose. A gown suitable for a fashionable tea shop but not too flashy to draw attention to me out on the street.

'He's pouring out his tea. He's taking a sip. No, wait. He's stopped. He hasn't let it brew for long enough. *I* could have told him that.'

'Robert. You know that's not what I meant,' I say sternly. I close my eyes and inhale the heady mix of tea and freshly baked sponge cake. The air resounds with the chink of teaspoons against china saucers and the steady hum of conversation from half-filled mouths.

The 'he' in question is, of course, our potential poisoner and scorpion-wrangler, Frank Churchill. He has charmed the women of Highbury with his bright eyes, easy manners and a smile so lascivious it makes even *my* cold heart beat a little faster. Emma is utterly enchanted. In fact, Jane seems to be the only woman in Highbury who sees through his act (apart from me). She's been giving him a wide berth since their tête-à-tête in the Coles' stable yard and the scorpion incident three days ago. And, as it seems that Frank is far more likely to be Mrs Churchill's poisoner than Jane, I've decided to relax my surveillance on Jane and spend some time shadowing Frank instead. I've billed it to Robert as an information-gathering exercise – a way to get dirt on Frank Churchill in a bid to break up his relationship with Jane. This is part of it, of course. The other part (the part Robert doesn't know about) is to catch Frank in the act of plotting another attempt on Mrs Churchill's life and ensure he doesn't get the opportunity to carry it out.

'You asked me what he's doing,' Robert insists. 'And, right now, he's demonstrating his ignorance of tea-making. Oh, good Lord.'

'What? What's happening?' I hiss, resisting the urge to turn round and look for myself.

'Really, it's quite shocking—'

'Robert, what?'

'I wouldn't have thought it of a man of his rank.'

'Robert!'

'He's putting the jam on first.'

'What?'

'The jam,' Robert enunciates, his voice laden with horror. 'Before the cream. *Monster*.'

'I don't think you're taking this seriously,' I say as the waiter appears with our Bath buns.

'On the contrary, I'm taking it very seriously. Everyone of taste and decency knows it's cream first, then jam. Honestly, you might end this whole sorry charade right now by informing Jane Fairfax that her future husband is a jam-and-cream man.'

'Robert!'

'How am I not taking this seriously?' His false moustache quivers.

I wasn't going to mention it, but since he's asking . . .

'Well, look at you.' I gesture towards his monocle. 'What exactly is this supposed to be?'

'I'm in disguise.'

'As what? A Prussian spy?'

'Yes,' he shouts, kicking the table in his excitement and I just manage to dodge the teaspoon that goes flying across the table as a result. It hits the floor with a satisfying clank. 'I wasn't sure you'd work it out.'

'Excuse me?' I can't tell if he's joking.

'Otto Ackermann, at your service,' he says in what I fear is supposed to be a German accent.

Apparently, he's not joking.

'Otto Ackermann?' I try to sound as unimpressed as possible (which isn't hard given the circumstances).

'Yes,' Robert says, grinning maniacally.

Clearly, it's not working.

'He's the fellow who was seen meeting Sir Reginald on the night of his murder.'

'Meeting Sir Reginald,' I say slowly. 'From your ... novel.' (I hesitate to use the word novel to describe what Robert is doing. I don't want to encourage him.)

'Yes. George has already become suspicious of the man, but Henrietta thinks he's making something out of nothing. Of course, I don't think Ackermann is involved in the murder itself,' Robert continues. 'That would be too ...'

Completely irrelevant to our current endeavours?

'Predictable,' he finishes.

Robert Martin is anything but predictable.

'Robert, what are you doing?'

He's picking the currants out of his Bath bun.

'I'm picking the currants out of my Bath bun.'

'But you like currants.'

'Yes.' He sighs, as if talking to somebody very stupid. (I suppose he's had plenty of practice out on the farm by himself.) 'But Otto Ackermann doesn't.'

'Doesn't he?'

'No,' Robert replies, seemingly unaware that he's discussing a figment of his own imagination. 'He detests them.'

'Of course he does.' I bend down to pick up the fallen teaspoon and count to five. 'I hesitate to ask you this,' I say, placing the teaspoon back on his saucer, 'but why, when we are supposed to be incognito, have you decided to disguise yourself as a Prussian spy? Don't you think it might make people a little suspicious of you?'

'Well, of course it will,' he says cheerfully. 'But they won't suspect me of being Robert Martin, tenant farmer, in pursuit of a man who has had the audacity to go to London for a haircut, will they?'

'I've told you. No man travels all the way to London for a mere haircut. He's up to something and I intend to find out what.'

'Really? And just what has he been up to so far, my dear Harriet?'

Frank Churchill might well have been up to a great deal. It started off promisingly enough when we followed him to the apothecary's this morning.

'Well, Robert,' I'd said, nudging his arm, 'off you go.'

'Excuse me?'

'Go and see what he's buying.'

Robert frowned and made no move to follow Frank. 'Why?'

'Why?'

'Yes, why?'

I could see this might go on for some time. 'He might be buying something incriminating.'

'Like what?' Robert asked, looking at me as if I'd just declared my love for Napoleon.

Poison, I wanted to say, but I couldn't exactly admit this to Robert. 'Just go and see,' I said, shooing him towards the window.

Not even Robert's raised eyebrow and signature smirk could dampen my spirits as he finally headed towards the apothecary's. I was right. We were about to catch Frank in the act or, rather, Robert was. I couldn't risk getting too close to Frank in case he recognised me later, despite my excellent disguise.

I paced back and forth for what felt like hours, but must only have been minutes, waiting for Robert to reappear.

'Cough drops,' said a voice behind me.

'Cough drops?' I demanded, whipping round to face Robert.

'Cough drops,' he affirmed and I could hear the I-told-you-so in his tone.

The cough drops were followed by boot polish, a cravat, a ball of twine (I'm still none-the-wiser about this one) and a silk handkerchief. All we had ascertained so far was that Frank Churchill loved to shop. We'd witnessed not the slightest hint of villainy. But Frank *is* a villain, I'm sure of it. It takes a con artist to know a con artist.

'He's leaving, Harriet.'

'What?'

'Frank Churchill has left the building.' Robert shakes me from my reverie.

I summon a waiter with lightning speed and pay our bill. Robert's eyes widen at the amount as he stuffs the remainder of his currant-less Bath bun into his mouth.

'Mrs Churchill is paying,' I say with a smile, although she might not be for much longer if things carry on like this.

I don't have high hopes for our afternoon following Frank. If the morning is anything to go by, it's not likely we're in for any wild excitement. I'm tempted to admit defeat and return to Highbury, but giving up is not in my vocabulary. Robert has become suspiciously quiet – no doubt he's plotting Otto Ackermann's next move in the Sir Reginald murder case. At least it keeps him occupied. Finally, I'm rewarded for my patience as Frank, with a furtive glance over his shoulder, disappears down a deserted alleyway with the promising name of Grope Lane.

This is more like it.

I grasp Robert's arm and feel him tense under my grip. It's not an unpleasant sensation. I had no idea farming could have such a powerful effect upon a man's physique. Not that this is the time to get distracted by Robert's biceps.

'You see,' I whisper in Robert's ear as I steer him towards the alleyway. 'I told you he was up to something.'

Now we just need to find out what.

We proceed with caution, keeping a safe distance between ourselves and our quarry. I'm not sure Mrs Churchill would be thrilled to hear that I've been spending my time following her nephew down dark alleyways instead of concentrating my efforts on Jane, but it's for her own good. And she certainly won't be hearing about it from me. Not unless I find something that incriminates Frank. I gag at the stench of rotting fruit, horse manure and something that smells suspiciously like stale urine.

I wish I wasn't wearing satin boots.

There's no cover in the alleyway and, if Frank were to look behind him, he would see us. I'm ready for such an eventuality. There are reasons enough for a man and a woman to seek seclusion in a deserted alleyway and I'm sure I could put on a good performance should the need arise. But it doesn't look like I'll have to resort to anything hands-on, because Frank is squinting at a scrap of paper he's just pulled from his pocket. He stops once or twice to study it and finally halts in front of an abandoned tavern at the end of the alleyway, looking up doubtfully at the fading sign of a beached mermaid tangled up in a fisherman's net. She's smiling beatifically, as if it were her intention all along to fall into the sordid grip of mankind.

Frank pauses under the sign and then takes three measured paces away from it, like a pirate hunting for treasure.

'What on earth is he—'

I put my finger to Robert's lips. We mustn't startle him now.

Frank appears to be performing some kind of elaborate dance. He stops, bends down, and reaches for something on the ground. I can't see what it is from this distance and in the gloom of the alleyway, but then there's a metallic creak, like a spring releasing, and a wooden panel rises from the ground, obscuring him from view. In a moment, it recedes with an agonising groan. I step towards it, impatiently.

Robert grips my waist. 'Harriet, he'll see,' he whispers, his fingers digging into my ribs.

But he won't see. Because Frank Churchill has vanished.

CHAPTER 6

Rule number six: If you hang around in dark alley-ways for long enough, you're sure to encounter a few rogues.

'Are we just going to stand here?'

'Do you have any better ideas?' I ask.

'Go home?' Robert says hopefully.

'And miss whatever Frank Churchill is doing here? I don't think so.'

'But what *is* he doing here?'

'Well, that's the point, isn't it?' I insist. 'We need to find out. It could be some sort of illicit gambling den. I've heard plenty of rumours on that front.'

Or maybe he's hiring an assassin to do away with his aunt.

'Perhaps he *is* just getting his hair cut.'

'Down a deserted alleyway, beneath a hidden trapdoor?' I ask, flinging my arms about with such abandon that I nearly smack Robert full in the face.

Honestly, Robert, I credited you with a better imagination than this.

'He might be,' Robert mumbles.

'What we need,' I say, ignoring his sullen looks, 'is somebody on the inside.'

'Well, unless you memorised Frank's little dance, I don't think we've got much chance of getting in any time soon.'

That's my Robert. Ever the optimist.

'Besides,' he adds, gesturing towards the trapdoor, 'he might not be coming back. It could be some kind of secret passageway. Frank might be on the other side of London by now.'

'Yes. Perhaps he's at the dockyards, procuring a fresh supply of scorpions.'

Robert shudders and peers down the alleyway, as if he expects an army of scorpions to swarm up out of the trapdoor at any second.

'We'll just give it another five minutes,' I say, trying not to sound like I'm begging.

'Harriet. He's been gone nearly half an hour. I think we have to accept he's eluded us at last.'

'This is so typical of you. Never any patience.'

'*I'm* impatient? That's rich coming from you, Miss We-must-go-to-London-right-now-because-Frank-Churchill-is-getting-his-hair-cut-and-I-don't-believe-him.'

I don't know why I'm picking a fight with Robert. Actually, I do. Because I *am* impatient. Nothing has happened all day and I don't want to write off this trip as a complete waste of time.

'He's not coming back, Harriet.'

I flinch at the loud metallic creak and pull Robert into the shadows as the trapdoor opens again. The silhouette of a man rises from the ground. It's not Frank. He's around the same age, but too broad in the shoulders, a few inches shorter, and he moves with less grace but more purpose than Frank. In fact, there's something disturbingly familiar in his movements. He whistles a jaunty little tune that has been stuck in my brain like a horribly persistent tic ever since I first heard it in the Derbyshire militia camp. I groan as I push Robert out of the shadows and into the path of our not-so-mystery man.

'Denny?' Robert squawks.

Of all the people we could have encountered down a piss-stained alleyway which, come nightfall, no doubt lives up to its name, it would have to be him, wouldn't it? Reuben Denny. Heartthrob of the Derbyshire militia, frequenter of debutantes' dreams and gentlemen's beds, although he vows he has given it all up in pursuit of a certain artistically inclined farmer. He's also the type to cheerfully inform his lover about his friend's plan to seduce a drugged woman at a ball for payment, rather than attempting to do anything to stop such a horror from occurring. Fortunately, unlike Denny, Robert has a conscience and half a brain.

It's not that I disapprove of Robert's lifestyle, but I'm not thrilled by his choice of partner or his blatant disregard for common sense and locked doors when Denny comes calling. I've seen rather a lot of Reuben Denny. Too much, some might say. But this is nothing compared to the visceral fear that one day it won't be *me* who barrels into the barn, or Robert's bedroom or, on one horrifying occasion, an actual pigsty – in front of the pigs, for crying out loud. And, when that day comes, the unfortunate interloper might not be as willing as I am to look the other way. In every other scenario, Robert is careful. Buttoned up. But then along comes Denny with his heroic scars and his crooked smile and that bloody uniform.

Denny starts and takes a step backward, raking his fingers through his hair while slipping something small and shiny into his pocket with his other hand. 'Robert? What are you— Why are you dressed like that?'

Robert removes his monocle, but seems to have forgotten about his false moustache.

Denny looks good. His hair is groomed, he's clean-shaven and, out of uniform, he seems smarter somehow. He's fuller in the face and looks all the better for it. Kinder. Although that might just be because he's gazing at Robert with an expression that's veering dangerously close to adoration.

'I'm running an errand,' Robert says as he realises Denny is still waiting for an answer.

Denny's lip twitches. 'For Harriet.' It's not a question.

'Yes,' Robert admits, voice hitching.

Denny sighs. 'Of course you are.'

'Denny,' Robert mumbles, reaching out and brushing a hand over Denny's shoulder.

'It's a shame you're busy running around after Harriet,' Denny says, his eyes roving over Robert's body. 'Otherwise

I would have asked if you wanted to go for a drink.'

'A drink?' Robert says, angling his hip towards Denny, as if he's forgotten why we're here. It's at times like this I think Robert's obsession with his landlord might not be such a bad thing. I can't imagine Mr Knightley trying to seduce anyone down a dingy alleyway.

'No,' Denny replies, taking a step towards Robert. 'Not a drink.'

Robert blushes, but doesn't retreat.

Don't mind me, Robert. It's not as if we're hot on the trail of a homicidal maniac.

'What are you doing here, Denny?' Robert asks, as if he's read my mind.

Denny stiffens and narrows his eyes. 'What do you mean?'

'Here.' Robert gestures. 'In a dark alleyway, clambering through a trapdoor?'

'Not jealous, are we?' Denny raises an eyebrow.

'Should I be?'

Please let it be true. If Denny has just emerged from a molly house, it will make things easier for me on two counts. One: it might finally break the spell of fascination that holds Robert in Denny's thrall. For, while it's Denny who trails around after Robert like a stray puppy, it's Robert who keeps feeding him.

Because he thinks he doesn't deserve any better.

And two: it would offer a convenient way to break up Frank and Jane. Frank would call off the engagement himself if he knew that *I* knew. No need to tell Mrs Churchill how I did it. Jane would be *gone*, just as my employer demanded, and neither Jane nor Frank would have any reason to poison Mrs Churchill then. Problem solved.

'You know I only have eyes for you,' Denny says, his fingers twitching towards his redingote pocket.

He's definitely up to something.

'It's not your eyes I'm worried about.'

Denny laughs and brings a hand up to cup Robert's chin. 'Why are you so bothered?'

'I – I just want to know what you're doing here.'

'Why?' Denny asks, withdrawing his hand. 'Why do you want to know?'

'Because you're up to something, Denny—' I say, stepping from the shadows.

'Harriet.' Denny's mouth settles into a sneer. 'Of course you're here. You're always here.'

'—and it may have something to do with my work.'

'I doubt that,' says Denny, smirking as he steps past Robert and into my path. He stands only an inch taller than me and the peppermint on his breath doesn't do enough to conceal the stench of whisky and tobacco.

'Just tell me where you've been,' I say, standing my ground.

'Why should I?'

'Because I know things about you. I've seen things.'

He bites the inside of his cheek as he glances at Robert

and then back at me. 'You wouldn't do that to him,' he says.

'Not to him,' I agree, bringing my lips right up to Denny's ear. 'But I'm sure you have plenty of indiscretions I could bring to light that don't involve Robert.'

Denny raises his chin and stares me down, eyes full of contempt.

Trust me, the feeling's mutual.

'Now, I'll ask you again. Where have you been? What have you been doing down there?'

Denny glances at the trapdoor, as if he's forgotten what this is all about. 'Fine,' he says, clearing his throat. 'If you must know, I was having my hair cut.'

Robert flashes me a triumphant smile. I pretend not to notice.

'You were having your hair cut?'

Of all the ridiculous things . . .

'Yes.'

'Then why the concealment? Why back alleys and secret codes and trapdoors?'

'He's a very exclusive barber. London's best-kept secret.'

Until now.

'Besides,' he adds, lowering his voice, 'he's French.'

'I see.'

It's not a great time to be French in Britain. Not a great time to be French in France, either, for that matter.

'Was there a gentleman there?' I ask. 'Handsome, tall, dark hair?'

'You mean Frank Churchill,' Denny says with a sly smile.

'Yes, I mean Frank Churchill.'

I think about asking Denny how he knows Frank, but I imagine he makes it his business to know all the handsome, rich society men.

'Yes, he's in there,' Denny says. 'Also getting a haircut.'

'And when you say a haircut—'

'I mean a haircut,' he says, gesturing towards his close-cropped Titus. 'See for yourself. He'll be up soon enough. Now, if that's all?'

I take a step back.

'Robert,' Denny says, eyes sweeping over him hungrily. 'Always a pleasure. Don't leave it so long next time.' He leans in and says something that sounds suspiciously like 'the moustache looks good on you'.

Robert blushes, his hand reaching towards his mouth.

'Harriet,' Denny says with a curt nod in my direction. 'I'll be seeing you.'

'Hopefully not too soon,' I say sweetly to his retreating figure.

We follow Denny to the end of the alleyway, which is just as well, because Frank reappears a few minutes later, sporting a stern expression and a rather fashionable Bedford crop.

'Well, of course, he had to have his hair cut,' I tell Robert. 'Otherwise people would have noticed the lie.'

'Right. The lie being ...'

'That he was coming to London to get his hair cut,' I

snap, realising exactly how ridiculous I sound. 'He's up to something,' I insist, with more confidence than I feel. 'You just watch.'

We trail him as he meanders through the streets, kicking loose pebbles as if he's been shorn of his sense of purpose as well as his hair. Finally, we follow him into Broadwood's on Great Pulteney Street.

'Go and see what he's looking at,' I whisper to Robert.

As Robert crosses the shop, Frank turns around and looks straight in my direction. I duck down behind the nearest pianoforte – an elegant instrument, not a grand, but a large-sized, square pianoforte of superior workmanship. It's remarkably like my mother's instrument – the one I assaulted with my clumsy childhood fingers until she coaxed them into diligent application. I had become proficient by the time she was gone, although I never did reach her level of mastery. I could sit at my mother's feet for hours, listening to Bach and Mozart flow from her fingers as if she had composed the melodies herself. She had a flair for improvisation and she rarely bothered with sheet music. 'It's all in here,' she would say, tapping her breast, when her admirers wondered at her skill.

I kept playing after she'd gone, as if it would keep a part of her with me. Father didn't approve. I suppose it was too painful a reminder of what he'd lost. It wasn't long before we had to sell the pianoforte and the building that housed it, along with everything else my mother left behind. Of course, I've played many a fine instrument in the homes of rich and impressionable gentlemen, but we moved so often from place to place that I never again had my own instrument.

'Can I help you, miss?' says a clipped voice behind me. I stumble against the pianoforte stool, but quickly recover myself. I peer over the instrument and see Frank at the counter, paying for his wares. I remain kneeling by the instrument, running my hand over it.

'I was just admiring the workmanship,' I say, turning in time to detect the raised eyebrow of the shop assistant, a bored-looking young man with a beaklike nose and the most outrageous Brutus hairstyle I've ever seen. (Perhaps he has paid a visit to a certain French barber.)

'Yes. It is fine workmanship.'

Too fine for you, his voice seems to say.

I'll show you, Mr Brutus.

'Would miss like to try the instrument?' he asks in the same clipped tone, no doubt expecting me to demur.

Well, I don't like to be predictable.

I glance over at the counter and see that Frank has retreated to the door. Robert stares at me, wide-eyed. I jerk my head towards the door, hoping he'll take the hint. He continues to stare at me, mouth hanging open like a dead fish, but, as I repeat the motion with added emphasis, he nods in acknowledgement and follows Frank out onto the street.

'Miss?'

'Yes,' I snap, turning my attention back to Brutus. 'I should like to try the instrument.'

'Very well,' he says, not attempting to hide his smirk as he pulls out the stool for me.

I sit down, fingers poised over the pianoforte.

'Would miss like some music?' he asks, still smirking.

'No, miss would not,' I say as I strike up the opening notes of Mozart's 'Rondo alla Turca'. *His* favourite. It wasn't what I'd meant to play. I didn't mean to conjure up the image of his enchanting smile as he watched me from his dutiful place beside his aunt, nodding in all the right places at her relentless monologue, his attention clearly fixed on me. If there was ever an incentive to memorise my music, it was those magical minutes when our eyes met over Mozart, both of us too stubborn to look away – propriety be damned. My fingers falter momentarily, but I couldn't stop if I wanted to. And I don't want to banish his smile. Because he'll never smile at me again.

It *is* a fine instrument. Not so fine as those I played in Vienna or Paris – or Derbyshire, even – but the comparison is an unfair one. I cannot expect perfection here. There's a softness in the upper notes that suits my style exactly. I hadn't meant to show off as much of my skill, but the shop assistant had been so superior that I wanted to wipe the smirk off his smug little face. By the end of my performance – for performance is what it is – a small crowd has gathered around the instrument. They break into astonished applause as I finish with a flourish.

'Madam,' Brutus simpers, his face flushed, 'I have never encountered such exquisite style. You must tell me, who is your music master?'

'I have no master,' I say as I rise from the instrument and glide towards the door, head held high.

Out on the street, Robert is watching a retreating carriage, foot tapping as his eyes dart towards Broadwood's. I'm thankful he wasn't around to witness my musical triumph. It didn't quite fit with my plan of keeping a low profile.

'Where is he?' I demand as I reach Robert.

'Gone back to Highbury,' Robert says, pointing towards the carriage in the distance. 'Should I follow him?'

'No,' I say wearily. 'I think we've done enough for one day. And I suppose I must collect Miss Bickerton from her aunt's house at some point.'

Robert looks relieved.

'What did he buy?' I ask, reluctant to abandon the last glimmer of hope that this hasn't been a wasted trip.

'Sheet music. *Irish Melodies.*'

'A present for Miss Fairfax, no doubt.'

'I expect so,' Robert agrees.

'Not exactly extravagant for a man of his means, is it? Hardly a grand gesture.'

'I suppose he has to be subtle about it. Small things that won't be noticed or can be explained away. He wouldn't want to cause a stir.'

Once in a while, Robert is utterly brilliant, though I'm careful not to tell him so.

'No,' I say, tapping my fingers against my arm. 'He wouldn't, would he? Wouldn't want anything that drew attention. Neither would Jane.'

Money doesn't solve everything, you know.

Jane Fairfax is right, of course. But it could solve *my* problem. Well, one of them, at least. I might not be any closer to proving who the poisoner is, but I may just have found a way to create a rift between Frank and Jane.

Perhaps this day hasn't been such a waste of time after all.

I take Robert's arm and steer him back towards Broadwood's.

'I think I have an idea,' I tell him.

And I think it might just work.

CHAPTER 7

Rule number seven: The only thing more intriguing than an extravagant gift is an extravagant gift from a mysterious benefactor.

Everyone is talking about Jane Fairfax's pianoforte. In fact, it's all everyone's been talking about all week. Right now, our esteemed hostess, Mrs Cole, is doing a spectacular job of grilling Jane about the tone, the touch, the pedal. But, let's be honest, there's only one question anyone really wants to know the answer to: who sent it?

Mrs Cole is far too polite to ask Jane outright and has instead alighted on the least scandalous option: Jane's guardian, Colonel Campbell. A gesture of paternal kindness for a girl who has an abundance of talent but no wealth to support it. Jane is a fine player and she deserves a fine instrument. She has that now, at least.

But it's not the sort of thing a middle-aged man springs upon his ward unannounced. No. Colonel Campbell is kind and this is not a kind gift. It is spontaneous. Ostentatious.

Just the type of thing a rash and entitled young man would send to his clandestine lover without considering the consequences. By the look on Jane's face, I can see she has reached this conclusion. Which is entirely the point.

I know what kind of damage a misplaced object can do. There was Lady Leighton's sapphire brooch, for example – the one that mysteriously appeared in Miss Eliza Wynne's bedchamber after she had admired it at the Leightons' summer ball. Disastrous timing for Miss Wynne, as she had been expecting a proposal from Lord Harbourne any day. Strangely enough, the brooch never made its way back to Lady Leighton.

And then there was the unfortunate incident of the maid who discovered Mr Cowan's cravat under Miss Clara Keen's pillow. Miss Keen was adamant that Mr Cowan hadn't stepped foot in her room, but then how did the cravat get there? Her protestations of innocence were not convincing enough for her father and she was packed off to the cottage of a maiden aunt in an insignificant Devonshire village. Mr Cowan, meanwhile, set his sights on a rich young heiress who disappeared (along with a great deal of Mr Cowan's silver) just hours before the wedding ceremony.

If a stolen brooch and a mislaid cravat can do such damage, imagine what trouble a pianoforte sent by a mysterious benefactor could cause.

I bet that Jane is regretting accepting the invitation to the Coles' dinner party right now – and as an evening guest at that. To suffer the indignity of being the source of after-dinner gossip and not to have even partaken in the dinner itself. But Jane Fairfax is in good company in the after-dinner crew tonight. For it turns out that Harriet Smith isn't good enough to sit at the Coles' table either. The Coles who are trying to claw their way up the social scale through the ill-advised purchase of garish paintings in gilt picture frames, marble statues of inelegant proportions and a grand pianoforte that gets about as much use as the Hartfield edition of Shakespeare.

'Really, it is ridiculous for Miss Fairfax to have a pianoforte at her aunt's house,' Emma tells me. 'There's barely any room for it in the parlour.' I'm sitting in my usual place by her side, fulfilling my customary role of chief flatterer and faithful confidante until she finds someone more interesting to talk to. Everyone in Highbury thinks that Emma is the centre of my universe but, the truth is, they only notice me when I'm in her sphere of influence. I'm Emma's little friend, lucky enough to capture her interest where so many have failed. I'm forever in her shadow, obscured from view. That's why I picked her. With Emma around, I can observe the Frank Churchills and Jane Fairfaxes of the world without them watching me.

Emma runs her fingers across the smooth silk of her new mauve gown. She has dressed herself with particular care tonight. Her hair is swept up off her face into an elegant bun, showing off her amethyst and pearl earrings. A simple amethyst cross hangs from her neck. Partly this is to remind the Coles of their place and the very great favour she is doing them by attending their little soirée. But mostly it is for Frank Churchill's benefit. Really, I should be encouraging her. It would help my cause if Frank could be persuaded to trade Miss Fairfax for Miss Woodhouse. But there's something about Emma's obvious attempts at seduction that sets my teeth on edge.

'If she'd wanted to practise on a superior instrument, she could have used the pianoforte at Hartfield. She need only have asked,' Emma adds, safe in the knowledge that Jane never would. 'I wonder who could have sent her such an extravagant gift.'

'Everyone is saying it's from Colonel Campbell.'

'Everyone is *saying* that. But what are they thinking?'

'Miss Woodhouse, whatever do you mean?'

Emma tosses her head like the Coles' Lipizzaner stallion. 'Only that it is such a generous gift. More the kind of thing you would expect from a lover rather than a father figure, don't you think?'

I frown, pretending to consider Emma's suggestion. 'But Miss Fairfax does not have a lover.'

Emma leans forward with a wicked smile. 'That we know of.'

I shake my head. 'I have hardly heard her talk of any men except for Colonel Campbell and Mr Churchill and her friend's husband, Mr Dixon.'

Emma clutches my arm. 'Well, it could hardly be Colonel Campbell or Frank. But Mr Dixon—'

'Mr Dixon is married,' I insist. 'And to Jane's best friend.'

'Yes,' Emma agrees, a glint in her eyes, 'and doesn't she look like a woman with a guilty conscience? Someone who's pining for a love she cannot have? Actually, she does look rather unwell, don't you think?'

I glance over at Jane. Her white muslin dress and pale skin give her an ethereal quality. She's tapping a finger unconsciously against the stem of her wine glass. 'I think she looks quite pretty actually,' I say quietly.

'No. She is too thin. And so lethargic. She has barely moved from her chair all night.'

I suspect this is a deliberate ploy on Jane's part to reduce the number of people who will quiz her about the pianoforte and to ensure she doesn't have to speak to Emma.

'I'm not convinced she should be here at all,' Emma adds. 'Perhaps I should speak to her aunt about it.'

I'm about to put a restraining hand on Emma's shoulder when I'm spared the necessity by the appearance of Frank Churchill. He's framed in the doorway, eyes roaming around the Coles' drawing-room. It's the first opportunity I've had to get a good look at him up close without a dark alleyway, or a tea-room menu, or a pianoforte between us. Frank is classically handsome. Tall, broad-shouldered, clean-cut. Perhaps a little too clean-cut for my taste, although it's hard not to be drawn in by those playful eyes, full of laughter, as if he's enjoying his own private joke but is perfectly willing to let you in on it.

Jane stiffens as she sees him, throwing herself into an animated conversation with her aunt. Frank steps into the room and sidles up to Jane, placing himself squarely in front of her. His smile falters as Jane turns away to speak to Mrs Cole. Frank hovers by her chair, exchanging pleasantries with Miss Bates, waiting for Jane to acknowledge him. Eventually, he gives up, nodding to Miss Bates and moving to the other side of the room, from where he can observe his fiancée's frowns at his leisure. He has an excellent vantage-point as he lingers behind Emma, who is too preoccupied with her mission to shoo me into an empty chair so that there is room for Frank between us to perceive that his interest lies elsewhere. Emma attracts his attention at last and Frank, apparently realising just how obvious he's being, sits down beside her.

'Mr Churchill, may I present my dear friend, Miss Harriet Smith,' Emma says with an unnecessary flourish.

'Miss Smith,' he says, taking my hand and raising it to his lips with such delicacy that I begin to understand what Jane sees in him. I lean towards him, breathing in the scent of lemon and jasmine and something wonderfully—

'Miss Smith?' Frank is making no attempt to hide his amusement.

I stare at him open-mouthed. Let him think I'm an imbecile. A wide-eyed damsel, completely in his thrall. I know his type, with his impossibly blue eyes and his teal cravat. The serial seducer, always eager to please, hungry for attention. I could have him eating out of the palm of my hand in seconds. Except I'm not here to ensnare Frank. I'm not going down that path again.

'Harriet. Mr Churchill was asking how you're enjoying tonight's gathering,' Emma says with a meaningful glare.

Apparently, I'm making her look bad.

I smile sweetly at Frank. 'Oh, it's wonderful. To be in such good company, I feel quite blessed.'

'Well said, Miss Smith. To good company.' Frank raises his glass and catches Emma's eye with a smirk.

She's so busy congratulating herself on her conquest that she doesn't register his furtive glance in Jane's direction.

The other gentlemen enter the room and Emma is forced to pay Mr Cole some compliments on his table and his wine and his grand pianoforte. We wait for her to finish but, when Mr Cole shows no sign of releasing her, Frank turns to me with a shrug.

'It appears we have been abandoned, Miss Smith. Your friend prefers our host's company to ours.'

His mirth is infectious. 'Frailty, thy name is woman,' I reply.

'You are fond of The Bard, Miss Smith?' Frank asks, appraising me.

I am, of course, but I didn't intend to let *him* know. Frailty, indeed. A minute or two in Frank's company and I'm already spilling my secrets. My father used to tell me: *Be accomplished, Hattie, but not too clever. A man has no need for a wife whose intelligence surpasses his own.*

Frank Churchill is precisely the kind of man who invites me to show off. His easy manners, his seductive smile, those eyes. Eyes that are now narrowed with a suspicion I need to erase as swiftly as possible.

'Oh, well, not so very fond,' I say, 'but Mrs Goddard has a nice edition of Shakespeare's *Collected Works* – quite a substantial volume and rather heavy. Although, I prefer Mrs Radcliffe myself. Have you read *The Romance of the Forest*?'

That ought to do it.

Frank's eyes have recovered their usual glint. 'I haven't yet had the pleasure.' He leans in and lowers his voice. 'Is it very horrid?'

I feel a blush rising to my cheeks as his breath tickles my neck.

Concentrate, Harriet.

'Most horrid,' I assure him, wrinkling my nose. 'The abandoned abbey is frightful. And the bit where Pierre has opened the chest and found— Oh, I should not say! You will have to read it for yourself.'

I fear I'm laying it on a little thick, but Frank is lapping it up. He *is* a man, after all.

'I shall do my best to acquire a copy post-haste. Although, I'm sure my aunt would not approve.'

I suspect he's right about that. I have a sudden image of Mrs Churchill in her nightdress, shivering and white-knuckled, pince-nez perched on the end of her nose as she squints down at a copy of *The Italian* by candlelight.

'Don't worry, Miss Smith. I'm sure I can find some dusty old volume from my uncle's library that won't be missed and secrete Mrs Radcliffe's masterpiece within its covers.'

'Honestly, Mr Churchill. That is quite shocking!' I shouldn't be flirting with Frank, but I find I can't help myself.

It's been a while.

'As shocking as *The Romance of the Forest*?' Frank asks, leaning in a little closer than is proper.

'Well, nothing is quite as shocking as that,' I say. 'Except perhaps *Udolpho*.'

'Ah, the black veil!'

'You *have* read Mrs Radcliffe.'

'On occasion. Even my eagle-eyed aunt cannot stop me if I really put my mind to something.'

Don't I know it?

Now that Frank is in front of me, drawing me in with those playful eyes, it's easy enough to forget that he might be plotting to murder his own aunt. He's a charmer; a smooth talker; the kind of man who gets what he wants with honeyed words and a sly smile. Then again, the way he's flirting with me, he doesn't come across like a man who has a disapproving fiancée glaring at him from across the room either.

Frank must feel her gaze upon him, for he glances over at Jane, and then back at me with a frown. 'Miss Fairfax doesn't look happy,' he says, his tone not quite neutral.

'Have you heard about the pianoforte?' I ask, knowing he could hardly have avoided the subject.

'I have heard of little else since I got here.'

'Poor Miss Fairfax is embarrassed by the attention, I think, though I don't know why she should be ashamed of a gift from the Campbells. If I had received a gift from such a quarter, I would be parading it around among my entire acquaintance. Although, I have to say, it *is* a rather generous gift, considering they are not even related.'

'The Campbells have been very good to Miss Fairfax,' Frank says.

'But this goes above and beyond what you might expect from *them*. Miss Woodhouse assures me it is a superior instrument. Now, if Miss Fairfax had a young man, I could well believe that he might buy her such a thing. It does seem like a gift of love.'

Of course, I know exactly who bought the pianoforte. Me. Well, technically, Mrs Churchill bought it, but it was my idea (with a little help from Robert). All in the name of chaos. Jane, of course, must assume that Frank has sent her the pianoforte – a reckless act that draws far too much attention to their secret engagement. And, if I can just convince Frank that Jane has a secret admirer who is bold enough to send her a love token as extravagant as a pianoforte, there's no telling what he might do. I'm just laying the foundations. I'm counting on Frank's jealous imagination to do the rest.

His mouth hardens as he stares at Jane. 'Yes, a gift of love,' he says finally. 'You are quite correct, Miss Smith. Your feelings do you credit. If you will excuse me,' he adds, rising from his chair. 'I've been meaning to talk to Mr Cox about . . .' He drifts off towards the door before he's obliged to use that pretty head of his to think up an ending to his sentence. He catches Jane's attention as he leaves, his eyes flitting back and forth between her face and the door. I see the 'no' form on her lips and the slight shake of her head, but she's out of her seat before Frank leaves the room.

Emma is still talking to Mr Cole and so I'm free to slip away and squeeze past Miss Bates as she talks a mile a minute at poor Mrs Cole. 'Really – such a generous present – but then the Campbells have always been so good to Jane – Mrs Campbell does write such fulsome letters – such neat handwriting – I was telling Mother the other day, "Mrs Campbell really does write so beautifully" – I cannot think where she has gone – Jane, that is, not Mrs Campbell—'

Mrs Cole looks every bit the fine hostess, her maroon silk dress perfectly complementing her hazel-brown hair, her figure surprisingly slight for one who has birthed four children within the past five years. She fiddles with her pearl necklace as she glances towards the door, evidently planning her escape. I stare at the necklace. The pearls are large and perfectly spherical, with a brilliant lustre. Years of rooting through rich heiresses' jewellery boxes has taught me how to spot a valuable piece and this one is of far better quality than I would have expected from the Coles. In fact, it looks an awful lot like one of the sketches that Mrs Churchill sent me of her missing heirlooms. But I don't have time to worry about that right now.

The corridor is eerily quiet after the bustle of the drawing-room. I peer through open doorways, conjuring up excuses to placate suspicious servants who might wonder why I'm lurking around in a deserted part of the house. I come to the end of the corridor without incident and I'm ready to turn back when I perceive the chink of light under the library door and the sound of hushed but frantic voices on the other side.

'—don't know what you were thinking—'

'A superior instrument, I hear,' Frank sneers. 'It shows a great deal of thought and affection. A gift of love, some might say.'

'Thought and affection!' Jane scoffs. I have never before heard such fire in her voice. 'Yes, I quite enjoy being the subject of Highbury gossip.'

'And you, of course, have done nothing to invite it,' Frank says, raising his voice.

It's good of him to oblige. My ear is getting rather sore from being pressed up against this door.

'Invite it?' Jane asks, matching his volume. 'I have been the soul of discretion. And what do I have to show for it? A love I cannot admit – that must remain a shameful secret, because I'm not good enough for your precious aunt. How can I marry a man who doesn't respect me? A man I cannot trust?'

'You cannot, of course,' Frank responds. 'It would be intolerable. Trust is the foundation of a strong relationship. Honour. Honesty. Perhaps you wish you had chosen differently.'

'Perhaps I do. Had I known the number of lies I would have to tell to conceal our relationship—'

'Yes, you have learned to lie very convincingly—'

'You have forced me to it. You have made me deny our connection. And yet *you* can flaunt it as much as you please, while *I* am the one left to deal with the consequences.'

'Flaunt the connection? What do you—'

I barge through the door with the force of a baby elephant, determined to intervene before all my good work is undone. 'Oh. Miss Fairfax. Mr Churchill—' I look from one to the other, mouth agape. 'Forgive me, I did not think— I was sure the library must be empty. It was so stifling in the drawing-room, I had to step out to catch my breath.'

'Yes, you're not the only one to be so afflicted, Miss Smith,' Frank says smoothly, gesturing towards Jane, whose face is angled towards the nearest bookcase. 'I found Miss Fairfax here complaining of a headache.'

'Oh dear. I do hope you are not ill, Miss Fairfax?'

She turns towards me to reveal red-rimmed eyes. 'My head feels much clearer, thank you,' she says, glancing at Frank, 'though I suspect the pain will take a while to subside. However, I know what I must do to cure it. Please excuse me,' she mumbles, hands shaking, eyes down, as she dashes from the room.

Frank snorts and slams his fist against the bookcase. Remembering his audience, he steps towards me with a smile too wide to be convincing. 'I think the occasion has got the better of Miss Fairfax. She is not cut out for society, I fear.'

'And what are you doing, hiding out in Mr Cole's library?' I say, arms folded. 'I'm sure your aunt taught you better than that.'

'I'm taking a lady's advice,' he says, scouring Mr Cole's bookshelves until his fingers alight upon *The Romance of the Forest*. He pulls out the first volume and presents it to me as if it's the crown jewels. 'I shall ask Mr Cole if I can borrow it. Or, better still,' he says leaning in with a conspiratorial smile, 'I shall spirit it away without his knowledge.'

'Well, you don't want it getting back to your aunt, do you?'

You have enough to conceal as it is.

He throws his head back and lets out a full-throated laugh.

'Precisely my thoughts. You're a clever girl, Miss Smith.'

I *am* clever. I'm not supposed to be showing him that, but there's something about Frank that tempts me to be myself. And I've never been much good at resisting temptation.

'From now on, Miss Smith, I declare I will be guided by you in all things.'

'Enjoy your book, Mr Churchill,' I say, slipping from the room before Frank's charm can work its magic. Dangerous though it is, I'm enjoying his attention. It reminds me of a seduction scam – the exhilarating chase, the intricate dance, the thrill of control. Except I don't quite feel in control with Frank Churchill. I don't have any proof that Frank is a poisoner, but he's certainly a master manipulator. And he has a temper too. As for Jane, the more I see of her, the more I'm convinced she has nothing to do with the plot against Mrs Churchill. I almost feel guilty about the hand I'm playing in her unhappiness, but I suppose she might thank me for it in the long run. From what I've seen of the Churchills, she would be better off steering clear of the lot of them.

Out in the corridor, Mrs Cole is berating a servant who is holding a bottle of wine out towards her. 'Not this one,' she snaps, pushing the bottle away in disgust. 'I will not insult my guests by serving them cheap wine. Go back to the cellar and find something more appropriate. And top up the port while you're at it.'

I creep up behind Mrs Cole, trying to get a good look at her pearl necklace. If it belongs to Mrs Churchill, there should be three tiny diamonds nestled in the clasp along with the engraved initials of Mr Churchill's great-grandmother. It's impossible to see from this angle. I'm going to have to try a less subtle approach.

'That's a beautiful necklace, Mrs Cole. Is it new?'

Mrs Cole starts at the sound of my voice but recovers herself quickly as she turns to face me with a broad smile. 'Oh, yes, my dear. How kind of you to notice! Mr Cole surprised me with it just this morning. He said it was a birthday gift. Well, my birthday isn't for another two months, but I'm not complaining.'

I return her smile with interest. 'Oh, but I think the clasp is loose and I would hate for you to lose it. I'm sure it must be very expensive.'

Mrs Cole's hand flies to the clasp of her necklace and she starts to fiddle with it. 'Did I fix it?' she asks as I peer at the back of her neck.

'No, not quite,' I say, stepping up beside her, unhooking the necklace and squinting at the clasp in the dim hall lighting. The tiny diamonds glisten and, as I angle the necklace towards a candelabra on the hall table, I catch the initials FMC upon it: Florence May Churchill. 'All done,' I say, fastening the clasp and taking a step backwards.

What on earth is Mrs Cole doing with Mrs Churchill's pearl necklace?

'You're a good girl, Miss Smith,' she says, patting my hand. 'It would not do to lose my pearls at my own party now, would it?' She lets out a tinkle of laughter, fingers trailing across her pearls to assure herself they are still in place.

I came here to break off an engagement. To get the measure of a would-be poisoner. I didn't expect to catch a thief as well.

CHAPTER 8

Rule number eight: Beware of new neighbours with sharp eyes and familiar faces.

'Of course, I don't suppose Mrs Cole is really a thief,' I say, plonking myself down on a bale of hay to watch Robert pick a stone out of the hoof of his skewbald Shetland pony, Toby. I stifle a sneeze as my boots kick up a cloud of dust. The scent of damp soil and wet fur has been replaced by that of freshly mown grass and blooming roses as we move towards summer.

'Then how do you think she obtained the necklace?' Robert asks, trying to hold Toby's leg steady as he wriggles and tosses his head.

'Well, when Frank wanted Jane to elope with him, he told her he'd get the money for it. Perhaps he's been selling off his aunt's jewellery to raise the funds.'

'Doesn't he have his own things to sell? Signet rings, fob watches, horses,' Robert adds, nodding towards Toby.

I snort at the image of Frank Churchill astride a Shetland pony, toes scraping the floor.

'But those are *his* things. The rich never part with their own possessions if they can help it – not when there are dusty heirlooms up in the attic that no one will miss.'

'Except Mrs Churchill did miss them,' Robert says, releasing Toby's hoof and patting his rump.

'Yes, well, Frank's obviously been getting a bit desperate.'

'My heart bleeds for him,' Robert mumbles.

'He need not bother about an elopement any more. Although, try telling Mrs Churchill that. Look here,' I say, waving a letter in Robert's direction. 'She says she will not pay me until she has proof that Frank and Jane's engagement has been broken off. How do you prove an absence? And she's insisting I retrieve all her jewellery before she considers the matter closed.'

I was quick to inform Mrs Churchill that I had recovered one of her pearl necklaces and not from Jane, which was half-true. I haven't yet acquired the necklace from Mrs Cole, but it should be easy enough. I also haven't shared my theory with Mrs Churchill that her dear nephew might be the one who poisoned her tea but, as I have removed his motive for murder, I think I can forgo *that* conversation.

'Honestly, I don't know what more she wants from me,' I say, rising from the hay bale as Toby snuffles at Robert's pockets, hunting for carrots. 'Frank is back in Yorkshire and he hasn't exchanged so much as a letter with Jane. My pianoforte plan worked. He's angry at her betrayal; she at his recklessness.'

Since Frank left three weeks ago, Jane has given up her daily walks to the post office altogether and the only correspondence she has received is a letter from Mr Dixon begging her to come to Ireland again. It turns out Mrs Bates has informed him about the scorpion incident and now he's more concerned than ever for Jane's welfare. But, if the danger he talks about comes from Frank, then Mr Dixon need not fear. Nothing untoward has happened to Jane since Frank's departure. In fact, barely anything has happened at all, except that Robert keeps abandoning me for increasingly indiscreet liaisons with Denny and Mr Elton has made a triumphant return from Bath with an inevitable wife in tow.

Which reminds me, I'm due at the Vicarage in half an hour to support Emma through a tedious meeting with the new bride. (Emma is even less a fan of Mrs Elton than she is of Jane Fairfax.) Honestly, when I struck up this friendship-of-convenience with Emma, I didn't realise all the advantage would be on *her* side. It's a wonder I've had any time at all to dedicate to Mrs Churchill's demands.

'Must dash,' I say, slipping a carrot to Toby, who nips at my fingers with startling enthusiasm.

'I do enjoy these little conversations of ours,' Robert says. 'They are so delightfully one-sided.'

'Well, perhaps if you didn't spend so much of your day shut up in your bedroom with Denny, I might have time to converse with you about something other than my job,' I say, stomping out of the barn to the crunchy accompaniment of carrot against pony's teeth.

✳

'Do have another macaroon, Miss Woodhouse,' Mrs Elton gushes, ignoring me entirely as she leans over to waft the plate in Emma's direction. Her accent is affected, overloud, but with the occasional Bristolian burr which belies her air of refinement. 'I simply dote on macaroons,' she says, nibbling the edge of her own sweet treat and leaving a trail of crumbs on her mustard-coloured silk dress.

She's a pretty creature, with china-doll features – rosebud lips, button nose – which could place her anywhere between twenty and thirty years of age, although the alacrity with which she married Mr Elton suggests she is closer to the latter than the former. Her mousy-brown hair is piled atop her head with tight ringlets framing her over-rouged cheeks.

'Mr E adores a macaroon,' she adds in a hushed voice, as if she's just revealed some scandalous secret. She slaps his hand away as he reaches for one. 'Although we must show restraint, must we not, my *caro sposo*? As you can see, Miss Woodhouse, Mr E had rather a lot of macaroons in Bath. It's a good thing we never made it to Maple Grove, for there would have been all manner of delicacies to tempt us there.' Mr Elton *does* look a bit fuller in his smug-but-handsome face since his return from Bath but, if he's had to listen to his new wife drone on about Maple Grove for hours on end, I can hardly blame him for using macaroons as a coping mechanism. 'Fear not,' Mrs Elton continues, keeping hold of her husband's hand lest he reach for the macaroons again. 'We will soon whip him into shape, I assure you.'

Mr Elton smiles at his wife – at least, I think it's supposed to be a smile, but his lip twitches as he nods to Emma and his free hand clenches into a fist. If there's one good thing about Mrs Elton holding court, it's that we no longer have to put up with Mr Elton's incessant flattery. He is cowed by his wife's presence, speaking only when she presses him to agree with her on some element of her appearance.

'Naturally you will have heard of Maple Grove, Miss Woodhouse,' Mrs Elton says with a wave of her hand.

Emma's jaw grinds against her macaroon. If nothing else, I'm enjoying her vain attempts at masking her obvious contempt for Mrs Elton.

'I see you are admiring my pearls, Miss Woodhouse,' Mrs Elton says when she realises that she isn't going to get a response from Emma about Maple Grove. Fortunately, Mrs Elton isn't the kind of person who requires a response. Just a captive audience. 'A gift from my sister, Selina, and her husband. The owners of Maple Grove,' she adds, as if this is a far more pertinent detail than the familial bond.

'Usually, I wouldn't dream of wearing pearls before midday,' she says, fingers trailing across the string of pearls bound tightly around her neck. They are not anywhere near as fine as Mrs Cole's pearls – or Mrs Churchill's, I should say. 'At least, not in my hair,' she adds, gesturing towards her poodle-like hairstyle. 'But one expects certain standards of a bride that need not be upheld by other women.' She casts a disparaging glance at my pearl-less attire before turning back to her husband. 'Mr E does so admire my pearls, don't you, Mr E?'

'Naturally, my dear,' Mr Elton murmurs, his eyes fixed on the plate of macaroons on the tea table.

As I have been pointedly left out of this conversation, I decide to amuse myself by counting the number of times Mrs Elton mentions her beloved Maple Grove.

'Of course, pearls are a common feature at Maple Grove.'

One.

'Selina insists on pearls when we have visitors, and there are so often visitors at Maple Grove.'

Two.

'Mrs Elton, how are you enjoying the Vicarage?' Emma asks, evidently not as great a fan of Maple Grove as her hostess is.

'Oh, I quite dote upon it, I assure you,' Mrs Elton declares, surveying her domain. She has clearly made herself at home. I detect Mrs Elton's touch in the elaborate flower arrangements scattered around the room and the overflowing potpourri vases on the tea table. 'It is not large, of course. Nothing like the size of Maple Grove.'

Three.

'But, then, it is not a fair comparison. So few houses could live up to Maple Grove.'

Maple Grove. Maple Grove. Maple Grove. It's reached the point where those three syllables no longer hold any meaning for me.

What would Frank Churchill make of Mrs Elton? I should think he could hold his own with her on the subject of great estates. I wonder how Maple Grove might measure up against Enscombe. I doubt we'll ever find out. It doesn't seem likely Frank is going to return to Highbury now things have ended with Jane.

I should be pleased events have resolved themselves with so little effort on my part. Easy money. Easier than I ever made with my father. Mrs Churchill won't be able to hold out on me for much longer. I'll recover her precious jewellery and convince her that Frank and Jane are no more and that there is now no danger of her being poisoned at the hands of a swindler (or an undutiful nephew). The thing is, as much as I complained to Robert about Mrs Churchill's fastidiousness, I was almost relieved by her demand for proof. You see, this job gave me a focus. A purpose. I have no idea what I'll do next. Mrs Churchill came to *me*. Father was always the one to sniff out a good target. I can't go back to the way things were with him. I don't have the means for the independent con any more. I need paying clients and I have no idea how to attract them. I can't exactly advertise, can I? Besides, I'm growing rather fond of life in Highbury with Robert. It's been a long time since I felt like I belonged anywhere. And while Robert isn't a great substitute for my father as far as work goes (particularly as he spends most of his time telling me I should be doing something more noble), at least I have someone to talk to. I'm sick of flitting from place to place, forever looking over my shoulder. And, as infuriating as he is, I'm not ready to leave Robert. I'm starting to think it wouldn't be so bad to put down roots somewhere. But the problem with putting down roots is that the past is bound to catch up with you eventually.

Mrs Elton is still droning on about Maple Grove but, now and again, she glances my way and catches my eye. Something in her expression suggests familiarity, as if she's not looking at Harriet Smith at all. She's looking at me. The real me. But she can't possibly know the real me.

Can she?

Now I think about it, she does look familiar.

It's feasible that I *have* encountered her before. Not in Derbyshire – I would have remembered – but, the truth is, I've clashed with so many women of marriageable age I can hardly be expected to remember them all, can I?

Augusta Elton may be one of them. And, if she is, I could be in a world of trouble.

✳

'I think Mrs Elton might know who I am,' I say, pacing up and down Robert's kitchen.

'Mmmm.' Robert is hunched over the kitchen table, papers sprawled everywhere, sucking on the end of his pen.

'Robert! Are you even listening?' I demand, snatching his pen away.

Robert sighs. 'It's hard not to when you're being so persistent about it. How am I supposed to finish my masterpiece when you are constantly interrupting me?'

'Shouldn't you be more concerned with running your farm? Mr Ingleby cannot do everything himself.'

'You'd be surprised,' Robert mumbles. 'And, as for Mrs Elton, I should think she probably does know who you are. She strikes me as the kind of woman who makes it her business to become well acquainted with her neighbours.' He snatches back his pen and starts scribbling.

It's nice to know where his priorities lie.

'No. Not Harriet Smith. I mean *me*.'

'Ah, well that is a problem,' Robert says, still scribbling.

'Yes, thank you. I'm well aware it's a problem. So what should I do about it?'

'Harriet, I'm a little busy right now. George and Rupert have just uncovered a major clue in the Sir Reginald murder case.'

'Rupert?' I stop pacing. 'Who on earth is Rupert?'

Robert frowns at me as if I really should be keeping up with the ridiculous nonsense that goes on inside his head.

'Rupert is George's dashing assistant,' he says, avoiding my gaze.

'What happened to Henrietta?'

'She wasn't working for me, so I had her seduced by some scoundrel (who may, in fact, be Sir Reginald's killer) and now she has sloped off in disgrace.' He lowers his voice. 'I fear she may be in the family way.'

Charming.

As if it wasn't enough for Denny to have robbed me of my assistant in reality by barricading Robert in his bedroom for hours on end, now he's supplanted me in Robert's novel as well.

Since Robert is continuing to ignore me, I pull up a chair and cast my eyes across the mountain of papers on the kitchen table in an attempt to find something to entertain me. A sketch of Sir Reginald's library. Some scrawls about the effects of cyanide poisoning. A love letter from Denny. The handwriting is barely legible, but I've somehow deciphered the entire thing before I can help myself.

'"Adieu, adieu, adieu. Remember me." Robert, you do realise this is what the ghost of Hamlet's father says to him when he's calling on Hamlet to avenge his "foul and most unnatural murder"?'

'Yes,' Robert says, not looking up from his notebook.

'Do you think Denny is aware of that fact?'

'Probably not.'

'Do you even like him?'

Robert puts down his pen and sighs. 'He makes me feel alive.'

'Which is all very well, but are you willing to die for him? Because that's what might happen if you continue to be so reckless. I wonder why you risk it all if you don't love him.'

Robert snorts. 'Don't you think you're being a bit hypocritical?'

'Hypocritical?' I demand. 'How so?'

He shakes his head and picks up his pen again. 'Forget I said anything.'

'No. I would like to know what you meant.'

His pen hovers over his notebook, ink dribbling from the nib. 'Well, a casual observer might suggest you're doing the same thing with Frank Churchill.'

'Excuse me?'

'Ever since he left, it's been Frank this and Frank that. He's all you ever talk about. Anyone would imagine *you* were the one secretly engaged to him. Why do you think I've been spending so much time with Denny?'

Well, really, this is too much.

'You know you can't get involved. Not if you want to protect that precious job of yours. I'd have thought you might have learned after last time.'

I feel my cheeks flush as I glare at Robert. He cannot possibly be comparing a casual flirtation with Frank with what I had in Derbyshire with—

'But it doesn't matter, does it?' Robert continues. 'You've achieved what you set out to do. Frank has gone, and broken poor Miss Fairfax's heart in the process. So now you can collect your fee and be on your way, Mrs Elton be damned.'

I don't think Mrs Elton would appreciate that sentiment. She is a regular visitor to Maple Grove, after all.

'Oh, dear Lord.' I slam my palm on the table with enough force to send Robert's notebook flying.

'What?' Robert is eyeing me warily.

'Maple Grove! If it truly is such a great house, then Mrs Elton could be the victim of one of my cons.'

Robert stares at me, jaw clenched, and I'm certain it's taking him a great deal of restraint not to voice his disappointment in me. 'And if she is? What are you going to do about it?'

'I don't know.'

'Surely you have procedures for placating vengeful victims who catch up with you?'

'My father used to deal with that.'

'Your father's not here,' Robert points out, folding his arms and leaning back in his chair.

'Yes, I'm well aware of that, thank you. If my father were here, I wouldn't be sitting around twiddling my thumbs on a job that's practically finished.'

'Well, what would he do?' Robert asks.

I'm not convinced 'What would Father do?' is the best motto to be adopting at this precise moment and I'm surprised Robert is proposing it given his opinions on the man, but it's not as if I have any better ideas.

'I suppose he would give them something they wanted.'

'You mean pay them off?'

I snort. 'Not if he could help it. But he has connections.' *Or, at least, he used to.*

'He would set them up in the kind of life they desired

– usually by conning someone else. He's cheap like that.'

'And they wouldn't object to the means by which it was achieved?' Robert asks, scandalised. 'You'd think after falling victim themselves—'

'You'd be surprised how willing people can be to relax their morals as soon as it benefits them. Not that it matters. I don't have those kinds of resources any longer.'

'Hmmm. It's probably for the best.'

'Yes, though my livelihood might be ruined, at least my conscience will remain clear,' I say, kicking his chair.

I was aiming for his foot.

'Well, what else can you do?'

There's always something you can do, Hattie, my father would say, usually when we were backed into a corner and he was counting on me to do something particularly unpleasant to get us out of it.

'Well, I could sit around and wait for Mrs Elton to approach me and reveal what she wants.'

'Why do I get the feeling you're not going to do that?' Robert asks, eyes narrowed.

'Because you know it's not in my nature to wait for anything. And, besides, I have a better idea.'

'Which is?'

'Mrs Elton has the advantage of me. It seems she knows precisely who *I* am.'

'So?'

'So I think it's time we found out a little more about Augusta Elton.'

CHAPTER 9

Rule number nine: Sometimes, you need to read between the lines. (Particularly if those lines are cross written.)

Honestly, this woman is a ghost. Nobody has heard of her beyond what she herself has told them. I was hoping the letter from my latest informant, the Master of Ceremonies at the Bath Assembly Rooms, would have given me something new. Something I could use. It pays to have friends in fashionable places. Well, usually it does. He can typically be relied on for the more salacious gossip but, this time, he hasn't told me anything I didn't already know. For the past nine days, I've been digging into Augusta Elton's history and he was my last hope of acquiring some useful information on her. I know that she is apparently the daughter of Mr Hawkins, a tradesman in Bristol. That her sister, Selina, clawed her way up the social ladder by marrying the distinguished Mr Suckling of Maple Grove. And that Augusta Hawkins turned up in Bath two months ago, full of stories about the Sucklings and Maple Grove, clearly on the lookout for a husband. But Augusta Hawkins hasn't enjoyed the same level of success in the marriage market as her sister. A humble clergyman can hardly measure up to the owner of an estate as magnificent as Maple Grove. Fortune-hunting favours the young – and Mrs Elton is no spring chicken. And perhaps she doesn't have the looks or the charm of her exalted sister.

Except that Mrs Suckling isn't Mrs Elton's sister. Because Mrs Suckling doesn't have a sister. Nor does her husband. I have discovered this much during my investigation into Augusta Hawkins' past. Not that she seems to have one. As far as I can tell, there never *was* such a person as Augusta Hawkins. So who on earth is she and what is she doing in Highbury?

I've taken to doing the only thing I can think of in the absence of any useful information: get up at the crack of dawn and keep watch on Mrs Elton at the Vicarage in the hope that she's about to slip out of the house to do something nefarious. Well, I finally struck lucky this morning. I duck down behind a hedge as she slips between the looming elms at the edge of the village, rising in time to see her slide her hand out of a hollow oak. She shakes the dirt off her gown and glances around surreptitiously. Satisfied, she turns on her heel and strides back towards Highbury.

I wait a few minutes to ensure she's well out of the way and no one has arrived to collect whatever mystery object she has deposited in the hollow. There's nothing beyond the dawn chorus and a brace of squirrels scuttling up tree trunks and leaping from branch to branch with wild abandon. Finally, I tiptoe over to the oak, reach inside and pull out a letter. I slide my finger under the seal and squint at the jumble of words spilling across the page. The letter is cross written and the handwriting so cramped that I can't make head nor tail of it in the dim light. If I could take it away with me, I'm sure I could decipher it, but I don't want to alert Mrs Elton to my thievery. Instead, I copy it into my pocketbook as accurately as I can from Mrs Elton's untidy scrawl, glancing over my shoulder after every few lines to assure myself that I am still alone. I pull out a pot of adhesive ointment – my father's secret recipe – and spread it across the letter's seal. Its thin and odourless properties mean that not even the sharpest eyes and most sensitive nose could detect it. I press my thumb over the seal until I'm sure the adhesive has done its job and then slip the letter back into the hollow. I retreat to the hedge, waiting to see who collects it. I don't have to wait long.

An adolescent boy the size of a brown bear crashes through the undergrowth on a piebald pony. The boy has high cheekbones and a dark, shaggy mane of hair which give him a certain allure. I know him. He's part of the Romani tribe who have settled on the outskirts of Highbury – if the Romani can be said to settle anywhere. They have been causing a great deal of hysteria among the village gossips, who have been delighting in rumours of black magic, ancient curses and stolen babies. Of course, the reality is much more mundane. They are just a group of people trying to make their way in the world, free from the stifling rituals of polite society.

I can definitely see the appeal.

And, like all good working folk, they won't give you something for nothing, as I discovered when I paid bear boy an obscene sum to hang around watching for signs of Frank Churchill's arrival in Highbury. And now, it seems, he is working for Mrs Elton. He swings his leg over the saddle and dismounts with surprising grace considering his bulk. He flits over to the oak tree, eyes darting from side to side as he retrieves the letter.

I could reveal myself and challenge him on where he's taking the note, but I suspect he will keep Mrs Elton's counsel if she's paid him enough for the privilege and I don't want it getting back to her that I've been stalking her through the woods at dawn. Of course, the ideal plan would be to follow bear boy to see where he delivers the letter, except that he's on horseback and I'm on foot. I stay crouched behind the hedge as he leaps back into the saddle and gallops away. And then I go to find the only other person who is mad enough to be awake at this hour.

There is nothing to do in Highbury. To be frank, it is much duller than Bath. There are no shops worth visiting. Such a small place. I do plan to visit London when I can. Lack of action dismays me. I hope, by the time you read this, I will be more happily employed.

I have not heard from my sister recently. I visited the silver smith she recommended in Bath. They have made some progress with her ring. However, there is a ridge in the silver that must be smoothed out. It cannot be done in a few days. Will inform you when gone. Will visit Bath in June to collect ring.

'Hmmm. Looks rather mundane to me.' Robert looms over my shoulder, staring at the message scrawled in my pocketbook. He stinks of sweat, straw and pig manure, and I wish he wouldn't stand quite so close. I'm in the henhouse, sitting cross-legged on a bale of hay, studying the message with the accompanying clucks of sleepy chickens. Like me, it seems that they are not fans of early-morning excursions.

'If it's so mundane, why was she hiding it in a hollow oak at the crack of dawn?'

Robert shrugs, bending down to collect some eggs from underneath a fierce-looking hen. She squawks at him, but shows no sign of moving. 'She said it herself. She's bored in Highbury. You're wasting your time with that. You won't get anything from it.'

'I already have something, thank you very much,' I say smugly.

'Really?' Robert raises an eyebrow in challenge. 'Go on then, genius.'

'For one thing, Mrs Elton is from a lower class than she claims to belong to.'

'And how do you figure that?'

'Well, her handwriting was small, cramped. Cross written.'

'My sisters cross write their letters,' Robert says, easing his hand underneath a sleeping chicken.

'Yes, and why do they do that?'

'To save space, I suppose.'

'Exactly. They want to fit as much as possible on a single sheet of paper. Compare it to this,' I say, sliding my finger under the seal of a letter from Mrs Churchill and wafting it in front of Robert. 'Mrs Churchill's writing is much larger. No cross writing. She's not afraid of blank space. She's rich enough to use as many sheets of paper as she pleases.' I place the letter beside me on the hay bale, unread, and turn back to my pocketbook. 'Mrs Elton's message is rather short. There was no need for cross writing. It is force of habit. And it makes it harder to decipher,' I add, wrinkling my nose. 'But there's something more useful in here – I'm sure of it. The sentence construction is odd – as if some of the words have been forced into place. So we look out for things that stand out. Oddities. Here,' I say, my finger tapping against a particular phrase.

Robert rises tentatively with an armful of eggs and peers at my pocketbook. 'Silversmith. What's so strange about that?'

'Not silversmith,' I say. 'Silver smith. Two separate words. Could smith be Smith?' I ask, pointing to myself. 'Harriet Smith.'

Robert rolls his eyes and turns back to the chickens. 'Of course, it has to be about you.'

'And where there's one name, there may be others. See here – frank could be Frank Churchill, perhaps?' I search the message for further names but find none.

'Frank is the third word in the sentence. Smith the fifth word in this one. Three and five. I wonder . . .'

I take my pencil and start scribbling down words.

nothing Frank worth small visit action time not Smith made ridge be gone Bath

Absolute nonsense. I shake my head and chew on the end of my pencil. There must be something else. 'The cross writing. What if there's another reason for it?'

'Like what?'

'Well, how about alternate lines? One from this way,' I turn my pocketbook on its side, 'and one from that.' I start scribbling frantically, reading it aloud for Robert's benefit.

There is nothing to do in Highbury. I have not heard from my sister recently. To be frank, it is much duller than Bath. I visited the silver smith she recommended in Bath. There are no shops worth visiting. They have made some progress with her ring. Such a small place. However, there is a ridge in the silver that must be smoothed out. I do plan to visit London when I can. It cannot be done in a few days. Lack of action dismays me. Will inform you when gone. I hope, by the time you read this, I will be more happily employed. Will visit Bath in June to collect ring.

Robert looks up from his hen harassment. 'That makes even less sense.'

'Yes. Hang on a moment.'

Three and five. I wonder . . .

There is nothing to do in Highbury. I have not heard from my sister recently. To be frank, it is much duller than Bath. I visited the silver smith she recommended in Bath. There are no shops worth visiting. They have made some progress with her ring. Such a small place. However, there is a ridge in the silver that must be smoothed out. I do plan to visit London when I can. It cannot be done in a few days. Lack of action dismays me. Will inform you when gone. I hope, by the time you read this, I will be more happily employed. Will visit Bath in June to collect ring.

Nothing from frank smith no progress small ridge plan in action gone by June.

Nothing from Frank.

Smith no progress.

Small ridge plan in action.

Gone by June.

I wave it at Robert triumphantly.

He frowns. 'What on earth is "small ridge plan"?'

'I have no idea,' I admit. 'But that's not the point. The point is, Mrs Elton is watching me and Frank and reporting back to someone.'

'You don't know who,' Robert points out helpfully.

'No. But it's a start. It's *something* after all these dead ends.'

'Hmmm.' Robert doesn't look convinced. 'What does her majesty want, anyway?' he asks, gesturing towards Mrs Churchill's letter.

Miss Smith,

I am long overdue an update on your progress. We have taken a house in London for the summer months. I trust that you will be able to manage the journey to deliver your news to me in person, although I assume you will have the good sense to wait until Frank is out of the house. You will find me at The Terrace, Richmond Hill, Richmond upon Thames. Bring the jewellery along with you.

Mrs Churchill

Robert shuffles over to my hay bale and snatches up the letter. 'Richmond? Why on earth would she come within nine miles of Highbury? If she's not convinced you've broken off the engagement, why would she bring Frank so close to temptation?'

'For that very reason,' I say, fist clenched, nails digging into the palm of my hand. 'She's testing me. She must have her proof.'

'It seems a bit illogical to me,' Robert says, handing back the letter.

'The rich, Robert. They don't play by our rules.'

'The rich have rules?'

'Yes, the main one being, ensure that anyone with less than five thousand a year is at your beck and call.'

I fold the letter and slip it into my pelisse with a grimace. 'I suppose I had better go and see Mrs Churchill then.'

CHAPTER 10

Rule number ten: If you want to get the measure of a man, speak to his servants. (Especially the impressionable young housemaid who is probably half in love with him.)

There is nothing of interest under Frank Churchill's bed. I hardly expected him to keep a vial full of cyanide in his bedroom, but I like to be thorough. If I'm going to convince Mrs Churchill to pay me what she owes, I need to return her jewellery and I don't think that one pearl necklace will quite cut it. If Frank has been selling off the family heirlooms to raise money for his elopement with Jane, and if the engagement is now off, it stands to reason that he might have bought back some of the pieces. Not Mrs Cole's necklace, of course. That is safe in the pocket of my pelisse and it only took some mild flirting with the Coles' footman, a good bottle of port and a few yards of silk rope to obtain it. I've looked in all the obvious places and the less obvious places and, as my current position indicates, several of the downright stupid places as well.

No such luck.

The most exciting thing I've discovered so far is a mouldy old handkerchief and a pencil that's been sharpened to within an inch of its usefulness. The butler let me in twenty minutes ago and, as Mrs Churchill is determined to make me wait, I thought I may as well take a look around while I had the opportunity.

I crawl out from under the bed, dusting off my gown, and lean in to slip my hand inside Frank's pillowcase.

Nothing.

I sigh and throw myself unceremoniously onto Frank's bed. If I were Frank Churchill, where would I conceal my stolen family heirlooms? Where did I hide such things from my father? The few keepsakes I managed to spirit away before his creditors got their grubby fingers on them. The last traces of my mother. I scramble over Frank's bed and stalk across to his chest of drawers, pulling it open and sifting through a sea of velvet waistcoats.

How many waistcoats does one man need?

I run my palm over the back of the chest of drawers, searching for a loose panel, a hidden compartment.

Nothing.

Sometimes a chest of drawers is just a chest of drawers. I tiptoe over to Frank's bookcase, trailing my fingers along the leather-bound volumes. Shakespeare. Milton. Richardson. Precisely what a young man should be reading. And not a Radcliffe in sight. I take out each book in turn, examining them for loose papers, but they don't even look as if they've been cracked open.

It's the same with the rest of the room. Everything is a little bit too tidy. It doesn't fit with Frank's reckless persona. There is very little of *him* here. It feels carefully curated. As if he fully expects people to be rooting through his belongings.

I move over to Frank's writing desk, feeling my way along its underside until I hit a glitch in the wood and pull hard to reveal a hidden drawer.

That's more like it.

My fingers fumble through a pile of half-written letters – orders for cravats and breeches and a pair of riding boots. Concealed beneath them is Mr Cole's copy of *The Romance of the Forest*. My heart beats a little faster at the realisation that Frank has heeded my advice. As I lift up the book, something drops to the floor. The diamonds glint as I stoop to retrieve them.

Mrs Churchill's earrings.

I slip them into my reticule. There's nothing else, except for a stash of blank writing paper and I don't think I'll glean much from it. But, just to be thorough, I snatch up the pencil I found under Frank's bed and rub it gently across the top page. It's a trick my father taught me, and it has borne fruit on more occasions than you'd imagine. I lean forwards as the letters begin to form themselves into words. Soft footsteps in the hallway rouse me from my work. A girl in a mint-green poplin dress flits past the door with the light tread of a housemaid.

I slam the drawer shut loudly enough to attract the maid's attention, kicking the rogue piece of paper under the desk behind me as it glides to the floor. The best way to catch the maid off guard is to make her think she's catching *me* in the act of doing something I most certainly shouldn't be doing.

Like sneaking around her master's bedroom.

The girl in the doorway is a handsome creature, fifteen or sixteen at most, but with shrewd eyes that seem older than her years. Her honey-blonde hair is swept back off her face and her muscular build suggests a life of manual labour before she made it into service. She is perfect for my purposes.

'Oh!' I exclaim, falling back against Frank's desk in a show of alarm. 'I didn't hear you come in.'

'Are you lost, miss?' the girl asks, a hint of a smile on her lips. 'This is Frank Churchill's room.'

'Yes. I know. That is—' I blunder, wondering how to deal with this girl who is appraising me carefully, foot tapping out a steady rhythm. I decide to go with some measure of the truth. 'Harriet Smith,' I say, giving her a quick curtsey.

'Matilda,' she replies. 'The housemaid.' There's a note of contempt in the final word.

'Really, Matilda, it's a bit embarrassing,' I say, lowering my eyes. 'I know Fra— Mr Churchill. We met at a ball in Weymouth last autumn and I haven't been able to get him out of my head since.'

Matilda stares at me impassively.

'It's a beautiful part of the world,' I say, in an attempt to get a reaction from her.

She snorts dismissively. 'A boring part of the world. I don't much like the sea.'

I don't much like it either, least of all at Weymouth. I can't think of the place without recalling the image of my mother standing outside The Golden Lion coaching inn, kissing the Colonel with a passion she had never shown my father. It had broken my seven-year-old heart. Two months later, Father sat me down and revealed that she had drowned in Weymouth Bay. And it was all downhill from there. I returned to Weymouth eight years after my mother's death, when my father was busy seducing a countess in Dorchester. I suppose I was ready to say goodbye at last. I told my father I was staying overnight with a friend in Abbotsbury and he was so busy with his newest conquest that he didn't even challenge the lie. After all, he knew I had no friends. He had seen to that. At the countess's insistence, I took her parlour maid and coachman along with me and I paid them for their silence about my real destination. When we reached Weymouth, I tortured myself by staying at The Golden Lion, the scene of my mother's betrayal. The last place I had seen her alive. I thought my visit would bring me peace. There was no peace for me in Weymouth, but I stopped mourning my mother after that trip. I finally let her go.

Yes, well,' I say, twirling my little finger around a loose curl of hair, 'I doubt Mr Churchill even remembers me, but I heard he had come to Richmond and I thought I should do him the courtesy of calling upon him and his aunt.'

'Mr Churchill isn't here,' Matilda says.

I already know this because, after a long, hot walk and a terrifying jaunt in a runaway stagecoach, I spent an hour lurking at the bottom of Richmond Hill waiting for him to leave.

'Yes, the butler informed me. I was supposed to be waiting in the drawing-room,' I say with a shrug and what I hope is a disarming smile.

'So what are you doing in here?' Matilda asks, perching herself on the edge of Frank's desk, legs swinging to and fro.

'Mrs Churchill was taking so long and I had such a curiosity to see Frank's room,' I hold up the pencil, 'and perhaps find some small token to remember him by.'

Matilda rolls her eyes and lets out a snort of laughter.

I laugh with her. 'It's rather pathetic, isn't it?'

'It is a bit,' Matilda agrees, 'although I don't expect you're the first girl to creep into his room looking for keepsakes. There's always some desperate young woman after him.'

Charming.

'No offence intended,' Matilda adds, reading my expression. 'Come on,' she says, hopping off the desk. 'I'm sure we can find you a better prize than a shoddy old pencil.' She shoos me away from Frank's desk and bends down to access the secret drawer.

Apparently, it's not so secret after all.

She rummages around for a minute, pulling out Mr Cole's copy of *The Romance of the Forest*. Frowning, she tosses it back into the drawer and slams it shut. 'Nothing in there today,' she pronounces.

I'm beginning to think Frank's careful organisation of his space might be warranted.

'I know!' Matilda rushes over to Frank's chest of drawers, pulling open the top drawer to reveal a jumble of silk cravats in every colour you could think of. 'One of these, perhaps,' she suggests, a glint in her eyes as she drapes a teal cravat around her neck.

'Oh no, I couldn't,' I say, running my fingers appreciatively over the smooth silk.

'He won't miss it,' she assures me. 'He's got dozens of the things. Besides, you're not like the usual, stuck-up misses he goes for. You remind me of my cousin, May. She's a good sort. You mustn't expect the mistress to approve of you, mind. I'm surprised she agreed to see you at all, except that she's so bored. Can you imagine if Frank Churchill tried to marry the likes of you or I? She would be furious!'

I'm not thrilled to be lumped in with Matilda the housemaid and her cousin, but if it gets me some information on Frank, I suppose I can bear it.

'Would she?' I say, wide-eyed. 'Well, I don't suppose she could do anything about if it Frank were really in love—'

Matilda snorts. 'In love? Frank Churchill? He knows nothing of love,' she says with the disdain of a woman twice her age. 'I've only been here a few months and he's had at least five, no, *six*, different women sniffing around him in that time. He likes the attention.' She sneers with a distinct air of sour grapes. I wonder how quickly he rejected *her*.

'Six? Goodness! And has he settled on one of them?'

'Ha! It wouldn't do him much good if he had. None of them are high and mighty enough to gain Mrs Churchill's approval.' Matilda shrugs. 'Why shouldn't you have a token to remember him by?' She is watching me expectantly as she pulls the teal cravat from her neck and holds it out towards me. It's not until she's pressing it into my hands that I realise it's the one he was wearing the night of the Coles' dinner party. I remember thinking how much it brought out the blue in his eyes as he smiled at me for the first time. I can't help but smile now at the memory of it as I lift the cravat towards my face and inhale its citrus scent.

'Lord, you do have it bad,' Matilda says as she closes the drawer. 'Best return to the drawing-room. It won't do for Mrs Churchill to find you in here.'

I snatch up my reticule from Frank's bed and bend down to stuff the cravat inside, along with the sheet of paper I kicked under the desk.

'She'll be down shortly,' Matilda says as I follow her into the drawing-room, 'although, I warn you, she's in a dreadful mood this morning.'

Matilda pours out the tea as I assess whether it's safe to drink it. (As Frank is well out of the way, I decide to take my chances.)

'Not that I can blame her,' Matilda adds, clearly enjoying having someone close to her own age to gossip with. She perches on the end of the chaise longue and leans forward. 'The lady's maid got her breakfast order wrong. Third time this week. Mrs Churchill only eats dry toast and yet Sophia brought it up buttered again this morning. I swear she only does it so she can help herself to the mistress's leftovers. I saw her in there yesterday, gobbling up toast as if she hadn't eaten for a week. Crumbs all over the place. Don't expect she'll last much longer. They never do. The last one had only been here a few months.'

'What happened to her?'

Matilda crosses her legs and helps herself to a biscuit. 'She had her head screwed on. Went off and found herself a husband. The good ones usually do. The mistress has been in a foul temper since we got here and Frank has barely stepped foot in the place. I dare say he would have preferred to settle in London. More to keep a young man entertained in town.'

'So it wasn't his idea to come to Richmond, then?'

'Oh no. It was the mistress who made that decision. And she always gets her way.'

Just as I thought. A test.

Matilda leaps up from the chaise longue and shakes the crumbs from her dress at the sound of Mrs Churchill stomping down the stairs.

'And if it happens again, you will not be around long enough to make your apology!' Mrs Churchill marches into the room as if she hasn't just been screeching at her lady's maid. She settles herself on the chaise longue as Matilda pours out the tea and then hovers behind her. Mrs Churchill sighs. 'That will be all, Matilda,' she snaps, without turning round.

'Yes, ma'am.' Matilda mouths 'good luck' to me as she scurries away.

'Miss Smith,' Mrs Churchill says finally. 'You are here.'

'I am. Although I'm not quite sure why *you* are.'

'You do not approve of my move to Richmond.'

'It's not my place to approve.'

'No. It is not. And yet you seem to have an opinion on the matter all the same.' *And I do not pay you to have opinions*, her tone implies.

'It's only that I'm at a loss to understand why you would wish to bring your nephew closer to temptation,' I say, although I know full well why she's done it. I just want to see if she'll admit it.

'Temptation?' Mrs Churchill asks, eyes blazing, as she slams down her teacup. 'But you yourself have assured me that it is all over between Frank and that girl. I expected you were here to inform me that you had done your job, Miss Smith. That you had rid us of Jane Fairfax once and for all.'

'You didn't ask me to drive her away from Highbury. Just from Frank. And, as I have already informed you, I have done that. I've watched Jane Fairfax very closely since Frank left, and I can assure you she has been thoroughly miserable. I'm certain she hasn't received a letter from Frank since he left Highbury. Frank has abandoned Miss Fairfax.' If my observations of Jane are anything to go by, it is she who has abandoned Frank, but I don't think this will play very well with Mrs Churchill. 'If ever he loved her, he is indifferent to her now,' I add, raising my teacup to my lips. The liquid burns my tongue, but it's a good barrier between myself and Mrs Churchill and so I keep drinking.

'Then this will be the perfect opportunity to test his indifference, will it not? If he has thrown over Miss Fairfax, there is nothing to worry about, is there?'

And there it is.

My hand reaches into my reticule and my thumb brushes against the silk of Frank's cravat as I feel around for Mrs Churchill's pearls.

'Besides, Miss Fairfax is not the only pretty young woman in Highbury, is she?' Mrs Churchill says, eyes gleaming. 'I am sure Miss Woodhouse will be pleased to see Frank more regularly,' she adds, watching me closely.

Ah. Miss Woodhouse. So that's her game.

'And my jewels?' Mrs Churchill demands.

Wordlessly, I hand over the pearl necklace and the diamond earrings.

'And the rest, Miss Smith? The second pearl necklace. The locket?'

'I have not yet found them,' I admit.

'Well, you will have to look harder, then. There are only so many places Miss Fairfax could have hidden them.'

'Jane does not have them.'

Mrs Churchill's head snaps up, eyes fixed on mine. 'Of course she does.'

'She didn't have the pearl necklace and I found the earrings in Frank's possession. I think he's been selling your jewellery to fund his elopement plan. I suspect Jane knows nothing about it.'

'Do you, indeed? And where is your proof, Miss Smith?'

'It's just a theory at present,' I admit, 'but it's the most feasible—'

'You have no proof, because there is none. That wretched girl has seduced Frank into stealing my jewellery to satisfy her own vanity. Frank has given them to her and, if they have ended up elsewhere, then she has sold them on to line her own pockets. She has done very well out of all this. My jewels. The pianoforte. No doubt she will try selling off that next.'

'If it wasn't for the pianoforte, she would still have Frank too,' I remind her.

'And how do I know she does not?' Mrs Churchill demands. 'I only have your word for it that your ruse has been successful.'

'Well, we'll know soon enough, won't we?' I say, taking another sip of my tea and giving her a simpering smile. She doesn't return it.

'I see it is not only Frank she has bewitched. I knew you were too green for such a delicate matter. You *like* her,' she taunts.

I take a deep breath and set down my tea. 'Has it not occurred to you, Mrs Churchill, that Jane Fairfax might not be the villain you're making her out to be? That the person who is trying to kill you might be a bit closer to home?'

'I hope you are not suggesting what I think you are suggesting, Miss Smith.'

'I am merely pointing out that your nephew has just as strong a motive as Miss Fairfax for getting you out of the way.'

'Insolent girl! Do you really dare to suggest that my own flesh and blood—'

'From what I've seen of him, I wouldn't rule it out.' I try to keep my tone even, but I can't help raising my voice to match her volume.

'I have had quite enough of your impertinence,' Mrs Churchill snaps, her face crimson with indignation. 'You will leave this house at once. I no longer require your services!'

A piercing scream rings through the house. It's pitch and length are enough to convince me that something is horribly wrong. I leap from the sofa, pulse racing, and I'm out of the room before Mrs Churchill can even rise from the chaise longue, taking the stairs two by two as I run towards the source of the sound.

Matilda is standing in the doorway, screeching at a dark shape lying on the Persian rug next to Mrs Churchill's four-poster bed. Slumped across the floor, face planted firmly in a puddle of her own vomit on Mrs Churchill's discarded breakfast tray, is what I can only assume is Sophia, the lady's maid. Or was, I should say. Because there's no doubt about it. Sophia is dead.

CHAPTER 11

Rule number eleven: Always have your wits about you. You never know where danger might be lurking and what face it might wear.

Matilda won't stop screaming. I understand why, but the sound is giving me such a headache that it takes all my restraint not to slap her round the face to get her to shut up. I grab her by the shoulders and move her towards the door, then turn back to deal with Sophia. Not that there's much I can do for her now.

I kneel beside the corpse, holding a hand to my mouth as I examine the vomit-covered toast on Mrs Churchill's plate. I roll Sophia over, noting the crimson shade of her face, the glassy eyes. Steeling myself, I break off a small piece of toast and sniff it.

Bitter almonds again.

I reach for my reticule, pulling out Frank's cravat and wrapping it round the toast. I'm not sure what I intend to do with it, but it feels important to hold on to some evidence of what's happened, so I stuff it into my reticule as Mrs Churchill sweeps into the room.

'Matilda, do be quiet,' she snaps.

Miraculously, Matilda falls silent. Perhaps I should have tried that, although I'm not convinced it would have had the same effect.

Stealthy footsteps in the corridor tell me the butler has made it upstairs. He looms in the doorway, gaunt and forbidding. He looks more like a funeral furnisher than a butler and I feel as if he's surreptitiously watching me and silently judging, though his eyes have been on Mrs Churchill the whole time.

'Wakefield, send for Dr Baxter,' Mrs Churchill commands without looking round.

He's too well trained to do anything other than nod and offer a clipped 'of course, ma'am', as he glances at the corpse and then back at Mrs Churchill.

'Take Matilda downstairs with you and fetch her some smelling salts,' Mrs Churchill adds, pushing Matilda towards the butler.

'As you wish, ma'am,' Wakefield says, ushering Matilda out into the corridor with the air of someone who has to deal with dead bodies and hysterical maids on a regular basis.

'She is dead?' Mrs Churchill asks. Her tone is neutral, but her skin is sallow and her hand shakes as she gestures towards the corpse.

I nod my assent, not trusting myself to speak, lest I follow Sophia's example and vomit all over the Persian rug.

Mrs Churchill dashes to the window with surprising speed for a woman of her age and draws back the curtain. She stares out of the window for a minute and then, with a sharp nod, moves over to her dressing table and starts rummaging through her jewellery box. It's odd behaviour for a woman whose lady's maid has just dropped dead on her bedroom floor, but I suppose she has her reasons. Mrs Churchill curses under her breath, shuts her jewellery box and stalks over to where I'm kneeling on the rug, next to the dead maid.

'Well, Miss Smith?' Mrs Churchill says as I struggle to my feet. 'Do you still think Miss Fairfax is innocent?'

Sophia's death has made me more convinced than ever that Jane has nothing to do with the poisoning plot. Good nature aside, she is not reckless enough to make such a mistake as this. But I'm not about to share my thoughts with Mrs Churchill. Despite her resolve to remove me from her house and her employ a few minutes earlier, she still seems to be looking to me for answers. And if she's choosing to forget that she has dismissed me, I certainly don't intend to remind her. I can do this. I haven't seen many dead bodies in my line of work, but I am good in a crisis. And reading people, digging up their secrets, it's what I do. This is a chance to prove myself to Mrs Churchill. Although, the way things are going, I'm not sure she'll like the results. Because things aren't looking good for Frank right now. He's the obvious culprit. Same poison. Same target. He'd been at the house just before it happened.

Hadn't stayed to watch his plot play out. Just like with the tea. Except . . .

I pick up Mrs Churchill's discarded teacup and inhale deeply. 'Did you drink the tea?' I demand.

'Yes. But I do not feel unwell.' She sits down on the bed nonetheless as I reach for the teapot and sniff it.

'That's because it wasn't in the tea this time,' I say, gesturing towards her breakfast tray.

She lets out an audible breath. 'Well, I suppose it will put a stop to her stealing my food.'

It takes me a moment to realise she isn't making a joke. Mrs Churchill is back to her unfeeling self and I find a strange sense of comfort in this.

'Did Frank leave before or after Sophia brought up your breakfast this morning?'

Mrs Churchill folds her arms. 'What does that matter? I know exactly who did this. It was *her*. She has decided that if she finds a way to dispose of me Frank will return to her.'

'But to have come all the way from Highbury to poison your toast—'

'A mere nine miles,' Mrs Churchill reminds me, flashing a triumphant smile as she stands over the corpse of her lady's maid.

Considering the trouble it took me to get here, I can't imagine Jane Fairfax managing the journey with her busybody aunt to contend with. But I can see that I'm not going to convince Mrs Churchill of this.

'I will leave you to it, Mrs Churchill. I'm sure you have arrangements to make for—' I gesture towards the rug.

'You will deal will Jane Fairfax?' she asks in a tone which suggests I won't see a penny more from her until I do.

It's not Jane. I'm almost sure of it. Most likely, it's a member of this household. And, despite Mrs Churchill's protestations, the member of the household who left the house shortly before the murder is top of my list of suspects.

'I will find your poisoner,' I vow, taking one last look at poor Sophia on my way to the door.

Mrs Churchill is staring out of the window again. 'See that you do.'

✳

Matilda is curled up on the chaise longue sobbing into her handkerchief. She raises her head as I enter the drawing-room.

'Oh, Miss Smith. Is it true? Is Sophia really—' She breaks off, takes a deep sniff of her smelling salts and reaches for a biscuit from the tea table, devouring it in three swift bites. She reaches for another.

'I'm afraid so. She was poisoned.'

Matilda's eyes widen. 'Poisoned?' She stares at the biscuit in her hand and quickly returns it to the plate.

'Apparently, she'd been at Mrs Churchill's breakfast again.'

'Then the poison was meant for Mrs Churchill?'

'It would seem so,' I agree.

'Oh, I knew I shouldn't have taken a biscuit. What if they are poisoned too? That's what got poor Sophia in trouble – eating food that wasn't meant for her.'

'The biscuits aren't poisoned, Matilda.'

'H-how do you know?' Matilda sobs.

'Because I had one myself,' I lie, 'and I'm perfectly fine.'

Matilda stops wailing and looks me up and down, searching for signs that I'm about to drop dead, I suppose.

'Besides,' I add, 'it must be fifteen minutes or more since you had your first biscuit. You'd be dead within minutes if they'd been laced with cyanide. Look how quickly it worked with Sophia.'

Matilda's face crumples. 'It's not safe. I'm not safe. I should never have come here,' she wails.

I want to ask her about Sophia's preparation of Mrs Churchill's breakfast, but it's obvious I'll get nothing sensible from her now. I hand her a fresh handkerchief and leave her to sob into it.

I tiptoe across the hallway and downstairs into the kitchen. There's tea and milk on the sideboard, a handful of eggs and half a loaf of bread. Hardly the feast I would expect for the Churchills, but I suppose they are still settling in. I bend over the loaf of bread and inhale deeply, enjoying its yeasty scent. My stomach rumbles mutinously. I left Highbury this morning without any breakfast, but what I've seen upstairs is enough to put me off breakfast for life.

'Can I help you, Miss Smith?'

Wakefield's face is more handsome than I had first given it credit for. He has piercing blue eyes and a strong jawline. I would put him at around five-and-thirty, although his stern expression may have added at least five years too many to my estimation. There's a scar across his neck that his high collar doesn't quite conceal and, though he walks with a light tread, he cannot mask the limp which I suppose is an old war wound. He has a military bearing – stiff and servile – which perfectly suits his role in Mrs Churchill's household.

'You know who I am? What I'm doing for Mrs Churchill?' I ask. Something tells me the direct approach will work best with Wakefield.

'I do,' he acknowledges.

'Then you'll know why I'm here,' I say, turning back to the loaf and giving it an experimental prod.

'There's nothing wrong with the bread,' Wakefield says.

'How do you know?'

He takes a step towards me and seizes the bread knife.

I stand my ground as he raises the knife.

'Move,' he instructs, pushing me away from the loaf as he leans in to cut a thick slice. He takes a large bite, chews and swallows.

We stand, staring at our feet for what feels like a lifetime. Finally, I look up. 'Well, you're still here,' I observe.

'So I see.' He doesn't sound the least bit surprised. As if he knew with absolute certainty the bread would do him no harm. And only one person could know that for sure.

He gestures towards the butter dish and removes the lid with a flourish. It's empty. 'It was like that when I came downstairs,' he says.

Which is awfully convenient.

'What were you doing in the kitchen?' I ask.

'Fetching the smelling salts for Matilda, as Mrs Churchill instructed, and I found the scene as you see it now.'

Someone has disposed of the evidence. Wakefield could easily have done it himself, but then why draw attention to its absence?

'Where was Matilda while you were doing this?'

Wakefield frowns. 'I deposited her in the drawing-room, out of the way,' he says in a tone which clearly emphasises his disapproval of Matilda's outburst.

'It must have been a great shock to her, discovering the body like that.'

'A servant should not show emotion,' he says. 'Our duty is to the household. We must be strong in the face of adversity.'

'I suppose Matilda does not have your experience.'

'What do you mean by that?' he snaps. It's the first time I've seen him lose his composure and he quickly recovers it.

'Just that, as a military man, you will have seen your share of violence, no doubt. Where did you serve?'

'Mysore.'

I hadn't expected him to respond and I'm not convinced he intended to, but it confirms my suspicions. I have heard stories of the horrors of Mysore. Horrors that could make a man lose his mind.

But there's a big difference between killing enemy soldiers on the battlefield and murdering inept lady's maids in your own household.

'Who made the breakfast?' I ask.

'Sophia herself.'

'Is that usual?'

'No. But our cook was taken ill on the road. We had to send her back to Yorkshire and couldn't find a suitable replacement at such short notice. A woman comes in to do the substantial meals, but we have been fending for ourselves in the mornings since we arrived. Breakfast isn't much of a problem because Frank avoids it and Mrs Churchill only takes tea and toast.'

'Dry toast?'

'Yes, but Sophia keeps— *kept* getting it wrong.'

'She was new to your household?'

'She had been with us just over two months, but the breakfast duties were new to her, of course.'

'And the cook—'

'Is well known to us.'

'Has anyone called this morning?'

'Just you.'

'Could anyone have entered the house without your knowledge?' I can't imagine that much happens in this household without Wakefield knowing about it.

Wakefield shakes his head. 'Not through the front door. I always lock it. Of course, someone may have entered through the back door. That is not locked during the day.

Nor is the garden gate.'

'Can I check?' I ask, slipping past him and into the hallway before he can respond. I'm startled by the scrape of a key in a lock.

I didn't expect the doctor so soon and, of course, he would not have a key. I leap through the nearest doorway and shut myself inside. I must have stumbled into the pantry because it's pitch black and stinks of rotting potatoes.

'Aunt Lavinia? Are you in?' Frank's voice rings through from the hallway upstairs. I hear the butler's footsteps on the stairs. 'Ah, Wakefield. It's as silent as the grave in here.'

'We were not expecting you back so soon,' Wakefield replies.

I was not expecting him back at all. I wonder what made him return.

Guilty conscience?

'I was halfway to town before I remembered I'd bumped into the Comptons yesterday and promised to call upon them this morning. I thought it best to get it out of the way now, for I never know when I'll be wanted in Highbury again.'

Wakefield's response is too low for me to hear.

'Something has happened, Wakefield. Is it my aunt?'

'It is my lady's maid,' Mrs Churchill booms from the landing. 'She has been taken ill.'

That's something of an understatement.

I wish I could see the expression on Frank's face. Is he surprised? Worried? Disappointed? Is he, even now, plotting further methods by which to dispose of his aunt?

What *is* certain is that I need to get out of here. Immediately. It would not do for Frank to catch me in his aunt's pantry. Even I would be hard-pressed to talk my way out of this scenario and I need, more than ever, to keep Frank on side.

In case he happens to be a homicidal maniac.

'You must not forget your engagement, Frank, now that you have come all the way back for it,' Mrs Churchill says, raising her voice.

If he has an engagement at all. Had I brought Robert with me to Richmond, he could have trailed Frank this morning and I would know whether Frank was lying about his whereabouts. But Robert is still preoccupied with Denny and, besides, I didn't want him to start up on my obsession with Frank Churchill again.

I'm roused by the creak of the stairs and receding footsteps. Frank must have gone up to his bedroom to change. I ease open the pantry door and steal out into the hallway and up the stairs. I'm almost at the front door when I hear Frank shout to his aunt, 'Have you seen my teal cravat?'

Wakefield nods to me as I open the front door. He doesn't look particularly sorry to see me go. I slip out into the street and glance up at the Churchills' townhouse. For a moment, I'm sure I see a form framed in Frank's window but, when I look again, there is nothing at all.

CHAPTER 12

Rule number twelve: Never enter a man's pigsty without knocking. It rarely ends well.

'Robert?' The kitchen of Abbey-Mill Farm is in utter chaos. Crockery piled high in the sink. A mop submerged in a puddle of dirty water which oozes across the floor. The kitchen table still buried under Robert's papers. I hope he's at least concealed those dreadful love letters from Denny. I retreat into the yard and look out over the fields. 'Robert?'

My over-familiar Welsh cow raises her head and lets out a plaintive moo. 'Where is he, girl?' She blinks at me stupidly. I'm roused by a series of snorts and squeals and decidedly human curses. 'Never mind,' I say, heading towards the pigsty.

Mr Knightley is flat on his back in the pigsty and Robert is writhing around in the mud beside him, wrestling with something small and pink.

'Oh,' I say, wondering how I've managed to stumble into one of Robert's fantasies.

Am I asleep? Has this whole day been one long nightmare?

A glob of mud flies across the barn and hits me full in the face.

Definitely not asleep.

Mr Knightley sits up and brushes off his breeches as the pink thing wriggles free of Robert's grip and charges straight at me. I throw my arms wide, bracing myself for impact and scoop up the piglet in one swift movement, depositing it back in the pigsty as Mr Knightley helps Robert to his feet.

'Miss Smith,' Mr Knightley says, hands on his knees as he catches his breath. 'How nice to see you.' There's a question in his statement and I'm fairly certain that it's something along the lines of: *What is an unaccompanied young woman doing sneaking round a gentleman's farm when all his female relations are absent?*

This was never something I had to worry about when I was with Father. He didn't care a jot about my honour. He would throw me at whatever rich man took his fancy, reputation be damned. Safety, too, as his stunt in Derbyshire proved. And yet, as the daughter of the so-called Earl of Dudley, I could do as I pleased. Nobody dared question me. But as friendless, parentless Harriet Smith – a girl with no connections – I have to be much more careful. The hypocrisy of it is infuriating. Emma Woodhouse can spend as much unaccompanied time as she pleases with Mr Knightley and nobody says a thing about it. As an heiress of thirty thousand pounds, Miss

Woodhouse is immune from scandal. I, on the other hand, have to fend it off with a saccharine smile and a good dose of injured innocence.

'Yes. How nice to see you,' Robert agrees in a tone which suggests the exact opposite.

'Queen Charlotte,' I blurt out.

Robert frowns. 'Excuse me?'

'I've come to see Queen Charlotte.'

Mr Knightley tilts his head and glances questioningly at Robert. 'I didn't know you were entertaining royalty.'

'She means my Welsh cow,' Robert murmurs.

'You said she was *my* cow,' I correct him. 'And that I could visit her whenever I pleased. So I have come to visit.'

'Then I will leave you to it, Miss Smith,' Mr Knightley says with a polite nod. 'You might want to clean yourself up, Robert,' he adds, casting his eyes over the farmer's mud-spattered form.

I watch Mr Knightley retreat and then follow Robert out of the barn and into the farmhouse, glancing around the kitchen for a distraction as Robert stomps off to his bedroom to change. I move over to the kitchen table and flick through Robert's research papers for his novel. My eyes settle on his notes on the effects of cyanide poisoning: headache; shortness of breath; rapid heartbeat; faintness; vomiting; seizures; cherry-red hue; loss of consciousness; death. Can kill within minutes, depending on dose.

Sophia couldn't have been dead long, given that Mrs Churchill had been screaming at her just before she had entered the drawing-room to speak to me. What agony must the poor girl have suffered in her final moments?

I flinch as the bedroom door swings open and Robert stalks out, still doing up his shirt buttons as he joins me at the kitchen table. He looks as if he's getting ready to berate me, but as he catches my expression, he decides against it. 'Who died?' he asks, apparently trying to lighten the mood.

'Mrs Churchill's lady's maid,' I say, rooting around in my reticule for Frank's cravat. I dump it on the table in front of him. 'Poisoned,' I pronounce, as Robert opens up the cravat and pokes at its contents. He leans in to give it a cautious sniff.

'Good lord. What *is* that?'

'Toast. Laced with cyanide. And vomit.'

Robert looks as if *he's* about to vomit as he wipes his fingers on his breeches. 'Please tell me you're joking?'

'Why on earth would I joke about something like this?'

Robert flaps his arms around like a startled crow. 'I don't know! But why would Mrs Churchill's lady's maid be murdered?'

'Well, she ate the poisoned toast, presumably.'

'Yes, I got that. But why?'

'She was hungry, I suppose.'

Robert sighs. 'No. I mean why was it poisoned?'

'Oh. It was Mrs Churchill's breakfast. Apparently, the new lady's maid was in the habit of bungling her mistress's breakfast order and then helping herself to the discarded food.'

Robert frowns. 'So it was meant for Mrs Churchill?'

'It would seem so.'

He narrows his eyes at me. 'I have to say, Harriet, you seem awfully calm about this. Almost as if you were expecting it.'

Here it comes.

'But, of course, you couldn't have expected anything of this kind. After all, you were only hired to break off an engagement and retrieve some family heirlooms, weren't you?'

I'm hoping his question is rhetorical.

'Weren't you, Harriet?'

I take a deep breath and hit Robert with my sweetest smile. He scowls at me.

'Well, it may be that I left out one or two details,' I admit. 'I *was* employed to do those things, but there was also the matter of Mrs Churchill's tea.'

'Her tea? What was wrong with her tea?'

'It had cyanide in it,' I say as quickly as possible.

'Cyanide?' Robert shouts, nearly upending the kitchen table as he leaps to his feet.

'You see. This is why I didn't tell you,' I say calmly. 'I knew you'd overreact.'

'Overreact? Harriet. You were hired to solve a murder.'

'Attempted murder,' I mumble.

'Well, it's murder now!' he shouts, pacing up and down the kitchen. 'I can't believe you got involved in this. I can't believe you got *me* involved. You have no clue what you're doing. This is insanity, even for you.'

He's right, of course, but the damage is done now. I stay silent as Robert continues to pace up and down the kitchen. He'll tire himself out eventually and then we can get down to business. Once we start talking suspects, his creative brain will kick in and he won't be able to resist the drama of it all.

Finally, Robert relents and throws himself into a chair, limbs flailing. 'So,' he says, gesturing towards the poisoned toast, 'who did it, genius?'

He's really not going to like this.

'Well, all things considered, Frank seems the most likely culprit.'

'Frank Churchill? The man you've been following around and flirting with and Lord knows what else—'

'Except he must have had an accomplice if it was him,' I say, ignoring Robert's jibe, 'because somebody disposed of the poisoned butter after he went out.'

'Could he have slipped back inside after the deed was done?'

'It's possible, I suppose. He has a key and he could have entered the house when we were all upstairs, but he would have had a very small window of opportunity before the butler and the housemaid went downstairs again. Of course, Mrs Churchill is convinced Frank is entirely innocent and Jane is behind everything.'

'Hardly surprising, is it? It would certainly help her case to get rid of Jane.'

'Hmmm. And I suppose we must consider the possibility that Mrs Churchill might have poisoned the toast herself.'

Robert raises an eyebrow. 'It seems a little extreme to kill off your own lady's maid just so you can blame it on your nephew's unsuitable fiancée.'

I'm inclined to agree with Robert on this one. I wouldn't put anything past Mrs Churchill when it comes to splitting up Frank and Jane, but this is a stretch, even for her. She didn't seem particularly upset at the loss of her lady's maid, but she was, at least, shaken by it.

'Who else do we have on our suspect list?' I ask, hoping to keep Robert distracted with detective work.

He shrugs. 'The housemaid?'

'Matilda? What's her motive?'

'Mrs Churchill isn't exactly a model employer,' Robert reasons. 'Or perhaps it's nothing to do with Mrs Churchill. Perhaps this Matilda had a grudge against the lady's maid and was after her position.'

I snort. 'She's hardly suited to her duties as housemaid. I doubt Mrs Churchill would promote her to the lady's maid position. No, Matilda would need a better motive than that. She doesn't appear to be the biggest fan of Frank and she certainly seems to know his business. There's a story there, perhaps. But if it's a servant you're looking for, Wakefield, the butler, is a much more likely candidate.'

'How so?' Robert leans over the kitchen table and picks up his pencil, twirling it between his fingers.

'Well, he had access to the kitchen to poison the butter

and to remove it. And we only have his word for it that the butter had disappeared when he returned to the kitchen to fetch the smelling salts for Matilda. He made a point of telling me the back door was unlocked during the day, which widens our field of suspects. Anyone could have walked in off the street, but they would need to have been very precise about their timing. I didn't have the opportunity to check to see if he was telling the truth about the door because Frank turned up and I had to hide in the pantry.'

Robert makes no attempt to suppress his smirk.

'There's something rather sinister about Wakefield,' I add, ignoring Robert's smirk. 'He's an ex-soldier, so he clearly has experience of killing people, and he knows everything that goes on in that household, including the task for which Mrs Churchill employed me.'

The more I talk about Wakefield, the more convinced I am that he could have done it.

'But what's his motive?' Robert asks, chewing on the end of his pencil.

'That is the question,' I admit. 'I haven't found one as yet but, be assured, there's more to Wakefield than meets the eye.'

'And then, there's Jane,' Robert adds. 'We can't forget her.'

'No. I suppose not,' I allow. But I don't like it.

'Well, we have our list of suspects,' Robert says, scribbling in his notebook. 'So which of them did it?'

'I have no idea,' I confess. This isn't really my area of expertise. I've been trained to rob people of their money, not their lives. Dead bodies. Murder. That's really more in Robert's line than mine. 'If this were your novel, who would you select as the culprit?' I ask.

Robert rubs the back of his head. 'I would pick the least likely candidate. Matilda or Jane or, better still, someone right on the fringe of the story. Someone we haven't considered. Perhaps we haven't even met them. Or perhaps we met them right at the start of this and now they've faded into the background. But there's a world of difference between fiction and reality. What makes a good story rarely works in the real world.'

I reach for my reticule and pull out the pencil rubbing I made from Frank's writing paper. Matilda's interruption and Sophia's subsequent death meant that I didn't get a chance to read it. I place it sideways on the table for Robert to see.

Monsieur Durand,

I regret that I was not able to pay you in full at our last meeting. I beg your forbearance a little longer. I expect to come into some money very soon and you can be assured that I will then be able to settle my account. In the meantime, I must insist that you do not call upon my aunt again. I will repay my own debts. They have nothing to do with her.

Your dutiful servant,
Frank Churchill

'That explains Mrs Churchill's strange behaviour,' I muse.

'What behaviour?'

'After we found Sophia, she went over to the window as if she was looking for someone in particular. I thought at the time it might have been Frank, but if this Durand fellow had been to the house threatening her, it stands to reason that this could have been him. A warning to Frank of what would happen if he didn't repay his debts. She was searching through her jewellery box, as if she expected something to be missing.'

'And was it?'

'I don't know, but it certainly opens up a new possibility. It sounds like gambling debts to me. Perhaps Frank *was* visiting an illicit gambling den in London and they just happen to do haircuts as well. In fact, Monsieur Durand is clearly a French name. Do you think he could be Frank's French barber?'

'It's a bit of a stretch,' Robert says, but I can tell he's considering it. If it's true, it means that Denny was lying to us. Perhaps this will finally be the thing to break Denny's hold over Robert.

'Frank expects to come into some money very soon, does he? And where do you suppose that is coming from? His soon-to-be-dead aunt? Frank won't receive his inheritance from his late uncle unless Mrs Churchill approves of his bride. Well, killing her solves *that* problem, doesn't it? Then all he has to do is win back Jane and they can live happily ever after at Enscombe.'

'Hmmm.' Robert's fingers tap against the table. 'How did Mrs Churchill take it?'

'Oh, she was her normal haughty self, but it was clear it bothered her more than she was letting on. It's not every day you find a dead body in your bedroom, after all.'

'No, I mean, when you told her you were dropping the job.'

I fold my arms across my chest and lean back in my chair. 'Come on, Robert. You know me better than that.'

'You can't seriously be thinking of carrying on? You admitted yourself that you're out of your depth.'

'I said no such thing.' I *am* out of my depth, but it's not something I'd ever admit to Robert. I'm sick of men telling me what I can't do.

'Harriet, you asked me how I would solve the murder in my novel. That's hardly the action of someone who knows what she's doing. You can't do this. You need to walk away.'

'I'm sorry, have I suddenly come into some money that I don't know about?'

'It's not just about money. A woman has been murdered.'

'You should be happy. I finally have a chance to do something more noble!'

'Harriet,' Robert warns, 'this is no joking matter.'

I know it isn't. I feel sick to the pit of my stomach at the memory of it.

'Which is why I need to see this through,' I say. 'I will honour my contract. I will find Mrs Churchill's poisoner. Sophia's killer.'

Robert shakes his head. 'You're insane,' he mutters, knowing the argument is lost.

'Are we going to talk about what just happened?'

Robert looks at me blankly.

I roll my eyes. 'Writhing around in the mud with Mr Knightley. What were you thinking?'

'I was thinking I needed to capture the escaped piglet,' Robert protests. 'Nothing more.'

'You're being far too obvious about your feelings for him. Any fool could see it, and Mr Knightley is no fool.'

'There is nothing going on with Mr Knightley.'

'No. And there never will be. Most likely he will marry Emma Woodhouse – the rich gravitate towards each other in most things, after all. And he is your landlord. You need to be very careful with Mr Knightley. I know how you feel about him, but you can't afford to get too close. Besides, what about poor Denny?'

'Poor Denny?' Robert scoffs. 'You hate Denny.'

'Yes, but he loves you. What do you think he'll do when he finds out?'

Denny has a vindictive streak a mile wide. It's bad enough to have it focused on me. But with someone he loves, someone who has betrayed him . . .

'Oh, and it has nothing to do with the fact that you want to interrogate him about Monsieur Durand and his so-called gambling den? Much easier to do if I keep him sweet for you.'

'Is that what you think of me? That I care more about this job than your happiness?'

He's not wrong about Durand, though. Denny doesn't like me, but it will be easier to get the truth out of him if he's still with Robert.

'I think you care about what's going to make you the most money,' Robert snaps.

And there we have it. What Robert Martin, my only friend in the world, really thinks of me.

'I'm trying to help you,' I say, doing my best to keep my composure. 'Whatever you choose to do with Denny, you need to stop this nonsense with Mr Knightley.'

'Yes, thank you, Harriet,' Robert says, pulling me to my feet and steering me towards the door. 'I don't think you're the best candidate to be giving me romantic advice, are you? But if I want any tips on how to shut myself off from love and die alone, you'll be the first person I ask.' He slams the door in my face.

I tramp back to Mrs Goddard's, heartsore and bone-tired. I head straight to my room, wondering what else could happen to make this day even worse than it already is.

They say bad luck comes in threes.

My foot slips as I enter my bedroom. I flail around, just about keeping my balance. I bend down to pick up the offending object. A single sheet of paper. I slump onto the bed as I unfold it.

The words are typed, cut from a book, and I recognise them immediately:

'Sblood, do you think I am easier to be play'd on
than a pipe? Call me what instrument you will,
though you can fret me, you cannot play upon me.

A warning. The one I've been waiting for. And it can only
mean one thing: he's finally on my trail.

CHAPTER 13

Rule number thirteen: In some circumstances, it's better to be the damsel in distress than the paranoid, pistol-wielding maniac who is perfectly capable of looking after herself.

My father gave me a copy of *Hamlet* for my eighth birthday. It was my first birthday without Mama and all the little customs she had invented for the occasion: the songs; the sweets; the silly parlour games with rules that only we understood. There was such a shroud of sadness spread over our house that I wasn't expecting anything to mark the occasion. My father had never given me a gift before and so I treasured this one. It offered me hope for the future: that there was life after Mama; that we could keep on going without her. As he handed it to me, he emphasised the resilience of Queen Gertrude, her cleverness in abandoning her husband for his brother, whom she preferred, and manipulating her new beau into disposing of the old one.

'There's a woman who knows how to deceive a man. Take her as your model and you'll go far, my duck,' my father said, patting me on the head, eyes focused on something beyond my sight.

I studied the play, learning Gertrude's lines by heart, but I couldn't understand my father's interpretation of it. I went to him one day, crawling into his lap as he bent over his accounts, brow furrowed.

'Father, I think you're wrong,' I told him with my childish confidence. He sighed and put down his pen.

'See here,' I said, finger tapping against Gertrude's lines. 'If Gertrude had plotted King Hamlet's death, wouldn't he have called down his vengeance upon her? Wouldn't he have appeared to challenge her?'

'He does appear to her,' my father said. 'In her closet. Where she betrayed him.'

'But she can't see him,' I reasoned.

He looked down at me with solemn eyes. 'Are you quite sure?'

Years later, my father took me to see the play in London, when he was posing as a recently widowed duke looking for some solace in his middle years, and I was the wild daughter who needed a firm, motherly hand to guide me. He leant over in the crucial scene and said, 'You see how determined the lady is to look through him? How she never quite meets his eye? That's her tell.' I saw it then, and have never stopped seeing it since.

Of course, Gertrude dies a horrible death by her lover's hand, or by her own if you believe my father's theory. Poison, of all things. My father always glossed over that part. He was never one to look to the end of the story – the happily-ever-after or the tragic demise. The former didn't serve his purpose; the latter would be his own fate soon enough, so why worry about it ahead of time?

My father had inscribed my copy, 'To Hattie, my little Gertrude'. I carried it with me wherever we went. I slept with it under my pillow at Mrs Goddard's. It isn't there now. He has taken it. The words on his warning note are cut from my own copy. My father cannot be played on like a pipe. I get the message loud and clear. He's coming for me. It's just a matter of when.

In my mind, he is already here. I see him lurking on every street corner. Every letter I read is in his hand. Every tread on the stair is made by his foot. If I could have avoided attending the ball at The Crown I would have done, but I wasn't about to throw away my first opportunity to see Frank since the day of the murder. For murder it is, even though the culprit did not hit their intended target. And I'm not about to let my father scare me off the case.

Frank spent his time pacing up and down in some agitation until Jane arrived. He flirted with Emma, but with no serious intent, was painfully polite to Jane as if regretting his split from her, and rarely glanced in my direction. On the one occasion I did catch him gazing at me across the ballroom, it wasn't with the admiration I had hoped to inspire. In fact, he didn't seem to be looking at me at all, but through me, as he contemplated some terrible fate. I was too preoccupied with images of my father ambushing me mid-dance and stabbing me with a poisoned fencing foil to be much bothered by Frank's sudden aversion to me. The problem with my father is he's a chameleon. He's spent his life blending in so, if he doesn't want to be seen, you can guarantee I won't see him.

Until it's too late.

I didn't want to come out this morning, but I saw Frank borrow a pair of scissors from Miss Bates last night and, as the old maid chattered on, he pocketed them. I'm sure he'll be dropping in on the Bateses' apartment this morning on the pretext of returning the scissors but, actually, to have another go at winning back Jane. I can't let him do that. Not if he's a cold-blooded killer.

Ordinarily, I could have charged Robert with protecting me against my father, but he's still not speaking to me after the whole Mr Knightley incident. And so, in Robert's absence, I've brought along Miss Bickerton again. I'm already regretting it, but my father is a cautious man and he's hardly likely to approach me with her in tow. I have other protections too, more reliable than Miss Bickerton. I'm hoping I don't have to use them.

'Must you walk so fast, Miss Smith?' Miss Bickerton is panting behind me, her cheeks flushed with the exertion, her flaming curls plastered against her neck. She's really not bred for heat or exercise, but beggars can't be choosers.

Yes, I absolutely *must* walk this fast. The elms looming over us add a sense of seclusion to this spot. It's the perfect place for an ambush and I'm not taking any chances with my father out here, baying for my blood. Because he could be anyone: a messenger; a servant; even a member of the rabble of Romani stomping towards us. They are a tightknit community, but if anyone could talk his way inside, it's my father.

Miss Bickerton lets out a shriek and grasps hold of my arm. 'Oh, Miss Smith,' she wails. 'We should not have come this way. Did I not tell you so?' She gestures frantically towards the Romani.

A wild-looking girl with coal-black hair and emerald-green eyes approaches us, pushing a basket towards me. 'Buy a trinket, miss?'

Poor Miss Bickerton can't take any more. Terrified by the gathering crowd, she lets out a shrill scream and runs off up the bank, calling on me to follow. She jumps the hedge like a prize steeplechaser and flees back to Mrs Goddard's, leaving me to face the Romani alone.

Some bodyguard she *is*.

Half a dozen scrawny children descend on me, headed by a stout woman with sharp eyes and a handsome face. By her side is my old companion, bear boy. He grins in recognition.

I'm jostled from side to side as the children vie for position, tugging at the hem of my gown. I'm really not in the mood for this today and I'm determined to catch Frank at the Bateses' apartment, so I pull out my pearl-handled flintlock pistol and point it at bear boy. The smaller children scatter, but bear boy stands his ground, smirking as he presses a letter into my unarmed hand.

'For you, m'lady,' he says with a mock bow.

'You there. Get away!'

I withdraw my pistol and slip the unread letter inside my pelisse as Frank Churchill charges at my assailants, head lowered like a raging bull. The remaining Romani flee the scene as if the devil himself is on their heels.

I let out a scream almost as shrill as Miss Bickerton's as I sink to the ground, waiting for Frank to come to my rescue.

'Are you hurt?' Frank is kneeling beside me, eyes blazing.

'Oh, Mr Churchill! I was so frightened. Miss Bickerton ran off up the hill, but I twisted my ankle and could not follow her. I don't know what I would have done if you hadn't come along.'

He appraises me carefully. 'I suspect you might have managed, Miss Smith. You strike me as a capable girl.'

This will not do at all. If Frank thinks me capable, I'll get nothing useful from him.

I try again as he helps me to my feet, leaning upon his arm and wincing to convince him of my injury. 'I thought you would have left for Richmond already.'

'It is my forgetfulness you have to thank for your good fortune. I borrowed a pair of scissors from Miss Bates last night and didn't remember them until this morning.'

The lie rolls so smoothly off his tongue I'm almost inclined to believe him, until I remember him slipping the scissors into his pocket as Miss Bates chattered on obliviously. Frank walks along in silence beside me, lost in thought, hand resting gently on my arm. It doesn't feel like the hand of a killer, but I'm determined not to waste this opportunity to interrogate him.

'I worry for the other ladies of Highbury with this rabble here,' I say, slowing my pace. I don't want to reach Mrs Goddard's before I've had chance to get anything out of him and, besides, I can't walk that fast on my poor twisted ankle, can I? 'If they were to approach Miss Woodhouse, or Miss Fairfax . . .' I watch him carefully to see how his ex-lover's name afflicts him.

Nothing.

Not even the tiniest flicker of emotion. It seems I must work a little harder for a reaction.

'I know they both walk this route,' I say, glancing behind me on the pretence of looking for rogue Romani, although in reality checking that my father hasn't taken advantage of my preoccupation with Frank to trail me back home.

Be mindful of your surroundings, Hattie, my father always said. *Don't be distracted by a pretty face. Concentrate on what is in front of you, and what lurks behind.*

I shudder and move closer to Frank. 'Are the women of Highbury to be so terrorised? And after the awful fate that befell your aunt's lady's maid.'

Frank's grip on my arm tightens. 'What do you know about that?' His voice is steady, but his fingers twitch against my pelisse.

'I heard Mrs Goddard telling Mrs Cole. The poor girl died, did she not?'

'A tragic accident,' Frank replies, dropping my arm.

'The doctor thinks she had a weak heart. I doubt you are so afflicted, Miss Smith.' He quickens his pace. 'I shall take you to Hartfield,' he pronounces, which is not what I want at all. Emma's house is much closer than Mrs Goddard's and we'll be there before I can break him.

I stumble, allowing my momentum to carry me forward so that I fall, accidentally, of course, right into Frank's outstretched arms. Pressed against his chest, I inhale the scent of lemon and jasmine and . . . bergamot. That's the third ingredient in his intoxicating cocktail. My pulse quickens at the rapid thump of his heart against mine. I need to pull away, but I can't seem to move.

'I'm glad to hear you say it was an accident, Mr Churchill. In truth, I had heard such dreadful rumours.'

'Rumours?' Frank draws back and holds me at arm's length. 'Such as?' He's smirking, as if at an indulgent child, but there's a hint of panic in his eyes.

'You will laugh at me,' I say, pouting.

Frank shakes his head, relaxing his grip. 'I will not, Miss Smith, I assure you.'

'Just the usual kind of thing. Thieves, brigands. Frenchmen,' I add, thinking of Durand.

'Frenchmen?' Frank's fingers dig into my shoulders.

'Yes,' I insist, eyes wide. 'There's talk of a Frenchman lurking outside your aunt's house around the time of the maid's death.'

'Why would a Frenchman kill my aunt's lady's maid?' Frank's tone is casual, but he's still gripping my shoulders.

'Well,' I say, shrugging off his fingers, 'you can't really trust the French, can you? You hear all sorts of things about them.'

Frank pats my shoulder, smiling now he's sure I'm plucking random theories out of the air. 'I think you've been reading too many of your Gothic novels, Miss Smith. I doubt there are many murderous Frenchmen lurking around Richmond.'

Anyone else would have taken him at his word, but I've been observing Frank for so long that I can hear the tinge of uncertainty in his tone. Of course, those rumours are a complete fabrication, but the fact that Frank is worried by them tells me all I need to know about the moneylender's character. If Frank is not my poisoner, then Monsieur Durand is definitely worth a look.

It's Frank who withdraws at last (and I flatter myself he does it with some reluctance). 'Can you walk?' he asks, and his solicitude sounds genuine.

I hobble forwards. Fall again, clutching at his arm. 'My ankle,' I say, shaking my head. 'Perhaps if I just rest a while . . .'

He sighs and smirks at me. 'I've got you,' he says and sweeps me up into his arms.

I close my eyes, enjoying the sun on my face as I'm lulled by the steady rhythm of his gait. I curl into his chest, my lips pressed against his neck. There's something about the way I fit into Frank's arms that is just so easy. So different from how it was with—

No. There's no sense in going back there.

And, while we're on the subject of ineligible men, now would be a good time to remind myself I'm in the arms of a potential murderer. I use our proximity as an excuse to slide my fingers into his redingote pocket, ever so gently, so he won't detect my presence. My fingers curl around a pencil, brush across a small, leather volume which is too heavy to remove without him noticing its absence and then finally alight upon something worth stealing. A letter.

That's more like it.

I swipe it from his pocket and slip it into my pelisse as Frank lowers me to the ground. I lean on him to limp those last few steps through the iron sweep-gate to Hartfield. Emma is soon upon us and I'm back to playing poor, empty-headed Harriet. I sink into a chair and stare at the fleur-de-lys design on Emma's writing box, tracing it back and forth with my eyes as Frank explains my predicament to Emma and then withdraws as quickly as humanly possible.

Does he feel it too? The undeniable spark between us.

As Emma ducks out of the room, I reach inside my pelisse for bear boy's note, unfolding it cautiously. Another warning, cut from my own copy of *Hamlet*, I'd wager:

When sorrows come, they come not single spies,
But in battalions.

If I was still in any doubt that the message came from my father, I'm under no illusion now. It could only ever be him. Keeping his distance, using the Romani to do his dirty work, is exactly his style. He's playing with his food. It's my father's way. It's the way he taught me. I have to wrap up this case, collect my fee and get out of Highbury as soon as possible. Before he goes in for the kill. Like Old Hamlet's Ghost, my father is not one to forgive and I'm certain now that he will not desist until he has had his revenge.

I open the second note – the one I liberated from Frank's pocket. There are five words inked across it in an elegant script that looks distinctly French.

Your time is running out.

I think it's time I paid a certain French barber a visit.

CHAPTER 14

Rule number fourteen: Sometimes, brute force gets you further than civilised conversation.

I'm wearing leather boots as I walk down Grope Lane for the second time. I didn't have the luxury of Emma's carriage today and, trust me, satin shoes and stagecoaches do not go together. But while my footwear has improved, the smell has not. If anything, the heat has made it worse. A swarm of flies crawls across something raw and rancid which I hope is a cut of meat stolen from the butcher's shop by a stray dog, rather than anything more sinister. Either way, I'm careful not to look too closely as I pick my way down the alley, trying to avoid the rotting meat and suspicious puddles of yellowish liquid and—

I stifle a shriek as a rat the size of a small dog runs across my boot. I'm not habitually squeamish. Scorpions I can deal with. Curious cows that try to lick you to death? No problem. But I draw the line at rats, with their beady black eyes and wormlike tails. If I was properly awake,

I would probably have done more than shriek, but I've been up most of the night contemplating my father's new warning and his possible connection to Mrs Elton. Right now, though, I need to forget about my father. I need to get through that trapdoor and take a look inside and speak to Durand if he is the French 'barber', as I suspect. My best hope is to wait until one of his customers appears and then rush them before the trapdoor closes. I've tried opening it myself and it won't budge. I even knocked a couple of times, but no joy. I suppose illicit French gambling dens don't open their trapdoors to just anyone. My head is pounding with the heat of the midday sun and the sweat is trickling down my back with such startling regularity that I feel like I'm melting. But I'm not going anywhere.

As the trapdoor groans and rises, a cautious head pokes out. I brace myself, ready to charge at the emerging figure. The sunlight hits his startled face as I hurtle towards him. Those broad shoulders. The scar above his lip. The familiar sneer I've seen directed at me so often. I've picked up too much momentum to stop now and so I end up barrelling into him. He hits the ground with a loud thud and exhales a breath full of whisky and tobacco right in my face as I land on top of him.

'Hello, Harriet.'

'Denny,' I say, trying not to gag at the stench.

'I'm flattered, darling, but you're really not my type.'

I roll off him and leap to my feet, brushing off my gown

as if this will expunge all trace of my contact with him. 'Trust me, you're not mine, either.'

Denny hauls himself to his feet, takes a step backwards and rakes his fingers through his hair. The movement triggers a memory. An image of Denny in this same alleyway slipping something into his pocket. Something glistening and gold.

'You had something in your pocket,' I say.

'I'm sorry?'

'When we ambushed you here last time. You had something in your pocket. What was it?'

'You hardly ambushed me,' he says, voice hitching as his thumb twitches briefly against his redingote pocket. He probably doesn't even realise he's done it, but the movement tells me that whatever was in his pocket that day is still there.

I sigh, throwing up my hands in mock surrender as I turn away. 'Fine, don't tell me. I can't imagine it's anything significant.' I'm a few paces away from Denny when I spin on my heel and charge at him. I catch him completely off guard – which was exactly the idea.

For the second time in the space of a few minutes, I knock him off his feet. This time, I'm not as quick to get up. I press my palm against his chest, feeling the thrum of his heartbeat against my fingers as I hold him down. My other hand works its way into his redingote pocket as he writhes underneath me, trying to buck me off. My fingertips are slick with sweat as they wrap around something small, hard and metallic. I draw my hand out of his pocket and hold it up to the light. A dainty, heart-shaped gold locket engraved with forget-me-nots with turquoise stones at their centre. I slide my finger against the catch to reveal the lock of hair inside a hinged, glazed compartment. The hair belongs to Mr Churchill's great-grandmother, I expect. Because there's no doubt about it – this is the missing Churchill heirloom.

'Care to explain this?' I ask, still sitting astride Denny.

Denny shrugs. 'Never seen it before in my life.'

I shift my weight, thighs digging into his hips. 'You're going to have to do better than that, I'm afraid.'

Denny sighs. 'Will you stop mauling me if I tell you?'

I smile at him sweetly. 'I thought you'd never ask.'

'I won it. In a game of whist.'

'From Frank Churchill?' I demand.

'Yes,' Denny mumbles.

'Down there?' I say, gesturing towards the trapdoor.

'Yes.'

'So I was right. It *is* an illicit gambling den.'

'He does hair too, though,' Denny says, as if this makes his lie by omission less morally objectionable.

'Why did you keep it? It's worth a pretty penny.'

'Well, I couldn't exactly sell it on, could I? It's rather distinctive, particularly with the old bat's hair inside.'

'You could have removed it,' I reason.

'Trust me, I tried. She won't budge.'

Sounds like a Churchill.

'Besides, it's much more valuable to Frank than it would be to any jeweller. Thought I'd give him the opportunity to win it back.' He grimaces and shuffles underneath me. 'Look, will you let me up now? It feels as if there's a walrus sitting on my stomach.'

'Fine,' I say, shifting my weight onto his chest to push myself up and off him. He winces, but doesn't complain.

'But you still have the locket,' I say, dangling the chain in front of his face as he scrambles to his feet.

'Yes, well, I haven't seen him for a few days. Which is odd for Frank. Usually he's here whenever he can escape from his tyrant of an aunt.' His eyes follow the locket as it swings back and forth.

'This gambling den. It's run by a fellow called Durand? French, is he? Your French barber?'

'How do you—'

'I have my sources.'

'The premises are his,' Denny admits.

'And does he lend out money to his patrons?'

Denny shakes his head. 'I wouldn't know about that.'

'Denny,' I say, leaning in so close that I can smell the sweat on his armpits, 'don't lie to me again. You knew I was looking for Frank. I asked you what you were doing down there and you didn't tell me the full story. And now a girl is dead.'

Denny's eyes widen. 'I didn't—'

'Don't make me beat it out of you. I'll ask you again. Does Durand lend money to his patrons?'

Denny holds my gaze. 'He makes a nice little sideline out of it. But you'd have to be desperate to borrow from him. He once loaned George Wickham a hundred pounds and, within a week, was demanding twice the amount in repayment. He didn't ask very nicely, either. Wickham had to seduce some empty-headed heiress for it. And it's a good thing he did, because I don't think he would have stood a chance against the brute Durand sent to collect.'

If Denny hopes to get a rise out of me by mentioning his friend Wickham – an odious cockroach who thinks it's perfectly acceptable to prey on semi-conscious women for money – he'll be sorely disappointed.

'Is Frank desperate?' I ask.

'Well, he's been on a losing streak for a while now.'

'Long enough to borrow from Durand?'

Long enough to consider poisoning his aunt to solve his problems?

If Frank is trying to win back Jane, and is in desperate financial straits as his correspondence with Durand suggests, he has two excellent motives for murder. If he gets rid of his aunt, Enscombe will be his and he'll be free to pay off his debts and marry as he pleases.

'Harriet.' Denny grips my elbow. 'Stay away from Durand. I wouldn't wish him on my worst— Well, I wouldn't even wish him on you.'

'I'm sure I could handle him,' I say, shaking off Denny's fingers.

'You need to leave it. Promise me.'

I pout at him.

'Harriet.'

'Fine. I promise.' I'm certainly *not* giving up on Durand, but I'm not going to get very far today with Denny standing guard.

In an uncharacteristically friendly gesture, Denny grasps my hands in his and squeezes. I feel the necklace slipping through my fingers and hold on tight.

Denny shrugs with a lazy grin. 'It was worth a try.'

There's no way I'm letting him take back the Churchill locket. This is going straight to Mrs Churchill. I want my money. I *need* it.

'Well, I'll be seeing you, Denny.'

'You will,' he says, grasping my arm and steering me out of the alleyway and onto the main street. The heat hits the back of my throat, but the air is fresher out here, away from the rats and rotting meat. 'I'm not leaving you there to attack the next poor sap who emerges from that trapdoor. Because he might be stupid enough to let you in.'

'I could have got past you if I had really wanted to,' I insist.

Denny laughs. 'And that would have landed you in a world of trouble.'

'What do *you* care?'

'I don't. But Robert would kill me if I left you to the mercy of Durand.'

'I doubt he'd be much bothered by it at the moment,' I mutter.

'He would,' Denny insists. 'He adores you in his own strange way. Whatever it is you're arguing about, he wouldn't want you to put yourself in danger.'

Perhaps I've been a bit hard on Robert. I suppose I wouldn't be thrilled if he started interfering in *my* love life.

Not that I have one any more.

'Harriet?' The smile drops from Denny's lips. 'Please don't tell Robert. About the gambling. He thinks I've given up. I promised him I wouldn't do it again.'

'Then why are you?'

'Well, look at what I have to compete with. Lord of the bloody manor.'

'Mr Knightley?'

Denny rolls his eyes. 'Give me some credit. I'm not blind. I know how Robert feels about him. He's not exactly subtle.'

'Then why don't you walk away?'

His laugh sounds more like a sob. 'If only I could. You should, though – from this. While you still can.'

He's wrong. I can't walk away either. I'm in as deep as he is.

As I wait at the coaching inn with a silent Denny by my side, I consider his warning about Durand. Denny keeps some rather dubious company, so if he says that Durand is dangerous, I'm inclined to believe him. It makes me wonder how long Frank has been in Durand's debt. If Durand is responsible for poisoning poor Sophia and the attempted poisoning of Mrs Churchill, perhaps that's not all he's responsible for. What if I was right that the boating accident in Weymouth wasn't an accident, but wrong about the culprit and the purpose of it? Because what if Durand's target isn't specifically Mrs Churchill, but anyone Frank cares about? If so, poisoning the lady's maid will not have served his purpose. He'll be looking to hit Frank where it hurts. Go after the person he cares about most in the world. And, if that's the case, then Mr Dixon was right. Jane Fairfax is not safe in Highbury.

CHAPTER 15

Rule number fifteen: It's easy enough to break into your neighbours' houses. It's getting out again that's the problem.

There's a dent in the front door of Abbey-Mill Farm, just underneath the doorknocker, in the shape of a horseshoe or a crescent moon, depending on the angle you view it from. I know this because I've been staring at it for the past five minutes. I haven't spoken to Robert since he ejected me through this door ten days ago and the memory of it doesn't make me eager to seek his help.

But it's not as if I have many options right now and so I steel myself to reach for the doorknocker and—

'Harriet?'

I whirl round, brandishing my father's mahogany cane, ready to strike.

Robert is in his shirtsleeves, mud spattered across his face and hair plastered against his forehead.

'What in heaven's name has happened to you?' I ask.

Robert runs his fingers through his hair, making it even worse. 'Your little Welsh cow decided she didn't want to be milked,' he says. 'Stubborn girl.' I wait for the lopsided smirk that will soften his features. It doesn't come. He pushes past me into the farmhouse, leaving the door wide open.

I suppose this is invitation enough.

Robert sits at the kitchen table, pulling off his muddy boots. I watch him struggle with them, not daring to help, lest he kicks me out again. Finally, he stops muttering to himself, the boots are off and we're both left staring at the floor, wondering who's going to break the silence. I lay down the cane and tap my fingers on the kitchen table, stopping abruptly as he slaps his palm against his knee. I sigh and sit down.

'So, how's the novel coming along?' I was always going to be the one to give in first.

Robert snorts as he glances up at me. 'Oh, you're being serious?'

'Yes, I'm being serious,' I snap. 'I would really like to know,' I add, softening my tone.

I think he's going to shrug it off, but then I detect the familiar curve of his lips and I know he won't be able to resist.

'I think George has made a breakthrough,' he says in a hushed voice. 'He's found a bloodied handkerchief stuffed up the chimney breast and wrapped inside is ...' He pauses for dramatic effect.

I lean in towards him. 'What?' I urge.

'Sir Reginald's missing ear.'

'No!' I say, trying to conceal my ignorance of the fact that Sir Reginald *has* a missing ear.

'Yes,' he says gleefully. 'And what else, do you think?'

'I'm sure I don't know,' I declare with more enthusiasm than I feel.

'A letter. From Rose Kent.'

I gasp, although I have no clue who Rose Kent might be. I'm trying to think of a better response than a mere gasp and Robert is clearly running out of steam too because he blurts out, 'How's the investigation going?'

Well, since I last saw you, I've been mobbed by Romani, stalked by my father, seduced by a potential poisoner and warned off the case by your lover, I want to say. I don't, of course. Partly because Robert already thinks I'm insane to pursue a murderer and I don't want to add fuel to the fire. And partly because if he realises what a desperate situation I'm in he'll never agree to help me. And I don't have a long list of potential assistants right now.

Robert is staring at me expectantly and I realise I still haven't answered his question.

'The investigation. Yes, it's fine. Coming along nicely, thank you.'

I expect Robert to make some cutting remark, but he just nods politely and says, 'Good, good,' before resuming his awkward silence.

Really, I'd rather he was insulting me.

'What's that for?' Robert asks, finally, gesturing towards the cane.

'I need to take another look in Jane Fairfax's bedroom,' I blurt out. 'And, this time, I'm taking precautions. I won't let another scorpion get the better of me.' It wasn't what I'd meant to say. There was supposed to be some sort of apology first, but Robert hasn't alluded to our argument and I don't want to be the one to bring it up.

'Why?' Robert asks, scratching the back of his neck with his thumb. 'You don't think Jane's the killer, do you?'

'No. But I fear she might become his next victim if she's not careful.'

'His?'

'Monsieur Durand,' I clarify.

Robert frowns. 'You found Durand?'

'Yes. Turns out he *is* the French barber, as I suspected.' I lower my eyes, hoping he'll leave it at that so I don't have to drop Denny in it.

'And how did you make this discovery?'

'I hung around in the alleyway and waited for one of his clients to emerge,' I say. It's as close as I can get to the truth without betraying Denny. I should tell Robert about Denny's gambling habit, but the look on Denny's face when he begged me to keep it quiet . . . In truth, I feel sorry for him. He doesn't stand a chance against Mr Knightley and perhaps he deserves one. He has stayed by Robert's side, despite Robert's wandering eyes. That has to count for something.

'And this client told you, just like that?'

I shrug. 'I can be very persuasive when I want to be. From the sound of it, Durand's a nasty fellow,' I add, remembering Denny's warning. 'And I started to think, if he's willing enough to threaten Mrs Churchill's life, perhaps he's after Jane as well.'

Robert clicks his fingers. 'The boating accident. The scorpion. You think it could all be him?'

'Exactly. So I need to search Jane's room again. Make sure he hasn't left her any more nasty surprises.'

'And how to you propose to search Jane's room?' Robert asks, as if he knows exactly what I'm here for.

I hit him with my most winning smile. 'That's where you come in.'

'Why do I get the feeling I won't like this one bit?'

'I don't understand you, Robert. You're perfectly happy to invent horrible murders, but when you're offered the opportunity to aid in a real-life murder investigation—'

'Yes, real life is the part I have a problem with. Just because I write about mutilated corpses doesn't mean I want to become one.'

'Well, it's not as if you'll be the one taking the risks. I just need you to play lookout. Jane and Miss Bates are taking tea with the Eltons today and Mrs Bates is over at Mrs Goddard's. The apartment will be empty. All you need to do is keep an eye on Jane and Miss Bates and raise the alarm if they make their way home before I've finished my search.'

'What's the signal?' Robert asks reluctantly.

I whistle a short melody, twice over, and wait for him to repeat it. His response doesn't faintly resemble the tune I've attempted to teach him. 'No. Low-low-high-low-high.'

He tries again. Low-low-high-high-low.

'Close enough,' I say, gesturing towards his muddy boots, strewn across the floor. 'Off to the Vicarage with you.'

'What, now?'

'Yes. Mrs Bates was due at Mrs Goddard's at eleven and Jane and her aunt left half an hour ago. They'll be settled with their tea and crumpets with Mrs E and her *caro sposo* by now.'

He sighs and reaches for his notebook.

'What are you doing?' I demand.

'If I'm going to lurk outside the Vicarage for hours on end, I'm taking something to occupy myself with.'

'I don't think so,' I say, snatching up the notebook. 'I will not have you being distracted by Sir Reginald's missing ear. This is serious, Robert. You must be on the alert.'

'Fine,' he says sulkily. 'I will do nothing except peer through the Eltons' drawing-room curtains at Jane like some sinister peeping Tom.'

'Good,' I say, keeping hold of his notebook, just in case.

I only glance over my shoulder about five hundred times on my way to the Bateses' apartment. There's no sign of my father, but that doesn't mean he's not there. Once, he pursued me all the way from Covent Garden to the Bath Assembly Rooms and I would never have detected his presence if he hadn't been so impatient to introduce himself to a recently widowed duchess that he pushed right past me en route.

The street is mercifully quiet as I prop my father's cane against the wall, slide a hairpin from the sleeve of my spencer and insert it into the lock of the Bateses' front door. The lock is stiffer than I had anticipated and I fear the hairpin will snap, but finally the door swings open with a loud creak. Cane under my arm, I slink into the dark passage, shutting the door softly behind me and ascending the stairs. I have no need for stealth now I'm inside. I make quick work of the second lock and creep into the apartment.

I slip into Jane's room, pulling on a pair of kid leather gloves to protect myself from scorpion stings and other such dangers. I open her dressing-table drawer and examine its contents before I touch anything. If Durand has set up a trap for Jane, my plan is to disable it, not fall prey to it myself. I poke at the contents of the drawer with my father's cane – the only thing of his I took with me when I abandoned him – until I'm certain there's nothing more dangerous inside than a bundle of letters secured with a crimson silk ribbon.

Well, now I'm here, I may as well take a look at her cor-respondence, too.

I untie the ribbon, sifting through the lavender-scented letters from Mrs Dixon and Mrs Campbell and Miss Bates. There's nothing from Frank. If Jane has kept Frank's letters, she's much too cautious to leave them where curious fingers might reach them. There's nothing from Mr Dixon, either.

I examine Jane's jewellery box again, but there's nothing new in there. The only other possessions I find in the dressing-table drawer are a pair of lilac gloves and an ivory fan. I move to her chest of drawers, poking at her muslin chemise dresses, petticoats and cotton stockings with my cane. There's a green velvet pelisse, which I rather fancy. An Indian shawl. A mauve silk parasol in the bottom drawer. There's a flash of movement as I prod it with the cane.

Please don't be another scorpion.

I kneel beside the drawer, picking up the parasol between my thumb and forefinger and shaking it gently. The creature scuttles to the other side of the drawer. It's bigger than a scorpion. I leap to my feet and raise my cane, ready to strike the dark, furry body of a—

Mouse. It's just a mouse.

I exhale loudly, bending down to scoop up the little creature. It wriggles out of my hand and disappears behind the chest of drawers. I shift the chest enough to see that there's a hole in the skirting board which bears investigating. I doubt there are any instruments of death concealed behind it but, if she still has them, this might be where I will find Jane's letters from Frank. The chest is too heavy to move further, so I have to lie on the floor and slide my arm behind it to reach into the hole. I ignore the dull ache in my shoulder as my fingers brush across cool leather. I pull it out slowly, shuffling inch by inch across the floor until I can see the pocketbook in my hand. I carry the pocketbook over to Jane's dressing table, sit down and untie the cord bound tightly around the book. A letter falls out as I open it.

Jane,

I returned to Weymouth to speak with the boatman. He says he was struck down with a mysterious illness the night before we were due out. He claims it must have been something he ate – he was sick to his stomach for two full days and did not leave his bed in all that time. I questioned him about the man who took out the boat, described him as thoroughly as I could, but he was none the wiser. He denies asking the man to take out the boat in his stead and is as anxious as we are to find him because of damage done to the boat, as well as his reputation, as a result of your so-called accident. I asked around and one man mentioned a fisherman called Parker who matched the description, but he had not seen him for some time. My findings support my supposition that you are in danger. I will continue to make enquiries. In the meantime, you must be on your guard.

Your friend always,
William Dixon

I flick through Jane's pocketbook. There's a sketch of a middle-aged man with shrewd eyes, light, curly hair and the hint of a cleft lip that gives the impression of a permanent sneer. The mysterious boatman, I suppose.

There's something oddly familiar about him, as if we've crossed paths before, but although I'm usually good with faces, I can't place his.

There's a ring tied to the pocketbook with a lilac ribbon – tarnished silver with a Roman onyx intaglio at its centre. A scorpion.

Interesting.

'Yes, Jane, dear, you would adore the rose gardens at Maple Grove, I assure you. My friends say there are none so fine as the roses at Maple Grove.'

Mrs Elton's strident voice leaves me paralysed. For one wild moment, I contemplate climbing under the bed but, thankfully, my brain thinks better of it before my body can comply. I stuff the letter back into the pocketbook and wrap the cord around it as quickly as possible. I don't have time to put it back behind the chest of drawers without being caught, so I slip the pocketbook into Jane's pile of Ann Radcliffe novels, nearly toppling them in the process.

'You do look fatigued, my dear,' Mrs Elton says loudly. 'Must be all that late-night reading. I insist that you sit down on the sofa. I will fetch you some tea. Here, let me take that.'

Mrs Elton bustles into the bedroom, Jane's pelisse draped over her arm. I freeze, cane held against my body as if it will somehow render me invisible.

She raises an eyebrow, her gaze sweeping across the room and settling on the chest of drawers, which is jutting out at an angle, as if she knows exactly what I've been doing. I wait for her to say something but, instead, she folds Jane's pelisse and lays it on the bed. Her gaze flits to the pile of books on Jane's dressing table and then to the chest of drawers. She retreats with an almost imperceptible nod.

I don't know why Mrs Elton is helping me and, while I'm grateful for it in the moment, I don't like owing people.

I dash over to the chest of drawers, sliding the pocketbook back into its hiding place, but I'm well and truly stuck. Even if Mrs Elton doesn't reveal my presence to Jane, I can't leave through the front door. Jane's bedroom opens directly into the parlour and, tired as Jane is, there's no hope of creeping out without her noticing. And, if I want to preserve the thin veneer of trust I've built up between us, she cannot find me here. There's only one way out if I want to avoid detection.

I tiptoe over to the window and lean out. The street is still quiet, but it's a long way down. I unscrew the top of my father's cane and pull out a length of silk rope. Opening the sash window as quietly as I can, I tie the rope around the middle of the cane, screw the cap back on and brace the cane against the window frame. Checking again that the street is clear, I step over the sill and tug on the rope, testing the cane's stability before I lower myself slowly out of the window. I let the rope go slack as my feet touch the ground and, with a flick of the wrist that took me months to perfect, I jerk the cane upright and pull on the rope. I reach out a hand as the cane sails through the window and hurtles towards me, plucking it from the air and tucking it under my arm in one smooth movement.

I haven't found any death traps in Jane's room, but the same theme keeps coming up. Mr Dixon. The boating 'accident' in Weymouth. I was right about it not being an accident, although I'm no closer to finding out whether Frank or Durand was responsible for it. But, as Jane has gone to so much trouble to catalogue and conceal the evidence, she clearly has her suspicions. If I've learned anything from sneaking around Jane's room for a second time, it's that the boating 'accident' is at the centre of this case. One thing's for certain: if I'm going to catch the killer, I need to find out what happened in Weymouth.

CHAPTER 16

Rule number sixteen: Don't flirt
with the enemy.

Today is my eighteenth birthday and I can't say I'm enjoying it so far. I've spent most of the morning prowling the corridors at Mrs Goddard's, waiting for another warning from my father. There's been nothing as yet and, since he hasn't given me a birthday gift for ten years, I don't know why I should expect him to start marking the occasion again now.

That's not to say I'm unaccustomed to receiving birthday gifts. For my ninth birthday, my father's lover, Lady Cockcroft, gave me a piebald Shetland pony. I named him Puck and, for two months, I barely left his saddle as we terrorised Lady Cockcroft's gardener by tramping our way through the pansies and peonies and, on one memorable occasion, the tiger lilies in the hothouses. I liked Lady Cockcroft. She had kind eyes and a wicked sense of humour and she smelled of roses and vegetable soap.

It was tucked away in her library, pining for my mother, that I first discovered the delights of Ann Radcliffe. Mrs Radcliffe took me to other worlds – of castles and ghosts and bandits; wicked uncles, secret marriages, forbidden loves. She made me gasp and shriek and shiver. For the first time since I lost my mother, I felt something other than sadness. So you see, these Gothic heroines of mine are not so ignoble as Robert suggests. They transported me to a place where I could feel and breathe and live. They gave me something to love again.

I was convinced my father would marry Lady Cockcroft but, instead, he dragged me from my bed in the middle of the night, loading handfuls of rubies and diamonds into Puck's saddlebags. The jewels were soon sold, and Puck along with them, and I didn't speak a word to my father for three months. I only relented when he threatened to send me away to a convent school in France. Father told me I could have another pony when we settled down somewhere, but I didn't want another pony and we never settled down again.

In the years that followed, I acquired an impressive collection of birthday gifts from my father's female companions and, later, my own suitors. Well, I would have done if I'd been allowed to keep any of them. A diamond tiara for my tenth birthday, a harp for my eleventh. A string of pearls, a gold brooch, a rosewood jewellery box, a forget-me-not ring, a gold locket. All sold to the highest bidder. Except for last year's gift. A turquoise and gold filigree cross. From *him*. It was his mother's and I knew what it signified when he fastened it around my neck. I knew what I was promising by accepting it. And I would have kept that promise, if it wasn't for my father. I should have left the pendant behind, but I couldn't bear to part with it. I shouldn't be wearing it now. There's no sense in it.

There's no use in being sentimental, Hattie, my father told me as he handed over Puck to an unscrupulous horse dealer all those years ago. And I've tried not to be. I'm not. My heart hardened with every birthday gift I was forced to surrender. But, once in a while, someone comes along to pierce my armour. I rub my thumb against the cross and let out a deep sigh.

I'm not completely empty-handed this year. Mrs Goddard has given me a new sewing kit. Miss Bickerton presented me with some lilac silk ribbon for my bonnet. Emma has bought me a pair of elegant amethyst earrings – more her taste than mine.

The best present is from Robert – a first edition of *The Romance of the Forest* with a dedication from Mrs Radcliffe herself. I don't know how he managed but, if this is the result of his guilt at abandoning me to a potential poisoner while he dreamed up dastardly deeds for his novel, perhaps I can cope with Robert's inattention now and again. In fairness to him, he's done some spectacular grovelling and he's been more useful to me in the past five days than he was during the entire length of my stay in Highbury before this. As penance for losing track of Jane on her way home from the Eltons, I have made him trail her around Highbury on every dull outing to her neighbours to ensure that no harm comes to her.

While Robert has been following Jane, I've had my eyes on Frank. Not like that. Well, perhaps a little like that. I have to admit, there have been a few choice moments when I've forgotten what I'm meant to be doing – namely, ensuring that he doesn't try to kill my client or provoke Monsieur Durand into doing it. The good news is there haven't been any further attempts on Mrs Churchill's life. The bad news is this probably means that one is imminent.

✳

'Really, Jane. I cannot understand why you are not more excited by the prospect. Mrs Smallridge is on excellent terms with my brother and sister. You will not find a better offer elsewhere, I assure you.'

Smallridge.

small ridge plan in action.

Hmmm. It looks like there *was* another name in Mrs Elton's coded letter, after all. But why is Mrs Elton so intent on getting Jane out of the way? And who else is in on the plan?

'I am much obliged to you, Mrs Elton, but, as I have told you before, I wish to spend some time with the Campbells before I seek a position. Indeed, I have promised them so.'

Having managed to avoid Mrs Elton for an entire week, I'm now suffering the misfortune of sitting in Mr Knightley's gardens at Donwell Abbey within earshot of her, although at least it means I get to keep an eye on Jane. (I couldn't exactly ask Robert to stalk her round the Abbey, could I? People would talk.) Mrs Elton is trying to convince Jane to take up a governess position she has found for her – one Jane never asked her to seek out – and Jane is standing her ground. Although, in truth, she looks about ready to keel over. Her skin is so pale it's almost translucent, there are dark rings under her eyes and she's slumped in her chair, as if she doesn't have the energy to hold up her head.

As for Augusta Elton, or Augusta Hawkins, or whoever she might be, I haven't been able to discover anything new. There have been no more exchanges with bear boy. No more coded letters. I keep waiting for her to approach me, to reveal what she wants, but she has resolutely ignored me so far. Perhaps she just can't see me over the brim of her enormous bonnet.

I was tempted to decline the invitation to Mr Knightley's strawberry party at Donwell Abbey, in an attempt to avoid any awkward conversations with Mrs Elton. But I couldn't leave Jane without a bodyguard and, if I can catch Frank on his own, I might be able to get him talking about Weymouth and the mysterious Parker.

If Frank ever arrives, that is.

'Mr Knightley, would you be so kind as to show us the gardens?' Jane asks, rising from her seat as Mrs Elton becomes increasingly insistent about the Smallridges. 'I would very much like to see all of the gardens.'

As the party trails after Mr Knightley, I find myself walking alongside the Eltons, the midday sun prickling my bare arms.

'Most shocking, Mr E, that Jane will not accept the offer at once. They won't wait around for long. I shall have to send her answer for her if she doesn't set her mind to it soon.'

'Quite right, my dear,' Mr Elton responds in a tone that suggests he's no longer listening to his wife, if ever he was.

'Perhaps Miss Fairfax doesn't want to take the job,' I say, before I can stop myself. I know I'm supposed to be laying low, but it is my birthday and, if I'm forced to spend it with the Eltons, I think I deserve a measure of self-indulgence.

'And what reason could she possibly have to refuse?' Mrs Elton says, glaring at me from beneath the brim of her ridiculous bonnet.

'Perhaps she prefers to stay in Highbury.'

Mrs Elton shakes her head and lowers her voice. 'I would have thought *you* of all people would recognise the benefit of Miss Fairfax's new position.' She gives me a cryptic smile.

And what exactly does she mean by that? Before I have chance to ask her, she has taken her husband's arm and turned in the opposite direction. I walk on, relieved to have some time to myself although, after a few minutes, I'm brooding over the mysterious Mrs Elton and the absent Frank Churchill. He should be here by now.

We retreat indoors for luncheon, enjoying the cool shade of the Abbey after a few hours in the blazing sun.

Frank has still not come. Mrs Weston fears her stepson has been thrown from his black mare. Mr Weston laughs off his wife's concerns, but I catch a glimpse of him pacing up and down by the window, fingers running absently through his thinning grey hair, as I help myself to the cold meats in the dining room. He's muttering something about Mrs Churchill as I walk past him studiously chewing on a mouthful of sliced ham. His nervous energy drives me out into the gardens.

What if something has happened to Mrs Churchill?

As I'm contemplating how quickly I can get to her house in Richmond and how long it will be before I am missed, I'm roused by the thunder of horse's hoofbeats. I look up, expecting to see Frank's black mare, but it's a messenger who throws himself from the saddle of his bay mount and presses a letter into Miss Fairfax's hands. He doesn't wait for a reply. Jane reads the message with a frown and turns towards the house, where she trades a few terse words with Emma and then flees towards Highbury.

Well, I'm not having that. Not when there's a murderer on the loose who may have their sights set on Jane. I set off after her, panting hard, my gown streaked with sweat.

I wish she would slow down.

My wish is granted a few moments later as Frank canters towards the Abbey on his black mare, pulling up as he spots Jane. I'm not close enough to hear their conversation, but I can perceive from Jane's stiff posture and Frank's animated hand gestures that it's a hostile exchange. As Jane tries to carry on walking, Frank steers his horse across her path and raises his voice. 'You're playing right into her hands.'

Jane's response is too low for me to catch as I creep closer under the shelter of the Abbey's sycamore trees.

Frank leans over his horse and reaches for Jane's hand. She flinches away from him and hurries off towards Highbury.

'This has to stop!' Frank shouts after her. His mare paws the ground as Frank stares at Jane's retreating form.

I have to make a quick decision. I can either follow Jane to ensure she doesn't get herself into any trouble or stick with Frank and try to get some information from him about what happened in Weymouth.

As Frank turns and catches sight of me, a flare of panic in his eyes, my decision is made for me.

Frank it is.

He attempts to conceal his discomfort as he dismounts and leads the black mare over to me, cheeks flushed. I stroke her muzzle as she snorts into the palm of my hand.

'You are not leaving too, Miss Smith?'

'Not now you are here,' I say smoothly as I turn and walk with him back towards the Abbey.

'I'm afraid you will not see me at my best today,' he says, ignoring my compliment. 'It's this damned heat. I don't know why I came at all.'

'I will not have you out of temper today, Mr Churchill, for it is my birthday and I am determined nothing and nobody will spoil it.'

'Well, now you shame me, for I do not have a present for you.'

'Your company will be gift enough,' I say, 'as long as you can throw off your ill humour.'

Frank sighs as he takes my arm. His shirt is damp and there's a faint tang of sweat mixed with his usual citrus scent. 'I fear, Miss Smith, though I always endeavour to please beautiful young ladies, I cannot satisfy you in this. As long as my infernal aunt insists on watching my every move, I'm not sure I know how to be anything other than ill-tempered.'

'She cannot be that bad,' I say, shifting subtly to feel the warmth of his shoulder against mine.

Although I'm quite hot enough as it is.

'She is insufferable. She doesn't want me to go anywhere unless she has approved it.'

'She allowed you to go to Weymouth,' I reason. 'And you were there some time, from what I've heard.'

'Well, yes. On that occasion she did allow me some freedom—'

'And Weymouth is such a lovely part of the world.'

'You have been to Weymouth, Miss Smith?'

'I have an acquaintance there by the name of Parker,' I say, ignoring his question. 'I wonder if you came across him during your visit?'

Frank shrugs. 'Weymouth is a busy place.'

He shows no hint of recognition at the name. No involuntary twitch. Nothing that suggests he is acquainted with this Parker. But I already know what a good actor Frank Churchill is.

'He has a pleasure boat. Takes out tourists. You went out on the water, I think.' If Parker is the boatman from Weymouth and Frank hired him to orchestrate Jane's accident, I'm sure I'll be able to tell from his response.

'Yes,' Frank says, swatting away a passing fly with surprising vehemence. 'But not for long. You've no doubt heard about Miss Fairfax's accident?'

There's nothing in the way he says it that suggests it was anything but an accident, or that he was in any way responsible. If Frank staged the accident himself to win over Jane, or if Durand meant it as a warning to Frank to encourage him to pay of his debts, Frank is giving nothing away.

'Yes, I did hear something of the sort from Miss Bates—'

'But, you see, everything is at my aunt's whim,' Frank continues, tugging on his horse's mouth in indignation. He will not be drawn on what happened in Weymouth. He is too fixated on his gripe with Mrs Churchill to pay heed to anything else. 'Take today, for instance; she knew very well of my invitation to Mr Knightley's strawberry party and so she chose to have one of her nervous seizures just as I was leaving. We would all be better off if she'd hurry up and die.'

He talks like a man who has already done the deed.

'You think me cruel,' he says as he turns to examine my face. 'I can see it in your eyes. I shock you with my candour.'

There's not much point in denying it and I'm not sure I could speak even if I wanted to.

Frank sighs again and drops the mare's reins. She wanders off to graze. 'It would be much easier if we could choose our family.'

I can't disagree with the sentiment. 'Isn't that what marriage is for?' I ask, finding my voice.

Frank lets out a bitter laugh. 'I forget your youth, Miss Smith. You are yet innocent in the ways of the world. If only I could settle down with a girl like you,' he says, sweeping a stray curl behind my ear, his fingers brushing against my cheek, 'then I'm sure I should be happy.'

I feel the tension leave his body as he tilts his head. My eyelids flutter shut as he leans in towards me. He's going to kiss me, and I'm going to let him, even though I know I shouldn't. I promised myself I wouldn't let it happen again, but for one blissful moment, I would like to forget about the rules and the job, and the fact that the man I'm contemplating kissing has just expressed murderous intent towards his own aunt. My client. It *is* my birthday, after all, and I don't want to be alone today. Besides, the longer I keep Frank occupied, the less chance he has of carrying out the threatened violence against Mrs Churchill.

He's so close, I can feel his breath against my lips.

Don't do it, Harriet.

It's too late now. I couldn't stop, even if I wanted to.

And I don't want to.

'Mr Churchill! You are here, at last. We had given up on you.'

My eyes fly open and I take two hasty steps backward, trip over my gown and fall flat on my bottom, fingers digging into the dry soil. Frank makes no move to help me up. He is already pulling his horse towards Mrs Elton, as if desperate to flee the scene of the crime. He's careful not to look back at me.

'Ah, Mrs Elton!' he exclaims, recovering his composure as he takes her arm. 'Did you think I could stay away from a gathering which numbers you among its guests?'

Mrs Elton swats at him playfully. 'Really, Mr Churchill, if my *caro sposo* were to hear you talk so!'

I remain where I landed, wrestling with a mixture of relief and disappointment as I brush the dirt from my gown. It's the relief that wins out as Mrs Elton glances over her shoulder at me with a sly smile. Because, as frustrated as I am by her interruption, I can't help but feel I've had a lucky escape.

CHAPTER 17

Rule number seventeen: Behave as if somebody is watching your every move. Because somebody probably is.

I am a complete and utter idiot. What was I thinking? I almost kissed Frank Churchill, who, most likely, is obsessed with another woman to the extent that he will kill for her, or is in debt to a man who is so dangerous that he's willing to kill Frank's loved ones in order to get him to pay it back. Either way, it's not a good move. Particularly not in public, in front of the woman who already has enough blackmail material on me to fill one of Robert's notebooks.

And, as for Frank, how am I ever going to face him now? Or Mrs Churchill? It's like Derbyshire all over again. Except I'm not in love with Frank. I'm not. Yes, he's well-dressed and charming and has amazing hair (thanks to a certain French barber/potentially murderous moneylender). And he smells divine. He's the only person I've felt I can show a remnant of myself to without fearing his disapproval.

He's hardly one to judge. He's an accomplished liar – I appreciate most women wouldn't look for this in a lover, but just think how good a con man he would be. He already is. And being my partner in crime would be a far better prospect for him than murdering his aunt. The two of us together would be unstoppable. I can't drag Robert along for the ride for ever. I do appreciate his help, but there's only so long I can have him tugging at my conscience before his righteousness starts to rub off on me. I need to think beyond this job. Look to the future.

Keep your head in the present, Hattie, and the future will take care of itself, my father always said. Well, he would, wouldn't he? He didn't want me to look to the future, for fear that I might discover one without him in it. And, now that I have, he's doing his best to sabotage that future. Who knows the depths to which he will sink to ensure that I'm as miserable and destitute as he is? The uncertainty is the worst part: waiting for the axe to fall; not knowing when, or where, or how it will.

But there's one thing I *am* certain of right now. I can't return to the Abbey. Not while Frank is there. I've had enough of the Churchill charm for one day. As for Mrs Elton, if I never see her again, I will not mourn the loss. Which doesn't leave me many options other than to walk through the woods in the shade of the horse chestnut trees, trying to ignore the scratching at the back of my throat and wishing I had a drink to hand. This isn't how I'd hoped to spend my birthday.

I walk down to the river and sit on the bank, losing track of time as I close my eyes against the sun, enjoying the scent of damp earth and oak leaves. It's quiet here, other than the chatter of sparrows and the shrill whistle of a solitary blackbird and—

Voices.

Raised in anger. Although the cadence carries, the words are obscured by distance and dense foliage. I rise reluctantly and tiptoe towards the commotion, seemingly snapping every twig in the wood on my way. I come to a break in the trees and, squinting against the sun, I can just make out two figures in the middle distance. One of them is Mrs Elton.

So much for avoiding her.

She's waving her arms around erratically at a tall, ominous figure who stands ramrod straight, arms folded across her chest. I catch a glimpse of her face as she turns away from Mrs Elton in disgust and, as her blazing eyes meet mine, I wish I had stayed by the riverbank. Mrs Elton storms off towards the Abbey, muttering under her breath. Mrs Churchill strides straight towards me.

Well, at least she's not dead.

Given the way she's glaring at me, it might have been better for me if she was.

'Miss Smith,' she says in that devastating tone of hers as she reaches the clearing.

'Mrs Churchill,' I say, with a nod. 'What are you doing here?'

'I tried to keep Frank away from Highbury today but, when that failed, it was clear to me that he had not given up on Jane Fairfax, as you informed me. And so I decided to deal with the matter myself. I had hoped to find Miss Fairfax at home – I had already put my coachman to great inconvenience, driving from Richmond to Highbury at such short notice. I did not expect to have him chasing round the countryside after Jane Fairfax. But it seems that Miss Fairfax cannot keep away from my nephew.'

I can't imagine Mrs Churchill or her coachman will be too pleased to discover that Jane has evaded them yet again. 'I do not see your carriage, Mrs Churchill.'

She raises her chin. 'I am hardly going to ride right up to the Abbey and demand to see Jane Fairfax in front of half of Highbury. My coachman is lurking about in the woods to keep out of sight, which is greatly beneath his dignity. I will have to give him a raise.'

Perish the thought.

'I didn't know you were acquainted with Mrs Elton,' I say, glancing towards Donwell Abbey.

'I am not,' Mrs Churchill snaps, sounding thoroughly offended at the prospect. 'I was simply asking her for directions to the Abbey when the insufferable woman started droning on about Mabel Grove and did I know a Mr Suckling who, it turns out – I did not ask, you understand – is her brother-in-law and a man who has recently purchased his own barouche landau. Why on earth should *I* be acquainted with a man who thinks the purchase of a barouche is something to shout about, I should like to know, and from Bristol of all places? I don't care how big his house is, I would not endure his company for all the world.'

Mrs Churchill's face is flushed, there's a sheen of sweat on her forehead and her breathing is laboured from the exercise and the heat of the summer sun. 'What are you doing skulking about in the woods?' she demands, the Sucklings already forgotten.

'I was . . . well, that is—'

'I do not pay you to lie around in the sun enjoying yourself.'

You do not pay me at all, I want to say, because all I've had from her so far is money for my expenses and nothing of my fee. No doubt she would say I hadn't earned it yet, and I suppose she would have a point.

'Jane is not here. Frank is at the Abbey. What else do you expect me to do?'

'Ensure Frank's affections are engaged elsewhere,' Mrs Churchill replies and I nearly have a heart attack. Surely she can't mean—

'Miss Woodhouse,' Mrs Churchill adds, looking at me as if I've just declared myself a French revolutionary.

Frank Churchill and Emma Woodhouse. It's a good idea. And one I'm sure won't happen now. Emma might have been in his power when he first arrived in Highbury, but she has long since vanquished Frank.

Perhaps I should ask her for some pointers.

'Which is why I was surprised, Miss Smith, to witness your own interaction with my nephew a short time ago. You need not play coy with me, girl. I saw what you were up to.'

'You were spying on me?'

She raises an eyebrow. 'I arrived at the opportune moment,' she says in a tone that suggests spying is beneath her station. 'Besides, I have a right to know how my money is being spent.'

'Mrs Churchill, whatever you thought you saw, I can assure you—'

'Do not think me so old that I fail to recognise the art of seduction when I see it,' she says with a knowing smile. 'I was skilled at it myself in my youth, believe it or not.'

Mrs Churchill has about as much charm as a fox in a henhouse, but I can well believe she was capable of bullying men into submission as a younger woman.

'I do not want you falling back into your old ways,' she says. 'I did not hire you to get rid of Miss Fairfax so that you could seduce Frank yourself. At least Jane Fairfax has some good breeding in her – and some suitable connections. Heaven knows where *you* came from, Miss Smith, but I tell you where you will not be going from now on: anywhere near Frank. Emma Woodhouse? That is a match. But Harriet Smith? I would sooner let him throw himself away on the Fairfax girl.' Mrs Churchill stops for breath, closing her eyes as she steadies herself against a nearby oak tree.

I'm shaking with anger, fists clenched. For a woman of her background – a nobody, who married far above her station – to declare that I'm not good enough for her precious nephew.

'I should have realised you were too young for this kind of work. A green girl who lets her emotions run away with her. You will stay away from Frank. In fact,' she reaches into her reticule and draws out a small parcel wrapped in brown paper and fastened with thick twine, throwing it at my feet, 'you are to leave my employ altogether. There is your fee.' She nods towards the parcel, expecting me to scrabble around in the dirt for it like the peasant I am, I suppose.

I hold her gaze, arms folded to indicate I'm not going to touch her money. I don't need it. (I do need it, of course, but I'm trying to prove a point here.)

'If you are not satisfied with my work, Mrs Churchill, I will be only too happy to part ways with you.'

She narrows her eyes. 'You are an insolent girl, Miss Smith. I do not wish to accuse my friend of poor judgement, but I fear that she has been greatly deceived in you.'

'I'm sorry I don't live up to your friend's recommendation. Although perhaps if you were really her *confidante in all things*, you would not have hired me in the first place.'

'How dare you. Do you honestly think—' Mrs Churchill breaks off for an ill-timed coughing fit. She slumps against the oak tree, taking large gulps of air. 'I do not ... I cannot—' She shivers so violently that even I think she's overdoing it.

I roll my eyes, hands on my hips. 'What's the matter, Mrs Churchill? Are you having one of your seizures?' I say with mock concern.

'The . . . girl.'

'What's that, Mrs Churchill? I can't comprehend you over all the bad acting.'

She pulls herself upright, eyes blazing.

'Yes, you don't have me fooled,' I jeer. 'Nor Frank, neither. He wasn't too impressed that you'd faked a seizure to keep him away from the Abbey. Well, it didn't work, did it?'

'You know nothing about it.'

'I know a lot more than you think,' I say, lowering my voice. 'Jane Fairfax has had a lucky escape from you.'

Mrs Churchill stumbles backward, her eyes flashing with something that looks a lot like terror.

Perhaps she's a better actress than I had given her credit for.

'In fact,' I add, looming over her, 'I wouldn't be surprised if you'd faked the whole thing. Not that I'd blame Frank for trying to do away with you. Would that he had succeeded!'

Mrs Churchill draws herself up to her full height, nostrils flaring. She looks as if she's about to deliver some scathing putdown, but then she spins on her heel and strides off into the woods. I would like to have followed suit, exiting in an equally dramatic fashion. However, Mrs Churchill's parcel is still lying where she discarded it and, while I might have been too proud to reach for it in her presence, I snatch it up eagerly in her absence. The twine is secured with a sailor's knot, which eludes my impatient fingers. There's a waft of lavender as I rip open the package to find a bundle of hundred-pound notes inside, wrapped in silver paper. There's a lot of money here. Far more

217

than we'd agreed on. I count the notes twice, just to be sure. Five thousand pounds. Five. Thousand. Pounds. I'm good, but I'm not sure I'm that good. I know of a very rich gentleman in Derbyshire for whom that would be half a year's income. Many other eligible bachelors who would think themselves fortunate with half the amount. I had settled on two thousand pounds with Mrs Churchill and I was surprised she agreed to *that*. As much as I would appreciate the additional funds, I don't like to accept more than my due. For the money means something and I'm certain it's nothing good. I know I would be foolish to accept it. For whatever reason, Mrs Churchill is trying to buy me off. But she'll soon find out that Harriet Smith is not for sale.

✳

I don't remember walking back to Highbury, but that's where my feet have carried me. I hover at the window of the haberdasher's shop, giving myself a moment to catch my breath. I know what I'm doing here, opposite the Bateses' apartment. I've come to check on Jane. The urgency of the messenger. The haste with which Jane withdrew from the Abbey. Her heated exchange with Frank. And all just before Mrs Churchill's arrival. Something has happened and I fear that Jane has placed herself in danger by coming home to confront it alone. The scorpion. The boating 'accident'. Mr Dixon's warnings. Jane Fairfax needs protection. A friend. And I'm free to be that friend now I'm no longer in Mrs

Churchill's employ. I feel a weight lifting from my chest as I cross the street. Perhaps it's for the best that Mrs Churchill has dismissed me. Now I'm rid of her, I might finally have the opportunity to do something for *me*. Follow my own path rather than the one my father set me on.

I raise my hand to knock on the front door of the Bateses' apartment, but it's already ajar. It swings open to reveal a body lying prone at the bottom of the stairs, a slight figure bending over it. The figure stifles a sob as she straightens up, her gaze steady as she extends a shaking hand towards the motionless body.

'Miss Smith, thank goodness you are here,' Jane says. 'I pushed her. I pushed her and I think she's dead.'

CHAPTER 18

Rule number eighteen: There are plenty of reasons to stand over a dead body looking guilty. Murder is just the most obvious one.

Oh Lord. Jane Fairfax has killed Mrs Churchill. Jane Fairfax has killed Mrs Churchill and it's all my fault. I wouldn't have believed it if I wasn't looking at Jane right now as she stands over Mrs Churchill's body, confessing to the crime. But this isn't like the other attempts. Pushing someone down the stairs is a spur-of-the-moment action. A crime of passion. Poisoning someone's cup of tea or toast is cold and calculated. And Jane Fairfax is not that.

'What do we do?' Jane is looking at me as if I can solve all her problems. I can't. I can't solve this. 'Harriet? What do we do?' Jane repeats, with a greater sense of urgency.

I don't know.

I'm used to taking orders, not giving them. This isn't my problem. I've got Mrs Churchill's money. I could leave, right now. Flee Highbury. Escape from my father.

Start again, somewhere new, where nobody knows my face.

I can't.

I can't do that to Jane. Not when I've played such a significant role in her unhappiness already. I can't abandon Robert without saying goodbye. And I owe it to Mrs Churchill not to leave her body sprawled at the bottom of the stairs like a sack of potatoes.

Jane blocks my path as I move towards Mrs Churchill's body. 'I didn't mean to— I didn't mean to—' she says, over and over, rocking back and forth.

'Jane, you need to let me through,' I insist, inhaling the scent of lavender as I wrap my arms around her and pull her away from Mrs Churchill's body. 'She may still be alive. I need to check.'

'She's dead,' Jane mumbles, tears streaming down her face as she sinks to the floor. 'I know she's dead. I did it. *I* did it.'

'What happened?' I ask, as I step around Jane and kneel down next to Mrs Churchill.

'We argued. I pushed her. She fell.' Jane wipes her swollen eyes and sniffs. 'You haven't asked me who she is.'

'I know who she is,' I say, sliding two fingers against Mrs Churchill's neck. 'She is Frank Churchill's aunt. No doubt she came here to ensure you had really broken off your engagement with Frank.'

'How do you—'

Mrs Churchill's eyes snap open and she scowls up at me.

I've never been so happy to be on the receiving end of the Churchill glare. It means that Jane is not a murderer. And my ex-client hasn't been horribly murdered within an hour of me accusing her of faking her illness and the attempts on her own life.

'Mrs Churchill? Mrs Churchill? Can you hear me?'

'Of course I can hear you,' she drawls. 'You're shouting right in my ear.'

If nothing else, it's clear the fall didn't knock any manners into her.

'Can you sit up?'

'Of course I can,' she says, hauling herself upright. 'I'm not an invalid.' She sways violently and digs her bony fingers into my arm to steady herself.

'She's alive!' Jane exclaims loudly (and somewhat unnecessarily). 'Thank goodness!' And although I hear the relief in her voice, her expression is troubled and her eyes keep flitting to the staircase.

As Mrs Churchill glances at Jane, I catch the flicker of surprise which she is quick to cover. But not quick enough.

'Should we call a doctor?' Jane asks, her gaze fixed on me.

'You most certainly should not,' Mrs Churchill barks, digging her knuckles into my thigh as she pushes herself to her feet. 'I am perfectly all right. I merely tripped on the stairs.'

Tripped? That's not what Jane said. Mrs Churchill would be the first person to accuse Jane if she really had pushed her, but she seems surprised to see Jane here at all. Could someone else have pushed Mrs Churchill? Durand, perhaps? Could he have been here to see Jane, but Mrs Churchill arrived first? But then why would Mrs Churchill cover for him? And why would Jane take the blame?

'I am quite ready to be getting home,' Mrs Churchill snaps, rousing me from my thoughts.

'I'm not sure you're in a fit state to travel, Mrs Churchill.'

'Nonsense! You will go and fetch my carriage and my coachman,' she says, waving in the direction of the Coles' stable yard.

There's a dull thump from somewhere above us. My head whips round towards the source of the sound. Jane doesn't react at all. 'Is there someone else here?' I demand.

'No,' Jane says, moving to the stairs to block my path.

I step towards her, ready to push past. I can take Jane Fairfax. She may be tall, but I guarantee you I'm much tougher than she is.

'My carriage, Miss Smith?' Mrs Churchill barks, stopping me in my tracks.

'I'll go,' Jane says, herding us out into the street and shutting the door behind her.

Mrs Churchill slumps against the window of the milliner's shop as she waits for her carriage. She clings to my arm with such force as I guide her into the carriage that I end up climbing in after her.

'Whatever are you doing, Miss Smith?'

'I cannot leave you to travel home alone in this state,' I say, much as I'd rather pack her off in her carriage and never speak to her again.

I expect her to protest, but she must still be feeling the effects of her fall because she leans back and closes her eyes with a deep sigh. 'Very well. But if you are coming, you had better be quiet about it. I have had a trying day and I am in much need of some peace.'

'I shall be as silent as the grave.'

'Hmmm.' Mrs Churchill nods and rests her head against the window. She's soon asleep, snorting like one of Robert's pigs.

I close my eyes to the image of Jane's swollen eyes and pasty face. Despite her admission, I'm sure she didn't do this. She was covering for someone. Someone who was hiding in the apartment when I arrived. She stopped me from going upstairs to investigate that noise. Drove us both out into the street. Locked the door behind her.

The steady rhythm of the carriage lulls me into a warm, hazy stupor. I feel like I'm floating, flying—

I jolt awake to a strangled sob. Mrs Churchill is writhing in her sleep, head lurching from side to side as she gasps for breath. Her eyes shoot open and she grasps my arm as I reach across the carriage to soothe her.

'Those eyes,' she moans, her own eyes full of terror. 'That face. Such hatred.' She sinks back into her slumber, mumbling to herself all the way back to Richmond.

Wakefield is at the carriage door as we pull up at

Richmond Terrace. He glares at me as I hand Mrs Churchill over to him, as if I'm the one responsible for her current condition.

'Wakefield? You will inform me if anything happens?' I say as he guides his mistress to the front door.

Wakefield turns towards me as Mrs Churchill stumbles inside, into the arms of the startled housemaid, Matilda. 'I will,' he says finally. He steps up to address the coachman. 'Escort Miss Smith back to Highbury.' The coachman nods as Wakefield hands me into the carriage, appraising me carefully as I lean out through the window.

'Take care of her,' I say, holding his gaze.

'I always do,' he replies, eyes fixed on mine. 'I always do.'

✳

It's the perfect day for a trip to Box Hill. The weather is fine, the scenery breathtaking. Up here, I can see for miles across the vast expanse of greenery that seems to go on for ever: box and yew and oak and ash; verdant meadows in their summer glory. If only I was in the mood to enjoy it. I barely slept last night, worrying about Mrs Churchill and Jane Fairfax and the mysterious figure lurking upstairs in the Bateses' apartment. I lay awake, staring at the ceiling, waiting for a message from Wakefield that never came. For me, this little trip couldn't have come at a worse time.

It's not just me, though. There's a lethargy about the entire assembled company. A want of purpose. A reluctance to engage with those beyond our nearest companions. Mr

Weston flits around like a concussed dragonfly, his valiant smile never faltering as he attempts to bring harmony between us. I trail behind Frank and Emma, dull and silent. Frank is resolutely ignoring me, as if yesterday never happened.

If only I could do the same. Yesterday I had a job. A purpose. Now all I have is five thousand pounds stuffed into my reticule and no idea what to do with it. I know it's insane to have it on my person, but I can't leave it at Mrs Goddard's, where any nosy parlour boarder could find it. Or, worse still, my father. He's already been in my room on at least one occasion, after all.

I don't feel right about the money. Having it here. It's not mine. I haven't earned it. I find myself asking the question I always used to pose when I was in a fix.

What would Father do?

He'd take the money and run. He's done it often enough.

But I don't want to be my father.

Perhaps I should wash my hands of the whole thing. Give the money to Robert. It would be enough to set him up in London to pursue his dream of becoming an illustrious novelist – and if it put some distance between him and Mr Knightley, all the better.

As the party halts, I sit down next to Frank on the picnic blanket, trying to attract his attention. He turns away to flirt loudly with Emma. I glance at Jane. She's not looking at Frank, yet it's obvious she can hear every word of his ode to Miss Woodhouse. Her cheeks are wan, despite the heat, and her eyes are glazed over as she nods in acknowledgement of her aunt's incessant chatter. Her knee jigs up and down as Miss Bates unpacks the picnic hamper and her fingers tap against the glass of wine Mr Knightley hands to her. Crimson drops spatter over her mauve muslin dress. Jane doesn't seem to notice.

'I do so like your ring, Miss Fairfax,' Emma says loudly, determined that she should be drawn into the conversation. 'Did it belong to your mother? It must be such a comfort to have something to remember her by. I had a beautiful ring from my mother. An arachnid.' She's watching Jane with a strange intensity.

'A spider?' Miss Bates leaps to her feet. 'There is not one here, I hope? I have never been fond of spiders – such unpleasant-looking creatures – Jane has never minded them, have you, Jane? Nor Mother. She says they are all God's creatures – which I suppose is true. I own, I would not mind them so much if they confined themselves to gardens, but they get indoors and it does so bother me seeing them scurrying along the floor—'

'No, not a spider, Miss Bates,' Emma says, unable to keep the impatience from her voice.

'The ring is not from my mother,' Jane says, steely eyed as she meets Emma's gaze. 'It was a present from Mrs Campbell. All I have left of my mother is her books. Well, *most* of them.'

'Yes, indeed, my sister was a great reader,' Miss Bates says, sitting back down now she's sure a spider attack is not imminent. 'That is to say, we both were. Henry Fielding and Ann Radcliffe – though Father never did approve of Mrs Radcliffe – I suppose it was the brigands and skeletons and the black veil—'

Emma turns away to whisper something to Frank as Miss Bates drones on. I can't make out what she's saying but, whatever it is, Frank clearly finds it amusing, because he's smirking at her in the most infuriating way.

'Ladies and gentlemen,' Frank declares with mock solemnity, cutting through Miss Bates's monologue, 'I am ordered by Miss Woodhouse to say that she desires to know what you are all thinking of.'

'Oh, well,' Miss Bates responds, 'I am thinking about my sister and Ann Radcliffe, but also about the weather – and the picnic hamper – I do hope the pork pie doesn't go off in this heat, but we packed it so carefully, I don't think it will – and how lucky I am to be with all my friends – and, oh, Miss Woodhouse, I hope you are not burning in the sun – but you have your bonnet and your shawl, of course—'

'To good friends and good weather,' Mr Weston exclaims, raising his glass. Nobody raises their glass in return. Mrs Elton sighs and whispers something to her husband. Jane has her head bowed and is staring at her fingers with rapt attention. Frank is deep in conversation with Emma again.

I'm certain Miss Woodhouse doesn't want to know what *I'm* thinking right now. Mainly, I'm fantasising about pushing her down Box Hill, and if she happens to break her pretty little neck in the process, so be it. Why she is flirting so publicly with Frank when she no longer cares for him, I don't know, unless it's to provoke Mr Knightley or Jane. The truth is, Emma always has to be the centre of attention and, while that sometimes works to my advantage, today I wish she would rein it in. I hardly think Frank is taken in by her. I can only suppose he's fawning over her for my benefit. He's obviously deeply disturbed by the idea of being in my power.

Fear not, Frank. I don't intend to hold you captive.

Frank clears his throat theatrically. 'Miss Woodhouse waives her right to know exactly what you are thinking and demands instead either one thing very clever, two things moderately clever, or three things very dull indeed.'

Mr Knightley rolls his eyes and turns his back on Frank.

Miss Bates comes to Frank's rescue. 'Ah, well, I need not fear – three things very dull indeed. I shall be sure to say three dull things as soon as I open my mouth, shan't I?' She looks from face to face with a nervous laugh. 'Do you all think that I shall?'

Emma and Frank share a smile which lingers a little too long on Emma's lips as she turns towards Miss Bates. 'Ah! But there may be a difficulty. Pardon me – but you will be limited as to number – only three at once.'

I inhale sharply and hold my breath as I wait for the truth to dawn upon Miss Bates: that Emma has taken her good-natured, self-effacing humour and used it as a weapon against her. I look towards Jane to see if she'll come to her aunt's aid, but she's staring off into the middle distance, oblivious to Miss Bates's plight and Emma's rudeness.

I'm certain Emma would not dare say such a thing to her social equal. To pick on Miss Bates, a woman who has fallen from her comfortable position in life into a state of comparative poverty – I didn't think Emma would stoop so low. I'm not excessively fond of Miss Bates myself, probably because I fear I'll end up just like her – unmarried and penniless, and although the former is of my own choosing, the latter is not. It's all very well for Emma. If she keeps up her resolution never to marry, she shall not become ridiculous. Because she has money. Property. She was born into it and has a father who will ensure it is preserved for her.

But, if I'm angry with Emma, I'm furious with Frank, who is still ignoring me, as if yesterday's near-kiss has been erased from his memory. I realise now that he has only spoken to me with candour and authenticity in private moments. He doesn't want to be seen conversing with me in public. It's just the same with Jane. He was happy enough to step out with her in Weymouth, to promise her the world when she was surrounded by the Campbells and the Dixons. Here, in Highbury, with her impoverished maiden aunt and the vulgar Mrs Elton by her side, he does not dare to declare himself.

Frank Churchill is a scoundrel. A fraud. A coward. Worse than that, he has destroyed Jane's character. She has lied for him, besmirched her own good name, gone against her very nature.

I glare at Frank as he shares a joke with his father. Mr Weston's rictus smile suggests he doesn't find it quite as funny as Frank does.

'And where did you slope off to yesterday?' Emma asks, nudging me out of my gloomy reverie as Jane and her aunt rise to take a walk with the Eltons, leaving their uneaten picnic behind them. Mr Knightley excuses himself almost immediately.

'Oh, I had a headache,' I say. 'Must have been the heat.'

'Yes, there was a lot of that going around,' Emma muses. 'First Jane Fairfax. Then you. Then the Eltons left soon after, complaining of the heat. It seems Mrs Elton's bonnet wasn't as effective as it looked.'

'Frank Churchill was complaining of the heat when he arrived,' I say. 'I expect he left early too?' He could have easily reached Highbury before me on horseback, even if his mount was tired from the ride to Donwell Abbey.

'On the contrary,' Emma says with a smirk, 'Frank was one of the last to leave. He was there to the very death. The Westons had trouble dragging him away once he'd settled in, though I dare say Miss Bates didn't help matters there.' A blush rises to Emma's cheeks as she mentions Miss Bates. 'But the Westons got away eventually and Mr Knightley sent Miss Bates home in his carriage.'

Well, there goes my theory. Jane cannot have been covering for Frank. Or her aunt. They were still at the Abbey when Mrs Churchill took her tumble.

So who could it have been?

I sit on the picnic blanket, nibbling at a strawberry tart, and praying for this interminable day to end. Finally, the walking party rove back into view and Mr Weston rises to greet the approaching carriages. Frank turns back to Emma.

'Miss Woodhouse, in truth, I'm glad we have a moment to ourselves. It was getting awfully crowded, and I only crave your company – and that of your charming friend, Miss Smith, of course,' he adds, with a stiff nod in my direction.

I arch my eyebrow at him, lips pursed, as I rise to follow Mr Weston towards the carriages. Mrs Elton is pacing back and forth, complaining about the heat again. Jane and Miss Bates amble towards us, arm in arm. Jane has her shawl wrapped tightly around her shoulders, staring at her feet and Miss Bates is strangely silent, her gaze darting across to Emma every now and again. Mr Knightley trots up on his black Friesian stallion, its coat glistening in the sunlight. He dismounts and strides over to Emma. She hangs her head and blushes as he speaks to her in a low voice. As Mr Weston hands Miss Bates into the Eltons' carriage, Jane pulls me aside.

'Is she all right? Mrs Churchill?' she whispers, watching her aunt settle into the carriage next to Mrs Elton.

'I think so. She has a hard head that one.'

Jane nods, lips pursed. Clearly she's not finished. 'Did she say anything to you? In the carriage?'

'Like what?' I ask.

Like who really pushed her?

Jane shrugs. 'I just wondered, that's all.' She glances up at the carriages and grasps my arm, steering me away from them. 'How did you know about all that? Mrs Churchill? Frank?'

I shake my head as her grip tightens. 'Not here. You need to trust me until this blows over. Then I'll explain it all. I promise.'

It's a promise I'm not sure I'll keep, but it should do the trick for now.

Jane drops my arm. 'You cannot keep your secrets for ever,' she says and steps towards the carriages.

I stand and watch the Eltons' carriage as it trundles away towards Highbury, my eyes fixed on Jane. 'You cannot keep yours either.'

CHAPTER 19

Rule number nineteen: Take pains to conceal your early-morning visitors from your nosy neighbours. (Particularly when they are uninvited visitors.)

Stones at the window. I wouldn't mind except it's seven in the morning and I've been tossing and turning all night, waiting for the message from Wakefield that Mrs Churchill is no more, which could mean that Jane Fairfax is a murderer and I have helped her to conceal the crime. Eventually, I drifted off to visions of the gallows, a heavy rope round my neck as I looked down upon the bloodthirsty crowd, with Denny, Frank and Mr Knightley elbowing their way to the front, vying for the best vantage-point.

Stones at the window again. Quite a handful, by the sound of it. I draw back the curtain and throw open the window as the person responsible for the disturbance scoops up another handful of stones. Bear boy.

'What do you want?' I hiss, conscious that Miss Bickerton is sleeping right next door. If she wakes up, the news of my early-morning visitor will sweep around Mrs Goddard's in a matter of minutes.

'A message for you, miss,' bear boy shouts, not bothered by any such qualms.

'Wait there,' I say, 'and, for goodness' sake, don't make any more noise.' I grab some coins from my purse – I have a feeling I'm going to need them – and tiptoe down the stairs and slip out into the yard. 'Well?' I demand, interrupting bear boy's tuneless whistling, which, in my book, constitutes making noise.

He grins, fixing his mismatched eyes upon me as he hands me the note. 'Some lad came over from Richmond with it, but was too scared to knock on the door so early. Didn't want to disturb folk.'

'Thank heavens you're not troubled by such niceties.'

'I'm not troubled by much, miss,' he says, his grin widening.

It's hard not to find him a little bit endearing, even if he is helping my father to terrorise me.

'And you just happened to be lurking outside my window when the messenger arrived, did you?'

Bear boy shrugs. 'Just on my usual early-morning walk.'

If that's meant to reassure me, it doesn't work. I glance down at the note.

Mrs Churchill requires your immediate attendance at Richmond. Time is of the essence.

Wakefield

My first thought is that Mrs Churchill is dead and Wakefield thinks it too delicate to put down on paper. My second thought is that he wouldn't have phrased it like this if she *was* dead. Perhaps she's too weak to write herself. Or too self-important. Whatever her reasoning, something has happened and, the sooner I leave, the sooner I'll know what it is.

'Any reply, miss?' bear boy asks.

'No,' I say, handing him a coin for his troubles. He salutes me and gives me a wink for good measure as he withdraws.

'Hang on,' I say. 'I wanted to ask you about the last message you gave me.'

'I deliver a lot of messages,' he says, shrugging his enormous shoulders.

'Trust me. You'll remember this one. You mobbed me with a gang of your friends and I pulled a pistol on you.'

'It's starting to come back to me.'

I smile at him. 'I thought it might. Now, if you could just let me know who gave you the message.'

Bear boy frowns. 'Well, miss, it's hard to recall all of my clients.'

'This might help jog your memory,' I say, handing him another coin.

He slips it into his pocket with a nod of acknowledgement. 'Toff, he was. Well dressed. Nice horse. Seen him around.'

'Recently?'

'Fairly recently, I'd say.'

'His name?' I ask, handing him another coin as he pretends to think about it.

'He didn't give it, miss,' he says, grinning maniacally. 'But I can assure you, you know him.'

'Anything else?' I press.

Bear boy shrugs. 'Like what, miss?'

'Distinguishing features?'

'Can't say he had any.'

Hmmm. Can't say because he's been paid not to, I suspect. Bear boy scuttles away before I can wheedle anything else out of him. That settles it. A toff. Someone I know. Someone willing to pay well to keep his identity a secret. It certainly sounds like my father. And he's clearly still hanging around. But I don't have time to worry about him right now. I need to get to Richmond and, for that, I need a horse. A fast one.

✳

I have to knock four times before the front door swings open at Abbey-Mill Farm.

'Oh God, it's you,' Denny mumbles, leaning against the doorframe, bleary-eyed.

'Delightful to see you too,' I say, peering past him into the farmhouse. 'Is Robert in?'

Denny huffs. 'No. He got up at the crack of dawn to do something or other to the cows and I haven't seen him since. Mainly because I've been unconscious. And I'd quite like to get back to it, if you don't mind.'

'Of course. Wouldn't want to deny you your beauty sleep. You certainly look as if you need it.'

'So do you,' he snaps, slamming the door in my face.

I spend a few minutes scouring the barns for Robert, narrowly avoiding a nip from Toby the pony as he searchers my pockets for the carrots I don't have. There's no sign of Robert. Wherever he is, he's not out on the farm, which is mildly inconvenient. It would have been easier to procure one of Mr Knightley's horses with Robert's assistance, but I'll just have to improvise.

The stables at Donwell Abbey are quiet when I reach them. It's easy enough to slip past the solitary groom in the yard to seek out a suitable mount. A chestnut Arabian mare whinnies a greeting and tosses her head as I pass her stall. She might do nicely. There's a Hackney horse in the next stall who flicks his ears back and paws the ground. He's a beautiful horse, but too highly strung. Mr Knightley's Friesian stallion raises his head and huffs gently as I approach him. He really is the most stunning creature. His coat glistens in the sunlight and his lustrous mane cascades down his neck. And he's already tacked up. Mr Knightley is probably planning to take him out for a ride this morning, but it feels like fate that I'm here and he's ready and waiting.

But first to get rid of the groom. I return to the Hackney horse and slide open the bolt of his stall door. He charges at the door, cantering through the yard and into the fields beyond. The groom tears after him, pitchfork still in hand. I return to the Friesian, swing myself up into the saddle and trot out into the yard. It's been a while since I've sat fully astride a horse rather than going through the ridiculous ordeal of riding side-saddle. It's good to be back here, even with my gown hiked up to my thighs and my legs prickled with goosebumps. I lean forward, whispering words of encouragement into the stallion's ear. We soar down the driveway, swerving to avoid a blurred figure who dives aside and squawks with indignation as we fly by. We're galloping so fast that we've left them far behind before I can worry about who it might be. Besides, they'll never catch up with us now. This is what freedom feels like. Pounding hooves, thumping hearts, the wind howling in your ears. It won't last, but if I close my eyes and give the horse his head, perhaps I can hold on to it that little bit longer.

＊

There's a boy at the door of Richmond Terrace – bright-eyed and neatly groomed. He's eager to take the reins as I dismount. I slip a coin into his hand as he leads away Mr Knightley's horse with a sense of reverence that only a seasoned stable-boy can exhibit.

'Miss Smith?' Matilda steps out into the street, watching me carefully. Her hair is spilling out of her haphazard bun and she looks as if she has slept even less than I have. Her expression is so grave I fear Mrs Churchill has met her maker.

'Mrs Churchill?' I ask as Matilda moves back to the doorway.

Matilda shakes her head and folds her arms, blocking my path. 'I saw you the other day, when you brought her home. People don't notice me, but I notice them. She was in a terrible state,' she adds reproachfully as if, like Wakefield, she thinks I'm responsible for Mrs Churchill's near-death experience. She glances over her shoulder and lowers her voice. 'She claims it was an accident, but I know better. I know it was *him*. She says she's better this morning, but I think she's putting a brave face on it. Still, she convinced Frank. He was happy enough to abandon her to visit some friends in town. Off he went at some ungodly hour this morning as if he didn't have a care in the world.'

'When you say you know it was him, do you mean Frank Churchill?'

Matilda shakes her head frantically, gripping my arm. 'I shouldn't have said. It isn't my place. It's just the shock of it all. I didn't mean anything by it.'

'Matilda, if you think Frank is a danger to Mrs Churchill, you must tell me,' I say gently.

'No!' Matilda snaps and looks as if she instantly regrets it. 'I'm sorry, Miss Smith. I have been working all hours since Sophia died and there is so much to do. And now with Mrs Churchill's illness . . .'

'Are you on your own? Is Wakefield not around?'

Matilda shakes her head. 'He's running an errand for Mrs Churchill. The footman has gone with Frank. I'm the only one here, except for the stable-boy. And Mrs Churchill, of course.'

Matilda hasn't asked me what I'm doing here, which is odd, considering that, as far as she knows, the only connection I have to Mrs Churchill is an unhealthy obsession with her nephew.

'I expect you're here about Frank and Jane,' she says as she finally moves aside to let me into the hallway.

'Excuse me?'

She rolls her eyes. 'There's no use trying to deny it. I hear things. I listen. I know that Mrs Churchill hired you to break up Frank and Jane.'

But not the rest, it seems.

'Mrs Churchill asked to see me,' I say, hoping she won't press me further.

She nods sagely. 'I thought so. This way.' Matilda leads me through the corridor and out into the garden at the back of the Churchills' townhouse. She grips my arm as I step onto the patio. 'You'll convince her, won't you, of the danger she's in? She won't listen to anyone else.'

Considering our recent exchange at Donwell Abbey, I doubt Mrs Churchill will listen to me either, but Matilda is gazing at me with the expectation of a stray kitten who has turned up on my doorstep looking for a saucer of milk and I find that I can't say no. 'I'll do my best,' I assure her.

It's pleasantly warm in the sun, bees are buzzing around the yellow rosebushes and red admirals congregate on the buddleia. Mrs Churchill is sitting at a cast-iron garden table with a pot of tea, crunching on a slice of unbuttered toast. She looks surprisingly healthy for a woman who was pushed down a flight of stairs two days ago.

'Good,' she says, when she catches sight of me. 'You are here.' She gestures for me to pull up a chair.

I wince as it scrapes across the patio. 'Mrs Churchill. You are looking better.'

'Well, of course I am,' she snaps.

I wait for her to mention our disagreement, or the five thousand pounds she threw at me, or the moment when Jane pushed her down the stairs, but she just carries on with her breakfast as if it's perfectly normal for me to be sitting opposite her in silence. The problem is, I've never been good at holding my tongue.

'What do you remember about your accident?' I'm going to refer to it as such until Mrs Churchill tells me otherwise.

She sniffs and stirs a spoonful of sugar into her tea. 'I remember waking up at the bottom of the Bateses' staircase with you looming over me. I remember you bringing me back here. Not much more than that.'

'What about before your fall? Did you see Jane? Did you speak to her?'

'I must have done, I suppose.'

'But you don't remember?'

'I am a very busy woman, Miss Smith. I do not have time to rake over the past.'

It's strange. By her terror in the carriage, her reference to the face full of hatred, it's clear someone pushed her. I would have expected Mrs Churchill to jump at the chance to accuse Jane of trying to kill her. Again. But, if she remembers being pushed by Jane, she has some reason for concealing it.

'Why did you summon me, Mrs Churchill? Do you want your money back? Is that it?'

I'm not giving it back. It's here in my reticule, but she can't have it. I'm past the point of consulting my conscience about it.

'You can keep the money,' she says with a wave of her hand, 'even though you failed to fulfil your duties.'

I pull the gold locket from my reticule and toss it onto the table. 'Well, here's another piece of your missing jewellery. I haven't failed at that. Turns out your dear nephew lost it in a gambling den and I'd wager that's where your other pearl necklace has gone too. But you know about Frank's gambling debts, of course. You've already had a visit from Monsieur Durand.'

'I do not know what you are talking about.' Mrs Churchill takes a long swig of tea.

As far as protestations of ignorance go, it isn't very convincing. A more natural reaction would have been to ask, 'Who?' But Mrs Churchill doesn't need to, because she knows exactly who Monsieur Durand is.

'That's why you checked your jewellery box after Sophia died. You thought it might have been Durand trying to collect on Frank's debt and leaving Frank a little warning.'

Mrs Churchill lifts her chin and looks me right in the eyes. 'Preposterous! Frank would not be caught up in something like that. He has everything he needs right here.'

'Except for the freedom to marry as he pleases.' I've given up being polite to Mrs Churchill now I have her money.

Her fingers tap against her teacup as she considers her response. 'Whoever this Durand fellow is, I can assure you he poses no threat to me or my family. The Churchills do not get mixed up with moneylenders and gambling dens or anything of that nature.'

'I never said that Durand was a moneylender.'

'You implied it. And, if that is the case, he certainly would not be acquainted with my nephew.'

'I wouldn't be so quick to dismiss Monsieur Durand if I were you,' I say softly. 'From what I've heard, he's a very dangerous man.'

But Mrs Churchill won't be told. Despite the threats she's endured in the past few months, the arrogance of the rich persists. She is a Churchill, if only by marriage, and Churchills are indestructible.

'Matilda!' Mrs Churchill barks. The maid comes scurrying across the patio. 'Bring me my post. And fetch Miss Smith a cup of tea. She looks as if she needs it.'

My instinct is to decline, just to spite Mrs Churchill, but I am rather thirsty after my long ride.

'Yes, ma'am,' Matilda says and scampers back into the house.

I sit in silence, watching a robin hopping along the garden fence. He swoops down onto the lawn and starts pecking at a wriggling worm with great enthusiasm.

Matilda tiptoes across the garden with a teacup in one hand and a parcel and two letters in the other. She hands Mrs Churchill her post, pours me a cup of tea and withdraws as quickly as she arrived. I take a grateful swig of tea. It's lukewarm and I drain the cup in three gulps.

Mrs Churchill frowns, setting down her own teacup. She tosses the letters aside and goes straight for the package, fingers working at the knot of the twine that holds it together. I catch a flash of bright white beneath the brown paper as she opens it. A thought niggles at the back of my mind, but I can't quite reach it.

Something is wrong.

Mrs Churchill leans in to examine the parcel's contents as a sweet, floral scent emanates from it.

'No, don't—' I slur, trying to pull her away from the parcel as my head pounds and my limbs become leaden. Everything is slowing down, and yet the world is slipping away from me far too quickly.

Mrs Churchill slumps over the parcel, eyes open but unseeing. My fingers twitch towards her, knocking her teacup from the table, and I can't—

CHAPTER 20

Rule number twenty: Your witnesses know more than they think they do. They just need a little encouragement.

I wake to the sweet scent of roses and the certain dread that I've missed something important.

Where the hell am I?

I raise my head to get a better look at my surroundings and I'm struck by a bout of nausea. I roll over just in time to observe the well-placed chamber pot on the floor beside the chaise longue and do my best to aim in that direction. I heave until I'm sure there's not a drop of liquid left in my body and my throat is so sore I feel as if someone has attempted to choke me to death.

There's something I'm supposed to be doing. Something I need to remember.

'Shhh. Go back to sleep.' There's a cool hand on my brow, a glass of water pressed to my lips.

Robert?

It might be, but before my voice can form the question, I'm slipping back into the fog.

✳

The chamber pot is empty now, but I can taste the acid at the back of my throat and my limbs are so stiff, I feel as if I've been trampled by a herd of Welsh cows. The room is dark and cool, curtains drawn, but my vision clears as I raise my throbbing head. I know where I am now. But how did I get here?

The garden. Something happened in the garden.

'Oh, thank goodness. You're awake. No, don't try to get up.' Matilda eases me back down onto the chaise longue. 'You must rest.'

I flinch as I settle back against the cushions and my fingers find a lump the size of a new potato at the base of my skull.

'You must have hit your head when you fainted,' Matilda says as she moves to open the curtains.

'Fainted?'

'The doctor says it was the shock of what happened to Mrs Churchill.'

That's not right. I didn't faint. I don't faint. I'm made of stronger stuff than that. I didn't faint when I was thrown from Captain Lacey's wild mustang at the tender age of thirteen and broke my leg so badly, I could see the bone poking through the skin. The groom fainted. So did Captain Lacey. But all I could think about was how furious Father would be that I'd put myself out of action. And then there was the time that poor coachman was trampled to death by his own carriage horses, right in front of me, innards splattered across the pavement. Everyone was losing their heads and their lunches over it. I was the only one who thought to pursue the horses to prevent another such accident. And it's a good thing I did, or else Lady Marchant would have lost more than one of her beloved King Charles spaniels.

I didn't faint at what happened to Mrs Churchill. Whatever it was that *did* happen to her.

'Mrs Churchill. Is she . . . gone?' I don't really need to ask that question. I know that she is.

Matilda is deathly pale and shivering, as if she's the one who is laid out on the chaise longue. She lowers her red-rimmed eyes to the floor and clutches a handkerchief to her breast, fingers twitching. 'I knew she was still unwell. I should never have let her get up this morning.'

'No. She *was* better,' I say, gripping her arm. 'It wasn't that. The parcel. There was something in the parcel.'

That's when it happened. She opened it, and she was gone. I was too. Some kind of drug that had done for Mrs Churchill and knocked me unconscious. There's something else about that parcel. Something important. It slips from my mind as I reach for it. But it was the parcel that killed her. I'm certain of it.

'Matilda.' My vision swims as I haul myself to my feet much too quickly. 'Who sent the parcel?'

'I don't know. There was no message with it.'

'When did it arrive?'

Matilda shakes her head. 'Yesterday. The day before, perhaps. But Mrs Churchill was not well enough to get up until this morning and she didn't ask for her post before then.'

'Well, which day was it?' I reach for the glass of water on the table with shaking hands.

'I don't—'

'Who delivered it?'

'No one. I found it on the hall table.'

'When did you first see it?'

'I don't—'

'Think, Matilda.'

She shrugs. 'It was after Mrs Churchill returned from Highbury.'

We're getting somewhere, but not as fast as I would like. I take Matilda's hands in mine. They're slick with sweat, and she tries to pull away, but I hold them firm. 'Close your eyes,' I command.

'What? Why?'

'Just close them.'

Matilda sighs, but assents.

'Take a deep breath.'

She inhales slowly.

'Let it out.' I grip her arm and guide her out into the hallway.

'Where are we—'

'Keep your eyes closed. You're walking through the hallway. You glance over and see the parcel for the first time. What do you do?'

Matilda's eyelids flutter as she presses her lips together in concentration. 'I walk over to the table to see who the parcel is for.'

'The lantern in the hallway. Is it lit?'

'Yes. I— I think so.'

'Do you recognise the writing on the parcel?'

'No. That is— It is block printed.'

As if someone is trying to disguise their handwriting.

Perhaps *that* was what had bothered me about the parcel. Why I had tried to warn Mrs Churchill.

'Had Frank returned from Highbury? Was he here?'

Matilda's eyes fly open. 'Yes.'

I put a hand on her shoulder. 'Keep your eyes closed.'

She nods, biting her lip.

'What was he doing?'

'Arguing. With Wakefield.'

'About what?'

'He wanted to see his aunt. But Wakefield said it was too late and she was not to be disturbed.'

'And then what did he do?'

'He came out into the hallway and asked me what I was still doing up. As if I would leave Mrs Churchill alone at such a time and with *him* in the house.'

Matilda has forgotten herself again. Though she was reluctant to admit it earlier today, it's clear she believes that Frank is a danger to his aunt.

'Did he see the parcel?'

'I don't know. If he did, he didn't comment on it.' Her eyelids flutter again.

I'm losing her.

Her eyes are open now and she's looking at me with the strangest expression. 'I did this. It's my fault.'

'What do you mean?'

Is she about to confess to murdering her mistress?

Matilda stifles a sob. 'If I hadn't brought the parcel to her, she'd still be here.'

Perhaps not.

'You couldn't have known. You can't blame yourself. I was sitting right next to her and I didn't do a thing to stop it.'

I take my hand from her shoulder and hurry down the corridor, slipping out into the garden.

'I will not stay in this house,' Matilda says as she follows me outside. 'Not now two women have been murdered. It will be me next. I'm not safe here.'

'Mmmm,' I say, tuning out Matilda's hysterics as my eyes adjust to the afternoon sunlight. I must have been out for longer than I'd thought.

It's not like the last murder scene I surveyed at Richmond. There's no corpse sprawled across the floor, no bodily fluids, no murder weapon in plain sight. In fact, you wouldn't know that anything out of the ordinary had happened here. The tea things have been cleared away, the chairs tucked neatly under the table. The parcel is gone.

'Where is Mrs Churchill?' I ask.

'I moved her,' says a cold voice behind me. Wakefield looks as unruffled as if he were talking about a piece of furniture rather than his dead mistress.

'What about the parcel?' I demand. 'The tea things?'

Matilda shakes her head. 'I cleared away the tea while we were waiting for the doctor. But the parcel, I don't know.'

'It was not there when I arrived home,' Wakefield says, an edge to his voice.

'Could someone else have moved it? The cook, perhaps?'

Matilda shakes her head. 'She's not arrived yet. Only the stable-boy was here, but I sent him to fetch Frank home. He's been such a long time. I do hope nothing is wrong.'

'When did he leave?'

'As soon as I found you both and recovered from the shock of it. I can't understand why they haven't returned.'

'If you'll excuse me, Miss Smith. There is much for me to attend to.' Wakefield retreats indoors.

Matilda steps towards me. 'Miss Smith?'

'Harriet, please. I think witnessing two murders together allows us a measure if intimacy.'

'Harriet. I don't wish to rush you off when you've had such a shock, but I must pack up my things before Frank returns, or else I'm sure I shall not have the courage to leave.'

'I cannot think you'll be in danger now Mrs Churchill is dead. Whoever killed her, it's clear she was the intended target. They have no reason to come after you.'

'Unless they think I know too much. Besides, with Mrs Churchill gone, there doesn't seem much point to me staying on.'

'Frank will still need a housemaid, I imagine.'

'Well, it won't be me,' Matilda says, glancing at Mrs Churchill's garden chair. 'I won't stay here. Nor at Enscombe. There's evil lurking within this family.'

Matilda says this in the doom-laden tone that only the servant class can really do justice to, but with two murders in the space of three weeks at Richmond, I can't really argue with her. Leaving so soon after Mrs Churchill's murder isn't really a good look, but if she fears that Frank is the murderer I suppose it's only natural. Besides, if Matilda *is* the mastermind behind the whole thing, she hasn't done herself any favours by being the only other person known to be in the house at the time of the murder and the one who handed the poisoned parcel to Mrs Churchill.

'You must let me pack up my things, Miss Smith. Harriet. Before Frank's arrival. You mustn't be here either.'

'Of course. You're quite right.'

There's no chance I'm leaving before Frank returns. I stumble against the garden table, clutching my head.

'Harriet!' Matilda rushes to my side.

'I just need a minute,' I say, sinking down into a chair. 'Go. Finish your packing.' I wave her off.

'If you're sure?'

I nod, closing my eyes. I don't open them again until I'm certain Matilda has withdrawn. I'm sitting where I was this morning, when Mrs Churchill, with her unbuttered toast and her steaming tea, informed me that she didn't remember anything about her fall down the stairs at the Bateses' apartment and that she was quite sure Monsieur Durand, of whom she had never heard, posed no threat to her or her family.

Perhaps if she'd been a little bit more forthcoming about the threats to her life, she might still be here.

But whoever heard of anyone using a parcel as a murder weapon? I wish I could remember more about the parcel, but I was too busy with my tea to pay it much attention. At that last moment, I knew that something was wrong, but I don't know how or why. And, by then, she was already gone.

There's something else that's bothering me. Why did Wakefield send me the summons from Mrs Churchill, and why wasn't he here when I arrived? It seems an odd time to be off running errands, given Mrs Churchill's fragile state. And why did Mrs Churchill summon me in the first place? She never did get round to telling me and I can't imagine what she could have wanted with me after everything that happened at Donwell Abbey and the Bateses' apartment. Whatever it was, it must have been important for Mrs Churchill to overlook the fact that I'd wished her dead and, worse still in her eyes, nearly kissed her nephew, a couple of days earlier.

'Harriet.' Matilda is hovering by the garden door. 'It's getting late.' She's clutching a small trunk which must contain all her worldly possessions.

'Surely you will not go without informing Frank?'

'I dare not stay.'

It would be better for me if Matilda did stay. It would give me eyes and ears where I most need them. I could talk her into it. It's exactly the sort of thing my father would do. Sweet-talk a vulnerable young girl into staying in a dangerous situation for his own means, without a second thought for her welfare. It's the sort of thing I would have done a few months ago.

I will not do it now.

'Where will you go?' I ask, rising from my seat.

She shrugs, staring down at her feet. 'To my uncle in Dorset, if he will have me back. He owns a coaching inn. It will be hard work and long hours, but it's safer than staying here.'

'You must send me your address when you're settled, in case I need to speak with you again.'

Matilda's face falls. 'I just want this to be over.'

'It will be,' I assure her. 'As soon as I find Mrs Churchill's murderer.'

Matilda's mouth hardens and she nods sharply. 'I don't think you will have to look far.'

A warm breeze rustles through the rosebushes and a scrap of silver paper flutters down the path towards the garden gate. I reach down to retrieve it, holding it between my thumb and forefinger. It could account for that flash of white I had seen when Mrs Churchill opened the parcel. I sniff it experimentally, but all I can detect is the faint scent of lavender. I try the latch on the garden gate. It slides open without any resistance. I remember Wakefield's earlier assertion that it is left unlocked during the day. Which means that anyone could have slipped into the garden to retrieve the package, including Wakefield himself, Frank, Durand, or even the mysterious figure from the Bateses' apartment.

I move back to the table. The letters are still there, unopened, but Mrs Churchill's gold locket has gone. I snatch up the letters and turn to Matilda. 'The locket that was on the table. Did you move it when you cleared the tea things?'

Matilda shakes her head. 'I didn't see a locket.'

Which means one of two things. Either Matilda is lying or someone stole it along with the parcel.

'Has the back door been unlocked all this time?'

Matilda hangs her head. 'I didn't think to lock it, what with the body, and the doctor and—' She breaks off with a sob.

I pat her arm. 'Nobody would expect you to think of it, in the circumstances. But could you do something for me before you go? Could you check to see that nothing is missing from Mrs Churchill's jewellery box?'

'You think someone has robbed her?' There's a strange look in Matilda's eyes, a challenge, almost, that makes me decide not to mention Durand. Perhaps Matilda has been helping herself to Mrs Churchill's jewellery. Perhaps she thinks I'm testing her.

'Probably not,' I say, not wishing to provoke her further. 'But it doesn't hurt to be thorough.'

The garden gate rattles. I clap my hand over Matilda's mouth as she lets out a little shriek. I pull her along the path and duck behind the buddleia, dragging her down with me. As I peer out from my hiding place, the garden gate inches open with a dull creak.

CHAPTER 21

Rule number twenty-one: If the murderer returns to the scene of the crime, don't let them find you there.

Why is it I never have my pistol to hand when I'm about to be confronted by a cold-blooded killer? It could be the cook, I suppose, but it's more likely to be the murderer returning to the scene of the crime, seeking a piece of incriminating evidence they left behind. That's how Robert would write it, in any case. And here I am: Harriet Smith, intrepid investigator, ready to pounce.

This is the moment where I catch them in the act.

The gate swings open and his feet crunch on the gravel. He dips his head to avoid colliding with a willow tree, cursing as a stray branch scrapes against his neck. I know exactly who I'm dealing with.

'Robert!' I clamber out from behind the buddleia, fingers raking through my hair to expel a few stray leaves.

'Harriet.' He half-shakes, half-embraces me. 'What on earth— You steal Mr Knightley's favourite horse, almost mowing me down in the process, and disappear with absolutely no thought for the consequences—'

Ah. So that's who I nearly killed on the way here. It could have been worse. It could have been Mr Knightley himself.

'Was he very angry?' I ask, twirling a strand of hair around my finger.

Robert sighs. 'With me, perhaps. He doesn't know you've stolen his horse. I told him I let you take it.'

'Oh. Well, that was decent of you.'

'I've been out looking for you all day. Where have you been?' There's an accusing note in his voice, as if he thinks I've deliberately set out to witness a murder and get myself knocked out in the process, just to inconvenience him.

'What do you mean, where have I been? I've been here. All day.'

Robert rubs the back of his neck with his thumb. 'I can assure you, it was the first place I thought to look, but the house was shut up, and no one came to the door when I knocked. The curtains were drawn and, oh—' Robert glances at Matilda's grim expression and then back at mine. 'Mrs Churchill. She's not—'

'Dead,' I say, nodding at Robert.

'Murdered,' Matilda adds, voice wavering, 'and she almost took Harriet along with her.' She starts gnawing at her fingernails as if her life depends on it.

Robert's eyes widen – whether at the revelation of Mrs Churchill's murder or at Matilda's use of my Christian name, I'm not sure – and he grips my arm so tightly, it feels as if his fingertips are fused to my bones.

'I'm fine, as you can see,' I say, shaking him off. 'I don't suppose the killer wished me any harm. I was just unlucky enough to be in the vicinity when Mrs Churchill opened the parcel.'

That's what I'm telling myself, anyway.

'Parcel?'

'Yes. It happened at this table. There must have been some noxious substance inside, because she collapsed as soon as she opened it, and I followed almost immediately.'

'And yet you survived,' Robert says, still squeezing my arm as if to reassure himself of this fact.

'I was further away. And I pride myself on having a stronger constitution than a fifty-five-year-old woman who was recovering from being pushed down the stairs.'

Matilda stops biting her nails and narrows her eyes. Apparently, Mrs Churchill didn't fill her in on everything that happened in Highbury, which is hardly surprising as she wouldn't even admit to me that she'd been pushed.

'What substance do you suppose could have killed her so quickly?' Robert asks.

'Well, I don't know, do I? I'm not a chemist.' Ironically, Mrs Churchill is probably the one person who would have been able to identify the source of her demise.

'Harriet, if I'd realised—'

'How could you?' I say, patting his arm. 'Besides, there was nothing you could have done.'

'When I couldn't find you here, I went back to Highbury. I looked everywhere. The farm, Mrs Goddard's, even Hartfield—'

'Hartfield? Good Lord. How am I supposed to explain to Emma why you're inviting yourself into her house, demanding to know my whereabouts?'

'I didn't present myself to Emma. I asked the coachman.'

'Don't suppose she won't hear of it. Gossip has a way of getting back to Emma Woodhouse.'

'Well, I'm sure you'll think of some explanation. Tell her I'm madly in love with you and stalking you, if you like.'

I've had my fill of stalkers, thank you very much, although Robert isn't to know. In fact, Father has been strangely silent since the Romani incident. Some might take this as a sign he'd given up. Not me. Not with *my* father. He'll be biding his time. Waiting for the perfect opportunity to present itself. He has much more patience than I do.

Patience is a luxury reserved for only the greatest of prizes, Hattie, he always said. *The trick is to learn when it's worth indulging in.*

I suppose he thinks I'll come running back to him now my new venture has failed so spectacularly. Regardless of what he did to me. What we did to each other. But I will never run to him again.

I don't know why I haven't told Robert about my father's threats. I suppose because he's so disapproving of my past,

I don't wish to remind him of it. Besides, he'd probably use it as proof that things are getting too hot for me in Highbury. But where else can I go?

I'm roused from my thoughts by footsteps and raised voices.

'Matilda?' Frank shouts from the hallway and then, in a lower tone, 'Where is that damn girl?'

Matilda drops her trunk on her foot, eyes wide. 'I did not expect— He mustn't find you here.'

Robert grabs me by the arm and pulls me towards the garden gate. 'We're leaving,' he assures Matilda.

She nods. 'You must,' she says and scurries into the house.

'Harriet, come on.' Robert squeezes my shoulder.

I don't think so. I'm not about to leave just as one of my prime suspects returns to the scene of the crime. And not without seeing Mrs Churchill's body. Who knows what sort of evidence the killer might have left behind?

'Give me a minute,' I say, shaking off Robert's hand and tiptoeing up the garden path. I slip through the door and into the corridor, edging towards the sound of conversation in the hallway.

'I don't understand.' Frank's voice hitches. 'She was so much better. I would never have left if I'd thought she was still in danger.'

'*I* did not think her better,' Matilda says, as if she's talking to a fellow servant rather than a member of the family. 'But the doctor said it would have been quick, at least.'

'Doctor?' Frank snaps. 'Who did you call?'

'Dr Phillips.'

'Phillips? He's a drunk. You should have called Baxter.'

'He had been summoned to a childbirth. So it was Phillips or nothing and neither of them could have done anything for her by then.' Matilda scowls at Frank, but he is too distracted to notice.

There's a loud thump and the chink of china against wood. 'We would have been here sooner, except that the stable-boy got turned around somewhere along the way, which is so unlike him. It was lucky he found me at all. If I hadn't stepped out to greet an old friend in the street, he might still be wandering around Knightsbridge. I should never have left her alone.'

I peer around the corner just far enough to see Frank, fingers tapping against his thigh, face ashen, eyes bloodshot. He doesn't look at all like a man who has just killed off the woman who is standing in the way of his earthly happiness.

'Will you be wanting anything?' Matilda asks, glancing in my direction.

Frank runs his fingers through his hair. 'No, Matilda. Not now.'

As Matilda withdraws, Frank sinks to the floor, head in his hands. My anger against him for shunning me at Box Hill immediately evaporates. His shoulders shake as he sobs and I want nothing more than to wrap my arms around him and smother his grief. I know what it's like to lose a mother, and Frank has lost his mother twice over.

I cannot countenance the idea that he played any part in Mrs Churchill's death.

I can help him. I *will* help him.

A hand tugs me backward as I step out into the hallway. 'Harriet,' Robert whispers in my ear. 'What in heaven's name are you doing?'

'What does it look like? I'm going to speak to Frank.'

'Are you insane?'

'It has been suggested. But look at him. He's distraught.'

'He's a skilful actor. We've already established that.'

'Well, if he did do it, I'll catch him unawares. He might confess something he means to conceal in the shock of it all.'

I don't for a second believe this, and Robert's raised eyebrow tells me that he doesn't either.

'Or, you'll blow your only chance with him. This is madness. What do you think he'll do if you confront him? You can kiss goodbye to your profession, for one thing.'

'I thought you didn't approve of my profession.'

'I also don't approve of you throwing everything away for a man as unprincipled as Frank Churchill. You'll gain nothing by it. We need to leave. Now. Get back home.'

Except Highbury isn't my home. I don't have a home. But I do have Mrs Churchill's five thousand pounds and, as rude as she was to me during our final encounter in Highbury, if I'm going to keep the money, I owe her something. I can't protect her any more, but I can find her killer.

✳

'You're quiet,' Robert says as we walk to the inn where Mr Knightley's horse is being fed and watered.

'I'm thinking.'

'About?'

'Jane Fairfax, if you must know.'

'You think she was involved?' Robert presses his lips together in a way that tells me he has something to say about this, but is doing his best to keep it to himself.

'I found her standing over Mrs Churchill's unconscious body at the Bateses' apartment. She admitted to pushing her.'

'And so you think she sent the parcel to finish the job?'

'No. She was clearly distressed when she thought Mrs Churchill was dead. I don't think her capable of premeditated murder. But there was someone else in the apartment, I'm sure of it. She was covering for them. And, whoever it was, if they were angry enough to push an ageing woman down the stairs, then they certainly wouldn't balk at sending her a poisoned parcel.'

'Do you have any idea who it could have been?' Robert asks in a tone which suggests he clearly has his own ideas about this.

'It wasn't Frank. According to Emma, he was one of the last to leave Donwell Abbey, along with Miss Bates. So it couldn't have been her, either.'

'Then who was it?' Robert asks, arms folded.

I shrug. 'Mrs Elton, perhaps? The Eltons left the Abbey just after I did. I was on foot. She could easily have got there before me if she used her carriage. And she has been clinging to Jane like a limpet since she got here.'

'Just because Mrs Elton might be the victim of one of your cons—'

'There is nothing to suggest it,' I remind him – except for the fact that I *know* I've met her somewhere before.

'—that doesn't mean she's murdered your employer to get back at you.'

'It's not that,' I insist, although trust Robert to bring this up. 'Mrs Elton clearly knows Mrs Churchill. I saw them arguing at the Abbey.'

'And did you ask Mrs Churchill about it?'

'Well, of course I did. I'm not a complete amateur.'

'And?'

'Mrs Churchill denied knowing her. Said she was asking for directions to the Abbey and Mrs Elton waylaid her.'

'Hmmm. Mrs Elton is enough to try the patience of the mildest of women and Mrs Churchill was certainly not that. And I don't see why Jane would cover for her. You'd think she'd be glad to get her out of the way.'

Robert's right, of course. Despite Mrs Elton's insistence that she dotes upon Jane, I can't imagine the feeling is mutual. But Mrs Elton is definitely up to something.

'Well then there's Durand, the moneylender.'

'Yes, but that assumes he really is the big bad crime lord you've convinced yourself he is. Can you really be so certain that Durand is a threat? You haven't even met the man.' Robert frowns. 'Have you?'

'No.' But only because Denny dragged me away from his lair before I could find my way inside. Robert's right, though. It's about time I met with Durand.

'Just how reliable is this witness of yours anyway?'

'I'm quite certain Durand is a dangerous character,' I say, ignoring Robert's question. 'I wouldn't put it past him to have done away with Mrs Churchill just to teach Frank a lesson.'

Revenge.

There's another suspect lurking at the back of my mind. Someone else who is seeking revenge, although not on Frank Churchill. But I don't intend to share the theory of my father's involvement with Robert. He would put it down to paranoia. Obsession. And he'd probably be right.

But the first warning note arrived just after Sophia's murder.

'You seem determined to suspect everyone but Frank Churchill,' Robert says.

'And you seem determined to suspect only him.'

Robert smiles. 'I suppose it's too much to ask you to drop this whole thing, while you still can?'

He's wrong. I can't drop it. It's too late for that.

'It's such a comfort that you know me so well,' I say. 'It saves a lot of time in unnecessary arguments.'

'I don't see why you're so intent on pursuing this. It's not as if Mrs Churchill can pay you now.'

'And everything is about money—'

'It usually is with you.'

'Perhaps I've decided to do something more noble at last,' I say, raising my chin.

'Not this, Harriet.'

'You can't pick and choose for me, I'm afraid.'

He rubs the back of his neck, narrowing his eyes. 'You're infuriating, you know that?'

'You may have mentioned it before.'

'If you're going to do it, promise me something.'

'Depends on what it is.'

'I'm serious,' he snaps, pulling me to a standstill. 'Don't trust anyone. Least of all Frank Churchill.'

'Is that all?' I say, rolling my eyes.

'Do you promise?'

'I promise,' I say, as we reach the inn. He looks deep into my eyes, searching for the loophole in my assent. Evidently, he can't find it because he nods and beckons for me to go ahead of him as we enter the stable yard.

'How did you get here?' I ask as Robert greets Mr Knightley's stallion. Robert gestures towards the chestnut Arabian mare in the next stall. 'I borrowed another horse from Mr Knightley. She's a bit tired from the ride, mind you, so we can't leave just yet.'

'You go. Take him back home,' I say, nodding towards Mr Knightley's stallion. 'I've got you into enough trouble as it is. I'll bring her back later.'

Robert shakes his head. 'I'm not leaving you to ride back alone. It's not safe.'

'Well, I got here on my own, didn't I? I'm as capable

a rider as you are. So if it's safe for you, it's safe for me.'

Robert looks as if he wants to protest, but settles for a shrug.

I reach out and squeeze his hand. 'Thank you.'

'For what?'

'For coming to find me.'

'Well, of course I came to find you,' he says, busying himself with the Friesian's saddle as his cheeks flush.

'I know things haven't been easy between us lately. We've both been distracted.'

Robert turns to face me. 'I will always be here when you need me. You know that.'

Actually, I didn't know that. I've never really had a friend before and so I don't know what to expect. My profession hasn't afforded me any time or space for friends, but I want to make room for Robert. I want him to be able to depend on me as I have come to depend on him. I don't tell him this, of course. I don't want him to think I'm going soft. And I don't want to make any promises I cannot keep.

I step forwards and draw him into an embrace. 'Even when I'm stealing horses from your ridiculously handsome landlord?'

He snorts against my neck. 'Even then.'

I pull away and hold him at arm's length. 'Robert, promise me something.'

'Anything.'

'Never give up on your dreams. And never promise me you'll do *anything* for me. You're setting a dangerous precedent.'

His chest vibrates with silent laughter as I lean in for another hug.

'Noted,' he says, his lip brushing against my ear as he gives me a final squeeze and leaps up into the Friesian's saddle. 'I'll see you in a few hours. Don't get up to any mischief in the meantime.'

I wave him away, wordlessly. I don't want to lie to him again. Not when we're having a moment. 'I will take you home,' I assure the chestnut mare, stroking her neck. 'There's just something I need to do first.'

CHAPTER 22

Rule number twenty-two: Avoid discovery at all costs. Even if that cost is your dignity

My ear is pressed against the garden gate as I slide the latch across and push.

Please don't be locked.

I'm not dressed for scaling garden walls this afternoon. I'm in luck, because the gate swings open and I tiptoe up the garden path, glancing at the upper windows.

The back door sticks as I turn the knob. I push my weight into it and give it a kick for good measure.

'Damn it all to hell!'

It's locked.

I pluck a pin from my hair and get to work on the lock. It takes less than thirty seconds to register that satisfying click.

I'm in.

I push my palm against the door. I'm *not* in. It must be secured from the inside. Talk about locking the stable door after the horse has bolted.

Time for Plan B.

My eyes sweep across the garden, searching for inspiration, until they settle upon the garden furniture that played host to Mrs Churchill's final moments. I lift the chairs up onto the table, assessing the stability of the new arrangement. Satisfied, I drag two plant pots full of ferns over to the door and position them between a sundial and a generously proportioned statue of Perseus, holding aloft Medusa's severed head.

I return to the garden gate, fingers fishing inside a velvet pouch I carry with me for just such emergencies and drop a gold cufflink onto the ground. Finally, I glance again at the upper windows and, when I'm sure nobody is observing me, I charge at the garden furniture, toppling table and chairs with an almighty clatter.

That should do it.

As the garden door opens, I'm busy concealing myself behind the ferns, hand resting on Perseus's thigh to steady myself. I stifle a groan as Wakefield steps out, his sharp eyes taking in the heap of garden furniture on the patio. I had hoped Matilda would have come to the door (if she hasn't left Richmond already) or, failing that, the footman. The butler will be much harder to get past.

Wakefield paces around the garden. He stoops to recover the furniture, setting it right with a precision that only a butler could manage. He pauses to scratch his nose with his little finger.

I flinch as a sparrow hops onto my shoulder and pecks at

the seam of my pelisse. Wakefield spins around as the ferns rustle. He edges towards the door, stops, eyes sweeping across the garden, then takes another step towards the ferns. I hold my breath, willing myself to stay as still as the chiselled Perseus I'm crouched beside. As Wakefield tiptoes towards my hiding place, the sparrow dives right at him. The butler ducks as the sparrow swoops over his head and I use his distraction to conceal myself behind the sundial.

Wakefield retreats towards the house, which is exactly the opposite of what I want him to do. Because I'm certain he'll bolt the door behind him and I'll be right back where I started. And I don't have a Plan C.

As Wakefield reaches for the doorknob, I scoop up a handful of pebbles, rise from my hiding place and lob them towards the garden gate. He turns so quickly that he sees them land, right next to the rogue cufflink. It glints in the afternoon sun and, as he steps forward and bends down to examine it, I slip out from behind the sundial and slide through the door into the house.

It's been a while since I performed the good old misdirection trick, but if Wakefield cares to investigate the mysterious cufflink, he'll find it belongs to Lord Marlborough of Inverness – a man with whom I have never crossed paths, due to the fact that he's been dead these past twenty years. I have a collection of trinkets set aside for this kind of occasion.

I scurry down the corridor and nearly collide with the footman who is wrestling with a ginormous trunk.

Fortunately, the trunk obscures me from view and I'm across the hallway before Frank's voice rings out, 'Through here, if you please.'

For one wild moment, I think he's talking to me, but he's facing the footman and gesturing towards the front door.

'There's another trunk to come from my room,' Frank tells the footman, 'but I haven't finished packing it yet.'

I'm out in the open here. If I can just slip upstairs to Mrs Churchill's room before Frank returns to his own room . . . I make a dash for the stairs. It's a risky move, but so is standing against a wall, hoping Frank won't turn round and notice me. And, as Frank is making quick work of packing up the house, this is likely the only opportunity I'll have to examine Mrs Churchill's body and retrieve the documents that connect me to her. I glide up the stairs and into Mrs Churchill's room, recalling the last time I was here and preparing myself to be confronted with another dead body. Mrs Churchill's bed is empty.

Hmmm. It's unlikely the funeral furnisher has already called, although I suppose Mrs Churchill may have been moved, ready for his attendance. Or perhaps she was never in the bedroom. Wakefield didn't specify where he had laid out Mrs Churchill's body. I had just assumed its placement. But something feels wrong about the absence of the body. As if someone is purposefully keeping it from me. Someone who fears what traces they might have left behind.

I crawl across the bed to Mrs Churchill's dressing table, hairpin at the ready. Matilda never got the chance to check her mistress's jewellery box for me, so I'll have to do it myself. Mrs Churchill has some extravagant pieces. I pick up a gold ring, set with amethysts, pearls and emeralds. A bit gaudy for my taste, but worth a pretty penny. Or, it would be, if it wasn't a fake. There's a yellow tint to the emeralds and I can't detect any of the imperfections I would expect from the real thing as I hold the ring up to the light. I rummage through her collection of brooches, rings, necklaces and earrings. Not a genuine piece among them. And the heirlooms I returned to her are nowhere to be seen.

My father would have pocketed the lot and sold them on to ignorant social climbers like the Coles. Mrs Churchill wouldn't have been duped by fakes. There's a reason she has filled her jewellery box with worthless copies. A method in her madness. But I'm not here to fathom the inner workings of Mrs Churchill's supercilious mind. I open the next drawer in her dressing table.

Got it.

I fold up the contract and slip it into my pelisse.

There's no way I'm leaving this where Frank could find it. I'm sure I could talk my way out of it if I had to, but I'd rather not put that theory to the test. I flick through Mrs Churchill's ledger, looking for further traces of Harriet Smith. My advance for expenses is right there. Not with my name against it, or any explanation of what it is, but it's there. 'Hibernian Sunset.' Mrs Churchill has a taste for fast horses, so I suppose she thinks this a natural enough explanation, should anyone ever cast an eye over her ledger. But if they really looked into it, I suspect they would discover that this particular nag doesn't exist. Trust her to keep accounts of her nefarious dealings. Well, I'm not about to let it be my downfall. I slide the ledger under my pelisse.

These aren't her only papers. There are a handful of letters, too, and to be thorough, I should take a look at them.

As I reach for a letter, my hand brushes against Mrs Churchill's paper knife. My fingers are around it before I can stop myself and I wave it in front of me. 'I want her gone,' I say under my breath in my best Mrs Churchill voice.

Footsteps in the hallway soon put a stop to my high jinks. I drop the paper knife on my foot and barely suppress my yelp of pain as I hear Frank's voice at the door.

'Wakefield, I wish to pack up my aunt's room next.'

'Of course, sir. I will fetch Mrs Churchill's luggage.'

I do the only thing I can manage at short notice. I push the drawer shut and roll under the bed.

'Mr Churchill,' the footman calls as Frank opens the bedroom door. 'Mr Weston is here.'

'Frank, my boy,' Mr Weston booms. He has followed the footman up the stairs, not content to wait in the hall as he was no doubt instructed. His disobedience may be my salvation.

'Father. This is a surprise,' Frank says in a tone which suggests it isn't a pleasant one.

'I set out as soon as I received your express,' Mr Weston says, oblivious to his son's disapproval. 'Such shocking news, although when the messenger came galloping up the driveway, we rather feared the worst. Mrs Weston was convinced that you'd fallen from that black mare of yours. But I had hoped it was Mrs Churchill. Well – not *hoped*, of course, but you know what I mean.' I hold my breath during the awkward pause that follows. Finally, when I'm about ready to burst, Mr Weston adds, 'How are you, son?'

'I'm . . . busy,' he finishes lamely. 'What are you doing here?'

'I came to pay my respects.'

'I'm not stupid, Father,' Frank says, lowering his voice. 'I know how things stood between you and my aunt.'

'It's true things were a little fraught between us. But you must know, I could not have wished this upon her.'

'No. Not like that,' Frank says, raising his voice. 'Put it down, for God's sake! Excuse me, Father. I must see to the packing before my worldly possessions are destroyed.'

'By all means, my boy. I will wait right here.'

I exhale slowly, realising that I'm still clutching Mrs Churchill's paper knife.

I wonder if I have time to return it to the dressing table.

I poke my head out from under the bed, just as Mr Weston slips into the room and slinks over to the dressing table. I freeze, hoping he won't look down at the lower portion of the bed to observe the coverlet in disarray and my head poking out. Fortunately, he's too intent on his task to pay attention. He's sifting through Mrs Churchill's letters with an urgency that matches my own.

What is he looking for?

He stops with a quick exclamation of triumph and slips a letter into his pocket. But he doesn't leave. His movements become more frenetic as he rummages through Mrs Churchill's chest of drawers and then drops down onto his knees with a groan, right next to the bed. Any moment now, he's going to lift the coverlet and find me wedged underneath Mrs Churchill's bed and I can't think of a single valid reason for my presence here.

There's an almighty thump from the corridor and the sound of approaching footsteps. 'Would you be careful with that!' Frank shouts. 'If you break it, it's coming out of your wages.'

Mr Weston swears under his breath and hauls himself to his feet with some effort. He withdraws from the room, whistling under his breath as he closes the door behind him.

'Well,' Mr Weston says with forced cheerfulness, 'I can see you're busy, my boy. I will not disturb you. You are right. Now is not the time to pay my respects.'

'Thank you, Father.' If Frank has seen Mr Weston slip out of his aunt's bedroom, he doesn't let on.

'Think nothing of it. You are well, though, aren't you, Frank?'

Frank sighs. 'As well as I can be,' he assures his father. 'Let me show you out.'

'I can find my own way out. You have a lot to do, I'm sure.'

'I do.'

'Take care of yourself. And visit us when you can.'

'I will, Father.'

Please don't come in. Please don't come in.

Frank enters the room. I see the tips of his boots through the gap in the coverlet. At least I had the forethought to rearrange it after Mr Weston left, so my presence shouldn't be immediately obvious, but I didn't have time to replace the paper knife. I'll just have to hope that Frank doesn't notice it's missing as he packs up his aunt's room.

As Frank rummages through his aunt's chest of drawers, I pull Mrs Churchill's ledger from beneath my pelisse and slide it towards the light. It's hard to read as I lie flat on my stomach with a crick in my neck, but I have some experience of contorting myself into small spaces. I flick through the ledger as quietly as possible, squinting at the entries in the dim light. It's a sad legacy to leave behind. Numbers in a ledger. A record of every transaction she ever made. The woman was certainly thorough and, fake jewellery aside, much richer than I gave her credit for. Or she knew how to spend her husband's money, at least.

I flick forward to the most recent entries in the ledger. Those of the past few days. There's no sign that she's given any money to Durand, but that doesn't mean he hasn't taken it without her consent. There *is* a record of the final payment she gave to me.

£5000 – *Jade Fanfare.*

There's thorough and then there's plain stupid. Why document the fact that she had paid me off? And would anyone believe she had spent so much on a racehorse? She could buy three horses of immaculate pedigree for that price and still have a tidy sum left over. Surely even a woman as rich as Mrs Churchill must have her limits? In fact, now I think about it, it's strange that she had the money with her when she met me at Donwell Abbey. She hadn't planned to dismiss me. It was only because she observed me with Frank that she decided to terminate my employment.

Did she habitually carry five thousand pounds around in her reticule for paying off underperforming con women who were intent on seducing her nephew? It doesn't make any sense.

I turn back a few pages, curious to see what else she has recorded in this confessional of hers. There's nothing out of the ordinary, except for one entry from autumn last year of three thousand pounds with the name 'Eden Pride' next to it. Another of Mrs Churchill's imaginary racehorses, no doubt.

And, if Hibernian Sunset stands for Harriet Smith, Eden Pride probably follows the same code. But then, why Jade Fanfare next to the five thousand pounds Mrs Churchill had given me? An amount I was not expecting, nor had she any reason to think she would have need to give to me that day.

As if the money wasn't meant for me.

Jade Fanfare. JF. Surely not? But she *did* meet with her. Although why she would be prepared to give Jane Fairfax five thousand pounds . . . unless it was a bribe to ensure Jane severed her connection with Frank for good. That, at least, might be worth such a sum to Mrs Churchill.

It's suspiciously quiet. I can no longer hear Frank banging around his aunt's room, packing up her belongings.

Perhaps he's gone.

As I peep out from underneath the coverlet, I'm confronted by a pair of feet.

Frank sighs. 'You can come out now, Harriet.'

CHAPTER 23

*Rule number twenty-three: Sometimes,
the best thing to do is brazen it out.*

I hold my breath and tense up every muscle in my body, clutching the paper knife to my chest. If I don't move, perhaps Frank will forget all about the fact that I'm hiding under his dead aunt's bed.

'Harriet.'

Or perhaps not.

'Do I have to drag you out?'

I fantasise about rolling out from under the bed, hurling the paper knife at Frank and making a run for it. Instead, I drop it onto the floor and kick it to the foot of the bed. It will give me one less thing to explain.

I have three options or, rather, three Harriets.

Harriet number one: the innocent maiden who is so simple she can barely spell her own name, let alone explain why she's been found in such a compromising position. But she doesn't have the brains to do anything nefarious, so why worry about it?

Harriet number two: the damsel in distress who would love to answer your question, but good luck getting her to string a sentence together between all the sobbing and wailing. Better have your handkerchief at the ready.

And then there's Harriet number three: the seductress. She'll tell it to you straight, but you'll be so distracted by her feminine wiles, you won't even care. What was the question again?

As I clamber out from under the bed and take one look at Frank's steely eyes and taut jaw, I realise the first two Harriets aren't going to work. He knows I'm not sweet little Harriet Smith and he proved himself immune to my 'damsel in distress' act when he rescued me from the Romani. Besides, there's no good explanation for why either of these Harriets would be hiding under Mrs Churchill's bed.

I cock my eyebrow and hold out my hand to him. 'Are you going to help me up, then?'

Frank tries to suppress his smirk, but his lip twitches against his will and he throws back his head and lets out that irresistible laugh of his. It takes me straight back to Mr Cole's library. He bends down and grasps my hand, pulling me to my feet. We stand chest to chest as I look up into his too-blue eyes.

'It's good to see you smiling,' I say, 'considering the circumstances.'

'I didn't mean to smile so soon,' he admits, 'but I find I cannot help it with you.'

My pulse quickens and my cheeks flush, which isn't a good look for a seductress. I'm meant to be in control. He's the one who is supposed to go weak at the knees at the sight of me.

He's good. Too good for my usual tricks.

I can see the suspicion in his eyes. He's waiting for an explanation.

I'd better make it a convincing one.

I sit down on Mrs Churchill's bed and hitch up my gown. I expect Frank to lower his eyes to follow my progress, but he holds my gaze as I unwind his cravat from my thigh. I've done a decent job of cleaning the vomit out of it and I've doused it in perfume, in case of any tell-tale odours. It can't hurt for Frank to have my scent in his nostrils. Give him something to remember me by. I like to be prepared for all outcomes and there was always a possibility that Frank would catch me doing something I shouldn't be at Richmond. Admittedly, I didn't think it would occur under his aunt's bed. It's hardly the most romantic of settings but, then again, I've seduced men in far more challenging circumstances than this.

I rise from the bed, dangle the cravat in front of Frank and drop it into his outstretched hands. 'I believe this is yours,' I say without a hint of embarrassment. That wouldn't work on Frank. He's a man who appreciates candour, which is probably why he never fell for Emma's charms.

'And how exactly did you get hold of it?' Frank asks, draping the cravat around his neck in a way that makes me want to undress him.

Not now, Harriet.

'I took it from your bedroom. Come, now, don't play coy. You know perfectly well this isn't my first visit to Richmond. You must realise I haven't been able to keep away from you since the night I first met you at the Coles'. You were wearing that very cravat,' I say, standing up and trailing my fingers along it, pulling Frank towards me.

'What were you doing in my bedroom?' Frank asks as he leans into my touch.

'I wanted to see where you slept,' I say, before I can stop myself.

Which doesn't make you sound at all like an obsessive stalker, Harriet.

His eyes widen and he takes a step away from me. I think I've pushed him too far, but then he's cupping my face, his thumb stroking up and down my neck in a way that makes me shiver.

'This isn't my room,' he murmurs against my ear.

'I heard footsteps and darted through the nearest open door,' I say.

'And you were hiding under the bed because?'

I shrug and smirk at him. 'I panicked.'

He sighs, his breath tickling my neck. 'Why are you here, Harriet?'

'To return your cravat,' I say, caressing the smooth silk. 'I should never have taken it.'

'Why did you take it?' He captures my hand in his.

'I thought we had a connection.'

'We did,' he says, pressing my hand against his chest so I can feel the rapid thrum of his heartbeat. 'We do.'

I almost believe him. I *would* believe him, if I hadn't seen the way he still looks at Jane, as if she's the answer to all his problems. But Jane doesn't want Frank any more. She didn't need Mrs Churchill's money as an incentive to walk away. She has seen through him.

'At Donwell Abbey, before Mrs Elton interrupted, I was sure you were about to kiss me.'

'I was,' he admits.

I bite my lip. 'It's just as well you didn't.'

'Why?'

'Your aunt would not have approved.'

He snorts. 'No. I doubt she would have.'

'Which is why I had to return this,' I say, gesturing towards the cravat. 'To put an end to my wicked thoughts.' I take a deep breath and a big risk.

Let's hope it pays off.

'I thought you might have started ignoring me out of duty to your aunt but, when she died, I hoped you would be free to make your own choice at last. I see now I was mistaken. You are not free. You have obligations. You will do your duty.'

Frank rests a hand under my chin and angles my head so that I'm looking into his eyes. 'Why are you here, Harriet?' he repeats.

I answer him honestly this time, my fingers fumbling with his shirt buttons. 'Because I couldn't keep away.'

He tugs off his shirt, pulls my pelisse from my shoulders and flings both garments across the room. Mrs Churchill's ledger drops to the ground with a dull thud, but there's nothing I can do about it. Besides, I don't think Frank is interested in the contents of my pelisse at the moment.

I don't mean to lean into him, but my body is propelling me forward, against my better judgement. I close my eyes, breathing in his jasmine scent as our lips meet and I feel him lifting me up and onto the bed. As my head hits the pillow, I'm crushed under the weight of his body, but not in a way that makes me want to do anything about it.

This is wrong on so many counts.

1) Frank is grieving for his dead aunt.
2) We're doing this on his dead aunt's bed.
3) He might have murdered his dead aunt.
4) He's still pining for Jane.
5) Robert will have a field day when he finds out what I've done and I'll lose the moral high ground I've been so enjoying when lecturing him about his own poor romantic choices. Plus, I really don't want to hear him say, 'I told you so.'
6) I vowed that my days as a seductress were over. This is my father's way of doing business. I don't want it to be mine.
7) I actually feel something for Frank and, while it isn't love, I don't wish to hurt him the way I've hurt so many others.

8) Despite expectations to the contrary, this is the furthest I've ever gone with a man and I'm not sure I want to cross that line.
9) I'm frightened about what might happen if I do.
10) I have vowed never to love again. I'm not sure I could if I tried. Because I'm still *his* – mind, body and soul – and I cannot give myself to another. Not even to save my own skin.

He never touched me like this. He would never have placed me in such a dishonourable situation. He was more of a gentleman than Frank Churchill could ever be. If he knew what I was doing now . . . But I'm sure he has long ceased to think of me and, if he ever does, I can guarantee they are not tender thoughts.

It was different with him. He didn't need to touch me to make my pulse race. A casual glance. A nod. He could walk into a crowded ballroom, oblivious to my presence, and even that was enough. It would have been easy to play a part – to give him what he wanted. His ideal woman. But I was always myself with him. Not Harriet Smith in any of her various guises. Me. And he liked me all the same.

What's happening here, now, with Frank, is good. Really. Very. Good.

Particularly that thing he's doing to my neck.

But it isn't *him*. And I'm not me with Frank. I'm back in Derbyshire, looking out across the Featherstones' ballroom, watching him. He's scanning faces in the crowd, frowning at everyone who isn't me. I know what he's planning to ask me tonight. I know what my answer will be and that Father will never forgive me for it. But then Father is handing me a glass of wine. I gulp it down gratefully. It's hot, so hot, in the ballroom and my head is pounding. There's a hand on my back, guiding me through the crowd and into an empty room. It's quiet and blissfully cool and I'm just going to lie down on the sofa for a while when I feel the hand on my thigh, the warm body pressed against me, chapped lips on my neck. And before I can push him away, the door swings open—

'Harriet.'

'Mmmm. Don't—'

'Harriet?'

Frank raises himself onto his elbows, eyes full of concern. 'What's wrong?' he asks, stroking my hair.

'Nothing,' I say, pulling him back down onto me. 'As you were, soldier.'

He rolls away with a huff. 'As I was? Do you even know what I was doing? Were you even there with me?'

Clearly, I have hurt his feelings.

'Yes, I was there,' I lie, resting my head on his chest. 'It was very . . . nice.'

'Nice?'

I try again. 'Heavenly. Thrilling. Like nothing I've ever experienced before.'

There's at least some truth in that.

'You were shaking, Harriet.'

'From the pleasure of it.' I don't sound convincing.

'You said no.'

'Are you quite certain? Perhaps it was "ohh".'

'I clearly heard you say no. Several times. Do you think I could have stopped myself otherwise?'

It's comforting to know Frank still has some gentlemanly impulses and that I haven't lost my feminine charms, despite their chronic lack of exercise in the past year.

'You are so beautiful,' Frank murmurs into my hair.

I raise my head to examine his features. He strokes my cheek, lips parted, eyes flicking from my lips to my breasts as he holds me at arm's length.

What about Jane? I want to ask him. Because although she has the resolve to give up Frank, I don't believe Frank has given up on her.

Yet I don't intend to throw away all my good work with Frank for the sake of my pride. I can't read him. He's not giving anything away. I suppose it's the gambler in him. He can bluff with the best of them and, apparently, he's willing to bet everything he has on this play. Which makes him a dangerous opponent.

'Stop.' I push my palm against his chest. 'We can't do this.'

'Why can't we, Harriet?'

I'm not sure if he means, 'Why can't we have carnal relations on my dead aunt's bed right now?' or, 'Why can't we run off into the sunset together, get married and have an impractical number of babies?' Not that it matters. It amounts to the same thing.

'I'm in love with someone else.'

And I always will be.

I've condemned myself to a life of spinsterhood at the tender age of eighteen because I can't let go of a man who must despise me.

Frank huffs as if he understands my predicament. He stretches out on the bed, giving me a delightful view of his bare chest and everything I'm giving up in this rejection of him. 'That is unfortunate. I can only hope he will make you happier than I ever could,' he says gallantly.

I sit up and slide off the bed, biting my lip against the tears as I snatch up my pelisse and slide Mrs Churchill's ledger underneath it.

I may not be able to get the measure of Frank Churchill, but I'm certain of one thing: I'll never be happy again.

As I slip out of Mrs Churchill's bedroom, I nearly collide with Wakefield. He's holding a pair of Mrs Churchill's silk gloves, staring at them with rapt attention, but it's clear he's heard every word of my exchange with Frank and everything we didn't say, too. I stand beside him, eyes on the gloves, desperately trying to think of something nice to say about Mrs Churchill.

'She was quite a character.' It's the best I can manage.

'She was,' Wakefield agrees in a reverential tone, 'but perhaps it is better this way.'

'Yes, she is at peace now, I suppose.'

Wakefield fixes his ice-cold eyes upon me. 'She will never be at peace. But to live in fear is no life at all.'

CHAPTER 24

Rule number twenty-four: Tears always work on a middle-aged man with a saviour complex.

It's dark as pitch as I lead Mr Knightley's chestnut mare back to the stable yard. I half expect Mr Knightley to be there waiting for me. Or Robert. I'm relieved to find neither of them. There are *certain* developments I would rather keep to myself and, knowing Robert, he'd be able to tell exactly what I've been doing with Frank Churchill.

Instead, I traipse back to Mrs Goddard's, feeling the weight of everything that has happened in this endless day. Was it really only this morning I was sitting with Mrs Churchill, gulping down tea and arguing about French moneylenders? I enter Mrs Goddard's, slip into my room and sprawl on my bed, fully clothed. I tuck my reticule, complete with Mrs Churchill's five thousand pounds, under my pillow. My eyelids droop as I shuffle onto my side, trying to get comfortable. Mrs Churchill's ledger, still secreted beneath my pelisse, digs into my thigh. I don't have the energy to wrestle myself out of the pelisse and so I roll onto my back, removing the ledger along with Mrs Churchill's unopened letters. I was so consumed by my encounter with Frank that I'd forgotten all about the letters I'd taken from the scene of the crime. The first letter bears Mrs Churchill's name, but no address or postal mark, as if it was hand delivered by the sender. I slide my finger under the seal and unfold it.

> *You have two days to acquire the funds. You do not want to find out what happens if I leave empty-handed.*

The note isn't signed or dated, but I recognise the elegant script immediately. I know Denny warned me to stay well away, but I think I'm going to have to pay a visit to *mon ami* Monsieur Durand all the same. I open the second letter.

> *Madam,*
> *You must forgive my earlier letter. It was written in haste and without thought. It was beneath me to pen it and unpardonable of me to send it. I beg that you destroy the letter and expunge it from your memory. I ask that you do not mention it to Frank. It will serve no good purpose.*
>
> > *Your obedient servant,*
> > *James Weston*

So this is what Mr Weston was looking for in Mrs Churchill's room. He had found the offending letter, but not this one – the apology that Mrs Churchill didn't live long enough to read. Which begs the question, what was in the original letter?

Something that could tie Mr Weston to Mrs Churchill's murder?

Mr Weston's longstanding feud with Mrs Churchill is common knowledge. And his attempt to remove all traces of the correspondence he had with her just before her death is hardly the action of an innocent man. Another thought occurs to me. Could he, like me, have had a dual purpose in stealing into Mrs Churchill's room? I was there to examine Mrs Churchill's body for evidence left behind by her murderer. Could he have been there to remove that evidence? My jaw clicks as my mouth stretches into a too-wide yawn. I feel as if I haven't slept in days.

Monsieur Durand is certainly worth a look, but Mr Weston has moved right to the top of my suspect list.

✳

My throat feels like someone has rammed Mrs Churchill's paper knife down it. I'm flat on my back, fully clothed, with Mrs Churchill's letters balanced on my stomach and five thousand pounds under my pillow. Just another normal day in Highbury. I didn't mean to fall asleep in my clothes, but I didn't even make it under the covers. I change my outfit hastily and run my fingers through my hair in a vain attempt to tame it. As I open my bedroom door, I walk right into Miss Bickerton.

'Oh!' she shrieks, as if she's surprised to see me emerge from my own room. 'Harriet, you do look unwell.'

I scowl at her. She always looks unwell, with her pasty face and stupid freckles and hair which she would tell you is chestnut but anyone else would call ginger, and yet I don't go around shouting about it at the crack of dawn, do I?

'When you didn't come down for breakfast, I thought you might be dead.'

'Dead?' That's a bit dramatic, even for Miss Bickerton.

'Yes,' Miss Bickerton insists. 'You didn't have any of Mr Knightley's apples, did you? Mrs Bates had a terrible stomach ache the other day after eating some of Mrs Goddard's apple pie and Mrs Goddard got the apples from Mr Knightley. So I thought you might have been killed by a poisoned apple. Like Snow White.'

'Who?'

'Snow White? The Brothers Grimm? It's really very good – there's this wonderful bit where the wicked queen is made to wear red-hot iron slippers and dance until she dies.'

'Good Lord. Is that what happened to Mrs Bates?' I say, raising my eyebrow.

'No,' she replies, missing my sarcasm entirely. 'She did rush off home rather sharpish after she'd eaten the pie, but I hear she made a full recovery.' Miss Bickerton sounds disappointed.

'Well, that's a relief,' I say, trying to step around her. She won't budge. 'As you can see, I am neither dead nor poisoned, and I've certainly not eaten any of Mr Knightley's apples.'

'Are you sure? You really do look dreadful.'

'If you'll excuse me, Miss Bickerton, I have some errands to run.'

And a killer to catch.

'Oh, well, don't stay out too long, will you? I wouldn't want you to keel over in this heat.'

'I'm sure it's better than the alternative of staying here with you,' I mumble, darting away before Miss Bickerton can think up some other fatal end for me.

I'm in enough danger as it is.

✳

Miss Bickerton is right – it *is* hot. My muslin gown is sticking to me, my head throbs and I feel as if I'm about to faint. Although, come to think of it, a fainting spell might work on Mr Weston. I'm sure there's nothing he likes more than soothing a damsel in distress. I toss my bonnet into a hedgerow as I approach the Westons' house and break into a run so that I'm panting by the time I pound upon the front door. A harassed-looking footman answers it, but Mr Weston is soon roused by the commotion.

'Oh, Mr Weston,' I say between gasps. 'I must see Miss Woodhouse at once.'

Mr Weston scratches his nose as he ushers me into the hallway. 'I'm afraid Emma isn't here, Miss Smith.'

I know Emma isn't here. In fact, I was counting on it.

'Oh! But I'm certain she said she would be sitting with Mrs Weston this morning.'

'So she is, my dear, but my wife has taken the carriage to meet Emma at Hartfield.'

'Oh, then I must beg your pardon for disturbing you.' I turn away from him, stumbling towards the door. Mr Weston reaches out to steady me and guides me into the drawing-room.

'You must sit and recover yourself, Miss Smith. You're in no fit state to go tramping across Highbury in this weather. I would have offered you use of the carriage if my wife had not taken it out. Bessie!' He signals to a snub-nosed maid hovering by the door. 'Please fetch some smelling salts for Miss Smith.'

'Sir,' she says with a quick curtsey and dashes from the room.

'You are very kind, Mr Weston,' I say, slumping down onto the sofa, 'but I must consult Miss Woodhouse on a matter of some urgency.'

Mr Weston is quick to accept my assertion that I cannot proceed without Emma's counsel – because a girl like me can't possibly think for herself when there's an officious heiress to do it for her – and so he willingly opens his door to me and drops his guard. Which is just as I planned it.

'I'm afraid I've done something terrible. Something I cannot fix.' I sniff loudly and dig my fingernails into the palm of my hand until my eyes water. Tears will work on a man like Mr Weston, who desires everyone to be as cheerful as he is. Soon I'll have him running around fetching me handkerchiefs and calling for cups of tea, although I'm not sure this will distract him long enough for me to locate the purloined letter. Right on cue, he whips out a handkerchief and presses it into my hand. I inhale its faint peppermint scent as I dab it against my eyes.

'I'm sure it cannot be that bad,' he says, sitting down beside me on the sofa. 'I know Emma is your particular friend but perhaps, in her absence, I can be of assistance.'

'I don't think so,' I say, twisting my finger around a stray curl of hair. 'You will think me very wicked.'

'I'm convinced you don't have a wicked bone in your body, my dear,' he says, patting my arm. His soft voice and gentle touch are almost enough to make me forget my purpose. Frank Churchill is lucky to have such a father.

Assuming Mr Weston doesn't turn out to be a cold-blooded killer, that is.

I sniffle into his now-sodden handkerchief. 'You are very kind, but it's perfectly dreadful. Something I can't take back.'

'A quarrel, my dear?' Mr Weston proffers a fresh handkerchief from who knows where. Perhaps he has a stash of them stuffed in his pocket for just such emergencies.

I suppose I'm going to have to work a bit harder to distract him.

I nod as I bury my face in the new handkerchief.

'Well, a quarrel is not such a bad thing. We've all said things we don't mean in the heat of the moment.'

I look up at him with wide eyes. 'I'm sure you have never uttered a harsh word in your life. You are so pleasant and patient. That's where your son must get it from. From what I've heard of his aunt, he cannot have learned it from *her*.'

Mr Weston's smile fades. I fear I've been a little too obvious, even for him.

I'm saved by a disturbance in the hallway that has us both on our feet. Mrs Elton sweeps into the room, followed by the red-faced footman who has evidently been unable to contain her.

'Miss Smith! Thank goodness I have found you. Indeed, you are not an easy girl to pin down.' Mrs Elton commands the space as if she is in her own house and *we* are her guests. 'You must forgive the interruption, Mr Weston, but I was running an errand for my *caro sposo* when I saw Miss Smith walking this way and I thought I must call in to see if she was still here. I did think to catch up with you, Miss Smith, but you strode off at such speed and I couldn't be expected to keep up in this heat, I assure you.' She sinks into Mr Weston's armchair and throws off her enormous bonnet. 'I am determined not to intrude upon your hospitality, Mr Weston. I recall there was a horrible little upstart who would descend upon Maple Grove without invitation. Selina used to dread his coming.'

The disdain in her voice is so convincing I almost forget that Selina Suckling is not her sister and her tales of Maple Grove are a complete fabrication.

The maid returns with the smelling salts and thrusts them into my hand. I nod gratefully as I retreat to the sofa and take a deep sniff.

'Can I get you something to drink, Mrs Elton?' Mr Weston asks with a wry smile.

'Oh, I have not the slightest wish to put you out. A glass of water will do, although I will own that a pot of tea is just the thing to quench my thirst on a hot summer's day.'

'Would you prefer tea, Mrs Elton?'

'No, no. Water will do just fine. But I see you are determined and who am I to stop a man from serving guests in his own house? I dare say you will send for a slice of Mrs Weston's famous sponge cake while you're at it, though, of course, I would not dream of requesting such an extravagance,' she says, fanning herself with her bonnet.

'It will be no trouble at all,' Mr Weston says, signalling the maid. 'Tea and cake for Mrs Elton and Miss Smith please, Bessie.' He ushers her out of the room before Mrs Elton can suggest anything else he must on no account furnish her with.

I'm desperately thinking of a distraction that will keep both Mrs Elton and Mr Weston occupied for long enough to search Mr Weston's study. But Mrs Elton makes the whole endeavour unnecessary on Bessie's return by upending Mrs Weston's best teapot and flinging her slice of the famous sponge cake across the room so that most of it ends up smeared across Mr Weston's waistcoat.

'Good Lord! How clumsy of me!' Mrs Elton exclaims,

leaping to her feet and swiping at Mr Weston's cake-stained form with her handkerchief. She appears to be making it worse.

'It is quite all right, Mrs Elton,' he says, trying to extricate himself from her handkerchief assault. 'If you ladies will excuse me, I will go and change.'

'Of course, Mr Weston. Do take your time. We are quite capable of amusing ourselves in your absence, I assure you.' She waves him away with her handkerchief and sinks back into Mr Weston's armchair. 'Lord, I thought he would never leave,' she says, dropping her airs and graces. 'So, you think it's him too?'

'I'm sorry?'

'Mr Weston. You think he's the one who killed Mrs Churchill,' she says with a satisfied nod.

'How do you know Mrs Churchill was murdered?' I ask, folding my arms. 'And, even if she was, why would Mr Weston have anything to do with it?'

Mrs Elton arches her eyebrow and I realise I'm asking the wrong question.

I try again. 'Who *are* you?'

'You don't remember me, do you?' Mrs Elton says, abandoning her refined accent in favour of the Bristolian burr I'd heard slip through on that first meeting.

Except, apparently, it wasn't our first meeting.

'From Yorkshire?' she prompts.

I shake my head. I know she's there, somewhere at the back of my mind, but I still can't place her. 'You're not Mrs Suckling's sister, I know that much.'

'No. I was her lady's maid, though I went by a different name back then. Before I gained my position with Mrs Churchill at Enscombe, that is.'

Those other interruptions: at the Bateses' apartment; at Donwell Abbey. She concealed my snooping from Jane. She stopped me from kissing Frank. She was helping me.

'You are Mrs Churchill's lady's maid?'

'I was there the day she hired you. I did worry you might have recognised me from our brief interaction in Mrs Churchill's study, although I took pains to change my appearance.'

'Emily? Or, rather not-Emily, I should say.'

Mrs Elton snorts. 'She was never very good with names. It's just as well because, when you didn't make quick enough progress for her, she sent me in to do my worst. She blamed me, of course, as I was the one who found you in the first place.'

'It was *you* who recommended me?'

'I did my research. You had some impressive credentials which made you well suited to tackling Mrs Churchill's Jane Fairfax problem, but it was your acquaintance in Highbury that moved you to the top of the list. I knew that Robert Martin would be a useful ally for you.'

Is this what it feels like to be conned? I suppose it's my own fault for forgetting my father's golden rule: *Never underestimate a woman.* But my father forgot it too. Or, I suppose he didn't realise I had become a woman. He does now.

'What about Frank?' I ask.

'What about him?'

'Didn't he recognise you?'

'He never so much as looked at me when I was at Enscombe. He's not one to mingle with the help, unless it's to order them around, and he had no authority over me. Plus, men in general are so unobservant.'

She has a point there. And, speaking of men . . .

'Mr Elton. Is he in on it?'

'Excuse me?' Mrs Elton asks, hands on her hips.

'Well, he's not really your husband, is he?'

'Not really my husband? Of course he is my husband! Do you suppose I would be keeping his house for him and rewriting his dreary sermons if I had not married him? I had to find some way of entering Highbury and nobody would suspect me as the glamorous new wife of the local clergyman.'

'You married him just to please Mrs Churchill?' I have to hand it to her. Mrs Elton certainly knows how to commit to the part.

'You need not pity me, Miss Smith. He's not a sensible man, but he's handsome enough and with a respectable house. It was as good an offer as I could have hoped to get anywhere else, and a better prospect than working as a lady's maid for Mrs Churchill for the rest of my days. Believe me, Mr E is a much easier person to please than my late mistress. And it is all above board. Mr Elton knows my true background. But a handsome dowry provided by

Mrs Churchill and his desire to snub Emma Woodhouse meant that he was happy enough to go along with it.'

'So when I saw you arguing with Mrs Churchill at Mr Knightley's—'

'She was berating me about my failure to convince Jane to accept Mrs Smallridge's offer. She said it had pushed her to do things that were *beneath her dignity*,' she says in her best Mrs Churchill voice, 'although, really, I don't think it was me she was angry at.'

'The coded letter you left in the hollow oak – that was for Mrs Churchill?'

'Ah, so you found that?' Mrs Elton nods her approval. 'Good for you.'

'Why do you think Mr Weston is involved?' I ask, careful not to give anything away.

Mrs Elton leans in. 'It's no secret that he hated her. He was furious at her when Frank was so late to Donwell Abbey. And then there was something Mrs Churchill said to me at the Abbey. "He's always had a vindictive streak, but that's the Weston blood for you." I assumed she was talking about Frank, but I wonder now if she was referring to Mr Weston.'

'And what makes you think I suspect Mr Weston?'

'Well, you're here, aren't you?' She gestures around the room. 'I can help.'

I study her expression, trying to assess whether I can trust this woman who has been following me around and lying to me and pretending to be something she's not. The maid's footsteps in the hallway remind me that I really don't have the luxury of time.

'Fine,' I say lowering my voice. 'I saw Mr Weston take a letter from Mrs Churchill's bedroom. I need to see what it says.'

'Well go on then,' Mrs Elton says, shooing me from the room. 'I will cause another distraction if Mr Weston returns.'

I slink across the hallway into Mr Weston's study. He's a straightforward man and I immediately find the letter in the top drawer of his unlocked bureau. Not very sensible, but I suppose he didn't expect anyone to come looking for it. I know I should slip the letter into my reticule and go back to the drawing-room before Mr Weston returns and notices I'm missing, but I'm sure I can count on Mrs Elton to keep him occupied if necessary.

Madam,

Do not suppose I would have written if not for my extreme disappointment in your conduct regarding my son. He has been your loyal servant these past sixteen years, subject to all your whims. I am sure he would have been more sensible of the duty he owed to my wife if he had not had to contend with your frequent seizures, which seem to have been conveniently timed to coincide with any attentions he proposed to pay to his family in Highbury. I have tried to keep the peace out of respect for Frank's regard for you, but I cannot stay silent when I see him suffering at your hands. Gone are the easy manners of his

youth, replaced with a snappishness and thoughtlessness which
I can only attribute to your influence. I beg you to release him
from the yoke of obligation while he can still recover his good
nature. If you will not do this for his sake, perhaps you will
do it for your own reputation. My darling Isabella told me
everything before she died – the lengths to which you went to
secure a union with her brother; the sordid secret you concealed
from him. If you do not treat Frank with more respect, I will
have no choice but to reveal that secret.

> *Your obedient servant,*
> *James Weston*

'Mr Weston!' Mrs Elton's shrill voice rings out from the hallway. 'I was just telling your maid that there is cake on the sofa and I fear that it will stain. Raspberry jam is such a challenge. My sister Selina once had a pot of the stuff spilled over her sofa at Maple Grove and nothing would get rid of it. She had to replace the entire suite in the end. Do let me show you.'

I return the letter to Mr Weston's bureau and slip out of his study and back into the drawing-room while he is bent over the sofa, examining the cushions at Mrs Elton's insistence.

It seems that Mr Weston is not quite the kind-hearted gentleman everyone takes him for. I wouldn't have thought him capable of threats and blackmail, but our familial bonds make us do things we're not proud of. Things we can't take back.

CHAPTER 25

Rule number twenty-five: When infiltrating enemy territory, find yourself an inside man. (Even if he doesn't want to be there.)

'So, what are we going to do about Mr Weston?'
Hmmm. *We.*

Mrs Elton seems to take for granted that she's one of the gang now. She was very helpful in distracting Mr Weston for me, but it doesn't mean I'm ready to trust her with all my secrets. Saying that, as Mrs Churchill's former lady's maid and undercover agent in Highbury, she may be privy to information I'm not, so I think it's worth keeping her on side.

'Well, first of all, we need to find out about this secret Mr Weston was threatening to reveal. Any idea what it might be?'

Mrs Elton shrugs as we walk down the drive away from the Westons' house. 'Mrs Churchill had a lot of skeletons in her closet, I assure you, and not many of them will ever see the light of day. I could tell you a few tales about her, but none that date back as far as her marriage to Mr Churchill. But, then, the daughter of an apothecary marries the owner of a great estate – well, there's bound to be a story there, isn't there?'

She's right. It all comes down to preserving the great Churchill name.

'Where are we going, anyway?' Mrs Elton asks.

I link arms with her and quicken my pace. 'We're going for reinforcements.'

✳

'For the love of God, will you bloody well keep still?' Robert is crouching over Queen Charlotte in the barn, reaching for her udders. She lets out a moo of indignation and gives him a good kick on the shin.

Can't say I blame her.

'Jesus Christ.' Robert falls off the milking stool and drags himself away from the cow's treacherous hooves.

Denny is sprawled across a bale of hay, open-shirted, eating an apple and cackling at Robert's attempts to placate the cow.

'You have to talk to her,' I say, edging towards Queen Charlotte and stroking her muzzle. 'Doesn't he, girl?'

'I *was* talking to her,' Robert says, pulling himself to his feet.

'Nicely, if you can do such a thing.' I hold her steady as Robert massages his leg.

'Who's your lady friend, Harriet?' Denny asks from his

hay bale, throwing his apple up in the air and catching it between his teeth. The juice gushes down his chin as he grins at me, apple still in mouth. He looks like a roast pig at a banquet.

If only he were as silent as one.

Robert rises to his feet and catches sight of Mrs Elton. 'What's *she* doing here?' he asks, brushing the straw from his breeches.

'Charming, I must say,' Mrs Elton replies with equal disdain.

Robert circles Mrs Elton as if she's some kind of wild animal. 'Why is she talking like that?'

'I can hear you, you know,' she says, raising her chin and glaring at him.

'Mrs Elton is here to help us.'

'Mrs Elton?' Denny says, dropping his apple and sitting up. 'This is Mrs Elton?'

'Yes, Denny.'

'*The* Mrs Elton? With her *caro sposo* and what's the name of that fancy house?' he asks, clicking his fingers.

'Maple Grove,' Mrs Elton supplies.

'Maple Grove. That's it.' Denny slaps his thigh and grins at her.

'I see my reputation precedes me,' Mrs Elton says, arching her eyebrow.

'Go on, say it,' Denny pleads. 'Maaaaaaaple Groooo-ooooove.'

'I'm not a performing monkey,' Mrs Elton snaps.

'Denny, will you please be quiet?' I say, stooping to retrieve his half-eaten apple and throwing it at him with more force than I'd intended. He catches it one-handed.

'You're prettier than I thought you'd be,' Denny says, eyes roving over Mrs Elton's body. 'You should really put her in your novel, Robert.'

'And we're all the best of friends now, are we?' Robert asks, ignoring Denny's suggestion.

'Yes, hang on, Harriet. I thought you'd conned her and she was out for revenge,' Denny says, tossing the apple back towards me. It lands at my feet with a dull thud.

I glare at Robert.

'Don't look at me,' Robert says, holding up his hands. 'You know what a gossip he is. I have no idea how he finds out half of what he does.'

Denny shrugs. 'I'm a very curious person.'

'It was a false alarm, if you must know. Not that it's anything to do with you.'

'As thrilling as this is,' Mrs Elton drawls, retreating into her grander-than-thou persona, 'don't you think it's about time we got down to business?'

'And our business is?' Robert asks, settling himself on the bale of hay next to Denny. Denny huffs as he's forced to move over to accommodate his lover.

'Finding Mrs Churchill's killer,' I say.

Denny claps his hands together with mad enthusiasm. Robert rolls his eyes.

'So, who's our prime suspect?' Denny asks.

'Well, Jane Fairfax claims to have pushed Mrs Churchill down the stairs at the Bateses' apartment—'

'And she had good reason for it,' Robert mumbles.

'—but I don't think she did it. She's covering for someone. And, whoever it is has to be on the suspect list for Mrs Churchill's eventual poisoning. If they had reason enough to push her down the stairs, they had reason enough to finish her off at Richmond when that didn't work. So we need to find out who Jane is covering for.'

'Last time we had this conversation, you thought it was *her*,' Robert says, gesturing towards Mrs Elton.

'That was after I saw you arguing with Mrs Churchill,' I tell Mrs Elton, 'and before I knew you were working for her.'

'I did not murder her, I assure you. And if you want to know my whereabouts at the time of her fall, you can ask my *caro sposo*. He had a bad back after all that strawberry picking and so I took him home and gave him a rather lengthy massage.'

I really didn't need that image in my head.

'So, if Mrs Elton here didn't murder Mrs Churchill, who else could it be?' Denny asks.

'Well, Mr Weston sent her a threatening letter shortly before her death and then stole it back to cover his tracks afterwards.' I hand the letter to Robert.

He reads it with a frown, Denny looming over his shoulder.

'What was the "sordid secret"?' Robert asks.

I shake my head. 'We don't know.'

'Not even her?' Robert nods towards Mrs Elton.

'I am here, you know. You can ask me questions directly.'

Robert ignores her.

'If anyone knows anything about Mrs Churchill's secret,' I say, 'it's bound to be Wakefield. The butler always knows something. But I doubt we'll get much out of him. He's an odd sort.'

'Odd in the homicidal maniac kind of way?' Denny asks.

'I wouldn't put anything past him.' Wakefield had looked at me as if *I* was the killer, although that could have been an elaborate double bluff to throw me off his scent. Working for Mrs Churchill would be enough to tip anyone over the edge.

'Wakefield is as straightlaced as they come,' Mrs Elton responds. 'I doubt he would consider it good etiquette to murder his employer. And, besides, if he did do it, I suspect he would be more subtle about it.'

'Is it possible Mr Weston was the person at the Bateses' apartment? Could Jane have been covering for him?' Robert asks, continuing to snub Mrs Elton.

'No. He was at Donwell Abbey all day. It couldn't have been him,' I say.

'Actually, he might not have been there the entire time,' Mrs Elton says. 'I saw him go outside as Jane rushed off, and he certainly wasn't around when I left shortly after.'

'So he could have followed Jane back to Highbury and argued with Mrs Churchill there,' Denny says. 'It's likely she would have wanted to have it out with him about the letter. He pushed her for being a miserable old bat. Down she went.'

'All right, so he may have pushed her,' I allow, 'but why would Jane cover for him? And, even if he did push her in a rage, why would he then send her a poisoned parcel to finish the job? As long as he held a secret over her, he had her in his power. He had no reason to kill Mrs Churchill. An accident. A crime of passion. I could see that. But the parcel was premeditated. Plus, he sent a second letter, showing his remorse for threatening Mrs Churchill. Why would he then kill her?'

Robert rubs the back of his head. 'So you're saying it wasn't Mr Weston?'

'I'm saying it doesn't seem likely. But we should keep an eye on him, just in case. Your job, Robert. Mrs Elton, you're on Jane. I don't believe she pushed Mrs Churchill down those stairs. We need to find out who she was covering for.'

I still don't fully trust Mrs Elton, and so sticking her with the person I think is least likely to have killed Mrs Churchill seems like the best bet. Besides, I still fear that Jane is in danger from Durand and I can't think of a more persistent bodyguard than Mrs Elton.

'What about me?' Denny asks. 'I'm quite happy to lounge around here looking pretty. Offer the odd bit of moral support, that sort of thing.'

'I'm afraid not. Denny, you're with me.' I draw him aside and lower my voice to ensure that Robert doesn't hear. 'We're going to follow the money.'

‹I would just like to let it be known I think this is quite possibly the worst idea you've ever had. And that's saying something. I tell you, I want no part in it.'

I raise my eyebrow at Denny. 'You're hardly in a position to refuse me, considering the secret I'm keeping for you,' I say, gesturing towards the trapdoor as it swings open.

Denny glowers at me. 'I'm surprised you haven't told Robert already, just to spite me.'

'The thought has crossed my mind,' I mutter as I climb down the ladder behind him. The truth is, if I had told Robert about Denny's continued gambling habit, I wouldn't have been able to use it to convince Denny to sneak me into Durand's lair.

I'm grateful for Denny's presence as I blunder down the cold, dank corridor. A row of feeble lanterns lines the walls, giving out enough light for me to see a few feet ahead. I stay close to Denny, clutching his elbow when something large and furry brushes against my ankle.

Please don't let it be a giant rat.

We reach the end of the corridor at last and stand in front of a large, oak door. Denny raps upon it, executing a secret knock so complex I suspect he's doing it to mess with me.

The door inches open with a groan to reveal a huge brute with a scar across his cheek and one eye missing. He holds a pistol to Denny's head. 'Password?' he demands. His voice is thin and reedy.

'Come on. You know me,' Denny says, slapping him on the shoulder.

'Password,' the brute repeats, unmoved by Denny's show of camaraderie.

'Denny, just give him the password.'

'Fine. It's *Udolpho*. But I can't see why you bother with the password when you know every person who comes in here.'

'I don't know her,' the brute points out, looking me up and down as if trying to assess the level of threat I might pose to his master.

'She's with me,' Denny says, sounding thoroughly dismayed at the prospect.

'If it helps,' I say, 'I'm a big fan of *Udolpho*.'

'It doesn't,' he replies. 'And, if I'm going to let you in, I'll need to take that pistol.'

Denny whips round and scowls at me. 'You brought a pistol?' he hisses.

'You're the one who keeps warning me how dangerous he is.'

'Yes, but I didn't mean—' Denny breaks off as the brute snatches up my pistol and steps aside to admit us.

The inner sanctum couldn't be more of a contrast to the dank corridor. The room is bedecked in teal and gold silk damask, illuminated by dozens of gold lanterns hanging from the ceiling. There's a velvet chaise longue in the middle of the room with a lithe, dark-haired man in a jade silk banyan draped across it. He has a cigar in one hand and a glass of wine in the other. His gaze sweeps across my body as I enter the room.

'And who might you be, *ma chérie*?' he says, propping himself up on his elbows. His accent is thick, but his English is as perfect as his décor.

'I have come to pay off Frank Churchill's debts.'

Durand sits up and puts down his glass of wine, tapping his slender fingers against the table. He nods towards Denny. 'Leave us.'

'Harriet, I don't think that's a good idea.'

'It's all right, Denny. It's better if I speak to Monsieur Durand alone.'

'I won't hurt the girl,' Durand assures him, waving his cigar in my direction. 'Not if it means I might get my money.'

'I'll be right outside if you need me,' Denny says, giving my arm a quick squeeze as he retreats.

It's not a huge comfort to know that Denny is my only line of defence against Durand. Well, apart from the dagger I concealed in my boot.

'Would you care for a glass of wine, Miss Smith? It's a Bordeaux.'

Considering all the poison that's been floating around recently, I would rather not accept the drink, but something tells me it might be more dangerous to refuse a Frenchman's wine than to risk being poisoned by it. Particularly when said Frenchman is a hardened criminal who happens to know your name.

'You know who I am,' I say, as he pours me a glass of wine and gestures for me to sit beside him.

'I make it my business to find out all I can about beautiful young ladies who hang around outside my establishment. Particularly when they turn out to be notorious con women.'

I remain standing as I take a sip of my wine. It smells of soil and pencil lead and tastes even worse. 'It's very good,' I say, arranging my features into a mask of contentment.

'It is excellent. Do you think I would offer a lady guest wine that was merely "very good"?' he says, imitating my accent. 'Even if she is an uninvited guest.'

'An uninvited guest with a gift for you,' I remind him, pulling Mrs Churchill's five thousand pounds from my reticule and handing it over.

He snorts. 'It's hardly a gift if it is my own money.' He rises from the chaise longue and hands it back to me, shaking his head. 'I'm afraid that will not cover it.'

'Not cover it? Good Lord! Who does Frank think he is – the Duchess of Devonshire? How much does he owe?'

'I cannot disclose my clients' personal business.'

'How am I supposed to pay you if you don't tell me how much he owes?' I hold my breath as Durand blows a cloud of cigar smoke into my face. My eyes sting and a lump forms at the back of my throat.

Durand's eyes move from the frayed hem of my gown to my scuffed leather boots. 'I don't think you could afford it, *ma chérie*. You seem like a nice girl. You don't want to get mixed up in all this.'

'I'm already mixed up in this, I'm afraid.' I hand him the anonymous note. 'You sent this to Mrs Churchill.'

He shrugs. 'You cannot prove it.'

'No. But I know it was you. And it's not the first time you've contacted her either. You'd already made a house call to Mrs Churchill and Frank wasn't very happy about it, was he?'

'Frank isn't really in a position to be unhappy with me right now,' he says, stepping so close that I can smell the jasmine and orange blossom on his skin.

I stand my ground. 'I'm afraid it's not just about debts and moneylending any more, *monsieur*. It's about murder.'

'Murder?' Durand frowns. 'I thought the old hag died of a seizure?'

'No. She was poisoned by an anonymous parcel. I was there. I witnessed the whole thing.'

'Ah, that is unfortunate.' I'm not sure if he's referring to Mrs Churchill's murder or my witnessing it.

'I imagine it might be bad for business if word got out that you were murdering your clients' relatives when they didn't pay up.'

His smile is all teeth. 'On the contrary, I suspect it would have the opposite effect. But, you see, there was no point trying to get the money from Mrs Churchill, for the simple reason that she had none. Or, at least, none that I could get at.'

The five thousand pounds in my hands says otherwise, as do the family heirlooms I've returned to her – although they are now missing, of course. I wonder if Durand has them.

'You're thinking of her jewellery,' Durand says, as if he can read my mind, 'but it was all fake, I'm afraid. Believe me, I checked.'

I'm not the only one who has been rummaging around in Mrs Churchill's jewellery box, it seems. She had obviously kept the heirlooms hidden away somewhere but, apparently, Durand doesn't know about these.

'She must have had other funds,' I say.

'Oh yes, she did. She's a clever woman. Or, at least, she was,' Durand corrects himself, 'before she got herself killed. She had squirrelled away quite the fortune over the years. But wherever she kept it, I couldn't find a way to get at it. I put my best men on it. Frank's inheritance was tied up, of course, until he turned twenty-five, but she had plenty of her own money. Including the trust she had set up for a Mrs Emily Parker. Thirty thousand pounds to be paid to her in the event of Mrs Churchill's death. We couldn't get at that either. Turns out Mrs Parker is already dead, along with her husband, but the trust has passed over to her brother-in-law.'

Emily Parker? Could this be Mrs Churchill's lady's maid? But why would Mrs Churchill leave such a large amount to a servant, however fond of her she was?

'This brother-in-law, Parker. Did he live in Weymouth, by any chance?'

Durand aims a puff of cigar smoke in my direction. 'You *are* well informed, *ma chérie*. Mr Ernest Parker of Weymouth.'

Mrs Churchill's lady's maid was related to the boatman in Weymouth?

It doesn't make any sense.

'When did you send the note to Mrs Churchill?'

Durand shrugs. 'The day of your little trip to Box Hill.'

You have two days to acquire the funds.

Mrs Churchill died the day after Box Hill. One day before Durand intended to collect the money. 'She died before she could read it,' I tell him.

'There wasn't really much point in me sending it if I was going to kill her before she opened it, was there? And before her time was up to acquire the funds, at that.'

'It could have been a double bluff. Something to make you appear innocent.'

He smiles. 'If it was, it evidently didn't work on you, *ma chérie*.'

But Durand is right. There was no sense in sending that note and then killing Mrs Churchill before the two days were up. If he was really planning to kill her, why incriminate himself by sending the note at all?

I don't think he did this. 'Thank you for the wine, Monsieur Durand.'

'You haven't finished it,' he says.

'I'm working.'

'Hmmm. Clever girl. Best to keep a clear head. Do feel

free to drop by again, won't you? When you're not working, of course. I have a feeling you'd do well at the card tables.'

'Perhaps a little too well.'

He laughs. 'Yes, perhaps you might. Still, I should like to see it.'

'Good day, *monsieur*.'

'*Au revoir, ma chérie*. And, if you happen to see Frank, tell him I want my money, or perhaps I'll pay a visit to that pretty little fiancée of his next.'

'I'll be sure to pass that on.'

I nearly knock Denny off his feet as I open the door. 'Come on. We're leaving,' I tell him as I retrieve my pistol from Durand's brute.

'Did you get what you came for?' Denny says, trying to pretend he wasn't eavesdropping.

'Ernest Parker,' I say.

'Who's he?'

'He's the key to solving Mrs Churchill's murder. And I think I know how to find him.'

CHAPTER 26

Rule number twenty-six: Use other people's ignorance to your own advantage.

'Oh, Miss Smith, so good of you to say goodbye to Jane – I know she'll be delighted to see you – that is, she is packing, but I'm sure – oh, Mrs Elton, put it over there, if you please—' Miss Bates is flapping around her apartment like an overgrown bat.

The morning sun streaks through the window as Mrs Elton carries a pile of Jane's books into the parlour and balances them on the edge of the tea table. It was too late to call on Jane when I returned from London yesterday and, besides, my interview with her will require some tact and so it's better that Denny is not with me.

'Goodness, you must think me a poor host, Miss Smith. I will fetch you some tea – or, perhaps you are too hot for tea – I always take tea on a hot day but some people—'

'Tea will be fine, Miss Bates.' I turn to Mrs Elton as Miss Bates bustles off to the kitchen. 'Jane is leaving?' I say softly.

'She has finally accepted the governess position at Mrs Smallridge's.' Mrs Elton lowers her voice to match mine.

'Well, Mrs Churchill has her wish, at last. It's a shame she's not here to enjoy it.'

'I suppose it was Mrs Churchill's death that pushed Jane over the edge,' Mrs Elton replies. 'I suspect she still thinks it was the fall that killed Mrs Churchill. I haven't corrected her.'

'I need to speak to Jane. Alone.'

'Leave it to me,' Mrs Elton says as Miss Bates appears with a tray.

'Now, Miss Smith – I'm afraid I could not remember – do you take milk or cream? Mother always takes cream when we have it, but Jane cannot stand the sweetness – Mr Knightley does not care for it either, though that's hardly surprising as he doesn't have a sweet tooth in general. I would have offered you a slice of apple pie – Mr Knightley gave us such wonderful apples – the last of his stock – except that it is all gone. So delicious. Mother had three whole slices. I think we may have some teacakes, although I'm not quite sure exactly where they—'

'Miss Bates, I must ask you a favour,' Mrs Elton says, before our hostess can give us a lecture on the culinary preferences of the entire village. 'I'm going out to purchase a farewell gift for Jane, but I don't know what to get her. I would greatly appreciate your opinion.'

'Oh, well, I'm not always the best person at making decisions, but I'm sure I will do my best – Jane is such a generous soul, of course, never asks for anything – except oughtn't I to wait until Miss Smith—'

'Miss Smith is fine here with her tea, aren't you, Miss Smith?' Mrs Elton says, linking arms with Miss Bates and steering her towards the door.

'Oh, well, if you're sure, Miss Smith—'

Mrs Elton drags her through the door before I have chance to respond. I can hear Jane shuffling around in her bedroom. I stand in the open doorway, watching as she folds her gowns with shaking fingers. She is colourless and painfully thin, as if all the life has been sucked out of her. I feel a pang of guilt at the thought of Frank's lips on my neck. Even though it's quite evident the whole thing is over. Jane is leaving Highbury – she'll finally be safe.

'You are leaving, Miss Fairfax?'

Jane doesn't turn at the sound of my voice. 'There is nothing left for me here,' she says as she removes another gown from her chest of drawers.

I'm itching to ask her about Weymouth and Ernest Parker, but I suspect she would clam up if I did. I need to work up to it. And she'll only tell me the full story if there's more than her own happiness at stake.

I think I've worked it out at last. Who really pushed Mrs Churchill. Someone I should have considered from the beginning. And, if I can convince them to own up, it might make Jane a little more talkative.

I step into the room and sit down on Jane's bed, careful

not to disturb her neatly folded gowns. 'Why did you push Mrs Churchill?'

Jane reaches into the drawer for another gown, avoiding my gaze. 'We were arguing,' she says finally.

'About what?'

'I don't fully remember.'

'It's funny. Neither did Mrs Churchill when I asked her.'

'Well,' she says, finally meeting my gaze, 'you already know about my secret engagement with Frank Churchill. It was about that.'

'She tried to pay you off? But you refused the three thousand pounds she offered you?'

'I would not take her money,' Jane says, throwing her gown onto the bed.

I'm certain now that Jane didn't push Mrs Churchill. She knows nothing about the money – or else she would have corrected me on the amount.

'Except she never offered you the money, did she?'

'How do you—'

'I know a lot more than you think I do,' I say, rising from the bed. 'Now, shall we try again? What were you arguing about with Mrs Churchill? Why did you push her?'

'I— I don't—'

'Who is Ernest Parker?'

Jane's eyes widen and she turns away in an attempt to hide her shock. 'I don't know what you're talking about.'

'Why did you push Mrs Churchill?' I ask again.

'Perhaps I didn't. Perhaps she tripped.'

'No. You said you pushed her. That's what you told me, in the heat of the moment. You pushed her. She fell. Hit her head. And now she's dead. You killed her.'

There are tears in Jane's eyes as she turns back towards me. She opens her mouth to respond, but she can only let out a strangled sob. She's not looking at me, but at the figure standing behind me in the parlour. The person I had been hoping to draw in.

'Jane didn't push Mrs Churchill,' says the voice from the parlour. 'I did. And I would do it again.'

✳

It was Mr Knightley's apples that finally got me there. I almost didn't notice it. Miss Bickerton talks such a lot of nonsense that I rarely pay attention to what she's saying. But then Denny was throwing that apple around at Abbey-Mill Farm and I suppose it got me thinking about it again. Mr Knightley has been very generous with his apples this year, but I've only heard of one complaint against them.

'Grandmama, don't,' Jane says as Mrs Bates steps into the bedroom.

And I bet if I'd bothered to check the date when Mrs Bates was taken ill after consuming a slice of apple pie at Mrs Goddard's, I would have discovered it was the same day as the strawberry party at Donwell Abbey. I hadn't even thought to check on her whereabouts. But who in their right mind would suspect frail old Mrs Bates of murder?

'Jane, please,' Mrs Bates says, laying a hand on her

granddaughter's back. 'This has gone on too long. I would never forgive myself if you took the blame for it.' She turns towards me with steel in her eyes. 'I pushed Mrs Churchill. I'm the one who killed her.'

'I think it might be best if we sit down,' I tell Jane, shepherding her into the parlour.

'I know everything that went on in Weymouth, you see,' says Mrs Bates, settling back in her armchair as I sink down onto the sofa, pushing aside one of Jane's embroidered cushions. Jane perches on the arm of the sofa, angled towards her grandmother. 'Jane's engagement to Frank Churchill. The boating accident. Mr Dixon told me all.'

Jane is shaking her head. 'Grandmama, why didn't you come to me about it?'

Mrs Bates smiles sadly. 'I was selfish. Mr Dixon wrote to me when he couldn't dissuade you from coming to Highbury, begging me to convince you to leave, but I did nothing. I wanted to keep you here. Our lives have been so much brighter with you around. But, after you found the scorpion in your room, I knew that Mr Dixon was right. You were in danger as long as you stayed in Highbury. As long as you were with Frank, I knew she was still out to get you.'

'Mrs Churchill didn't send the scorpion, Grandmama.'

'No,' I say. 'That was Emma.' I'm only just realising it now, but it makes complete sense.

Jane whips round to face me. 'You can't possibly know that.'

327

'But I'm right, aren't I? It was something Emma said about you the first time I met her. "She knows how to hold a grudge. And sometimes grudges can go too far." I thought she was just being dramatic but, the more I saw you together, the more I realised there was something in what she said. You knew the scorpion was from Emma, as soon as you laid eyes on it. There was a message in it that I couldn't understand, but you did. And then there was the box your scorpion came in. I knew I'd seen it somewhere before. Emma has a set of them at Hartfield. I was staring right at one of them the day Frank rescued me from the Romani.' My cheeks flush as I feel Frank's arms around me. Fortunately, Jane is too preoccupied to notice that I'm blushing over her ex-fiancé.

'We never got on,' Jane admits, staring at her hands. 'Not even as children. It was little things at first. Emma broke my doll. Stole my music master. Humiliated me in front of Mr Knightley. I could cope with that. But the last time I was in Highbury, two years ago, she pushed it too far. She took a book of mine. *The Italian* – my mother's copy – and lost it. She didn't even apologise. I tore up her room looking for it, but it wasn't there.'

'And so you took something from her in retaliation. A ring. A silver ring with a scorpion intaglio.'

I see the shame in her eyes as Jane raises her head. 'I knew it had belonged to her mother. Knew what it meant to her. So I took it. I wanted her to know how it felt.'

'And she went one better and sent you a real scorpion

to welcome you back to Highbury. Or, more likely, to drive you away again.'

Emma Woodhouse doesn't do things by halves . . .

Jane raises her chin. 'I suppose I deserved it.'

Mrs Bates is shaking her head. 'No. Mrs Churchill sent the scorpion,' she insists. 'She was still a danger to you. I saw her through the window at Mrs Goddard's and so I made an excuse and rushed home to warn you.'

'It was you who sent the messenger to Donwell Abbey,' I say. 'To warn Jane that Mrs Churchill was in Highbury.'

Mrs Bates nods. 'Jane came home in a terrible state. I sent her to lie down. When Mrs Churchill turned up, ranting and raving about Jane's relationship with Frank and how she was going to put a stop to it all, I couldn't let her do it.' She turns towards Jane. 'I didn't want you to end up like poor Hetty, penniless and ridiculed. So I pushed her.'

'I must have fallen asleep,' Jane says, 'because it wasn't until I heard the noise on the stairs that I realised anything was the matter.'

Mrs Bates's features harden as she turns from Jane to me. 'I'm not sorry,' she says, folding her arms. 'After what she did to Jane in Weymouth—'

'Grandmama.' Jane shoots her a warning glance.

I turn back to Jane. 'I think it's time you tell me what happened in Weymouth. I cannot help your grandmother unless you do.'

'You will help us?' Jane asks, leaning forward to clutch my arm.

'I will do my best.'

Jane looks to her grandmother.

'Best to make a clean breast of it,' Mrs Bates replies.

Jane takes a deep breath and nods. 'It was a few weeks into my stay at Weymouth when Frank proposed to me. I was so swept up by the romance of it all, and the worry of what would become of me now Miss Campbell was betrothed, that I almost said yes there and then. But my duty to the Campbells and my aunt and Grandmama caught up with me before I could get too carried away. More than that, I was worried about how Frank's aunt would respond, for it was clear he hadn't spoken to her before approaching me. Frank is like that. He's led by his heart and doesn't often think of the consequences.'

I've been there.

'I told him that, although the Campbells had been very kind to me and given me a first-rate education, they had no dowry to bestow upon me. That must be reserved for their daughter.'

'And what did he say?'

'He said it didn't matter if I hadn't got a penny to my name. He was convinced that, once his aunt met me, she would fall in love with me, just as he had.'

The idea of Mrs Churchill falling in love with a penniless orphan who was angling to marry her nephew is a bit of a stretch, even for a dreamer like Frank.

'This is one of Frank's many faults, I'm afraid,' Jane says, reading my expression. 'He's lived such a life of luxury, he cannot imagine a scenario in which money and status actually matter. He's never had to do without them.'

'So you refused him?'

Jane hesitates. 'I didn't accept him. But I didn't refuse him either.'

Which, to a man like Frank Churchill, would be taken for tacit assent.

'The next day, we were to go on a boat trip. The Campbells. Mr Dixon. Frank, too. Mr Dixon had arranged it all but, when we got there, the boatman was nowhere to be seen. He had been taken ill and another man took his place. He told us he was a local fisherman who knew the waters well. There was something about him that made me want to stay on dry land, but the others seemed satisfied and so what could I do? He looked nervous to me. Shifty. He kept giving me sideways glances when he thought I couldn't see him and, when I turned in his direction, he would always make a point of busying himself with some non-existent chore.

'A couple of hours in, when the others were readying our picnic, he took me aside and asked me if I was Miss Fairfax, the lady who was keen to catch a glimpse of some puffins. I suppose he'd heard me saying so to Miss Campbell. He said we were just coming up to a spot where they were known to nest among the cliffs and that, if I positioned myself at the stern of the vessel, I would get a good view of them. I forgot my dislike of him in the excitement of it all: I really did want to see the puffins. And so there I stood, alone. Watching. Waiting. I thought he was still behind me. I turned to ask him if I had missed the nesting site, but he had disappeared.'

Jane shivers and slides from the arm of the sofa onto the seat beside me, tucking up her legs to her chest. 'Suddenly, there was a violent jolt and I felt myself plunging over the rail. I was sure it was over right then. A single thought went through my head: *At least I don't have to worry about my future any more.* Because not knowing how I would make my way in the world, how I would survive without the Campbells, had been pure torture. But then I felt Mr Dixon's hands around my waist and he was pulling me back on board. Miss Campbell was screaming. Frank was shouting. But the boatman was as silent and pale as I was. I caught his gaze for a second, read the guilt in his eyes, and I knew it had been no accident.'

'And what made you suspect Mrs Churchill?'

'How do you know that I did?'

'Come on, Jane. It doesn't take a great leap of logic to arrive at that conclusion.'

Jane shrugs. 'I'm sure I saw her in Weymouth, the day Frank proposed to me.'

'Did you tell Frank?'

'How could I?' she asks, throwing up her hands. 'I had no proof. But the next time he asked me to marry him, I said yes.' Her lips curve up into a defiant smile.

I have a newfound respect for Jane Fairfax. To think Mrs Churchill's attempt to prevent Frank and Jane's engagement was the very thing that ensured it. I had been so certain Frank was behind the boating accident. But it all makes sense now.

I want her gone.

Mrs Churchill had very nearly succeeded that day.

'I killed her,' Mrs Bates says, rising to her feet. 'I am ready to face the consequences.'

'Sit down, Mrs Bates,' I say. 'You are no murderer.'

Mrs Bates frowns. 'But I pushed her.'

'It wasn't the fall that killed her.'

'Then what did?' Jane asks.

'A parcel laced with poison. Did you send her a parcel?' I ask Mrs Bates.

She shakes her head, confused.

'Did *you*?' I ask Jane.

'I did not,' she replies. 'Much as she might have deserved it.'

'Then you have nothing to worry about.'

'Why did you let me think my grandmother had killed her?' Jane asks, fiery-eyed.

I shrug. 'Mrs Bates was more likely to confess if she thought she was protecting you from an accusation of murder. And I suspected you would be more motivated to tell me what you knew if you feared your grandmother might be punished for the crime.'

Jane looks thoroughly disgusted at my subterfuge, but I'm past pleasing Jane Fairfax. There are more serious things at stake.

Like catching the real killer.

'You were looking for the boatman, with Mr Dixon's help. You found him, didn't you? I saw Mr Dixon's letter. Parker. Ernest Parker. *He's* the boatman.'

EP. Eden Pride. The name in Mrs Churchill's ledger. Mrs Churchill had paid Ernest Parker three thousand pounds to do away with Jane. And he had failed. Or perhaps his heart wasn't really in it once he met Jane. It's one thing to agree to arranging an 'accident' for a complete stranger, but once he had looked upon Jane's angelic face, who could blame him for not putting all his efforts into ensuring her demise?

It might also explain why Mrs Churchill has sold off all her jewellery and replaced it with cheap copies. He could have been blackmailing her. But, then, what about the connection to Emily Parker? Ernest Parker's sister-in-law. Mrs Churchill's lady's maid. Why leave her a fortune? And why transfer it to Ernest Parker after her death. Unless—

Mrs Churchill's sordid secret. Could it really be—

'You are well informed, Miss Smith. It seems you hardly need me at all.'

'Well, I know the boatman's name. But even if he's still in Weymouth, it won't be an easy task to find him.'

Jane smiles. 'I think I can help you with that,' she says, rising from the sofa and retreating to her room. She returns a minute later, clutching a letter in one hand and Emma's ring in the other. She presses the ring into my hand along with the letter. 'You will see that it is returned to Miss Woodhouse?'

I nod, slipping the ring into my pocket.

'Mr Dixon would not let the matter drop. He has been corresponding with the real boat owner in Weymouth for some months.'

'He has been a good friend to you.'

'He has. The mistake was that we were looking for a fisherman. Well, he *was* a fisherman, but not now. Since September last year, he has been the proprietor of a coaching inn. See for yourself,' she says, gesturing towards the letter.

I glance down at the address.

The Golden Lion, St Edmund Street, Weymouth.

No. It can't be.

Because I know that address. I've been there.

The Golden Lion, Weymouth. The place where I lost my mother.

CHAPTER 27

Rule number twenty-seven: *The sins of the father are inevitably visited upon the sons. If he doesn't have any sons, a long-suffering daughter will do.*

I've long since tried to purge my memories of Weymouth, although it's become increasingly difficult of late. The sand between my toes; the stink of fresh fish in my nostrils; the screech of gulls that were almost as big as I was. The starfish I found washed up on the beach, which I scooped up along with handfuls of shells. I lined them up on the garden wall when I got home, but the starfish blew away in the wind. I cried for a day. It wasn't really about the starfish, of course, but I'd already lost the thing most precious to me in the world and the starfish was the final straw.

I was seven years old when I climbed out of bed in the middle of the night at The Royal Hotel in Weymouth, past my snoring father, who was sprawled across the bed with a bottle of whisky gripped in his outstretched hand. I had shut my eyes tight against my parents' screaming match earlier in the evening, feigning sleep as I wrapped my pillow around my ears to muffle their venom. The fighting had been a feature for a while and I was fast learning to block it out. But all was quiet now, apart from Father's snores and the click of the bedroom door as my mother slipped out. I was afraid she was abandoning us, or else I never would have dared to follow. She couldn't leave me here with Father's rage and half-filled whisky bottles. If she was leaving, I was going with her.

I was halfway down the Esplanade before I missed my pelisse, but it was too late to head back for it. Mama would be furious if she knew I was out alone at such an hour, but I wasn't really alone. She was within shouting distance if anything went wrong, so I wasn't afraid. Mama would always protect me. She took a sharp right off the Esplanade and I ran to keep up, heart pounding. So long as I could see her, I felt safe. I had to duck back into the shadows as she slowed her pace and glanced nervously behind her, but I raised my head in time to see her slink into The Golden Lion. I couldn't think what she was doing there at this time of night; I could only wait for her to come out again.

The sun was rising as she tiptoed out of the inn, the air reverberating with the shouts of fishermen as they loaded their boats, and I could barely move from the cold. I tried to rise to greet Mama, no longer caring what she would say about my nocturnal escapade, but my legs were numb and I slumped to the ground, grazing my knee as the Colonel stepped out beside my mother and kissed her full on the lips. I knew the Colonel. He was a friend of my father's, with a fine moustache and pockets full of carrots which he let me feed to his dapple-grey mare. I had thought him kind. But he was a serpent who had tempted my mother away from us. I ran all the way back to our hotel, shook my father awake, wrestling the whisky bottle from his determined hand, and told him what I had seen. Mama never returned. So, you see, it's my fault. *I* broke up our family and destroyed my father in the process. I couldn't leave him, because I'm the one who drove him into his con-man life and turned him into an obsessive, unforgiving husk of a man.

The Weymouth connection. The Golden Lion. It cannot just be a coincidence. What if my father has been on my trail for much longer than I anticipated? What if he orchestrated this whole job, just to bring me back into his sphere of influence? What if Mrs Churchill's death is all because of me?

✳

I seem to be spending a lot of time staring at Robert's doorknocker nowadays. It's a nice doorknocker.

'Hello, Harriet,' Robert says, looking suspiciously ruffled as he opens the door just wide enough to admit me. Well, I squeeze through, in any case.

'Are you busy?' I ask as I stride into the kitchen.

'Actually, I was just about to—'

'Good. Because I could really use your help,' I say, pulling up a chair at the kitchen table and laying out my father's notes.

Robert leans forward to examine them. 'What are these?'

'Threats,' I say calmly. 'From my father. The first one arrived just after Sophia the maid died.'

'And you're telling me this only now because ...?'

'I would have told you at the time, except we'd just had a huge argument about your ill-judged love life—'

'I thought it was about your suicidal determination to start up a murder enquiry.'

'In any case, it wasn't good timing.'

'And this one?' he asks, waving the second note in front of my face. 'Why didn't you tell me about that?'

'Because I knew you'd blame it on Frank.'

'If the shoe fits—'

'It doesn't fit, though,' I say, placing Jane's sketch of Ernest Parker in front of him.

He looks at the sketch and then back at me. 'I'm sorry, what is this supposed to prove?'

'I found this sketch in Jane's room a while ago, along with a letter from Jane's friend Mr Dixon about the boatman who took them out on the water in Weymouth. When Jane had her accident. And then Monsieur Durand told me that some of Mrs Churchill's money was tied up in a trust to an Emily Parker of Weymouth and that it had passed on to her brother-in-law, Ernest Parker, after her death. And then Jane gave me—'

'Hang on. You went to see Durand?'

'Er, yes.' It's too late to backtrack now.

'How on earth did you manage to—' Robert breaks off as realisation dawns. 'I see. Your *witness*.'

'Now, don't blame Denny. He didn't want to take me there. I forced him into it.'

'I don't think Denny could be forced into anything.'

'Well, he tried to talk me out of it. Anyway, you're missing the point,' I say with a wave of my hand. 'Jane told me Mrs Churchill tried to kill her in Weymouth. She hired a boatman to dash Jane over the side of the vessel.'

'Is that why Jane pushed her down the stairs?'

'That wasn't Jane. It was Mrs Bates. But—'

'Mrs Bates? Are you sure?' Robert is staring at me as if I've just declared that Byron has taken holy orders.

'Yes, I'm quite sure. But that's not important right now. It turns out Ernest Parker was the boatman from Weymouth. And Mr Dixon discovered that he is now the proprietor of The Golden Lion in Weymouth.'

Robert shrugs and scratches his ear.

'The Golden Lion. It's where I last saw my mother. Where I caught her with the Colonel.'

'So?'

Is Robert really this dense?

'Can't you see? This whole case. It's *him*. It's all him. One big con.'

'Harriet, you're not making any sense.'

I'm making perfect sense. He's just not listening.

'Jane told me Mrs Churchill paid a boatman in

Weymouth to arrange a little accident for her and, meanwhile, I get hired to get rid of Jane. And the boatman happens to live at an address that has particular significance for my father.'

'So, you're saying . . .' Robert leans over the table, looking at me as if I've just escaped from a lunatic asylum. 'What are you saying, Harriet?'

'That this Parker fellow, the boatman, clearly has something to do with my father. My father set the whole thing up. This case. My job with Mrs Churchill.'

'Why would he do that?'

I slam my fist against the table, nails digging deep into my palm. 'Because he wanted me to fail. Because he couldn't stand the thought of me abandoning him, like my mother did. He wanted to show me that I needed him. So, he got Mrs Elton to recommend me to Mrs Churchill and he set me up on a job he knew I couldn't handle.'

'And Mrs Churchill's murder?'

I hadn't let myself dwell on it, but I have to voice my suspicions now, if I'm ever to get Robert back on side. 'He killed her. He did it to punish me. To show me that I can't work alone. That I can never escape him.'

Robert edges round the table and kneels beside me, taking my hands in his. 'Harriet, you're my best friend, so please know this comes from a place of love. You must realise that this is completely insane. Can't you see what he's doing to you?'

I sigh and roll my eyes. 'You still think it's Frank?'

Robert shakes his head. 'I don't know if it's Frank. I don't care if it's him, other than how it affects you. But I can guarantee with absolute certainty that your father didn't murder Mrs Churchill. He didn't set this whole thing up. He isn't in Highbury. You've been so convinced he'd catch up with you and exact his revenge, you didn't stop to consider he might not care enough to come after you.'

'No. You don't know him like I do.'

Father wouldn't leave me.

'I know him well enough to see he's abandoned you, just like your mother did.' He trails his fingers through my dishevelled curls. 'You haven't been forging your own path here in Highbury. You're still following in your father's footsteps. This elaborate solution has been conjured up by your fevered imagination. Please, you need to let this go. You need to stop chasing your father. Because he's not chasing you.'

I thought Robert would understand. I thought he would be on my side. 'You're wrong. You don't know anything.' I pull his hand from my hair.

'I know you can be so much more than this. If you just let him go.'

'Oh, yes, and you're an expert at letting people go, aren't you, Robert? How's Mr Knightley?'

Robert bows his head, cheeks flushed with anger. 'You were right about Mr Knightley. It was stupid of me to ever think of him. Dangerous. I've let him go, Harriet. He can marry Emma Woodhouse or whoever he will. I've made my peace with that.'

I snort in contempt. 'But you haven't learned, have you? You don't love Denny. You're using him. You're a hypocrite, Robert Martin. You criticise me for my deception. What about your lies to Denny? You'll be kicking him out of your bed as soon as the next Mr Knightley catches your eye.'

I hear a thump from the bedroom. Robert is still looking down at his feet as Denny stumbles into the kitchen, doing up the buttons of his rumpled shirt. He looks utterly crushed.

'Denny, I'm sorry. I didn't know you were—'

'It's all right, Harriet,' he says, patting my shoulder as he avoids looking at Robert. 'You didn't tell me anything I didn't already know.'

'Denny— Denny, wait.'

Denny turns towards Robert, finally, steel in his watery eyes. 'I've waited long enough.' He flicks me under the chin. 'Look after him, will you? Somebody needs to.'

I nod, despite the fact I'm in the middle of a blazing row with the man he's asking me to care for.

'Robert. I'm sorry. I wouldn't have said it if I'd known he was here.'

Robert laughs bitterly. 'No. You were being honest for once in your life.'

'I want to fix this, Robert. I really do, but I have to go to Weymouth right now.'

'That's right. Time to leave. It's what you do when things get tough. You did it with your father. You did with—'

'Don't you say his name.'

'Fitzwilliam. Colonel Francis Fitzwilliam. I don't know why you're so scared to say it. You did him a favour by abandoning him. He's had a lucky escape from you.'

I slap Robert so hard that he staggers backwards against the kitchen table. 'You said you'd always be here when I needed you,' I shout as he scrambles to his feet. 'But I suppose you're only willing to fulfil that promise when it suits you.'

'You don't need me right now, Harriet. You need *you*.' Robert pushes past me, leaving me standing in his kitchen, staring after him as he strides through the front door.

Robert is right about one thing. I'm the one who needs to step up. This is between me and my father, so it's just as well I'm on my own now. It's about time we had this out, and I need to stand on my own two feet to do it. It's time to return to Weymouth.

CHAPTER 28

Rule number twenty-eight: Never mind your money or your life. When travelling by mail coach, your most valuable commodity is personal space.

The mail coach stinks of whisky, piss and a baby's milky vomit. Said baby is currently wailing like a banshee and drooling over my pelisse, while its harried mother jigs it up and down on her knee, her meaty thigh pressing me into near non-existence. The balding, fat man sitting opposite is taking up three-quarters of the highly inadequate leg room afforded to the two of us and trying to engage me in conversation every time we knock knees. He finally gives up when I request, very politely, that he remove his hand from my leg after the third time he *accidentally* places it there.

Whoever designed the mail coach clearly never intended to travel by one. Every time I close my eyes in an attempt to imagine I'm anywhere else but here, I'm startled by the violent but sporadic snores of the drunk who is currently trying to nuzzle into the harried mother's neck, which pushes her further into my space. In the opposite corner is a rakishly handsome but emaciated young man who is reading Byron's *The Corsair*, looking around with disinterested contempt every few minutes and sighing loudly. I resolve to ignore him. If he looks good and reads Byron, he's probably trouble. And I'm in enough trouble right now.

I would have preferred to hire a private coach, but it would have been much more expensive and conspicuous. I didn't want to draw attention to myself as a lone woman out on the road. If someone is following, which I have no doubt they are (my father would hardly trust me to get to Weymouth all by myself), it is better to be in company. Even this company. It would have been cheaper to take a seat on the outside of the coach, but it's a long journey and I've heard horror stories of travellers dying of exposure to the elements and the coachman not even noticing until they reached their destination. Not that this is likely to happen in late June. I was loath to dip into Mrs Churchill's five thousand pounds because I still have a nagging doubt about keeping it, but I *am* doing this to catch her killer, so I suppose she would accept it as a necessary expense. In truth, I was lucky to get a seat at all at such short notice. There were already four passengers booked inside the coach before I arrived – five if you count the baby – but the coachman evidently decided that he could make a little extra money on the side by squeezing me in as well.

Byron boy has been glancing over at me with such

alarming frequency for the past half-hour that I'm starting to think he might be one of Father's spies. It's dark when we stop at the next coaching inn to change horses. I rummage in my reticule for Mrs Churchill's money and approach the coachman as he harnesses the new horses with impressive efficiency. There's no waiting around with the mail coach. They have a schedule and they will stick to it, leaving their passengers behind if they tarry too long.

'Are there any seats on the outside of the coach?' I ask, gesturing to the empty seats above him.

The coachman snorts. 'Not enjoying the company, love?'

'I would like some fresh air,' I say stiffly.

'Sorry, love, they're all taken.'

I haven't seen anyone up there during any of our stops other than the guard, but the coachman says it with such finality something tells me not to argue the point.

I climb back into the coach and squeeze myself into my corner. Despite the stink of sweat and vomit, the unbearable heat in the coach, and the persistent shrieks of the demon child who keeps grabbing at my face with sticky hands, I somehow fall asleep pressed up against the window.

I awake with a jolt. The coach is quiet, it's pitch black outside as I draw back the curtain, but I hear frantic shouts on the wind, the thunder of approaching hoofbeats and three distinct pistol shots. You hear horror stories of highwaymen holding up mail coaches in the middle of the night, but I came prepared for such an eventuality.

I reach for my own pistol, pulling it out from under my pelisse. I turn away from the window in time to see that Byron boy is awake, eyes on my pistol, but he quickly feigns sleep when he realises I'm watching him. I listen hard, ear pressed against the window as I wait for the coach to pull up, my pistol pointed firmly at the door, ready to blow away whichever poor bastard has had the bad luck to interrupt my journey. But the horses never slow and the shouting fades away as I'm lulled back to sleep by the steady rhythm of the coach.

Byron boy is staring determinedly out of the window when I awake at the next inn, pistol still in hand, and he leaps from the coach before I can catch his eye. As I slip out of the coach to stretch my legs, I see a hooded figure with a slight limp slipping into the shadows. I'm about to follow when the harried mother presses her sticky baby into my arms and hurries towards the coaching inn, clutching her stomach. The baby promptly starts wailing at me, sabotaging any attempt I might have made to trail the mysterious passenger. As the mother emerges from the inn a few minutes later and reclaims her baby, I wait by the coach, foot tapping. If the mystery man returns, I'm determined to see him coming.

'All right, ladies and gents,' the coachman shouts. I linger by the door.

Come on. Where are you?

'Are you coming, miss?' the coachman demands.

I nod, stepping into the coach as it jolts forward. As I peer through the window, I think I see a flash of black flitting towards the coach, but it's too dark to be sure. Byron boy has not returned either. I suppose my pistol has scared him away.

I drift off to visions of Weymouth beach. My skin peels in the scorching sun as my mother wades into the sea. I'm building an ambitious sandcastle with multiple turrets and a moat. Mama is waving to me from the water, shouting something I can't hear, but I need to finish my sandcastle so I turn away as her head bobs under the water. I bend down to scoop up a dead starfish from the sand, placing it triumphantly on the uppermost turret. I can't see Mama as I look back towards the sea, but suddenly my father is looming over me. He walks straight through my sandcastle fortress, destroying it completely and I watch with tear-filled eyes as my starfish sweeps out to sea.

'Miss. Miss?' There's a hand on my shoulder, shaking me awake. 'We're here,' the coachman says.

I take a deep breath and stretch out my limbs in the empty space. I jump down from the coach, my eyes watering as I squint against the morning sunlight. The muggy air takes my breath away and I'm soon throwing off my pelisse and longing for a good sea breeze. Seagulls squawk and dive at passing tourists. My nostrils are filled with the scent of sea salt, damp sand and fresh fish. I walk along the Esplanade, dodging hordes of screaming children and courting couples and one cackling little boy who is chasing after his poor sister with a crab in his outstretched hand. It feels like a different place altogether from the route I walked on the night I trailed my mother to The Golden Lion.

I make a detour to King George's not-so-subtle statue. I've always found it a bit tasteless, but there's a sense of familiarity to it which I'm craving right now. The locals are obsessed with King George (hence the massive statue), but who can blame them? He's transformed their humble little town into a fashionable seaside resort and now business is booming, even though he stopped visiting some years ago. If they hoped the statue would lure him back, it hasn't worked. Perhaps he grew bored of being the town celebrity. It must be a bit wearisome to be constantly followed around by a brass band who strike up a rousing rendition of 'God Save the King' every time you emerge from your bathing machine.

I feel eyes on my back. I can't see anything suspicious as I glance over my shoulder, trying to be subtle about it. I step off the Esplanade and onto the golden beach, the sand like a velvet carpet beneath my feet. I look out across the beach, thinking of the last time I was here. The last time I saw—

There's a hint of movement behind me and it takes all my restraint not to turn around to confront my pursuer. Instead, I quicken my pace, heading for a gaggle of young women who are promenading across the beach at surprising speed. I dip my head, weaving between them. One of the girls tuts at me and whispers something to her companion. Her companion shakes her head and glares at me. As I lower my gaze, I spot a gangly, blonde-haired girl of about seven or eight scrabbling through the sand a few feet away, her fingers grasping at a stranded jellyfish. I sidestep the group of young women and drop down into the sand, crawling over towards the intrepid explorer.

'Don't touch it,' I say, pushing her hands away from the jellyfish.

She wrinkles her freckled nose at me. 'It's dead,' she says, leaning in to give it another jab with her slender fingers.

'It's dangerous,' I counter, keeping my head down, hoping I've lost my pursuer. 'Jellyfish can still sting when they're dead, you know.'

She tucks a strand of hair behind her ear and raises an eyebrow. 'It's a *chrysaora hysoscella*. The sting barely hurts. *You're* more dangerous than it,' she says, giving me a sideways glance.

'Hmmm,' I say, surveying the crowds for any signs of my pursuer. The beach is busy, but nobody is paying us any attention. 'You might have a point there.'

The girl has gone back to examining her jellyfish, nose perilously close to its stingers.

'Can I ask you a favour?' The girl ignores me. 'Can you walk a little way down the beach with me?'

She snorts as she raises her head. 'Mother says I shouldn't speak to strangers.'

'It's a little late for that. Besides, you don't have to speak to me. Just walk.'

She narrows her eyes. 'What's in it for me?'

I offer her a coin.

She sighs loudly. 'I don't need money. I want *that*,' she says, pointing to the outline of the pistol under the pelisse draped over my arm.

'I'm not giving you a loaded pistol,' I hiss.

'Well, that's what I want,' she says, folding her arms.

'Look,' I say, fumbling around in my reticule. 'I can't give you my pistol, but I'll let you have some shot.'

She sighs again, but grabs the shot before I have time to question the wisdom of my decision. 'I suppose I'll have to find my own pistol,' she mumbles as she leaps to her feet. 'Come on, then,' she says, brushing the sand from her dress, dead jellyfish forgotten.

She chatters away as we walk, despite her mother's warnings. It's close to midday when we reach the Esplanade and I bid her adieu. 'Don't kill anyone with that,' I say, gesturing to the shot in her fist.

'Don't talk to any strangers,' she replies and skips away across the beach in search of new jellyfish to torture, no doubt.

I glance over my shoulder as I take a right onto St Edmund Street. If my pursuer is still behind me, they must be a long way back. I approach the inn and stare up at the golden lion statue above the door, recalling my mother's face as she stood beneath it, kissing the Colonel.

I ball my hands into fists and blink back tears. Now is definitely not the time to be thinking of my mother. My eyes dart to the sign to the left of the door. *Proprietor: Mr E. J. Parker.*

Is this the setting my father has picked for our inevitable confrontation? Is he lounging at the bar with a glass of whisky and a cigar, waiting for me?

I push open the door and slip inside. The stench of sweat and stale ale hits the back of my throat, making me gag. There's a bearded old man in the corner, slumped over a tankard, murmuring to himself. He looks like part of the furniture; a permanent fixture. He *is* that. He was sitting in the very same corner when I stayed here two years ago.

My father isn't here. The man behind the bar glances up at me as I cross the room. He has curly blond hair and a cleft lip. I recognise him immediately from Jane's sketch, but I'm careful not to show it. I don't want to spook him.

'Can I help you, miss?'

'I hope so,' I say with a smile. 'I'm looking for a room.'

'One moment,' he says, retreating into the corridor and shouting up the stairs. 'May! Young lady wants a room. Do you plan to stay long, miss?' he asks as he returns to the bar.

'Just a couple of nights.'

'Have you visited Weymouth before?' He picks up a stray glass from the bar.

'Yes. In fact, I've stayed here before. A few years ago. You were not the landlord then.'

'No. We have been here less than a year.'

A handsome girl with honey-blonde hair and the same shrewd eyes as Parker steps up to the bar.

'Ah, May. Room four is free, I think.'

'Yes, Father. They left this morning.'

'I would not have returned, except a friend of mine recommended it,' I say casually.

'And who is your friend?' he asks, smiling.

I hold his gaze. 'Mrs Churchill.'

The smile drops from his lips. He turns towards his daughter, but not quickly enough to conceal the glimmer of fear in his eyes. 'Don't think I recall a Mrs Churchill. Do you, May?'

'No, Father.'

'Perhaps you have the name wrong.'

'Perhaps,' I agree.

'I've just remembered, I already promised room four to a young man some half-hour ago.'

May frowns. 'It's not in the book.'

'No. I forgot to put it in. All our other rooms are full. You might try The Royal Hotel, down the street. It's a much bigger establishment than ours. I would advise your Mrs Churchill, too, that The Royal Hotel would be more to her taste. We're simple folk around here. We don't want any trouble.'

Either Ernest Parker doesn't know that Mrs Churchill is dead or he's pretending he doesn't.

'I know what you did for Mrs Churchill,' I say, lowering my voice. Parker glances nervously at his daughter. 'I know about the thirty thousand pounds that she left to your sister-in-law, Emily Parker, as well. And that it passed to you after her death.'

Parker turns towards May. 'Room four could do with a clean before the gent returns for it.'

May nods obediently and retreats towards the stairs, eyeing me warily as she goes. Parker watches her leave.

'Your brother was a coachman, was he not?'

'He was,' he says, turning back to me.

'He worked for Mrs Churchill at Enscombe. It's where he met Emily.'

'Yes.'

'Mrs Churchill was very upset when Emily left. She begged her to stay, didn't she?'

'So my brother told me.'

'Because Emily wasn't just Mrs Churchill's lady's maid, was she? She was her daughter. *That's* why she left all that money to her.'

Parker shrugs. 'Emily never wanted the money. *I* don't want it either.'

'But it's not your money, is it?' I say, realisation dawning. 'There was a reason Emily ran off with your brother in such a hurry. She was pregnant,' I add triumphantly.

Parker's shoulders slump as his eyes dart involuntarily towards the staircase.

It's all starting to make sense now.

'I don't want any trouble,' Parker hisses.

'Nor me,' I assure him, but it's too late for that. Trouble is already hurtling towards us like a runaway stagecoach and there's no stopping it now. I need to see this through.

The sunlight stings my eyes as I step out onto the street. The clock of St Mary's Church chimes midday. A group of young men are loitering across the street, glancing over at me with curious eyes and nudging each other encouragingly. One of the men, a muscled fisherman with golden curls, winks at me and takes a step forward. A carriage clatters down the street at breakneck speed. I hear the desperate shout of a voice I recognise somewhere behind me but, before I can turn to see who it is, I feel two firm hands on my back. They shove me hard, right into the path of the oncoming carriage.

CHAPTER 29

*Rule number twenty-nine: Your enemy's enemy
is a darn sight better than your enemy.*

I reach out my hands to break my fall, but it won't do much good if I'm trampled to death by a pair of tearaway carriage horses seconds later. On the plus side, the carriage is a glistening black barouche landau, so at least I'll go out in style. I had hoped the last thought I ever had would be a little more profound than this, but time isn't really on my side. And, as Hamlet would say, the rest is silence.

Except it's not silent. There's the thundering of the horses' hooves, their frightened whinnies as the driver attempts to pull them up, the futile shouts of pedestrians, and that low voice in my ear which says, 'I've got you, Harriet,' as strong arms encircle me and pull me backwards.

Father?

He wraps his limbs around me to break my fall and his momentum rolls us over so I end up sprawled on top of him in a very unladylike fashion.

'Hello, Harriet.'

It's not my father. It's Frank Churchill.

Frank smirks and pushes a curl of hair from my eyes. 'Fancy seeing you here.'

Meanwhile, the driver of the barouche has pulled up and leapt out, abandoning his passengers. 'Miss, I— I'm sorry. I— I didn't see you until it was too late to stop.' He's in worse shape than I am. One look at his pallid face prompts me to haul myself off Frank and rise to my feet more quickly than I would have done otherwise.

A calloused hand grips my elbow and I turn to see the golden-haired sailor from across the street peering down at me with anxious eyes. 'Are you all right, miss?'

'She's fine,' Frank says, brushing off his breeches and pulling me away from the sailor, fingernails digging into my forearm. 'You're fine, aren't you?'

'I am, thank you,' I say, directing my words at the handsome sailor, who bows out gracefully when he sees I'm already spoken for. Frank drops my arm and starts walking in haphazard circles, scanning the crowds. He stops, nods and takes my hand, tugging me towards the beach.

'What are you doing? Where are we going?' I ask, running to keep up as Frank weaves his way through the tourists.

'We're going to find out who just tried to kill you.'

Frank strides forward with purpose, as if he's following someone, but there are so many people on the beach I don't know how he could track a single figure. I'm enjoying the squeeze of his fingers against mine as he pulls me along.

There's a reassuring *I've got you* in his grip, but there are too many unanswered questions to savour the sensation for long.

'Frank, what are you doing here?'

'I followed you,' he says, skidding to a halt to avoid tripping over an obese pug who is waddling across our path. The pug snorts like a demon out of hell as its stubby legs propel it forwards and then plonks itself down on top of a sandcastle, sounding as if it's having a particularly violent asthma attack.

'You followed me? All the way from Highbury?' Could I really have been so distracted that I didn't notice? Father would be ashamed of me. But, then, Father is the reason I'm so off my game. 'Why?' I add, trying to read his expression.

'Because I don't trust you,' Frank says as he drags me across the beach. 'Because I knew you were up to something the moment I saw you sneaking out of our lodgings at Richmond the day the maid died.' He ducks behind a bathing machine and pulls me after him. 'And then there was the time I caught you under my aunt's bed,' he says, peering round the bathing machine like an absolute lunatic.

'Frank, what exactly are you looking at?' I ask, following his gaze as he stares at something in the middle distance.

'The person who pushed you,' Frank says, stepping from behind the bathing machine and striding across the beach again. 'And don't change the subject.'

This isn't the way to enjoy Weymouth beach. It should be leisurely walks and bare toes digging into the cool sand, not having your arm tugged out of its socket by a maniac who's pursuing someone you can't even see.

'I know you were working for my aunt,' Frank says, picking his way through a rabble of children who are digging a deep trench in the sand with determined fingers. 'I'm fairly certain now that you were hired to drive Jane away. Love her though I did, my aunt was accustomed to getting her own way and didn't much care who she had to hurt to achieve it.'

'She thought Jane was trying to kill her,' I say, feeling the sudden urge to defend Mrs Churchill.

It's not as if she can stand up for herself any more.

Frank stops and drops my hand, eyes roving across my face as if he's reading a book. 'You can't be serious?'

'I'm deadly serious. *Someone* was trying to kill her.'

'Kill her?' Frank asks, frowning. 'She told you that?'

I shrug. 'She showed me the evidence.'

'Of course, she would think it was Jane, wouldn't she?' Frank says, throwing up his hands as he resumes the task of stalking my invisible attacker. 'And you believed her?'

I shake my head. 'No. Not really. I thought it was *you.* But then the poor lady's maid was poisoned—'

'Poisoned?'

'Oh come on,' I say, rolling my eyes. 'You didn't really believe that nonsense about her weak heart, did you?'

Frank presses his lips together and quickens his pace.

'And then I considered it might have been Durand.'

Frank's head jerks towards me. 'You know about Durand?'

'Oh yes. I know everything you've been up to.'

He snorts. 'I doubt that. But you're wrong about Durand. He's a nasty piece of work, but even *he* wouldn't go that far.'

'Yes, I came to the same conclusion after I met him. It didn't make sense that he would send Mrs Churchill a warning note and then kill her before the time limit he'd given her to get the money.'

'You went to see Durand?'

'Of course I did. He was one of my prime suspects.'

Frank shakes his head in disbelief. 'I knew you weren't quite right in the head, but you really have no regard for your own safety, do you?'

I cock my head at him and smile. 'Admit it, you're a little bit impressed.'

He doesn't return my smile. 'What I can't understand,' he says, lengthening his stride, 'is what the hell you're doing now. My aunt is dead, if you hadn't noticed.'

'Yes. And it's my fault.'

'I'm sorry?'

It's very hard to have this conversation with Frank when he's pursuing some phantom assailant at a ridiculous pace in the midday heat.

'I was supposed to keep Mrs Churchill safe,' I say, 'but it turns out that *I* was the reason she wasn't safe all along.'

Frank glances at me, a hand brushing across his forehead. 'I don't understand.'

'Frank, I'm sorry, but I think my father poisoned your aunt.'

Frank stops and stares at me like I've completely lost my wits.

Perhaps I have.

'Your father?'

'Yes. He's a con man. We used to work together, but we had a falling-out last summer and, since I've been in Highbury, he's been sending me threatening notes cut from the copy of *Hamlet* he gave to me for my eighth birthday. It's all very dramatic.'

Frank's grip on my arm tightens as he pulls me along the beach. 'I don't see how this connects to him murdering my aunt.'

'Neither did I, until I found out about The Golden Lion.'

'The inn you visited?'

'Yes. When I discovered from Jane that it was the address of the boatman who took you out on the water in Weymouth—'

Frank's brow creases. 'When Jane had her accident?'

I take a deep breath. 'It wasn't an accident.'

'I'm sorry?'

'It wasn't an accident,' I repeat. 'Your aunt hired someone to kill Jane. A Mr Ernest Parker. Do you know him?'

Frank shakes his head, bewildered. 'My aunt used to have a coachman called Parker. He ran off with—'

'Emily. Your aunt's lady's maid.'

'Yes. How do you—'

'Ernest Parker was the coachman's brother. He was a fishermen, but he's the landlord of The Golden Lion coaching inn now. That's how I know for sure that this is my father's doing. You see, The Golden Lion has a special significance to him. He *has* to be involved. He set up this whole job to punish me. To prove to me that I can't work without him.'

'Let me get this straight. Your father killed my aunt to teach you a lesson?' He's looking at me with the same expression Robert did when I shared my theory with him.

'He didn't do it directly,' I say. 'That isn't his style.'

No. I see it now. He had an accomplice. Someone to do his dirty work. Someone who would gain a great deal from Mrs Churchill's death. My father is very good at reading people. Exploiting their weaknesses. Positioning them in the line of fire so that he can walk away unscathed.

'Then how did he do it?' Frank asks.

I shake my head. 'We will find out soon enough.'

'What on earth did you do to your father that makes you think he would resort to murder? I'm no stranger to family grudges, but *this*?'

'I abandoned him,' I say, head down. 'And this is his revenge.'

'Harriet—'

'It's like he said, "Call me what instrument you will, though you can fret me, you cannot play upon me."'

'Harriet, that wasn't your father.'

'No, I know. It's Hamlet.'

'No,' Frank says, stopping to scan the beach ahead. 'I mean, he didn't send the notes.'

'What?'

'Those notes. Your father didn't send them,' he says, cheeks flushed.

'How can you possibly know that?'

He reaches into his redingote pocket and pulls out a battered leather volume that is far too familiar. 'Because I did,' he says, handing me my mutilated copy of *Hamlet*.

'No.' I shake my head, pushing it back into his hands. 'I don't believe you.'

I don't *want* to believe him.

'It's true,' he says, sliding the book back into his pocket when it's evident I don't want it. 'I took it from your room after I first saw you at Richmond.'

'You couldn't know to take *Hamlet*. You couldn't know its significance.'

'You quoted *Hamlet* at me that night in the Coles' library. The book was under your pillow. It had an inscription inside. I guessed it had some value to you.'

'Why would you send those notes?'

'I wanted to warn you off. I was worried you were influencing Jane. After she broke off the engagement, I thought I could win her back, but you kept getting in the way.'

Frank pulls me forward as the crowds begin to thin around us. If my would-be murderer had come this way, surely we would have seen them by now?

'So you decided to terrorise me and stalk me all the way to Weymouth? Hang on,' I add, realising exactly how stupid

I've been. 'You set the Romani on me. You paid them to accost me and pass me the note so that you could swoop in and rescue me.' He doesn't deny it. 'And then you followed me here and you were brazen enough to take a seat on the very mail coach I was travelling in.'

Frank frowns at me. 'I wasn't on the mail coach.'

'You were,' I insist. 'On the outside of the coach.'

'I hired a horse and was following behind. I nearly lost you several times when I couldn't change horses quickly enough.'

'I don't believe you.' Somebody was on the mail coach with me, watching me. I know it.

'During the night, my horse was spooked and he bolted. I got too close to the coach and the guard fired several warning shots at me as I tried to pull back. I suppose he mistook me for a highwayman.'

'How many?'

'What?'

'How many shots?'

'I don't— Three. There were three shots, that I heard.'

I had heard them too. 'But I saw you, slipping from the coach,' I insist. 'It was dark, but I saw a figure in a black, hooded cloak.'

'Like that?' Frank says, gripping my arm and pointing a way along the coast, towards Bowleaze Cove.

I squint at the tiny figure who is making good progress up into the hills. Before Frank can stop me, I break into a run.

I fly down the beach towards the cove, chest heaving, a knife-sharp pain in my throat. I hear Frank shouting behind me, but I soon outstrip him. I kick up a cloud of sand as I run. Towards answers. Towards my father. I don't care what Frank says. If it wasn't Frank on the coach, there's only one person it could have been.

Except that means your own father tried to kill you.

I push the thought away as I sprint along the curve of the cove, slowing finally as I reach the steep terrain of the hills surrounding Bowleaze Cove. I can't see the black-clad figure from here, but I keep going, knowing that this is the way my father was heading. I bend over, hands on my knees, to catch my breath as I reach the crest of the hill. I can see King George on his white limestone horse over on Osmington Hill.

I quicken my pace again as I hurry along the clifftop. It's strange that my father would bring me here, to the place I sought shelter from him after I told him of my mother's affair. And his way of dealing with it? Getting rip-roaringly drunk and accusing me of making it up for attention. He had hurled his precious whisky bottle at the wall and a shard of glass had lodged just above my eyebrow. I had run from him then, down the Esplanade, across the beach, all the way to Bowleaze Cove.

I see a flash of black on the clifftop, but I'm distracted by Frank's call of 'Harriet, wait!' as he makes it to the top of the hill and, when I turn back again, there's nothing up ahead. The wind whistles in my ears, waves lap against the cliff and, although Frank isn't too far behind me and my father must be concealed near by, I suddenly feel very alone up here on the clifftop as I slip my arms into my pelisse and button it up. I'm my seven-year-old self again, heart pounding, palms sweating, as I seek the courage to face what lies ahead. I tucked my feet up to my chest that day, sobbing into my knees, waiting for someone to save me.

But nobody did. Eventually, exhausted and shivering, I skulked back to The Royal Hotel, where my father was passed out on the bed, vomit dripping from his chin. My mother was nowhere to be seen, but her clothes and luggage had disappeared. To this day, I don't know whether she carried them off herself or if my father threw them out in a fit of rage. But there's someone here now. I hear the soft tread of boots through the heather behind me.

'All right, Father,' I say, drawing my pistol and turning to face him. 'Let's have this out, once and for all.'

He lowers the hood of his cloak and looks me right in the eyes. Except it's not my father.

'Wakefield? I don't understand.'

The butler steps aside to reveal a tall figure standing ramrod straight behind him.

'Miss Smith,' she pronounces in that now-familiar tone of distaste. 'I did not expect to see you again.'

I didn't expect to see her either. Because she's supposed to be dead.

CHAPTER 30

Rule number thirty: When your murdered client comes back from the dead, make sure you're not hallucinating. And then demand an explanation.

Mrs Churchill doesn't look at all well. Better than dead, I suppose, but not by much. Her face is pale and gaunt, her gown hangs loosely from her body and her hair is so windswept that she looks like a heroine from a Gothic novel, caught in an ambush on some lonely moor.

I reach out and poke her with my pistol.

'You were dead,' I tell her. 'I saw.'

Those glassy eyes staring at me. I was sure then. I had failed her. I felt the shame of it. The guilt. And she used that against me.

'You saw what I wanted you to see, Miss Smith.'

'But the parcel,' I insist. 'I saw you open it. You collapsed. I collapsed.'

'I made up the parcel myself,' Mrs Churchill says, momentarily distracted by something behind me. I'm curious to know what it is, but I'm not about to turn my back on a woman who has just risen from the dead. 'There was nothing in it.'

The flash of white – the silver paper. The same paper Mrs Churchill used to wrap up the five thousand pounds. That's what had bothered me about the parcel. And the floral scent – lavender. I'd smelled it on her money, too. I thought I'd finally worked out who had killed Mrs Churchill. But it turns out she did it to herself.

I shake my head. 'But if there was nothing in the parcel—'

'I dosed your tea with a strong sedative and then feigned my own collapse.'

'But the doctor – he confirmed your death—'

'I instructed Matilda to call Dr Phillips rather than Dr Baxter,' Wakefield says. 'I told her that Dr Baxter was busy delivering a child.' He has positioned himself between me and Mrs Churchill, pistol drawn and aimed in my direction.

'You weren't really out on an errand,' I say, nodding at Wakefield. 'You were waiting for Mrs Churchill to drug me so you could swoop in and make sure that nothing went wrong.'

Wakefield's mouth twitches but he remains silent.

'Dr Phillips is a drunk,' Mrs Churchill adds. 'I knew he would barely examine my body and that Wakefield would step in if necessary. Besides, once you lost consciousness, I took a sedative strong enough to fool the sharpest of eyes. A much more potent concoction than the one I had administered to you. It is a very tricky formula – lethal if any of the ingredients are measured out imprecisely, but my father taught me well—'

'So, Matilda—'

'Did not know a thing about it,' Mrs Churchill replies, glancing over at Wakefield.

'And the funeral furnisher—'

'Was paid for his silence. They will bury a weighted coffin. For all intents and purposes, Mrs Churchill is dead.'

'What about Frank?'

'He had no idea. He was so distraught about my death that it was not difficult for Wakefield to keep him away from my body.'

I had hoped to hear a note of shame in her tone, a hint of remorse. There's nothing but cold, hard reason.

'But why? Why go to all that trouble? What was the point?'

Why do that to Frank?

'The point, Miss Smith,' Mrs Churchill snaps, 'is that I realised the only person who could protect me from the danger posed was me myself.'

'And my father? None of this has anything to do with him, does it?'

Mrs Churchill raises her chin. 'I have never met your father, Miss Smith, and, from what I have heard of him, I would not wish to.'

I lower my pistol.

Father isn't coming.

There's a dull ache in the pit of my stomach. Robert was right. I concocted this mad theory because I wanted my father to be pursuing me. I wanted him to care enough to track me down. But he doesn't care. He's never cared about me. I was a good con partner and when I wasn't that any longer, I ceased to be anything to him.

My mouth hardens as I glare at Mrs Churchill. 'You murdered poor Sophia. Why?' I thought that Sophia's death was a tragic accident. That Mrs Churchill had been the target. But with Mrs Churchill standing here in front of me, having made a miraculous recovery from her own untimely murder, I realise it's something else entirely.

Mrs Churchill folds her arms. 'That was not me.'

'I don't believe you,' I say, taking a step towards her.

She backs away, eyes wide. At first, I think it's me she's scared of but then she hisses, 'You brought him here?'

There's a shout on the wind and I turn to see Frank standing a few feet behind me. With his hair swept across his face and his lip curled into a snarl, he reminds me of a caged lion I once saw in the Royal menagerie. He has the same look of fear tinted with rage in his eyes as his gaze flits from me to his aunt. 'I don't understand,' he says, when he finally recovers enough to form his thoughts into words. 'Why would you do this?'

'Frank,' Mrs Churchill says, reaching a hand towards him. He shrinks away from her. 'You have to understand, it was the only way.'

'The only way to what? To stop me from marrying Jane?

To ruin my best chance of happiness? You set the whole thing up. Tried to make Jane look guilty. Hired Harriet to stop her. Faked your own death and let me mourn you. Do you realise what you've done?' He clenches his fist to suppress the tremor in his hand. A man like Frank is reluctant to show weakness, especially to a woman.

Mrs Churchill lets out a startling bark of laughter. 'I have done you a favour. It would never have worked between you and Jane. You need a firm hand.'

'A firm hand? I'm not an untamed horse! You cannot force people to bend to your will, or dispose of them when they don't comply.'

'That is not what I am doing,' Mrs Churchill protests.

'You tried to kill Jane!' Frank shouts, voice shaking with anger. 'Here in Weymouth. You paid a man to arrange an accident for her right in front of me. Harriet has told me all about it.'

I give Mrs Churchill an apologetic shrug. 'In my defence, I thought you were dead,' I say, gesturing towards her with my pistol.

Frank steps closer to me, eyes still on Mrs Churchill as he knocks the pistol from my grip and catches it in one smooth movement. 'Give me one good reason why I shouldn't shoot you right now?' he asks, hand steady as he approaches his aunt, pointing the pistol straight at her head. He has regained control of himself, and it's far more frightening than his rage. If I hadn't thought him capable of killing his aunt before, I believe it now. He will do it if I let him.

Mrs Churchill laughs. 'I am already dead.'

Frank cocks the pistol. 'Jane could have saved me. I could have been a good man. I *needed* her.'

'Frank.' I take a step forward.

'Don't move,' he warns, whirling round to face me.

I hold up my hands in surrender. 'Frank. You don't want to do this.'

His mouth stretches into a slow smile. 'I really think I do.'

'What about Jane?' I need to appeal to his Achilles heel. I need to draw out the fiery lover – ardent, impassioned. Because passionate people let their guard down. Make mistakes. Passionate people can be manipulated.

'It's too late for that,' he says, pistol aimed at his aunt once more.

'It will be if you pull that trigger. You have the capacity to be a good man. She brings it out in you.'

Frank shakes his head. 'Jane doesn't want me.' He scowls at his aunt with tear-filled eyes. '*She* has seen to that.'

'What will you do,' I ask, 'once you've killed your aunt?'

Frank shrugs. 'Perhaps I could partner up with you on your next con. We do make a good team.'

I try to look as if I haven't spent hours on end fantasising about this very thing. 'That's not what you want,' I say. It's not what I want either, tempting though it may be. I edge towards him. 'Put down the pistol, Frank, and you can fix this. Put down the pistol and you can go home to Jane.'

I'm lying, of course. Jane will not take him back. But if I can make him believe it, even for a second, then I can gain control of this situation.

And I need to be in control.

I try a different tack. 'What will Jane say when she hears what you've done? What will she think?'

The pistol twitches in his grip.

'She will think that it is *her* fault. That she has driven you to this.'

Frank's gaze slides from his aunt to me.

I have him now.

'She will not be able to live with the guilt of it.'

Frank shakes his head. 'It is not her guilt to bear.'

'But she will bear it anyway.'

He knows that I'm right.

Frank raises his head heavenward and closes his eyes. When he opens them again, I see that he has made his choice. 'So be it,' he says, lowering the pistol and dropping it to the ground in disgust. Mrs Churchill lets out a long-held breath as I bend down to retrieve my weapon and aim it in her direction.

It's time to take back control.

'Now, Mrs Churchill. We need to get a few things straight.'

Mrs Churchill snorts. '*You* will not shoot me.'

'No? Would you like to stake your life on that? Are you a gambling woman?'

'She won't do it, ma'am,' Wakefield says, pistol trained

on me. But I see the flicker of doubt in his eyes. And that's all I need.

'Poor Sophia didn't deserve to be murdered just to make the threat to your own life seem more convincing, Mrs Churchill. Jane didn't deserve to be terrorised by you. *I* didn't deserve to be used.'

'Frank, think about Jane,' Mrs Churchill pleads. 'She would not want this. You can go back to her.'

Grovelling really doesn't suit her.

I laugh. 'Frank's right. It's too late for him and Jane. I was only saying that to stop him shooting you.'

'And why did you stop him?'

'Because I wanted to do it myself.'

'He will not let you,' Mrs Churchill says, glancing at Frank, but she doesn't sound too convinced.

I turn towards Frank. 'It's a nice idea, us running off into the sunset, partners in crime. We could make a fortune.'

He bites his lip and nods as if he's actually considering it, but I can't tell whether it's real desire or just good acting. I can't tell if I'm acting, either. There's still something about Frank that calls to me. Something familiar but thrilling all at once.

'We just have to tie up a few loose ends first.' My finger caresses the trigger of my pistol.

'Frank. You will not let her do this?'

Frank shakes his head and turns away.

Mrs Churchill stares deep into my eyes. She wants me to look at her when I do it.

She's brave – I'll give her that.

I take a deep breath, finger on the trigger and—

'Tell me about your daughter.'

Mrs Churchill blinks. Clearly, she wasn't expecting this. 'Who?' she snaps, but there's no force behind it.

'Your daughter.'

'Daughter?' Frank turns towards his aunt. 'You don't have a daughter.'

'That's what Mr Weston was threatening to reveal to Frank, wasn't it? Your *sordid secret*. The fact that you conceived a child out of wedlock and then trapped Mr Churchill into marrying you. What happened? Were you further along than you imagined and you realised you couldn't pass it off as Mr Churchill's child for much longer? So you went away, pretended to lose the child? Gave it up?'

Mrs Churchill says nothing, but the way she drops her eyes tells me I'm right.

'But you couldn't quite let go, could you? You kept an eye on her over the years and, when she was old enough, you brought her to Enscombe as your lady's maid.' I pause for effect. I really want it to hit home. 'Emily.'

'Emily?' Frank's expression softens.

'It was a reckless move. But perhaps it would have worked out if it hadn't been for your coachman – John Parker.'

I see the fire in Mrs Churchill's eyes as she raises them to meet mine.

'It was the usual story,' I continue, keeping my tone casual. I know that it will vex Mrs Churchill. 'She fell in love. He got her pregnant.'

'It was madness,' Mrs Churchill says, her face distorted with hatred. 'They had nothing to live on. They had to stay with his brother.'

'Ernest Parker.'

'Yes. I told her I would find a good home for her baby. That she could keep her job. But she left with the coachman. Married him. She died in childbirth,' Mrs Churchill adds, voice breaking, 'and her husband took to drink. He joined her within a year.'

'But the child survived?'

Mrs Churchill nods, no longer able to speak.

'And she was brought up by her uncle here in Weymouth. You checked in on her every now and again, paid her way. You transferred Emily's trust to her, in the care of Ernest Parker, so she would have something to live on after your death. But then you got careless.

'Frank came to Weymouth and met Jane Fairfax. He planned to marry her. You couldn't stand for that. You were desperate to split them up, preserve the Churchill family honour. Jane reminded you too much of your own lowly origins, perhaps. So you paid Ernest Parker to arrange an accident for Jane. And, in the process, you got too close to your granddaughter and she found out who you really were. She wouldn't settle for the inheritance. She wanted to be part of your life. And you couldn't say no.

'That's when things started to go wrong. The poison in your teacup. The dead maid. You realised your granddaughter was trying to kill you. Perhaps she decided that the money was worth more to her than a place in your family, after all. Perhaps she grew impatient for it. It could have been her plan all along – to kill you to get at her inheritance as soon as she could.'

Mrs Churchill looks as if she wants to say something in response but, if she does, it seems as if she cannot get the words out. The great Mrs Churchill, rendered silent at last. If only I could take the credit for it.

'That's why your jewellery box is full of counterfeit pieces. So much of your money was tied up. This was a way to get at it quickly, without alerting anyone. You sold off the real jewels to fund your escape plan. It's why you were so keen to have the stolen family heirlooms back – so that you could sell them off too. What was it that finally convinced you to go through with your plan of faking your death to escape her?'

Mrs Churchill stares at me stony-faced.

'She got to you at last, didn't she?' I say, remembering Mrs Churchill's performance at Donwell Abbey. Collapsing against the tree. Gasping for breath. Except I realise now that it wasn't a performance. 'You really were ill at the Abbey, weren't you? Somehow, she'd managed to get the poison past you. You were already in a bad way before Mrs Bates pushed you down the stairs.'

'It seems you have it all worked out, Miss Smith.' Mrs

Churchill folds her arms in defiance, but she can't hide her relief that it's finally out in the open.

'That's why you're in Weymouth, isn't it? You came to warn Ernest Parker that your granddaughter was out of control.'

Those shrewd eyes. I should have worked it out much sooner.

'She was there at The Golden Lion when I confronted Ernest Parker. She heard everything I said and she knew then that I was too close to the truth. She pushed me in front of that carriage and, when that didn't work, she followed us here.'

I don't need to turn around to know that she is standing behind me, listening to the whole sorry tale. I see it in Mrs Churchill's expression.

'Didn't you, Matilda?'

CHAPTER 31

Rule number thirty-one: Money may be the root of all evil, but family comes a close second.

Matilda is on me before I can aim my pistol, wrestling it from my grip and kicking it away. The pistol skids across the ground, coming to rest a few feet in front of Wakefield. I will him to bend down and retrieve it before Matilda can make her next move, but he's standing stock-still, staring at Matilda as she turns towards Mrs Churchill.

'Hello, Grandmother.' Her honey-blonde hair is blowing around her head in a tangled mess, her eyes are wild and bloodshot. The string of pearls around her neck looks horribly out of place. Mrs Churchill's missing necklace, I'd wager. The one I couldn't locate. Matilda draws her cloak around her body and shivers as a violent gust of wind almost knocks us off our feet. She ignores Frank entirely.

Wakefield angles himself towards Matilda, finger on the

trigger of his pistol. I glance at *my* pistol on the ground before him. If I could just get a bit closer, I might be able to reach it.

'It *was* you who pushed me in front of the barouche,' I say, eyes on Matilda as I inch towards Wakefield.

Matilda shrugs. 'It's nothing personal. I thought you were coming for me.'

If only I'd been a bit quicker, a bit smarter, I could have prevented this whole encounter. I should have realised back in Highbury when I'd first laid eyes on Jane's sketch of Parker. Matilda has those same shrewd eyes. And after Mrs Churchill's apparent death, she had told me of her plan to seek work with her uncle in Dorset who ran a coaching inn. But it wasn't until I came across Ernest Parker's daughter at The Golden Lion that I started to put it together. May. Matilda's cousin. The one she spoke of so fondly during our first exchange at Richmond. There's a strong resemblance between them, although Matilda has a hardness to her which I didn't detect in May.

'Harriet, I don't understand,' Frank says, looking from me to Matilda.

'Ernest Parker is Matilda's uncle. Matilda is Emily's daughter.'

It had nothing to do with my father and my own connection with Weymouth. Robert was right – it was all in my head.

Frank frowns at his aunt. 'You paid your granddaughter's uncle to kill my fiancée? That's low, even for you.'

'He did not do his job,' Mrs Churchill says, as if it makes her crime less heinous.

'Job?' Frank scoffs. 'Destroying my future is a job, is it?'

Mrs Churchill shakes her head. 'I would not expect you to understand.'

'Then explain it to me. Why are you so intent on destroying everyone else's happiness, you miserable old bitch?'

'Don't you dare call her that!' Matilda shouts, eyes blazing. 'She doesn't deserve it.'

'But she deserves to be dosed with cyanide does she, Matilda?' I ask. 'Not enough to kill her. Just enough to let her know someone is out to get her?'

'I never meant to hurt her,' Matilda mumbles, glancing in my direction. 'I was careful with the dose. I was just trying to protect her. From him.' She waves an accusing finger in Frank's direction.

'Me? Oh, yes, *I'm* the dangerous one.'

'Why did you kill the maid, Matilda?' I shout as the wind whips up, carrying my words away with it.

Matilda glares at me, lips pursed.

'It wasn't a spur-of-the-moment thing. You clearly planned it. First, you poisoned the cook, so she had to return to Yorkshire. That gave you much easier access to your mistress's food. Then you planted the poisoned butter, knowing Sophia would put it on Mrs Churchill's toast and Mrs Churchill would never touch it. You knew poor Sophia wouldn't be able to help herself. You told me yourself that you'd witnessed her eating Mrs Churchill's discarded breakfast the day before. You knew exactly what you were doing. Were you jealous of Sophia?' I ask. 'Because you wanted to be Mrs Churchill's lady's maid? But she could hardly appoint you to that role without raising suspicion, could she? I'm sure Wakefield was disapproving enough that you'd been brought into the house in the first place.'

Wakefield nods in agreement, finger still poised on the trigger of his pistol. 'I advised Mrs Churchill not to hire her. Of course, I didn't know why she *had* hired her at that point.'

'But she told you later, Wakefield, when she realised her mistake?'

'She did,' Wakefield assents. 'But, by then, there was only so much we could do. I did not wish to resort to such extreme measures to deal with Matilda, but she made it necessary, I'm afraid, when she killed Sophia.'

'I wasn't jealous,' Matilda says sullenly. 'Sophia was getting too inquisitive. Kept asking questions. She would have spoilt everything.' Her lip quivers and I see for the first time the fifteen-year-old girl in the murderess who stands before me. 'And I *should* have been lady's maid. Like my mother.'

'You are nothing like your mother,' Frank says quietly. 'She was kind and decent and sane.'

Matilda whips round towards Frank. 'What do you know about my mother? What right do you have to speak of her? *You* stole her place. Her role. The Churchills should never have adopted you. If my mother had been recognised as part of the family, if Mrs Churchill had given her the love and attention that she bestowed upon you, then she would never have run off with my useless father. She would never have had *me*. She would never have died.' Her voice breaks on the final word.

'I did what I could for her, Matilda,' Mrs Churchill says. 'I gave her a position. Security.'

'Yes, and how do you think she felt running around after *him*,' Matilda shouts, jabbing a finger towards Frank's face, 'knowing that he had taken her place? *You* did this,' she says, eyes fixed on Frank. 'You're the reason I poisoned Sophia and Grandmother. This is all your fault.'

'But why, Matilda? Why would you do that?' Mrs Churchill asks, taking a step towards Wakefield. Wakefield glances at Mrs Churchill and some silent communication passes between them.

Matilda is sobbing silently now, head bowed. 'Because it was the only way to get you to take the threat seriously. The only way you would leave him.'

'Me?' Frank asks. 'Why should she leave *me*?'

Matilda's head jerks up and she sneers at Frank. 'Of course you wouldn't understand. You've never appreciated a single thing she's done for you.'

'Excuse me?'

'No,' Matilda shouts. 'You're not excused. She took you in when your mother died, despite her dislike for your reckless father. She took care of your education, your love life, your inheritance, and you threw it all back in her face. You're entitled and ungrateful and you don't deserve her. Not like *I* do.'

'You're delusional,' Frank says.

Matilda's mouth stretches into a horribly wide smile. 'Did you know it was quite by chance I discovered the truth? I didn't mean to eavesdrop on my uncle's conversation with her, but he was raising his voice and he has such a vile temper. I was worried he might hurt her. That's when I discovered who I was – who she was, and what my uncle had done for her – and I saw my opportunity to get out of here. I didn't want to be stuck in some stupid seaside resort all my life. I can't even swim! So I begged her to take me with her. Of course, we couldn't tell anyone who I really was. It was our secret. And I would have been happy at Enscombe. I would have kept to myself and done my job and never caused any trouble if it hadn't been for you.' She jabs a finger towards Frank again. 'The way you treated her. The endless complaints about her to your father and Miss Smith and anyone else who would listen. The gambling. Bringing that dreadful Frenchman to her door, demanding money. And how you carried on with that Fairfax girl, sullying the Churchill name.'

Frank walks to the cliff edge and looks out at the sea below. As he spins on his heel to face Matilda, he dislodges a rock which plunges over the cliff edge. I don't hear it land.

Frank laughs. 'Yes, *I'm* the one sullying the Churchill name.'

'She was so intent on disposing of Jane Fairfax, when she should have been getting rid of you. I tried to show her that you were no good. That you were a danger to her. But she never would believe it of you.'

'I bet you got a shock when she keeled over in the garden,' Frank says, smirking at Matilda with such frustrating poise that it's likely to tip her over the edge.

Apparently, Frank Churchill has a death wish . . .

'I thought it was *you*,' Matilda mumbles. 'I thought you had killed her so that you could be with Jane. You ruin everything. But it's all right now,' she says, turning towards Mrs Churchill. 'You're alive and we can be together again. We can go anywhere in the world. Just the two of us.'

Mrs Churchill steps away from Matilda.

'Ha! You think she'd go anywhere with you?' Frank shouts, gesturing at his aunt. 'Look at her! She can't stand to be anywhere near you.'

'You lie!' Matilda snarls, eyes on Frank. 'You're trying to break us apart, just like you did with my mother. I won't let you. You can't have her. You can't—' There's a glimmer of silver as Matilda reaches into her cloak and then charges at Frank. Wakefield raises his pistol but I already know he will miss. The angle is wrong and Matilda is moving too fast. I don't have time to retrieve my own pistol, but I have to stop her. I've never been more certain of anything in my life. And I can only see one way to do it.

I throw my full body weight at Matilda, raising my hand to protect myself from her weapon, which I notice, as it slices through my palm, is Mrs Churchill's paper knife.

I certainly don't covet it now.

I push my bloodied palm into Matilda's face and she claws at me with flailing arms as we teeter on the cliff edge.

And then we're falling.

CHAPTER 32

Rule number thirty-two: If you're going down, make sure you take the homicidal maniac down with you.

Matilda clings to me, mouth open in a silent scream. I pray the sea is deep enough to break our fall – and I'm really not the praying kind, so it'll be just our luck if we dash our brains out on the rocks on the way down.

I feel strangely at peace as we hurtle towards the sea. It hardly matters now, if I'm not going to live to enjoy the achievement, but I feel as if I've finally done something noble. (If I can say it's noble to throw myself off a cliff to protect a womanising cad from a misguided adolescent girl who clearly hasn't had any positive role models in her life.)

I've never considered myself in need of a higher purpose but, now I've suddenly found one, it might have been nice to pursue it for more than the few seconds it's going to take me to fall to my near-certain death. Perhaps I'll get lucky and the water will be deep enough that I'll drown instead.

I tuck myself up into a ball (or as close an approximation as I can with Matilda clamped onto me like a limpet), and take a deep breath in, holding it as I plunge into the cool water.

I cough up about a gallon of sea water as I break through the surface. The good news is, I'm still alive. The bad news is, I might not be for much longer if Matilda doesn't stop dragging me down with her.

I shake her off for long enough to unbutton my sodden pelisse and peel it from my waterlogged form. Matilda is bobbing up and down in front of me, arms flailing as she attempts to gain deeper waters. But it's evident she wasn't exaggerating when she said she couldn't swim. I kick off my shoes and undo my gown one-handed to shed some more weight. It sinks down into a watery grave as I swim out in pursuit of Matilda. It's all very Ophelia-like. Matilda is further out than I would have imagined possible, given her non-existent swimming technique, but I'm confident I can reach her. She's flagging now and, with one final burst of energy, I'll be upon her.

As I reach out to grab her arm, she places her palm on the top of my head and pushes me under the water. I take a big gulp of air as I fight my way to the surface.

'Harriet!' Frank peers over the cliff edge, cupping his hands to his mouth. 'Harriet! I'm coming in.'

As Matilda pushes me under again, I choke on a mouthful of seawater and, by the time I've recovered enough to warn Frank not to follow, he has already removed his shoes and shirt and is getting ready to jump. His limbs flail as he falls. He's approaching the water at completely the wrong angle. He's going to—

Frank hits the water with a loud clap and doesn't resurface.

Meanwhile, Matilda has an arm around my neck, choking the life out of me. I reach behind me, grasping at Mrs Churchill's pearls in the hope it will be enough to distract Matilda. The necklace breaks as I give a sharp tug and the pearls shoot off in all directions. One floats in front of me as my head becomes heavy and my vision blurs. I need to do something quickly.

I go limp against Matilda's body and, when she relaxes her grip, I kick back hard. She lets out a sharp gasp as her fingers slide from my neck and she's left grabbing at the waves. There's still no sign of Frank.

Matilda is thrashing around in the water behind me like a fish on a hook. 'Harriet, help me!' she screeches, reaching for my hand. I don't want her to drown and I certainly don't want her to get away, but Frank has been underwater for too long. And I can't save them both. Matilda, I expect, doesn't want to be saved. She just wants to take me down with her. But Frank's a grown man and Matilda's a fifteen-year-old girl. It doesn't seem right to leave her to sink into Weymouth Bay.

'Harriet!' Matilda goes under.

I scan the water, searching for signs of life. I take a huge gulp of air and dive down towards a dark shape sinking into the seabed. The weight of the body drags me down, but I find a reserve of strength I never knew I had as my arms encircle it and I fight my way upwards. My chest is so tight I think it's about to explode, my head is pounding and my vision blanks out as I reach the surface. I drag the body onto the beach, collapsing beside it. There's a hacking cough in my ear and a mouthful of water sprays me right in the eyes as I turn my head.

'Sorry,' he rasps. 'And thank you.'

'You're welcome,' I say, patting his hand as I blink away the seawater.

My head swims as I sit up too quickly. I squint out across the water, looking for any sign of Matilda.

Perhaps she got away. But perhaps it's better if she didn't. Because what did she have left to look forward to? Life on the run with only her conscience for company and, eventually, the end of a rope. Better to be a sacrifice to the sea.

✳

We climb back up to the clifftop as soon as we have enough energy to move. Mrs Churchill has long since cleared out with Wakefield, but at least Frank is able to retrieve his shirt and shoes and redingote, the latter of which he wraps around my shoulders to cover my sodden petticoat.

'That was a reckless thing you did, jumping off a cliff with Matilda,' Frank says as he tears a strip off his shirt and wraps it around my still-bleeding palm. I wince, feeling the sting of the seawater as my makeshift bandage turns crimson.

'She was going to kill you,' I say, staring at my injured hand.

'I don't know,' Frank says, folding his arms. 'I think I could have taken her.'

'You definitely couldn't have taken her.'

Frank lets out a laugh, not the full-throated one that does strange things to my stomach, but the soft chuckle of someone who has just been through a harrowing ordeal but is determined to put a brave face on it.

I walk over to the cliff edge, peering into the turquoise abyss. My foot knocks against something hard and metallic. My pistol. I had assumed Wakefield would have taken it, but he had his own weapon, I suppose, and I did do him a favour by throwing myself off a cliff with Matilda. One less problem for him to deal with. Or two, if I didn't resurface.

'Where do you think she'll go?' I ask Frank as he steps up beside me. 'Your aunt.'

He shrugs. 'She can't exactly return to Enscombe, can she? But you can rest assured she'll be all right, wherever she ends up. Aunt Lavinia's a survivor.'

'I wish someone had told me that before I took on this damn case.'

Frank nudges my shoulder. 'But then you wouldn't have met me, would you? Which would have been a great shame for all concerned.'

I roll my eyes, hoping it distracts him from my flushed cheeks. 'Yes, thank goodness your aunt hired me to sabotage your love life.'

'I think I may have done that all by myself,' Frank says, head bowed.

He's not wrong.

'You know, I really was fond of Emily,' he says when I don't contradict him. 'She was kind to me. I suppose now I know why. She used to sneak me bread and butter from the kitchens when I'd misbehaved and been sent to bed with no supper.'

'You, misbehave?'

He grins at me, but it soon fades. 'I wish I'd known about Matilda,' he says, gazing out to sea.

I wish I had too. I might have been able to stop her before it came to this.

'Would you have treated her any differently if you had known?' I ask.

Frank sighs. 'Probably worse,' he admits.

'Families are complicated beasts. Blood ties aren't all they're cracked up to be.'

'No,' Frank agrees. 'I suppose they're not.'

'While we're in confession mode—'

'Are we?' Frank asks. 'I don't remember agreeing to that.'

'Well, I am, at least. We'd be up here all week if you got started on yours.'

'Charming.'

'I should probably tell you I sent Jane the pianoforte.'

'You?' Frank drops his arm from my shoulder. 'Why on earth did you do that?'

'To create discord between you. I knew Jane would assume it was from you and would be furious at the position you'd put her in. The lies she would have to tell on your account. And it didn't take much to convince *you* she had some secret lover. In the meantime, Jane got the instrument she really deserved, and all at your aunt's expense.'

'You're a wicked woman, Harriet Smith.'

'Yes, well, I'm working on that.'

'And *I* need to work out what I'm going to do now Jane has thrown me over. I thought she could make me a better man because she's so good herself. But it turns out she didn't want to save me. She said she only agreed to marry me because she was worried what would happen to her otherwise. But she decided, in the end, she would rather be a governess than my wife.' He leans in, arm brushing against my shoulder. 'Perhaps it's not such a mad idea, us working together. I wasn't joking when I said we make a good team.' He hits me with those too-blue eyes.

I sigh, reach for his hand and squeeze it. 'Frank, the truth is, *I* don't want to save you either.'

He laughs, interlocking his fingers with mine. 'Fair enough.'

We stand together, holding hands, looking out over the water as the sun sets. It's all very romantic.

'What will you do now?' Frank says finally, breaking the mood.

'Oh, I have a few ideas,' I say, gazing out over Weymouth Bay.

'I suppose I should get going,' he says, dropping my hand and stepping away from the ledge as the wind picks up. He's shivering in his shirtsleeves and wet breeches. 'Are you coming?'

I shake my head. 'I think I'll sit here for a while.'

'Stay safe, Harriet.'

I wave my pistol at him in reply.

I sit listening to the waves lapping against the cliff face as the sun goes down. I huddle into Frank's redingote, which smells faintly of citrus and bergamot, thinking it would be somewhat ironic to survive jumping from a cliff with a homicidal maniac who promptly tried to drown me, just to die of pneumonia up here in my petticoat. But I'm not quite ready to leave yet. I want to do something for Matilda – mark her passing – except with no body and no personal effects, I'm not left with many options.

As I stand up and peer over the cliff ledge, I see something glinting in the moonlight a few feet below. I don't know what would possess me to scale a cliff in the darkness to reach something shiny. Perhaps my latest near-death experience has given me delusions of immortality. I take off my shoes to get better purchase on the cliff ledge and inch slowly towards my prize. I slip several times but, somehow, I know I'm not going to fall. I feel the stretch in my shoulder as I reach for it, fingertips inches away. With an agonising groan, I swing myself across those final few inches, my fist closing around the mysterious object. As I haul myself back up onto the clifftop, I realise what it is.

I trace my fingers across the emeralds and rubies and pearls at the hilt of Mrs Churchill's paper knife. No wonder it cut through my palm. The blade has been sharpened since I last saw it at the Churchills' house in Richmond, as if Matilda knew she would have to use it as a weapon. She must have been back to Richmond and found the paper knife under Mrs Churchill's bed. It's not even Matilda's really, but she was the last person to wield it, and it belonged to someone she really did love, so it will have to do. I'm about to wipe my blood from the blade with my sodden petticoat, but in the end, I leave it. A trace of my contact with Matilda and Mrs Churchill. I plan to toss it over the cliff with a few brief words for Matilda, but then I remember how much she despised the sea. Instead, I slip on my shoes, walk down into Bowleaze Cove and bury it deep in the sand.

'Farewell, Matilda. Be at peace.'

I feel lighter as I stand up, shake the sand from my fingers and look out over Weymouth Bay. As if I've buried a piece of myself too.

CHAPTER 33

Rule number thirty-three: If you want to control your future, you must let go of your past.

'Help me, Harriet!' Matilda is calling to me, her skin ghostly pale, her eyes bloodshot. I reach for her outstretched arm, grabbing at her fingers. They come away in my hand. She's a bloated, rotting corpse and I can't save her.

'Harriet!' The voice is my mother's. Her golden hair turns mousy brown as she sinks into Weymouth Bay.

'Mama!'

I dive down towards her, but it's too late. She's gone.

I jolt awake, choking on a mouthful of sand, my petticoat drenched in sweat. There's an awful crick in my neck which I'm going to feel for a least a week. I hadn't meant to fall asleep, but I suppose the excitement of the last few days has finally caught up with me. The sun is just rising and Bowleaze Cove is blissfully quiet, apart from the squawking seagulls and the susurration of the waves. It's almost enough to lull me back to sleep.

Every part of my body is throbbing with the dull ache of chronically underused muscles. My palm is sore but, as I unwrap the blood-soaked scrap of Frank's shirt, I'm relieved to see it's stopped bleeding. I'll have a nice, heroic scar, though.

I half expected Frank to be here when I awoke, but I'm glad he's not. I don't do well with temptation, although I'm sure he would hardly find *me* tempting in this state. With any luck, he's well on his way to Highbury by now. I'm not sure I'll be too far behind.

The truth is, I've grown rather fond of Highbury and its residents. It's been nice to have a settled position, even if I've had to put up with giggling schoolgirls at Mrs Goddard's and a moody soldier who is far too comfortable walking around with his shirt undone at Abbey-Mill Farm. There's a sense of reassurance in the everybody-knows-everything-about-everybody world of Highbury, which I didn't know I was craving. I've never really been part of a community before. With Father, I was always looking ahead to the next location, the next con. But, apart from my ludicrous fantasies of running away with Frank, I haven't been thinking ahead in Highbury. I suppose I was too busy looking over my shoulder, waiting for my father to catch up with me. But Robert was right. He's not chasing me. I can finally stop running.

That's my biggest regret about this whole experience. Not that my father has abandoned me, but that I've abandoned Robert. Kind, funny, infuriating Robert who is the only person I've met who has ever had my best interests at heart. I suppose that's why I had such trouble accepting it. I see now that Robert was only trying to protect me. To help me become the person he always knew I could be. He has so much more faith in me than I have in myself. At least, he did, before I ended up screaming at him for having the courage to tell the truth and then accidentally sabotaging his love life. I've let him down and I need to put it right.

What I really ought to do now is take a leaf out of Jane Fairfax's book. Poor Jane. How the residents of Highbury pity her fate. To become a governess rather than a wife! Well, at least a governess gets paid for her services. She can leave when she chooses. Jane has chosen to control her own fate rather than let a man control it for her. She has chosen to save herself. I see nothing tragic in that.

'Harriet.'

I let out an involuntary yelp of as I whip round to face Robert and then a hiss of pain as I remember too late the crick in my neck.

'Jesus Christ, are you trying to kill me?' I demand, to cover my shock.

Robert offers me a lopsided smirk, but he can't hide the worry in his eyes as he takes in my bedraggled appearance. 'It looks like you've already tried that.'

You don't know the half of it.

'Did you know that William Wordsworth's brother drowned just over there?' I say, pointing towards Weymouth Bay.

'I didn't,' Robert replies, sitting down next to me, cross-legged, fingers tracing nervous patterns in the sand.

'Yes. Captain John Wordsworth of *The Earl of Abergavenny*. He might have saved himself, but he decided to go down with his ship.'

I feel as if I've been clinging to a sinking ship for far too long. I think I'm ready to let go at last.

I turn towards Robert, examining him closely. He looks dreadful and wonderful all at once. His mop of dark curls is wilder than ever. His skin is a little too tanned, as if he hasn't been taking care to keep out of the sun, and there are charcoal-grey bags under his eyes which suggest he hasn't slept for quite some time.

I'll always be here when you need me.

And he is.

'How did you know where to find me?' I ask, watching his fingers tap out an erratic rhythm against a conch shell he's dug out of the sand.

'Mrs Elton.'

'Mrs Elton? How on earth did she know where I'd be?'

Robert shrugs. 'I don't know. I assumed you'd told her.'

I shake my head. I didn't tell anyone where I was going, which wasn't very sensible now I think about it. I suppose she must have spoken to Jane and they worked it out between them.

'Well, she likes poking her nose into other people's affairs, doesn't she?' Robert adds. 'She seemed to think you might have got yourself into a spot of bother.'

Another favour I owe Mrs Elton. They're certainly stacking up.

'Yes, well, it's all done now.'

'You found Mrs Churchill's killer?' Robert asks, a note of surprise in his voice.

'In a way, yes. And before you ask, it wasn't Frank.'

Robert holds up his hands. 'The thought never crossed my mind.'

'You're a terrible liar.'

'So, it was Jane, was it?' he teases.

I sigh. 'It's complicated. I'll tell you on the way back.'

'You are coming back, then?'

'If you'll have me,' I say, taking the conch shell from his hand. 'You were right about my father. In fact, you were right about all of it.'

'Can I have that in writing?'

'Do you mind? I'm trying to get through a disgustingly heartfelt apology.'

'Apologise, then. But do it slowly, so I can savour it and bask in the glow of being right.'

I drive my elbow into his ribs and start talking again before he can recover himself enough to get in another playful jibe.

'My father never cared about me. It was always about the con. He was never going to come after me. That was his revenge for my betrayal.'

I watch the froth of the waves spill across the sand, hissing and fizzing, the bubbles glistening like diamonds.

The ferrous tang of seaweed fills my nostrils as I stare out to sea. I realise now that I don't want my father's forgiveness. And I don't forgive *him* for what he's taken from me. I left him because I had to. I needed to get away. I thought I was escaping when I came to Highbury, but all I did was carry on being the person he wanted me to be. I can only break free of his influence by abandoning my life as a con artist altogether. And I can only do that if I forgive myself.

'I'm sorry for what I said to you – about Mr Knightley and Denny. It's none of my business. And I'm sorry if I've cost you your relationship with Denny.'

Robert waves away my apology. 'Denny will get over it, I imagine. Or, if he doesn't, it's probably for the best. *I'm* sorry for what I said about Colonel Fitzwilliam. He didn't have a lucky escape from you.'

I smile sadly. 'He did. You were right about that, too.'

He's better off without me.

Robert sighs. 'We're a sad pair, aren't we? Young, devilishly attractive, and not a handsome man between us.'

'Honestly, Robert, there's more to life than men.'

Robert snorts. 'Like what?'

'Like doing something more noble,' I say, a glint in my eyes. 'Like Harriet Smith: Private Enquiry Agent.'

'Good Lord,' Robert murmurs.

'Well, what do you think?' I hold my breath. I don't have quite enough confidence in myself yet to do this without Robert's approval.

'I think it's a terrible idea.'

My heart sinks.

'You should definitely do it,' he adds. 'Although, it will be hard to achieve in your current state.'

'Well, I'm hardly going to walk around looking like a half-drowned corpse, am I? And with Mrs Churchill's five thousand pounds, I'll be able to afford as many new gowns as I desire. Perhaps even that satin reticule I've been after.'

Robert huffs. 'No, I mean your current state. As, you know—' He clears his throat, seemingly reluctant to continue. '—an unmarried woman.'

'Yes, heaven forbid a single woman make a name for herself.'

Robert shakes his head. 'It's not even your real name.'

'So?'

'So it shouldn't be that much of a hardship to trade it for mine.'

'I'm sorry. Are you suggesting what I think you're suggesting?'

'If you think I'm suggesting that we should get married to enable you to carry out your business more easily, then yes.' Robert's tone is casual, but his expression is deadly serious.

'Are you insane?'

Robert shrugs. 'Probably, to consider marrying you.'

I slap him on the shoulder. Hard.

'Ouch. I'm trying to help you here. To help you avoid scandal.'

'I don't need to avoid scandal,' I say, tossing my head.

'To help *me* avoid scandal, then. You're always going on about how reckless I am with Denny.'

'Hmmm. And what about Denny? What will he have to say about it?' I ask, folding my arms.

'Very little, I should think, seeing as he's not even talking to me at the moment.'

'I don't think I'm cut out to be a farmer's wife. Although, considering the number of times you've left poor Mr Ingleby in charge of Abbey-Mill Farm, I'm not sure he'll willingly hand it back to you now. He probably has some legal claim to it.'

Robert laughs. 'Let him have it, for all I care!'

'Oh yes? And what will we live on?'

'Your earnings, of course. And, you're forgetting the fortune I stand to make from George and Henrietta's adventures.'

'Oh, it's back to Henrietta, is it? Poor Rupert has been ousted, this time.'

Robert shrugs. 'Let's just say Henrietta has proved herself worthy, after all.'

I roll my eyes. 'Of course.'

I can't believe I'm actually considering Robert's offer. But, then, I suppose he's right that it would help us both. After all, he can hardly marry Denny, can he? And, seeing as I've sworn off men for good, this is probably the only opportunity I'll get to walk down the aisle. And I do like a good party.

I throw up my hands in mock surrender. 'Fine. Have it your way. I suppose we can get married if that's what you really want. Perhaps we could have a double wedding with Emma and Mr Knightley.'

Robert laughs. 'Yes,' he agrees. 'I'm sure Miss Woodhouse would be thrilled to share the limelight with you on her wedding day.'

'Even better,' I say, clicking my fingers at him. 'We'll have our wedding before hers. Steal her thunder. We'll have a huge wedding party and I'll ride up the aisle on Queen Charlotte. And Mrs Elton can follow behind on Toby the pony. And perhaps some pigs to bring up the rear.'

'Hmmm. We can discuss ways to upstage Emma Woodhouse on our way back to Highbury.'

'Wonderful,' I say, taking his arm. 'I have so many ideas. There's just something I need to do first.'

✳

When my father told me Mama had drowned in Weymouth Bay, two months after she left us, my first thought was that he had killed her. My second thought was that it was *my* fault. But it's not true. I buried the truth here at The Golden Lion, the site of my mother's betrayal of us. Her abandonment of me.

Ernest Parker eyes me warily as I cross the threshold of The Golden Lion in my stiff petticoat and Frank's redingote. I must look like the sole survivor of a shipwreck. His restless fingers tap against the bar.

'Mr Parker.'

He goes very still, as if he can sense I'm here to deliver some terrible news.

'I'm very sorry. It's about your niece. Matilda.'

'Yes?' he asks, eyes down, as if he knows what's coming.

'I'm sorry, Mr Parker. There was an accident.'

'She's dead?'

'I'm afraid so.'

'I always knew that girl would come to a bad end,' he mumbles, picking up an empty glass and pouring himself a generous measure of port with trembling hands.

I linger at the bar.

'Is that all?' he snaps, wiping his eyes against the back of his hand.

'I thought you might like to know that Mrs Churchill is gone.' I reach a hand across the bar and touch his elbow gently. 'You should forgive yourself for what you've done. You're not the only one she convinced to do her dirty work.'

He looks at me with watery eyes and nods.

'There's one last thing,' I say. 'I need to see one of your rooms.'

✳

I wasn't sure it would still be here after all this time but, as I crawl under the bed and remove the loose floorboard, I find the letter tucked neatly underneath, exactly where I left it two years ago. I unfold it reverently.

My dearest Harriet,

I know you saw me on the beach today. I am sorry I turned away, but I feared you would make a scene. I want you to know that I do not blame you for telling your father. It was a blessing, really. It meant that I could finally be happy. I hope that you find happiness too, Harriet. I know you love your father but I hope, one day, you find the strength to leave him. This is for when you do.

All my love,

Mama

So you see, The Golden Lion isn't the last place I saw my mother. As I walked from Weymouth beach across to Bowleaze Cove, ready to burn a candle in her memory on the eighth anniversary of her drowning – the first one I'd been able to mark – I saw her walking down the beach, hand in hand with the Colonel and a little girl who looked an awful lot like me. My mother had turned in my direction, a smile frozen on her lips as she glanced at me and then carried on her way. I thought she hadn't recognised me, until I received this letter. She must have followed me back to The Golden Lion that afternoon, scribbled a few lines in haste and entrusted them to the landlord. By the time he handed the letter to me the next morning, my mother had gone. I couldn't read it then – I wasn't ready to listen to her excuses for abandoning me. And so I tucked it away here for when I *was* ready. But it turns out she didn't think her behaviour needed to be excused. Instead, she forgave *me* for betraying *her* to my father. Well, I don't need her forgiveness. Not now.

I drop the letter in disgust and count out the accompanying bank notes. Two thousand pounds. Less than half of what Mrs Churchill gave me. That's what my mother thought I was worth.

I rip the letter into tiny pieces and scatter them out of the open window, watching them blow away on the sea breeze. I pocket the banknotes. I descend the stairs and head for the door, nodding to Mr Parker as I leave.

'Take care of yourself, miss,' he says.

That's exactly what I intend to do.

Robert is waiting outside The Golden Lion in a shiny black barouche that looks suspiciously like the one that almost ran me down yesterday.

He flings the door open, grinning down at me as he proffers his hand. 'Are you ready, Harriet?'

I'm almost certain I am, but something is stopping me from taking Robert's hand. Something is still weighing me down. I reach into Frank's redingote and pull out my battered copy of *Hamlet* and flick to the final scene.

Good night sweet prince:
And flights of angels sing thee to thy rest!

There's nothing sweet about my father. He doesn't deserve to be remembered. To be mourned. I haven't lost my father. He has lost me. I let the book slip from my fingers, kicking it under the carriage as it falls to the ground.

Now I'm ready.

I grin back at Robert as I reach for his hand and step up into the barouche. 'Let's go home.'